RED KNIFE

RED KNIFE

A CORK O'CONNOR MYSTERY

WILLIAM
KENT KRUEGER

ATRIA BOOKS

New York   London   Toronto   Sydney

ATRIA BOOKS

A Division of Simon & Schuster, Inc.
1230 Avenue of the Americas
New York, NY 10020

First Atria Books hardcover edition September 2008

ATRIA BOOKS and colophon are trademarks of Simon & Schuster, Inc.

For information about special discounts for bulk purchases, please contact Simon & Schuster Special Sales at 1-800-456-6798 or business@simonandschuster.com.

Designed by Davina Mock-Maniscalco

Manufactured in the United States of America

1 3 5 7 9 10 8 6 4 2

Library of Congress Cataloging-in-Publication Data

Krueger, William Kent.
Red Knife : a Cork O'Connor mystery / by William Kent Krueger.—
First Atria Books hardcover ed.
p. cm.
1. O'Connor, Cork (Fictitious character)—Fiction. 2. Private investigators—Minnesota—Fiction. 3. Minnesota—Fiction.
4. Gangs—Fiction. I. Title.

PS3561.R766R43 2008
813'.54—dc22
2007048175

ISBN-13: 978-1-4165-5674-9
ISBN-10:   1-4165-5674-5

To my friends and colleagues, past and present,
in Crème de la Crime,
who have done their best to keep me honest

RED KNIFE

MISKWAA-MOOKOMAAN
(RED KNIFE)

It was not yet dawn and already he could smell death. It came to him in the scent of the bear fat mixed with red ochre that was the war paint smeared across his face. It was in the sulfur odor of his powder horn and in the stink of his own sweat-drenched body as he bent to the stroke of his paddle. It was in the air itself, something crisp and final, as if these were the last breaths he would ever draw, and it made his nostrils burn.

In the east, the sky hinted at color, a faint flush of red. The dark lake surface around the canoes carried a suggestion of the same hue, blood mixed with the juice of blackberries. The only sound was his own breathing and the occasional liquid gurgle of water as he swept his paddle back.

His name was Diindiisi, which meant Blue Jay. He was sixteen years old. He was Anishinaabeg, one of the Original People. This was his first war party.

For years his father and the other men of his village had been preparing him for this moment. Several days earlier, they'd painted him black, a sign that in this business he was not yet initiated. The night before, they'd forced him into the bitter-cold water of the lake, where he'd washed himself clean. Afterward they invited him to join in the preparations for battle. They painted their faces. Those who had the honor of doing so adorned their hair with eagle feathers, symbols of the enemies they'd slain. They attached the *penasewiam*, holding charms for invulnerability, to their belts or armlets or headdresses.

Now Blue Jay was among them, a warrior, his knife sharpened, his war club at hand, his flintlock cleaned and loaded. His father knelt in the stern of the birch-bark canoe. Blue Jay had the bow. He was afraid, more afraid than he'd ever been. He was also excited, and the two emotions waged a battle inside him that no man looking at his face could see.

There were ten canoes, two warriors in each, a small war party. The enemy were Dakota from the south. That alone was enough to get them killed. But they were hunters as well, trespassing, taking game the Anishinaabeg would need for their own people in the coming winter.

The canoes neared the shoreline. Blue Jay leaped silently to land and lifted the bow so that the bark of the hull wouldn't snag and tear. His father followed and together they settled the canoe on the shore. They gathered their weapons. In the gray light of early morning, they followed the others along a deer trail into the trees.

Blue Jay knew where the hunters were camped, which was in a clearing next to a fast-running stream. He knew because the enemy had been scouted and because he smelled the char from the fire they'd lit the night before. It was only a faint scent on the breeze, but in the deep woods it was profoundly distinct, especially to the heightened senses of a young man on his way to war.

Ozhaawashkwaabi, Black Eye, who led the party, lifted his hand, signaling them to stop. He pointed left and right, and the warriors fanned out. Blue Jay crept to a twisted-trunk cedar tree only a stone's throw from where his father knelt behind an uprooted pine that a powerful wind had pushed over sometime before. In the clearing in front of them lay a circle of ash from a fire. Strewn around it were the blanketed forms of the sleeping Dakota. Blue Jay counted thirteen.

His hand went to the hilt of his knife, then to the war club shoved into his belt. He slid the powder horn from his chest and set it at the base of the cedar. He raised his flintlock and waited. His heart beat so furiously he was afraid the tree he leaned against would begin to shake.

In his mind, he went over the things his father had said to him the night before.

"Choose one of the enemy and aim carefully. Wait until you hear Black Eye give his war whoop, then shoot. Shoot well. Bring your enemy down as you would any animal you hunt in the forest. Give your own war whoop. Make it fierce. It will fill you with courage and it will strike fear in the heart of the Dakota. Run to your enemy with your war club in your hand. Be wary. A man down is not a man dead. Smash the bone of his skull. And then take his scalp in the way I have told you. The scalp is important. It is proof of your kill, proof you are a warrior."

One of the Dakota began to stir. He sat up and stretched. He stood, scratched at his crotch, and lightly kicked the blanket of the man lying next to him. He spoke in a language Blue Jay didn't understand and then he laughed. The other blankets began to move. One by one the enemy awakened.

The sun had touched the tops of the aspen trees that edged the stream. A jay on a high branch began a long string of grating screeches. One of the enemy turned to look, picked up a rock, and threw it to no effect. Blue Jay sighted his rifle barrel on the back of that enemy. With his thumb, he drew back the hammer of the flintlock. There was the smallest of clicks as the hammer locked, hardly more than the snap a very small twig might make. The Dakota nearest him turned suddenly in his direction. He peered directly at the cedar that shielded Blue Jay. He spun and shouted something to the others. At that same moment, Black Eye let fly his war cry.

Blue Jay squeezed the trigger. The hammer released. The flint hit the strike plate. The powder exploded. Through the drift of smoke that materialized in front of his face, Blue Jay saw his enemy jerk and collapse. Other Dakota hit the earth, though Blue Jay didn't hear the shots that brought them down, he was so intent on his own actions.

He dropped his flintlock and drew his war club. He gave a yell, so loud and harsh it seared his throat, and rushed forward into the clearing. All around him rose the cries of battle, sharp and desperate. He heard and did not hear. His mind was on the enemy he'd felled with his musket ball. The man lay on the ground, facedown. The ball had hit him in the right shoulder blade and blood welled up through a hole ragged with white bone fragments. The man didn't move. There appeared to be no breath in him, no life. Blue Jay gripped his war club in his right hand. With his left, he grasped the Dakota's shoulder and turned him over.

He was surprised. It was not a man but a boy not even as old as he. He was surprised again when the boy's eyes sprang open and his hand flew upward, thrusting a knife blade toward Blue Jay's belly. Blue Jay spun away, but not before the blade sliced his flesh. He swung his war club and knocked away the hand that held the knife. With a powerful sweep of his leg, the Dakota boy kicked Blue Jay's feet out from under him and he went down. The boy was on him. They grappled, rolling in the wet grass. The Dakota was strong and lithe, but the musket ball had weakened him. Blue Jay felt the boy's strength ebbing quickly. He wrenched his right hand free and swung his war club again. It hit the Dakota's head with a sound like chopping rotted wood. Blue Jay rolled away and came to his feet, but his enemy didn't move. He planted his foot on the Dakota's chest and swung his war club again and again, until the enemy's face and forehead were a bloody mush.

He stood breathing in gasps, staring down at what he'd done. He didn't feel elated. He didn't feel powerful. He felt only grateful that it was not him lying dead in the meadow grass.

Cries went up in celebration. He scanned the clearing where the slaughter was nearing an end. His father, tall and blood spattered, strode toward him, a scalp clenched in his fist. He looked down at the dead Dakota and nodded his approval.

"Now his scalp."

Blue Jay drew his knife. He'd skinned animals all his life, and skinning the head of the Dakota was easy. He slit the forehead just below the hairline, cut behind an ear, drew the blade across the base of the skull, then finished at the other ear. From the forehead back, he peeled the scalp away and held it up before his father. He'd done well. Now he felt the pride.

When it was finished, the war party gathered. They left the clearing, left their enemy unburied, left the bodies and pieces of bodies to be eaten by the scavengers of the forest. In the stories the Anishinaabeg would tell of this battle, they would call the clearing Miskwaa-mookomaan—Red Knife—for the color that flowed across their blades on that triumphant autumn morning.

Two hundred years later, on that same bloody acre, the citizens of Tamarack County, Minnesota, would build a school.

ONE

The words on the note folded around the check in his wallet read: *Here's $500. A retainer. I need your help. See me today.* The note and the money were from Alexander Kingbird, although it was signed *Kakaik*, which was the name of an Ojibwe war chief. It meant Hawk.

Five hundred dollars was a pretty sound enticement, but Cork O'Connor would have gone for nothing, just to satisfy his curiosity. Although the note didn't mention Kingbird's situation, it was easy to read between the lines. In Tamarack County, unless you were stupid or dead you knew that Alexander Kingbird and the Red Boyz were in trouble. How exactly, Cork wondered, did Kingbird think he could help?

Kingbird and his wife, Rayette, lived on the Iron Lake Reservation. Their home was a nice prefab, constructed to look like a log cabin and set back a hundred yards off the road, behind a stand of red pines. A narrow gravel lane cut straight through the trees to the house. As Cork drove up, his headlights swung across a shiny black Silverado parked in front. He knew it belonged to Tom Blessing, Kingbird's second-in-command. It was Blessing who'd delivered the note that afternoon.

And it was Blessing who opened the door when Cork knocked.

"About time," Blessing said.

He wasn't much more than a kid, twenty-one, maybe twenty-two. Long black hair falling freely down his back. Tall, lean, tense. He reminded Cork of a sapling that in the old days might have been used for a rabbit snare: delicately balanced, ready to snap.

"The note said today. It's still today, Tom," Cork said.

"My name's Waubishash."

Each of the Red Boyz, on joining the gang, took the name of an Ojibwe war chief.

"Let him in." The order was delivered from behind Blessing, from inside the house.

Blessing stepped back and Cork walked in.

Alexander Kingbird stood on the far side of his living room. "Thank you for coming."

He was twenty-five, by most standards still a young man, but his eyes weren't young at all. They were as brown as rich earth and, like earth, they were old. He wore his hair in two long braids tied at the end with strips of rawhide, each hung with an owl feather. A white scar ran from the corner of his right eye to the lobe of his ear. Cork had heard it happened in a knife fight while he was a guest of the California penal system.

Kingbird glanced at Blessing. "You can go."

Blessing shook his head. "Until this is over, you shouldn't be alone."

"Are you planning to shoot me, Mr. O'Connor?"

"I hadn't thought of it, but I may be the only guy in this county who hasn't."

Kingbird smiled. "I'll be fine, Waubishash. Go on."

Blessing hesitated. Maybe he was working on an argument; if so, he couldn't quite put it together. He finally nodded, turned, and left. A minute later, Cork heard the Silverado's big engine turn over, followed by the sound of the tires on gravel. Everything got quiet then, except for a baby cooing in a back room and the low, loving murmur of a woman in response.

"Mind taking your shoes off?" Kingbird said. "New carpet and Rayette's kind of particular about keeping it clean."

"No problem." Cork slipped his Salomons off and set them beside a pair of Red Wing boots and a pair of women's Skechers, which were on a mat next to the door.

"Sit down," Kingbird said.

Cork took a comfortable-looking easy chair upholstered in dark green. Kingbird sat on the sofa.

"You know why you're here?" he said to Cork.

"Instead of twenty questions, why don't you just tell me."

"Buck Reinhardt wants me dead."

"You blame him?"

"I'm not responsible for his daughter dying."

"No, but you're hiding the man who is."

"And you know this how?"

"Popular speculation. And he's one of the Red Boyz."

"I want to talk to Reinhardt."

"Why?"

Kingbird sat tall. He wore a green T-shirt, military issue it looked like. On his forearm was a tattoo. A bulldog—the Marine Corps devil dog—with USMC below.

"I have a daughter of my own," he said. His eyes moved a hair to the right, in the direction from which the cooing had come. "I understand how he feels."

"I don't think you do. Your daughter is still alive."

"My daughter will also never use drugs."

"In that, I wish you luck."

"Reinhardt and some of his men threatened one of my Red Boyz yesterday. He needs to understand that anything he does—to me or any of the Red Boyz—will be answered in kind. I've seen wars, O'Connor. It's easier to stop them before they get started."

"Then give him what he wants. Give him the man responsible for his daughter's death. Give him Lonnie Thunder."

The suggestion seemed to have no effect on Kingbird. "Will you arrange a meeting?"

"Why me?"

"Because you're not just another white man. You've got some Ojibwe blood in your veins. Also, you used to be sheriff around here and I figure that gives you a certain standing. And—" He held up a card, one of the business cards Cork routinely tacked to bulletin boards around Aurora. "—it's how you earn your living."

"How do I know, and how can Buck be sure, that you won't just shoot him as soon as he shows up?"

"Let him name the place and the time. You'll be there to observe and to maintain the peace."

"Five hundred dollars isn't nearly enough to get me to step between blazing guns."

"I'll be unarmed. You make sure Reinhardt is, too. And the five hundred dollars is a retainer. When this meeting is done, you'll have another five hundred."

Rayette Kingbird strolled into the room carrying her child. Misty had been born six months earlier. When Alexander Kingbird looked at his wife and his daughter, his face softened.

Cork stood up. "Evening, Rayette."

"Cork."

"Bedtime for Misty?"

She smiled. She was full-blood Ojibwe. Her life before Kingbird had been hard. Abandoned by her mother and raised by her grandparents, she'd been into every kind of trouble imaginable. When Cork was sheriff of Tamarack County, he'd picked her up a few times, juvenile offenses. She'd skipped childhood through no fault of her own and he'd thought that any youth she might have had had been squeezed out long ago. Then she met Kingbird and married him and things changed. She looked young and she looked happy.

"Past bedtime," she said. "She wants a kiss from her daddy."

Rayette held the baby out and Kingbird took his daughter. He nuzzled her neck. She gurgled. He kissed her forehead. She squirmed. "Night, little turtle," he said. He handed her back to his wife.

Rayette left with the child. Kingbird looked after them a moment, then turned to Cork.

"We've named her Misty, but her real name is Tomorrow. Every child's name is Tomorrow. You, me, Buck Reinhardt, we're Yesterday. Kristi Reinhardt shouldn't have died. No child's life should be cut short of tomorrow."

"Nice sentiment, Alex, but what are you going to offer Buck? What do I tell him that will make him agree to meet you?"

He ignored the fact that Cork had used his given name, not the one he'd taken as a member of the Red Boyz. He said, "Tell him he will have justice. Tell him I give my word."

TWO

Buck Reinhardt was a son of a bitch and he'd be the first to tell you so. He could be mean, selfish, bullying, insensitive, and offensive, and grin at you the whole while. It was nothing personal; he was that way with everyone. Everyone except his daughter Kristi. Her he'd done his best to spoil rotten.

Kristi was the only child born from Buck's second marriage. His first wife was dead and the children from that marriage were all adults. Most of them had fled to the four winds to escape their father. With Kristi, it seemed that Buck Reinhardt was determined not to make the same mistakes he'd made before. He went on making mistakes; they were just different ones.

Reinhardt built a place on Skinner Lake five miles west of Aurora, where he had the area pretty much to himself. There was public access on the far side, but it wasn't often used because the lake was shallow and if you were a fisherman looking for the big ones, you wouldn't find them in Skinner.

Cork turned onto the narrow gravel road that skirted the lake and wove his way through a fine stand of sugar maples that Reinhardt tapped each year. The man may have been a bona fide bastard, but he boiled down a great maple syrup, which he gave away in small bottles as gifts at Christmas. Cork could see the lights of the house through the trees and again where they reflected off the black water of the lake. It was a big, sprawling place, begun small and added onto over several decades as Reinhardt's growing fortune allowed. He'd done all the work himself; the house ended up as quirky as the man whose mind had conceived it. There was no eye to a unifying design. Buck

Reinhardt built whatever suited his fancy at the moment he picked up saw and hammer. It had started as a one-bedroom cabin, but over the years had grown into a multitude of additions put together side by side or on top of one another. In the end, it resembled nothing quite so much as the random construction a child might create with a handful of building blocks. It wasn't ugly exactly. It was certainly unusual, and very big, especially now that Buck and Elise, his second wife, lived there alone.

Cork parked in the drive and climbed the steps of the front porch, which overlooked the lake. The porch light was on. It was early May, too soon for moths. Another three or four weeks and they'd be swarming around the light. He knocked. Almost immediately the door opened.

Elise Reinhardt was younger than Cork by several years, early forties somewhere. Reinhardt had met her while she was carting cocktails in the bar of a four-star resort near Grand Rapids. Shortly after that, the first Mrs. Reinhardt moved out and six months later was dead of pancreatic cancer. Within a year, Buck had married again.

Elise Reinhardt was a strong woman. Any woman who'd marry an old piece of tough leather like Buck Reinhardt had to be. She was an attractive, blond, blue-eyed, big-boned Swede whose maiden name was Lindstrom. Although she was no longer a young woman, she kept herself in shape and knew how to look good. Men in Aurora noticed. Reinhardt liked that about his wife, liked that men looked at her. He often said as much. Said, too, that he'd kill her if he ever caught her looking back, but only said that part after he'd had too many boilermakers.

When she opened the door, she wasn't at all the woman who'd catch a man's eye. Her own eyes were tired and puffy, her face plain, her skin sallow, her lips set in a snarl. She was a woman in mourning and she wore her grief with an awful fury.

"What?" she said.

"Sorry to bother you, Elise. I'm looking for Buck."

"Look somewhere else. He's not here."

"Any idea where I might find him?"

"Like I could give a good goddamn." She took a couple of seconds and pulled herself together. "Try the Buzz Saw. He's probably getting shit faced with the boys. He does that a lot these days."

The truth was that Buck had always done that a lot. Reinhardt owned a tree-trimming business. He'd secured a number of lucrative contracts with power and telephone companies to keep the lines clear of limbs, and he had a dozen crews operating throughout the North Country. He didn't pay all that much, but in an area where the iron mines had mostly closed and logging wasn't what it used to be, Reinhardt was a decent employer. If you worked for Buck, you never missed a paycheck, never got called on the carpet for a sexist or racist slur, and never, when you went drinking with him, paid for your own booze.

"Thanks. If I miss him, mind telling him I want to talk? It's important."

"What about?" Elise said.

Cork couldn't see any reason to hold back. "Alex Kingbird wants to meet with him."

Elise looked dumbfounded. "What could he possibly have to say to my husband?"

"He claims he has something to offer Buck."

"Yeah, what? His heart at the end of a sharp stick?"

"I think it would be a good idea for your husband to hear him out."

"You'd have to hog-tie Buck to get him in the same room with Kingbird."

"Tell him I'll drop by again after church tomorrow morning."

"Buck doesn't go to church anymore."

"I do. Round noon okay?"

Her lips went tight and she stared at him. Finally she said, "I'll tell him."

"Elise, I'm sorry about Kristi."

She nailed him with her ice blue eyes. "No, deep inside you're just so damn happy it wasn't your daughter."

He wasn't going to argue the point. In a way, she was right.

"I'll see Buck tomorrow."

"Lucky fucking you," she said and slammed the door.

THREE

The Buzz Saw stood along Highway 2, a few miles south of Aurora in a little unincorporated municipality called Durham. There was a big neon sign on the roof that appeared to spin like a ripsaw blade. The parking lot was less than half full when Cork pulled in. He didn't see Reinhardt's truck, which was hard to miss because of the rack of floodlights mounted on the cab. Buck claimed he needed the lights for whenever the tree trimming went late and things got dark. Most people suspected the real reason was that Reinhardt shined deer. On the door on either side of the cab was a big image of a green tree with REINHARDT TREE TRIMMING printed boldly in black below.

It was Saturday night, but things at the Buzz Saw weren't buzzing. That was because it was early May, still several weeks away from the onslaught of summer tourists. A few tables were full, but mostly the customers had scattered themselves around the big barroom in singles or pairs. When they weren't talking, they were listening to Mitch Sokol and the Stoned Rangers belt out an ear-splitting mix of electric bluegrass and country rock. Ropes of blue cigarette smoke coiled up everywhere, and the air was a choking mix of that, the odor of spilled beer, and the aroma of deep fry.

Cork stood just inside the front door for a minute, looking the place over. He saw a lot of folks he knew, but he didn't see Buck Reinhardt or anyone who worked for the man. He shook a few hands as he made his way to the bar, where Seneca Peterson was tending that night. She was midtwenties, statuesque, sported a silver stud in one nostril and a ring through her lower lip, and had close-cropped hair that was a striking mix of jet black and cotton candy pink. Cork had known her since she was a baby, when the only pink on her was the natural tone of her skin. She'd been baptized at St. Agnes, made her First Communion there, had sung in the choir, and even once played Mary in the yearly Christmas pageant. Now she was tending bar, with a stud in her nose and a tattoo crawling up the back of her neck like a green spider.

"Hey, Sen," Cork shouted above Sokol and the Rangers.

She stepped up and wiped the bar in front of him. "What'll you have, hon?"

"Leinenkugel's Dark."

"One Leinie's coming up."

She brought him the draw.

"Seen Buck Reinhardt tonight?" he asked.

"Yeah. Left a while ago. Pissed."

"Why?"

"I cut him off."

"He'd had too many?"

She shook her head. "Mostly he was shooting his mouth off. You know Buck."

"What was his gripe?"

"About what you'd expect given what happened to Kristi. Lot of talk about f'ing Indians."

"Red Boyz?"

"That, sure. But f'ing Indians in general. A lot of my customers have some Ojibwe blood in them. I don't need Buck Reinhardt getting everyone riled up."

"He left easy?"

"I'd say so."

"Doesn't sound like Buck."

"The Green Giant and Turner escorted him out." She was talking about Derek Green, the bouncer at the door, and the bar manager, both more gorilla than man.

"Was he alone?"

"Yeah."

"Drunk would you say?"

"I've seen him way worse. Mostly he was"—she thought a

moment and scratched at the stud in her nose—"belligerent. Hell, who can blame him? But I told him he had to do his drinking and his bitching somewhere else."

"Any idea where he might have headed?"

"If he was going in the general direction of home, the next logical stop would be Tanner's on the Lake."

He left her a five as a tip—he liked the idea that she'd kicked Reinhardt out for badmouthing the Ojibwe—and headed to Tanner's. Reinhardt wasn't there either and hadn't been. Cork tried the Silver Horse, the Chippewa Grand Casino bar, and finally the bar at the Four Seasons, all with the same result. It was a quarter of eleven by then. He didn't want to call Reinhardt's house and risk disturbing Elise. He stood on the empty deck in back of the Four Seasons, looking at the spray of the Milky Way above Iron Lake. The temperature was in the low fifties, not bad for that time of year. He had on a light jacket but a good flannel shirt would have done as well. Up the shoreline, the lights of Aurora were like stars fallen to earth. The night was still and quiet. It would have been a pleasure to stand there awhile longer taking in the stillness, the stars, the air that smelled of apple-wood smoke from the fireplace in the Four Seasons's lounge. He decided to call it a night and head home. He would hit Reinhardt's place first thing after Mass in the morning. That would give Buck a chance to recover a little if he was hungover. He was a son of a bitch sober. Hungover, he just might get it in his head to take a chainsaw to Cork.

Corcoran O'Connor lived in an old two-story frame house on an old residential street in Aurora called Gooseberry Lane. Lights were still on downstairs when he parked in the drive. Inside, he found his wife, Jo, on the sofa watching a video. Nine-year-old Stevie was asleep with his feet on his mother's lap. Jo didn't get up when Cork came in, but Trixie, the family mutt, jumped up from where she'd been lying and came bounding toward him with her tail wagging a blue streak.

"Nice someone's glad to see me," Cork said. He patted Trixie and kissed the top of Jo's head. "What are you watching?"

"The last few minutes of *Abbott and Costello Meet Franken-stein*." Cork had introduced his son to the old comic duo, and Stevie loved them, though Jo wasn't a particular fan. "Took you a long time. How'd it go with Alex Kingbird?"

"Let's talk in the kitchen."

She gently maneuvered herself from under her son and left him sleeping soundly on the sofa. In the kitchen, she plucked a couple of chocolate chip cookies from the jar on the counter, gave one to Cork, and they sat down at the table.

"So tell me," she said.

"He wants to meet with Buck Reinhardt."

"Whatever for?"

"To avert a war, he says. He thinks the shooting's about to begin."

"I wouldn't put it past Buck to haul out the firepower. What's Kingbird offering to entice him to a meeting?"

"Justice."

"What's that mean?"

"I don't know. He wouldn't say."

"Justice." She frowned, bit into her cookie, and looked thought-ful.

Kristi Reinhardt had been eighteen when she died. She'd been one of those girls life had drenched in promise. A stunning beauty with hair the color of dark honey. Smart, athletic, a talented swimmer and diver. She was also reckless and a thrill seeker, traits she got from Buck. She had a fondness for motorcycles and for the kind of guys who rode them. It was one of those guys, a biker named Aaron "Crunch" Bergman, who'd introduced her to meth. When it became clear she had a drug problem, Buck and Elise sent her to Hazelden, the renowned treatment facility near the Twin Cities. She came home clean, but within a couple of months of returning to Aurora, Kristi died while under the influence of the drug. It had happened during a late-night party at the park above Mercy Falls. According to wit-nesses—other kids present—she'd poised herself at the lip of the rocky ledge on top of the falls, as if she was preparing to dive in one of her competitions. No one thought she'd do it. It was never clear whether she'd fallen or had actually dived. She hit the pool at the bottom of the falls headfirst. The pool was shallow. She smashed her skull on a rock two feet below the surface and died instantly.

In his statement to sheriff's investigators, Eric Neiburg, one of the kids at the party, said that he'd seen Kristi smoking ice: crystal meth. She'd told him that she got it from an Indian—Lonnie Thunder—in exchange for oral sex. When sheriff's deputies executed a search warrant for the trailer on the reservation where Thunder lived, they found meth and they found photographs of Kristi Reinhardt that would make any parent's blood run cold. They also found photographs and videos that Thunder had made of Ojibwe girls, some of them minors. They didn't find Thunder. He'd vanished. The general speculation was that he was hiding somewhere on the reservation, protected by the Red Boyz. Buck Reinhardt had made it clear that he was holding Alex Kingbird personally responsible.

"You don't think he's going to turn Lonnie Thunder over to Buck?" Jo asked.

"So Buck can skin him alive? I don't think so."

"Will Buck agree to meet?"

Cork finished his cookie. "Want some milk?"

"No, thanks."

He got a tumbler from the cupboard, went to the refrigerator, and pulled out a half-gallon carton of Land O' Lakes 2 percent. "I tried to track him down. Hit half a dozen bars, no luck."

"Ah, that's why you're so late and smell like an ashtray."

He put the milk back in the fridge and sat down again. "Where's Annie?"

"She went to the movies with Cara Haines."

Cork gulped his milk. "I'm bushed."

"What about Buck?"

"He's a lot older than me and drunk. I'll bet he's bushed, too."

"I mean when will you talk to him?"

"Tomorrow after church. Figure I'll catch him while he's still a little groggy. That way if he tries to shoot me, his aim'll be off."

She looked troubled and reached across the table and put her hand over his. "I don't like the idea of you in the middle of this, sweetheart. Buck Reinhardt has always been a little crazy. Who knows what losing

Kristi could drive him to do? And if Alex Kingbird is really dealing drugs, god, I don't want you anywhere near them when they meet."

"Kingbird gave his word to come unarmed. I'll work the same promise out of Buck or it won't happen."

"His word? You'd take his word? And Buck's?"

"Look, I'll figure something out, Jo." He eased his hand free.

She sat back, unhappy. "This is serious, Cork."

"I know, believe me. But I think Kingbird's right. Unless somebody does something, all hell could break loose around here. He's trying to do something and he's asked me to help. What can I say?"

"Are you getting paid for this?"

"Five Franklins up front and another five when the meeting goes down."

She drilled him with her cold blue eyes. "What kind of casket can I possibly get with that?"

FOUR

Lucinda Kingbird was happy and that made her afraid. Though she had struggled all her life, all forty-four years, in the pursuit of real happiness, it had eluded her. So many people seemed happy that Lucinda had to accept on faith that it was a true thing. In a way, it was like the story of the Blessed Virgin and the conception of Jesus: illogical, irrational, a circumstance she had never experienced—never would experience—yet a whole world, a whole history of people, most far smarter than she, had believed and defended it, so how could it not be true? Happiness for her had always been a question of faith, not experience.

Lately, however, miraculously, she'd been happy. But having discovered happiness, she was terrified that it might be snatched from her.

That Sunday morning as she drove up the eastern shoreline of Iron Lake, all around her shafts of sunlight shot through the pines like gold arrows from heaven. She was a small, pretty woman with dark eyes and the light tan skin of a Latina. Her hair, long and black, still showed no hint of gray. She sang softly to herself, an old song from her childhood, one that her grandmother had crooned to her.

> "'Duérmete mi niño.
> Duérmete solito.
> Qué cuando te despiertes,
> Te daré atolito.'"

Until recently, she'd forgotten the sweet little lullaby. Now she often sang it to her granddaughter as she held the baby in her arms and felt, deep in her heart, a warmth she knew must be happiness.

As soon as she crossed onto the reservation, she took Pike Road east and followed it until she came to the gravel lane that cut off to the right through a stand of red pines that hid the house of her son Alejandro. She parked near the front door and waited. She was expected. Every Sunday morning, she drove from Aurora to pick up her daughter-in-law and her granddaughter and take them with her to Mass at St. Agnes.

She genuinely liked her daughter-in-law. Rayette was a smart cookie, tough, devoted to her husband and her child. Rayette often told Lucinda how much she appreciated her help with the baby. She seemed to enjoy as much as Lucinda did the Sunday drives to St. Agnes. Much of the time on the way there and back, they talked family, talked motherhood, even talked sometimes about deep things, things like God, which Lucinda never discussed with anyone else. She thought of her daughter-in-law as a friend and felt blessed.

There was so much now that made her happy.

The front door didn't open, and Rayette didn't appear with Misty in the car-seat carrier. Running late, Lucinda decided. With a baby, it was understandable. She got out, went to the door, and rang the bell. From inside came the sound of voices and the baby's incessant crying.

Pobrecita, thought Lucinda. Poor little one.

She rang the bell again, then knocked long and hard to be heard above the baby's wail. Finally she tried the knob. The door was locked, but she had a key, which she used.

"Rayette? Alejandro?" she called.

She knew that using her son's Christian name—or the Spanish version of it, which was how she'd always addressed him—didn't please him these days, but she refused to use any other. Alejandro was a good name. It would still be his long after this Red Boyz business had passed.

The talk, she discovered, came from the television, tuned to an infomercial hyping a revolutionary piece of exercise equipment. Except for the crying from the baby's room, the house felt empty. Lucinda slipped her shoes off and left them beside the others already on the mat by the front door. She found her granddaughter in the crib, tangled up in her pink blanket.

"Oh, sweet one," she cooed. She untangled the blanket, lifted the child, and held Misty against her breast. "Shhhhh. Shhhhh. It's all right, *niña*. Grandma's here."

But where were Rayette and Alejandro?

The baby continued to scream while Lucinda checked the bedroom, where the bed was still neatly made. Had it been slept in at all? She returned to the baby's room and changed Misty's diaper, trying to keep her mounting sense of dread at bay. In the kitchen, she made a bottle of the formula Rayette kept in the cupboard. She settled in the rocker in the living room with Misty in her arms. The baby greedily sucked the bottle dry. Lucinda burped her and little Misty fell asleep almost immediately.

Now Lucinda allowed the worry to overwhelm her. No mother would willingly desert her child this way. And Alejandro, for all his macho posturing, was a good father and husband. He, too, would not be absent if he could help it.

She stood slowly and tried to return Misty to her crib, but the baby began to wake and Lucinda decided it was best to hold her a bit longer. Once again she checked the rooms of the house. Nothing seemed out of place, nothing amiss, though she wondered at the shoes on the mat beside the front door. In addition to her own, there were a pair of Skechers she knew belonged to Rayette, and a pair of Red Wing boots that were probably Alejandro's. It seemed odd that these items were still there. Rayette usually picked up before she retired for the night. And if they'd gone out this morning, why hadn't they put on their shoes?

She grabbed the soiled diaper she'd left on the changing table and took it to the utility room off the kitchen to dispose of it in the trash bin. The room had a door to the outside, facing the garage. The door frame was splintered, as if by a powerful blow, and the door itself stood open.

"*Madre de Dios,*" Lucinda whispered, hoarse with fear.

With the child still in her arms, she stumbled outside through the open door and gulped in the cool, pine-scented air. She hurried to the garage and peered in a window. Both her son's Explorer and the Toyota Corolla that Rayette drove were parked inside. She stepped back, stepped into something slippery, and she looked down. She stood in the middle of a dark, irregular shape that might have been spilled oil, but looked more like blood.

Her legs went shaky. Misty felt too heavy in her arms. Something had happened, she knew it absolutely. Something bad.

"Call Will," she said, speaking aloud to give herself courage. Her husband would know what to do.

The backyard had been carved out of a meadow, and tall wild grasses grew up against Alejandro's neatly mowed lawn. A gathering of crows, noisy and contentious, fluttered about in the high grass a few yards into the meadow. She wanted to ignore their greedy cries, but crows were scavengers, she knew, and she found herself drawn toward them, pulled slowly across the yard by the dark need to know what it was they fought over. As she drew nearer, she saw an outline pressed down in the meadow grass where the birds had gathered. The sun had climbed above the pines along the east side of the meadow, and grass shimmered with drops of yellow dew and beads of a garnet color.

At her approach, the crows lifted, a black curtain rising, and they flew away.

When Lucinda saw the prize that had drawn them there, she screamed. The baby woke and echoed her.

FIVE

Occasionally on Sunday mornings in church, Cork just wasn't there. His butt was in the pew but his mind was a million miles away. That was a blessing of ritual: Some Sundays you could fake it. This was one of those Sundays, and Cork went through Mass without thinking about it. In his head, he was going over the talk he would have with Buck Reinhardt afterward. It would be tricky, but he liked the challenge of bringing Buck and Kingbird together. The truth was that he was dying to know what the leader of the Red Boyz had to say. What was it he was willing to offer Reinhardt? Giving up Lonnie Thunder, turning him over to the sheriff, didn't feel right. A gang—any brotherhood—was strong because of the integrity of the whole. Solidarity was the foundation, and its erosion was the end. Giving up Thunder would be too great a risk. Kingbird had to understand that. So what do you offer as justice, Cork wondered, when justice was impossible to offer?

He was pulled from his reverie when his daughter, seventeen-year-old Annie, left the choir loft and joined another teenager—Ulysses Kingbird—in front of the chancel rail for the offertory. Annie sang a medieval hymn that the young Kingbird had arranged. Ulysses accompanied her on guitar. They'd been practicing for weeks. Cork had heard Annie singing in the bathroom, in her bedroom, humming on the stairs. This was the first time he'd heard her with the accompaniment and he was moved. It was extraordinary.

After the service, Cork and Jo caught up with Ulysses Kingbird in the common room in the church basement. This was where the congregation usually gathered to socialize. Refreshments were kept simple: juice or punch for the children, coffee for adults, cookies for all. The kitchen abutted the common room, and there were always several women visible through the wide serving windows, bustling around in an important way.

Ulysses stood in a corner with his father, Will Kingbird, who had a cell phone to his ear. Ulysses was sixteen—barely. His skin had the shadowy cast of the Ojibwe, courtesy of his father, but his features were sharp, his face narrow, his lips thin and soft, all evidence of the Hispanic blood on his mother's side. In a couple of years, he might grow handsome, but at the moment he was awkward and pimpled. Standing beside his father, he looked as if he'd rather be anywhere else on earth.

"Ulysses," Jo said, approaching him with a warm smile. "That was an absolutely beautiful piece you played."

"Thanks." His dark eyes dropped to the linoleum. "It was Annie, you know. She's got the voice."

"Don't go selling yourself short. You play the guitar wonderfully. And that arrangement was extraordinary."

He shrugged off her compliment. It was clear that if there had been a way, he would have disappeared.

"Where's your mother?" Jo asked. "I can't believe Lucinda would miss this."

His father flipped his cell phone closed. "That's what I was just trying to find out." Will Kingbird was full-blood Ojibwe. Powerfully built, he stood well over six feet tall. He was Cork's age, staring fifty in the face, and his black hair, which he kept military short, was salted with gray. He held himself impossibly rigid, the result, Cork figured, of thirty years in the marines. "She was supposed to pick up Rayette and Misty and bring them to church like she always does. Can't get her cell phone and nobody answers at Alex's place."

"Car trouble maybe," Cork suggested. "If they're on the rez, it's hard to get a cell phone signal."

"Or baby trouble," Jo said. "They can be a handful."

Kingbird frowned at their casual suggestions. "I think Uly and me'll head out there, see what's going on."

Annie worked her way toward them through the post-Mass gath-

ering. When she reached Ulysses, she playfully punched his arm.
"Awesome, dude."

A smile slid briefly across his lips. "No, you were."

"Oh, like you and your guitar were totally not there." She put her
arm around him in the way Cork had seen her do with her softball
teammates. She glanced at Will Kingbird, cordial but not friendly.
"Morning, Mr. Kingbird."

"Morning."

"Wasn't he incredible?"

"You both did a nice job."

"Dude," she said to Ulysses, "your mother would have loved it.
Where is she?"

"I don't know."

"We're about to find out," Will Kingbird said. He gave them all a
nod in parting. "Let's go, Uly."

Cork watched them weave their way across the basement. Halfway to the door, the parish priest, Father Ted Green, met them and
spoke to Kingbird for a moment. They followed the priest toward another door where Cy Borkman, in his deputy's uniform, was waiting.
They all went upstairs.

"What was that about?" Annie said.

"No idea," Cork replied. But it didn't look good.

Jo turned to head away. "I'm going to find Stevie. I'll be right
back."

A few minutes later, Father Ted returned to the common room.
He approached Cork, a look of anguish on his youthful face. "There's
someone in my office who wants to see you."

"Who is it?" Cork said.

"The sheriff."

"What's up, Ted?"

"I think you'd better talk to the sheriff."

Cork turned to Annie. "Tell your mom I'm upstairs."

He followed the priest to his office. Inside, Sheriff Marsha Dross
was waiting, standing at a window, looking out at the sunny May
morning. She turned when she heard them enter.

"Mind, Father?" she said.

"No, I'll be happy to wait outside."

"And would you close the door?"

When they were alone, Cork said, "What's going on, Marsha?"

"Alexander and Rayette Kingbird were killed last night."

"Oh, Jesus."

"Lucinda Kingbird found their bodies this morning."

"How'd it happen?"

"Before I answer that, I need to ask you a few questions, Cork."

"Go ahead."

"What was the nature of your relationship with Kingbird?"

"Until last night I had no relationship with him to speak of."

"What changed last night?"

"He asked me to come and see him. I went to his place and we talked."

"What time?"

"I got there about eight thirty, left maybe twenty minutes later."

"He was alive when you left?"

"Of course he was alive. Haven't you got a time of death yet?"

She lifted her hand to hold back his questions. "In a minute. What did you talk about?"

"He wanted me to arrange a meeting with Buck Reinhardt."

"Why?"

"To keep things from getting out of hand. Kingbird told me Buck and some of his men threatened one of the Red Boyz."

"Did you arrange a meeting?"

"I couldn't find Buck."

"Where'd you look?"

"His house first, then four or five bars. I gave up a little before eleven and went home."

Dross was thirty-five, not a pretty woman exactly—big bones, broad face, hair kept short. She was wearing jeans and a blue flannel shirt with the sleeves rolled back. She pulled a paper evidence sack from the breast pocket of her shirt and handed it to Cork. He opened it and saw that it held one of the business cards he gave out for the work he sometimes did as a private investigator. There was dried blood on the card. He closed the sack and handed it back.

"We found this on Kingbird," she said. "That's one of the reasons I wanted to talk to you." Her eyes were brown and, at the moment, edged with a look that might have been anger. "It was an execution, Cork. Their hands were taped. They were shot in the back, close range, a shotgun. Preliminary estimate of time of death is between eleven P.M. and one A.M. Ed and his team are working the scene. BCA's on the way. Would you mind going out there with me? Something I'd like you to take a look at."

"Sure. Just let me tell Jo."

Father Ted was outside, staring down the hallway toward the open door to the sanctuary, where sunlight through the stained-glass windows fell on the pews in colorful, broken pieces.

"Is there anything I can do?" he asked. He was not quite thirty, had been the priest at St. Agnes for a little over two years, and was full of a naive and vibrant energy that Cork sometimes found exhausting.

Cork put a hand on the priest's shoulder. "You know any prayers for peace, Ted, now's the time to haul 'em out."

SIX

Y ou could have had a deputy do this," Cork said as they drove south along Iron Lake in the sheriff's cruiser.

"I wanted to talk to you myself," Dross said. "Ever since Kristi Reinhardt died, I've been worried something like this would happen."

"Still no luck locating Lonnie Thunder?"

"The people who could help live on the rez—and you know how much they like white folks in uniforms."

"A lot of them wouldn't mind one bit if you arrested Thunder."

"No one's come forward to tell me where he is."

During the third year of his first term as sheriff, Cork had hired Marsha Dross as the first female law enforcement officer in Tamarack County. She was approximately his height and not too dissimilar in build. One evening nearly two years earlier, in the soft light of dusk, a sniper had mistaken her for Cork and put a bullet into her. She'd survived, but the damage had killed any hope she might have had of ever conceiving a child. She wasn't married—the shooting had ended her engagement to a man who desperately wanted children—there were no prospects on the horizon, and Cork didn't know if the question of marriage and children was one she even pondered much these days.

"Taking a lot of crap lately from a righteous and outraged citizenry?" he asked.

She gave a snort that passed for a laugh. "You see Hell Hanover's editorial in this week's *Sentinel*?"

She was referring to Helmuth Hanover, publisher of the area's weekly newspaper. Anyone who'd ever been the target of one of his venomous printed diatribes pretty much figured that he was in league with the devil. Hence, the name by which he was generally known: Hell.

"Yeah. And come to think of it, you do resemble Barney Fife with a bra."

Dross rounded the southern end of the lake and began to head north, up the eastern shoreline toward the rez.

"Makes you feel any better," Cork said, "Hanover took a lot of shots at me when I wore the badge."

"Hanover's an ass, but he's reflecting a pretty significant sentiment. This Red Boyz horseshit's got everybody pissed. It's bringing out the bigot in people."

"You think it's horseshit?" Cork asked.

"Don't you?"

"There's stuff I disagree with, but I can understand the reasoning."

"You're not going to give me a sociology lecture about poverty, are you? Because with the casino, every Ojibwe in the county is getting a nice chunk of change now."

"That's not exactly true and you know it. But it's not about money. The Red Boyz are all young, a lot of them raised by parents who weren't much more than kids themselves and didn't give them any sense of who they are or what they could be. All they know is that they're Indian and looked down on, generally speaking. A brotherhood is one way for them to find some self-esteem, to belong to something that makes them feel important, especially a brotherhood with its roots in Ojibwe ethics."

"Ethics? The Red Boyz? The ethics of thugs maybe."

"The Red Boyz stand pretty firm against drugs and alcohol. They don't use and they do everything they can to discourage it on the rez. Bet if you tracked the numbers, you'd find that since Kingbird organized the Red Boyz, arrests for drug use and related crimes in this county have gone way down."

"I do track them and you're right. But"—she held up a cautionary finger—"that doesn't mean there's no crime going on. The Red Boyz all drive nice, new, big vehicles, and I can almost guarantee they didn't pay for them with what they get from the distribution of the casino revenues. DEA's convinced the Red Boyz operate a narcotics depot on the rez. They warehouse the merchandise and distribute it all over the Midwest."

"Where other people's children buy it."

"Exactly."

"I told you there's stuff I didn't agree with. That's some of the stuff."

"What else don't you agree with?"

"It's a charismatic organization. Its strength depends too much on Kingbird's influence. He was the one who gave it direction, who set the guidelines."

"Guidelines? You think Lonnie Thunder was operating under guidelines, Cork? You ought to see the videos he made."

"I don't know what to make of Thunder."

"Kingbird's gone now, so what'll the Red Boyz do?"

"I wish I could say there was somebody capable of stepping in to fill his shoes. Tom Blessing was basically his right hand, but Tom's no Alexander Kingbird. Things could easily fall apart, get real messy."

"That's exactly what I'm afraid of, this whole situation getting out of hand. I'd feel a lot better if I had Lonnie Thunder in custody. That might go a long way toward pacifying everybody." She gave him a sidelong glance.

"This is what you wanted to talk to me about?"

She kept her eyes on the road ahead. "You're part Ojibwe. People on the rez trust you."

"Trust me more than they trust you anyway. It's a situational kind of thing. For a lot of Shinnobs, I'm still way too white."

"Cork, I don't have a single deputy with a drop of Ojibwe blood in him."

"No one to creep around the rez and snoop unnoticed? No one to go looking for Lonnie Thunder? That's what you want me to do?"

"That's where I was headed, more or less."

"I would do this why? For the sake of friendship or some other sentimental crap?"

"There's something you need to see at Kingbird's place."

* * *

Captain Ed Larson headed up major-crimes investigation in Tamarack County. He was midfifties, a tall, studious-looking man who wore wire-rims and preferred button-down oxford shirts and suede bucks. When Dross and Cork arrived at the Kingbird home, Larson was out front deep in conversation with Agent Simon Rutledge from the Bemidji office of the BCA, the state's Bureau of Criminal Apprehension. Cork knew Rutledge well. He liked the man and respected his abilities.

Rutledge seemed surprised to see him. "Cork?"

"Hey, Simon." He shook the agent's hand, then Larson's. "Morning, Ed."

Larson appraised Cork's attire: sport coat, white shirt, tie. "Church?"

"I snatched him after the service," Dross said. She exchanged a handshake with the BCA agent. "Thanks for coming, Simon."

Rutledge wasn't an imposing figure. A couple of inches under six feet, he had reddish thinning hair and a hopelessly boyish smile. He was, however, one of the most effective interrogators Cork had ever worked with. It was his style, full of sympathy and very winning. Cork had seen him coax confessions out of suspects whose lips were sealed with distrust, anger, contempt. People in the cop business who knew Rutledge called his style of interrogation "Simonizing."

"You don't mind me asking, what's O'Connor doing here?" Rutledge said to Dross. "No offense, Cork."

"None taken."

"I asked him here in a consulting capacity. Have you had a chance to look things over?"

"Ed walked me through the scene. Your team's doing a good job."

"What do you guys think?" Dross asked.

Larson nodded toward the garage. "We found blood on the grass over there. Isolated and, as far as we can tell, not related to the shootings themselves. Kingbird had a head wound. Somebody clubbed him pretty good. A lot of bleeding but not much swelling, so looks as if it happened just prior to the killing."

Dross glanced at Cork. "How was he last night?"

"Nobody had clubbed him when I left."

Rutledge looked confused. "You were here last night, Cork?"

"We'll get to that in a minute, Simon," Dross said. "Go on, Ed."

"What it looks like is that Kingbird came outside and was as-saulted near the garage. My guess would be that he was drawn out. But he was careful. He left the doors locked behind him. Whoever it was who assaulted him had to break into the house through the door to the utility room. I imagine they were after Rayette. She was prob-ably a witness. Or maybe the assailant had planned all along to make her a victim."

"Any 911 calls?" Cork asked.

Larson shook his head. "The phone line was cut. And we're too far out for a cell to be able to pick up a signal."

"Lucinda Kingbird found the bodies, is that right?"

Larson nodded.

"Where is she?"

"Deputy Minot took her home."

"How was she doing?"

He shrugged. "Soldier's wife. While I interviewed her, she didn't shed a tear, just worried about the baby."

Rutledge squinted at Cork. "The suspense is killing me."

"Suspense?" Cork said.

"I'm dying to know what you were doing out here last night."

Cork explained the circumstances.

"Buck Reinhardt," Ed Larson said, as if it made perfect sense.

"I know about the Reinhardt girl's death," Rutledge said. "Tell me about her father. Is he the kind of man who could do something like this?"

Dross considered his question. "You have a daughter, Simon. If you believed someone was responsible for her death, think you might be capable of something like this?"

Rutledge glanced at Cork. "You said you didn't find him last night."

"That's right."

Larson took off his wire-rims and carefully cleaned the lenses with a white handkerchief he'd pulled from his pocket. "When I'm finished here, I'll head over to the Reinhardt place, interview Buck."

"Might be a good idea if I went along," Rutledge suggested. "You talk to Reinhardt, I'll talk to his wife, see if we get the same story."

"Who else should we be talking to?" Dross asked.

Larson said, "DEA's convinced the Red Boyz are deep into the drug trade. Cold-blooded executions and drugs pretty much go hand in hand."

"Match made in hell," Dross said. "Call DEA, Ed. Run this by them."

"What about the Red Boyz themselves?" Rutledge said. "Is it possible there's a power struggle going on or some kind of ideological rift, anything that might have led to this?"

They all looked to Cork.

He held up his hands defensively. "It's not like there's a pipeline that runs between me and the Red Boyz. Don't forget, I hauled some of them in as juveniles."

"You know their families," Dross said.

"I'll do what I can, okay?"

Larson slipped his wire-rims back on. "Marsha, did you tell Cork about the business at the back of the house?"

"What business?" Cork said.

"It's what I wanted to show you." Dross turned and led the way.

They walked carefully through the yard, along a path Larson's people had marked for entry and egress from the scene. In the high grass beyond the mowed edge of the backyard, deputies were still working. The bodies of Alexander and Rayette Kingbird were gone, but the long green blades of wild grass were still splashed with spatters of dark red.

"Tom Conklin's already at Nelson's," Dross said, speaking of the man contracted as medical examiner for the county. He did his autopsies in one of the prep rooms in the basement of Nelson's Funeral Home. "He seemed pretty eager to get started. Turn around, Cork."

Cork turned and looked back at the house. "Jesus. Is that what I think it is?"

"We've taken samples," Larson said. "We'll have them analyzed to be certain. But, yeah, I'm pretty sure it's blood."

Across the wall of the house, painted in large, ragged letters each a foot high and dried now to the color of old rust were the words DED BOYZ.

SEVEN

Annie O'Connor had learned how to cook from the best. For the first fifteen years of her life, most meals at the O'Connor house were prepared by her mother's sister, Aunt Rose. Rose was a cook with an outstanding reputation, and Annie was an apt pupil. Though she preferred sports to most domestic pursuits, cooking appealed to Annie's sense of order and, in a way, her enjoyment of competition. Since Aunt Rose had left—married and gone to Chicago—Annie regularly took a turn preparing the evening meal. Her father's schedule was erratic, especially since he'd started his sideline business as a private investigator. He wasn't an inspired cook, preferring to stick with the staples: mac and cheese, hot dogs, chili, sometimes a passable meat loaf. And once Sam's Place opened for the season, he wouldn't be home most evenings until very late. Her mother often worked long hours at her law office and had always been a cook with a reputation for disasters in the kitchen. Although she had improved some since Aunt Rose left, the truth was that almost everyone in the family preferred Annie's cooking, and Annie liked being the best at things.

Sunday dinner was always at one. That afternoon the main dish was pot roast, simple but succulent, and the smell of it filled the house. Annie and her mother worked together in the kitchen, both agreeing that Annie was in charge. Stevie's job was to set the table. It was all a familiar pattern, yet that day felt anything but usual to Annie. Before he'd gone out to the reservation with the sheriff that morning after church, her father shared with them what had happened to the Kingbirds, and she couldn't stop thinking about the tragedy.

She knew Rayette Kingbird mostly from visiting with her at St.

Agnes. She'd liked Rayette, liked that at first glance she appeared to be a hard woman but in fact was quite kind and very sensible when you got to know her. Alex Kingbird she knew only a little. She'd seen him around town with Rayette. They'd stopped together at Sam's Place a few times for burgers and shakes. He was quiet, but he seemed to laugh often when he was talking with Rayette. Annie knew the stories about him: kicked out of the marines, an L.A. gang member, prison time, and the Red Boyz. What she saw was a man who seemed to be a good husband and a good father, someone in love with his wife and his child.

She knew Ulysses Kingbird best. Again, this was through the St. Agnes connection, where music brought them together. At school, he didn't fit in anywhere. He wasn't a brain. He wasn't a jock. He wasn't a preppie or a stoner. Despite his musical talent, he didn't hang with the band geeks or the artsy kids. Mostly he was quiet and tried to disappear. Moving down the hallway at school, he reminded her of a piece of driftwood floating, purposeless, down a river.

He might have been successful at being overlooked if it hadn't been for the fact that his brother was Alexander Kingbird, head of the Red Boyz. As a result, kids at school hit on Uly for drugs. Teachers made assumptions about him. His asshole classmates—and there were a lot of assholes—tormented him with insults. Since Kristi Reinhardt had died, things had become worse. Uly might never have come right out and said anything, but the music connected him and Annie in a powerful way. When they got together to practice the songs Uly had arranged for Sunday's service, Annie sometimes got him to talk. Not a lot, but through the crack in the door that opened, Annie saw much.

Uly's biggest problem, it seemed to her, was that his father was Will Kingbird. Him, she didn't like at all. Mostly she saw him at Mass, where he sat so stiffly he looked as if he'd been carved out of the pew itself. He made her think of the old Louisville Slugger her parents had given her when she started playing softball: hard and perfectly capable of delivering a good, solid smack. Mrs. Kingbird often seemed to have a wary look on her face, and though Uly never talked about abuse, it made Annie wonder.

Her father came home a few minutes before the potatoes were

done. He went upstairs to wash his hands. When he came back down, everything was on the table and ready.

At first the conversation was about Jenny, Annie's older sister who was nearing the end of her first year of college at the University of Iowa, and who'd called to check in, as she always did, after the family came home from church. But Annie was dying to know what exactly had happened at the Kingbird place. Her father didn't want to talk about it, except to say that it was true, Rayette and Alexander Kingbird were dead. They'd been shot.

Stevie, who seemed not to know better, kept pressing. "Where?"

"They were found in the meadow behind the house."

"I mean where were they shot?"

Her father looked up from dishing roasted potatoes onto his plate. "In the back," he replied after a long pause.

"Was there lots of blood and stuff?"

"Stephen," his mother said, "that's enough."

"I was just wondering." He lingered over his green beans. "Why did they want you there?"

"Alex and Rayette were Ojibwe. The sheriff thought that because I'm part Ojibwe, I might be able to answer some questions they had."

Annie used this as her opening to ask about something that had been on her mind for quite a while. "You and Mr. Kingbird were friends once, right, Dad?"

"We're not unfriendly now."

"I mean like tight."

"We played football together. Because we shared Ojibwe blood, he probably talked to me a little more than other people. Folks saw that as tight, I suppose, but I never really knew him. I don't think anybody did. He never let anybody that close."

Annie said, "I like Uly's mom better."

Her father smiled. "You want to know the truth, so do I."

"But she seems, I don't know, subdued. Like she's afraid of him."

"That might be a cultural issue," her mother said. "She's Latina. I believe it's not unusual to be submissive to your husband, at least in public."

"I think Uly's afraid of him," Annie said.

Her father said, "Has he told you that?"

"Not in so many words. I just get that feeling."

Stevie piped in, "Uly sure plays the guitar good."

"He's always seemed a little troubled to me," her mother said. "Do you ever see him at school, Annie?"

"He's only a sophomore, so we don't have any classes together. But I see him sometimes, yeah. He gets picked on, mostly by guys who're huge losers and looking for somebody they think might be a bigger loser than them. Allan Richards, for example."

"Richards?" Her father looked up from his plate. "That wouldn't be Cal Richards's boy, would it?"

"That's him."

"Cal Richards." He shook his head. "Now there's one sick soul. Sounds like the apple hasn't fallen far from the tree."

"Will you help the sheriff?" Stevie asked.

"A little bit maybe. I'm going back to the reservation this afternoon to talk to a couple of people."

"Oh?" Annie's mother said. She didn't sound thrilled.

"I need to talk to George LeDuc, Jo. And as long as I'm out that way, I might as well drop by the Blessing place and have a word with Tom."

"Mom, can Trixie come in?" Stevie asked.

"Yes, but don't feed her at the table. I've put some scraps aside for her for later."

Stevie got up to let the dog in. Annie waited until she thought he couldn't hear, then asked the question that had most been on her mind.

"Do the shootings have anything to do with Kristi Reinhardt?"

"I don't know, Annie." Her father stabbed another piece of pot roast, but paused before he put it on his plate. "Buck Reinhardt is a strange man. But, you know, if this is all about his daughter, I can almost understand."

He seemed ready to say more, but Stevie came back in with Trixie at his heels, and her father went back to eating.

What she would remember whenever she thought back on that conversation was the powerful confusion of compassion and anger she saw on her father's face. That and how much the look scared her.

EIGHT

Thomas Blessing lived with his mother, Fanny, in a one-story frame house that, as long as Cork could remember, had been in desperate need of a new coat of paint. The house was a god-awful purple, something out of a psychedelic nightmare, and Cork had often wondered if one reason Fanny didn't paint it was that nobody was stupid enough to manufacture the color anymore.

The house stood near a crossroads on the eastern side of the rez. On the other side of the road stood the abandoned ruins of an old gas station, a gray derelict that stared hollow-eyed at the Blessing place. Several years before, a photographer for *National Geographic* had shot the old place, and the photo appeared in the publication, run with an article about the plight of the rez: the deterioration, the drunkenness, the desperation. It hadn't been an unfair article, Cork had thought at the time, but it had made the situation on the rez sound hopeless. The Ojibwe may have lacked many things, but they'd never lacked for courage and they'd never lost hope.

Behind the Blessing house was a marsh full of cattails and red-winged blackbirds. In the summer, the marsh was home to great blue herons that waded among the lily pads with awkward majesty and bent with a formal-looking stiffness to snatch at fish and crawdads.

It was Fanny Blessing who answered Cork's knock. She appeared to be headed out. A big black purse hung on her shoulder and a jean jacket was slung over her arm.

"*Boozhoo*, Fanny," he said, offering the familiar Ojibwe greeting.

"If you're here to arrest Tommy, I ain't going to stop you," she said.

She was a heavy woman. She was also a smoker, had been since she was a kid, and she was paying the price: emphysema. She wore a tube that ran from her nostrils, over both ears, and down to a small green oxygen tank, which she pulled around beside her on a little wheeled cart. She was a couple of years younger than Cork and had been a wild one in her day. Fanny had loved a good time, loved Wild Turkey with a beer chaser, loved dancing in bars and at powwows, and loved men, no-good men especially. She'd had three children by three different fathers. One had died young, a drowning. The middle one, a girl named Topaz, had run away when she was sixteen and, as far as Cork knew, hadn't been in touch with Fanny since. Thomas, her youngest, was the only one left with her, but she didn't seem particularly inclined to want to keep him.

"I know whatever you're here for, he probably done," she said. "All that crazy Red Boyz shit."

"I haven't done anything," Tom Blessing said from somewhere in the room behind her. "And even if I did, he wouldn't be taking me anywhere, Mom. He's not the sheriff anymore."

"Just here to talk to Tom, if you don't mind," Cork said.

"He's the one you got to convince." She waved away her responsibility. "You two go at it. Me, I'm heading to the casino." She let the screen door slam shut behind her and maneuvered past Cork with her oxygen cart in tow.

Thomas Blessing stepped into the light that fell through the doorway into the living room. "I keep telling you," he called after her, "it's like taking water from a lake and just pouring it back in."

Cork figured he was speaking about the checks each registered tribal member received as a share of the profits from the Chippewa Grand Casino, south of Aurora. Fanny took the money then gave it right back at the slot machines.

"What do you want me to do?" she called as she opened the door of her big white Buick, which was parked next to her son's black Silverado. "Sit around all day listening to the preachers on television? Least at the casino I can smoke without you giving me a lot of crap for it."

She settled her oxygen tank in the passenger seat, kicked the engine over, backed onto the road, and shot toward Aurora.

Blessing looked at Cork coldly through the screen door. "What do you want?"

"You heard about Alex and Rayette?"

"Nothing happens on the rez we don't know about it right away."

"What do you think?"

"I think Buck Reinhardt just bought himself a ticket to hell."

"You think it was Reinhardt?"

"What are you doing here? What's with all the questions?"

"You have any idea why Alex—"

"His name was Kakaik."

"You know why he wanted to see me?"

"No."

"He asked me to arrange a meeting with Reinhardt."

That seemed to surprise him. "What for?"

"Said he wanted to offer Buck justice."

"Looks like Reinhardt decided to deliver his own form of justice first."

"You have any idea what Kingbird—sorry, Kakaik—might have been thinking of offering Reinhardt?"

"You mean besides a bullet between the eyes?"

"I'm wondering if he was thinking of turning in your cousin, Lonnie Thunder."

"No way. He wouldn't do that. He'd never disrespect one of the Red Boyz that way."

"Seems to me Lonnie had already betrayed the Red Boyz. He dealt drugs here in Tamarack County. It's my understanding none of the Red Boyz is allowed to do that."

"Where'd you get your information?"

"It's what I heard. I want to talk to Thunder."

"Go ahead."

"I've got to find him first, Tom."

"My name is Waubishash."

"If anybody knows where your cousin is, I figure it's you."

"Even if I did, why would I tell you?"

"Because it would be in his best interest to talk to me."

"Yeah? And why's that?"

"I think a good case could be made that he killed Rayette and Alex."

"That's crazy."

"Is it? What if he was afraid Alex was going to turn him over to the sheriff?"

"I already told you Alex wouldn't do that."

"You mean Kakaik."

"Fuck you."

"I'll make a deal with you. Tell Lonnie I want to talk to him. He can arrange it anywhere, anytime he likes, in any way he thinks will make it safe for him. If he's able to convince me that he had nothing to do with killing the Kingbirds, I'll stop dogging him. Otherwise, I'll find him on my own and drag his sorry ass to the sheriff myself."

"I'd love to see you try that, old man."

Cork held him with his gaze. "I'm thinking that now Kingbird's gone, the Red Boyz are going to look to you for leadership. Believe me, Tom, I wish you luck. Talk to your cousin and have him call me. Or call me yourself." He held out a business card. Blessing made no move to open the screen door and accept it, so Cork slid it into the crack between the edge of the door and the frame. "If I don't hear from one of you by the end of the day, I start hunting Thunder."

Cork turned around and headed toward his Bronco. At his back Blessing called, "You come onto the rez, maybe it's you who gets hunted."

Cork kept walking.

NINE

Will returned in the late afternoon. Lucinda had finally been able to get the baby to nap, and when her husband came in the front door, she put her finger to her lips.

"She's sleeping," she whispered and waved him to the kitchen.

He looked dumbfounded at the plates and pans of food that filled the counters—casseroles, salads, breads, desserts.

"What's all this?"

"People have been bringing things all afternoon so I don't have to worry about cooking. It's been kind of them, but it's also been hard to get the baby quieted."

He sat at the table while she made coffee. The whole while he stared at the window above the sink and said nothing.

She'd been numb all day, focused both on the baby, who'd cried most of the time, and on being cordial to the good-hearted people who dropped by with food. She thought the grieving would come when she wasn't so busy, so tired, and when she was alone. The grieving for Rayette anyway. The grieving for her boy Alejandro had been done long ago. The man who called himself Kakaik—what a horrid sound, like a hungry bird—she didn't really know. In so many ways, he had become like his father: a stranger to her. Who knew what was in their heads or in their hearts? Frightening, if you thought about it too much, that you could live with a man for twenty-six years and not truly know him. Was she alone in this?

"They'll release the bodies tomorrow," Will said when she brought his coffee. "I talked to Nelson at the funeral home. He'll take care of things. The visitation will be Tuesday evening. The service will be on Wednesday."

"Thank you for taking care of things," she said.

He sipped his coffee and stared out the window.

Rayette had told her that Alejandro was a warm, loving man but that she didn't always know what was going on with him. He would sit for long periods and stare, and where his mind was he wouldn't share with her. Rayette suspected that in those times he was somewhere in the past, because often he would clench his teeth and his jaw would go rigid. He didn't talk about the past, she said, except in generalities, and she thought there were a lot of things that had hurt him. Lucinda knew what some of those things were. There had always been tension between Alejandro and Will, often open hostility. Will said it was natural. Sons always challenged their fathers, and it was a father's duty to prepare his son for the challenges of life. If that was true, then Will was perfect for the job. He was a hard man, a hard father.

"Where's Ulysses?" Will asked.

She began to wipe the counter. "He left a while ago. He took his guitar. You know how he is. He needed to get away by himself and play his music and think."

"I wanted to talk to him."

Good, she thought, with a brief sense of hope. *Uly needs to talk.*

"He left the damn garage door open again," Will said.

She turned and glared at her husband. "Did you love him?" The words came out before she'd even thought them; if she'd thought first, she might not have spoken. She stared into his eyes, those dark Ojibwe windows that he never let her see through.

"What?"

"Did you love Alejandro?"

"He was my son."

"You barely spoke to him in the last two years."

"We said what needed saying. We understood each other."

"Do you think he loved you?"

"He respected me. That's more important. Why talk about this now, today?"

Yes, why? The worst possible time to talk about what could not be changed.

But she pressed on. "He came to me once when he was twelve. It was when you were stationed at Lejeune. He asked me, 'Mama, does God love me?' And I said of course he loves you. And he asked, 'Does God love Uly?' And I said yes, very much. And he asked, 'Does God love Papa?' And I said God loves everybody. And he looked at me with such disappointment in his young eyes and he said, 'Then it doesn't mean anything, does it.' And he walked away."

"What did he mean by that?"

"I don't know. He never brought it up again."

"Why would you think of that now?"

"It's not just now. I've thought about it from time to time. I always intended to ask him someday what he meant. Now it's too late." She hadn't looked away from his face. She almost never focused on him this way. It made him uncomfortable to be watched. "Will, who killed them?"

"Who do you think? Buck Reinhardt, that's who."

"What do we do?"

"We wait to see what the sheriff does."

"And then?"

He got up and rinsed his cup at the sink. "I'm hungry, Luci."

He was finished talking about this. She knew that no matter what she said now, the discussion was over.

"Come back and sit down," she said with a sigh. "I'll fix you something."

He kept his back to her. "You'll eat, too?"

She took his cup and put it in the dishwasher. "It's not good to eat alone," she said and turned her mind to the meal.

TEN

In addition to being the elected tribal chairman of the Iron Lake Ojibwe, George LeDuc was a successful businessman. He ran the general store in Allouette, the larger of the two communities on the rez. He was in his early seventies, a bear of a man with hair gone gray, but still plenty of vigor in him, enough to have fathered, a couple of years earlier, a daughter of whom he was magnificently proud.

His wife, Sarah, was half his age and had plenty of energy herself. She'd convinced LeDuc to have an addition built onto the store, and she'd put in a little coffee shop she called the Moose Mocha. It had done well, become a gathering place for folks on the rez and also for whites using the new marina and boat-launch facility that the tribe had built at the edge of town, on Iron Lake.

The store was closed on Sundays, but the Moose Mocha was open and doing a good business when Cork walked in. Sarah was behind the counter, steaming milk for a latte. Sarah's sister Gloria was at the register. LeDuc was nowhere in sight.

Cork approached the counter. "*Boozhoo*, Sarah. George around?"

She peeked from behind the big stainless-steel coffee machine and smiled. "In back, taking out the garbage." She had to speak loudly, above the hiss of the steam. When the sound stopped, she said more quietly and with great concern, "We heard about Alex and Rayette. It's all anybody's talking about. What a tragedy." She carefully poured the steamed milk into a cup containing espresso. "We heard you were out there, too."

"For a little while," Cork said.

She paused in spooning foam onto the surface of the drink and her face contorted, as if she was in pain. "Shot in the back, we heard, like it was a hit or something. Is that true?"

"It appears that way."

She was a plain woman but her dark eyes were beautiful and when she was happy there was a sparkle to them, as if they were full of stars. It was her eyes, LeDuc often said, that had won him over. They didn't sparkle now. "Drugs?" she asked.

"That's one of the possibilities."

LeDuc came in from the back. "Cork! Thought I heard your voice."

Sarah handed the latte to her sister and turned to her husband. "He says it's true, George."

"What's true?"

"About the Kingbirds. Shot in the back."

LeDuc's face showed all the emotion of a sandstone wall. "I've called a council meeting for tomorrow."

"Got a few minutes free, George?" Cork said.

"Okay?" he asked his wife.

"Go on," she said.

They stepped outside into the warm late afternoon. Across the street stood the new community center where the tribal council met. It also housed a free clinic, a number of the reservation business offices, a gymnasium, and a recreation room. LeDuc said, "I'm listening."

"George, I'm looking for Lonnie Thunder."

"I haven't heard anything. Talked to his father a couple of days ago. Ike says he hasn't seen Lonnie in a while, but that's not unusual. He's probably hiding. Hell, Buck Reinhardt's running around loose out there. I was Lonnie Thunder, I'd hide." He looked past Cork, at Iron Lake, which was visible through a stand of oaks, its surface satin blue. "Think it was Reinhardt killed the Kingbirds?"

"If I was sheriff, he'd be at the top of my list. But I'm thinking there are other possibilities."

"Some folks around here are saying it was because of drugs."

"Maybe. I'd like to talk to Lonnie Thunder about the shootings."

"Why Thunder?"

"I spoke with Kingbird last night. He wanted me to arrange a meeting with him and Reinhardt."

"Kingbird and Reinhardt? I'd like to've had a ringside seat for that. What was he thinking a meeting would accomplish?"

"He told me he was going to offer Buck justice."

LeDuc chewed on that. "Any idea what he meant?"

"It might be that he was considering giving Thunder over to the sheriff."

"And Thunder got wind of it and killed him and Rayette?" He didn't look convinced.

"Maybe he didn't start out thinking he'd kill Kingbird, it just ended up that way. Things got out of hand."

"Maybe. Nobody ever accused Lonnie Thunder of having any sense." The lines around LeDuc's eyes went deep and he was quiet. "I was Kingbird, I'd have given Thunder over without a second thought. Everybody on the rez knows about those videos, knows what he was up to with those young girls. Any of us got our hands on him, believe me, we'd deliver a little Ojibwe justice before we turned him in." He shook his head. "I can't understand him protecting Thunder. Kingbird was smart. There was a lot to admire about him. A few weeks ago he came into the store. We talked for a good hour. I challenged him on the whole drug thing, told him the Red Boyz were a blight on the Anishinaabe name. Accused him and his gang of preying on the weakness of others. Know what he said? Said the Chippewa Grand Casino did the same thing, just had the power of law behind it, and law didn't make a thing right. Had himself a point there, I suppose. This was before anybody knew what Lonnie Thunder had been up to with those young Shinnob girls. Kingbird got pretty quiet after that. You know he'd been seeing Henry Meloux?"

Meloux was a Mide, a member of the Grand Medicine Society, a healer of the body and spirit. He was god-awful old and lived by himself in an isolated cabin far north on the rez. He was also a man Cork respected and loved above all others.

"I had no idea," Cork said.

"You want to know the truth, once you got past all the things you think about gangs, Alex Kingbird had a lot to recommend him. Shame he wasted it on the Red Boyz and the likes of Lonnie Thunder."

ELEVEN

For an hour and a half in the afternoon, Annie played softball at the high school field. It wasn't a scheduled practice, but many of the girls from the team liked to get together this way on the weekends. They were leading the division and wanted to keep their edge. Besides, they all loved the sport and loved each other and loved being young and totally free on a warm May Sunday.

They finally broke up and went their separate ways. Annie walked toward home with Cara Haines, who played first base. Cara was like a grasshopper, with a slender body and long arms and legs. Normally Annie had to walk double-time to keep up, but as the two girls made their way together through Aurora, they moved slowly and hardly spoke.

They were seniors, with graduation less than a month away. In the fall, Cara was going to college at Concordia, in Moorehead, Minnesota. Annie was going to college, too, although that hadn't always been her plan. Before she entered high school and softball became one of her greatest passions—maybe her greatest—she'd intended to become a nun. It had been a clear vision for her since she was very young. By her sophomore year, however, both her love of softball and her growing interest in boys had blunted her sharp resolve, and her intentions had altered slightly. She'd decided that she would first go to Notre Dame, pitch for the Fighting Irish, and then, perhaps, give herself over as a bride to Christ. Unfortunately, Notre Dame hadn't offered her an athletic scholarship, but the University of Wisconsin had. So at the end of August, Annie was headed to Madison, and the question of what path lay beyond that, spiritual or otherwise, was put on hold.

The two young women had spent their lives in Aurora, had followed the same streets, passed the same houses, taken for granted all the details that had outlined and helped define their existence. College didn't mean they were traveling to the ends of the earth, but they weren't just leaving Aurora, either. They were leaving their childhoods behind. Something important was ending, and often these days Annie found herself trying hard to notice everything about her hometown, to gather up all the small perfect pleasures and store them in her heart.

"I got a job this summer," Cara said. They were walking past the shops on Oak Street, most of which were closed on Sunday except in the summer-tourist season.

"Yeah? I thought you were going to work with me at Sam's Place. I already told my dad you would."

"My uncle has this friend who runs some kind of outfitter thing in Montana, near Glacier. He's giving me a job."

"Doing what?"

"I don't know exactly. But it's Glacier. I was there a couple of years ago. It's awesome."

"So when do you take off?"

"The day after graduation. Unless we make it all the way to the state championship. I'll stay for that."

Annie had the sudden, sinking feeling that they were already drifting apart. "It's all going to change, isn't it," she said.

"Don't go all sloppy on me."

Annie stopped and stared down Oak Street where the concrete was shaded by all that was familiar: Pflugelmann's drugstore, the tall clock tower of the county courthouse, the old Rialto theater, Johnny's Pinewood Broiler, and the dozens of other shops and alleyways and street corners that were already beginning to feel lost to her.

"Sometimes I think all I want is for nothing in my life to change, ever," she confessed.

Cara turned and gazed down the street in the direction from which they'd just come. "I guess I know what you mean. But we'll be back. You know, Thanksgiving, Christmas. And, hey, we can party without the whole town knowing every detail."

Annie laughed. "I've seen you when you drink. Girl, you're so loud the whole frigging state can hear you get crazy."

From up ahead came music in a familiar style. Annie recognized the pluck and strum of Uly Kingbird on his guitar. She spotted him sitting alone at the top of the county courthouse steps. His eyes were closed and he seemed lost in his music.

"Come on," Annie said, and started toward Uly.

Cara held back. "Oh, God. You heard what happened to his brother?"

"Of course."

"Look, I don't know him. He's always creeped me out. What am I supposed to say?"

"It'll be all right. Come on." She crossed the street. "Hey, Uly," she called from the bottom of the courthouse steps.

He opened his eyes and stared down at her. His fingers kept working the strings. It sounded familiar, but Annie didn't recognize the tune. It sounded like it might have been Bob Dylan, whose music Uly loved, partly because of the connection with the Iron Range. Maybe a Dylan tune Uly had rearranged.

"I heard about your brother," Annie said. "I'm sorry."

Beside her, Cara said, "Really sorry."

Uly sang, "And now you're gone forever and now you're gone for good."

"Are you okay?" Annie asked.

Uly sang, "You've taken that long lonely walk into that dark wood."

"Look, if you need to talk or anything—"

Uly strummed a sudden, harsh cord, cutting her off.

"Jeez," Cara said. "She's just trying to be nice."

"I'll follow you there someday," Uly sang. "The choice it isn't mine. I can see the end a'coming like a freight train down the line."

Cara grabbed Annie's arm. "You're not going to stick around for this, are you? Let's get out of here."

Annie shook off her hand. "I'll go when I'm ready."

"Fine. I'll walk home alone."

"Fine."

Cara spun away and crossed the street in long, angry strides.

Annie turned back to Uly, whose fingers never left the strings of his guitar.

"Is that Dylan?" she asked.

"Does it matter?"

Annie climbed the steps and sat beside him. "You okay?"

He stopped playing and put a finger below his right eye. "See any tears?" He struck a stage smile. "Military family. We don't cry." He strummed a couple of chords, then shook his head. "Alex was a lot older than me. We weren't what you'd call close." He looked away from her. "You're welcome to stay, but I don't really feel like talking now."

She sat with him and he bent to the music as if nothing existed but the song.

TWELVE

Cork watched a flock of Canada geese wing their way north above Iron Lake. They flew in a shifting V, dark and purposeful against the butter yellow sky where the sun was setting. Along the lakeshore, the poplar and birch were already leafed out. It had been a mild winter; actually, it had not been much of a winter at all. There'd been hardly any snow, the lakes had frozen late, and the ice had gone out early. The resorts, usually buzzing with the activity of snowmobilers and ice fishermen, were empty. April, which folks in the North Country called "mud season," had been dry as well. There was common agreement that the seasons weren't what they used to be. Global warming, everyone said, and shook their heads helplessly.

Cork should have spent the day getting Sam's Place ready for the summer. Sam's Place was an old Quonset hut on the shore of Iron Lake just outside the official limits of Aurora. Long ago, an Ojibwe named Sam Winter Moon had converted it to a burger and shake joint that had become popular with both locals and summer visitors. When Winter Moon died, he'd passed the place to Cork, who'd been like a son. Normally, Cork opened in May, on the day of the fishing opener, and didn't close until mid-November. In that time, he grilled thousands of burgers and hot dogs and served up a sea of shakes and soft drinks. His children worked with him, and that was the aspect of the operation he loved most. This year Annie would be there from the beginning—working on weekends and around her school softball schedule—with some of her friends hired to help. Come June, Jenny would be home from college for the summer and she'd work, too. Stevie often helped out as well, though much of his time was spent hanging out on the old dock with Trixie, fishing for bluegills and sunnies.

At the moment, Cork's mind wasn't on Sam's Place. It was working in the old mode, the cop mode, asking questions and probing dark corners for answers.

He passed the Buzz Saw and didn't see Buck Reinhardt's truck in the parking lot. He didn't see it at Tanner's or at the casino. When he came to the turnoff to Skinner Lake, he took it and headed toward Reinhardt's home.

Elise answered the door. She looked different from the night before. Not happy exactly, but less aggressively angry. She was wearing makeup again. From behind her came the sound of music. Soft jazz. She had a drink in her hand. From the smell and the lime wedge among the ice cubes, Cork guessed it was a gin and tonic.

"Still looking for Buck?" she asked.

"Yeah."

"Not much point in it now, is there? Kingbird's dead. Doesn't matter anyway. Buck's not here. Check the bars."

"I passed the Buzz Saw. Didn't see him there, either."

"He told me they kicked him out last night. Buck's a grudge holder. It'll be a while before he gives them his business again."

"What time did he get home last night?"

She stiffened up and her face seemed to prepare itself for anger. "The sheriff's people asked the same question. Look, Buck got home maybe fifteen minutes after you left. He came straight home from the Buzz Saw. After that he was here with me all night. So if you're thinking he killed the Kingbirds, think again." She took a drink from the glass in her hand.

Cork said, "You know that it wasn't Alex Kingbird who sold the stuff that got Kristi high."

"He wasn't just an innocent bystander, either."

"Rayette was."

"She chose her man."

"As did you." They stared at each other. Cork said, "Suppose the Red Boyz go hunting for a little justice of their own now, Elise. You want to be right there beside your husband when the bullets start flying?"

"I can handle a rifle."

"Let's hope your hands aren't taped and your back isn't turned." He knew it was over the top, and he reined himself in. "Sorry. That was uncalled for."

"You bet it was."

The door banged shut in his face, and he turned to leave. Before he reached his Bronco, another vehicle came up the road and pulled into the drive. Cork waited while it came to a stop beside his own. Dave Reinhardt killed the engine and stepped out. The vehicle was a police cruiser from Yellow Lake, where Dave was the chief.

David Reinhardt was Buck's youngest child from his first marriage. The other children from that marriage had scattered, and Cork couldn't recall the last time he'd seen any of them back in Tamarack County. Alone among them, Dave Reinhardt had elected to stay. He'd attended the University of Minnesota at Duluth, then done his police training in Minneapolis, where he'd served for four years before coming home. Cork had hired him as a deputy in the Tamarack County Sheriff's Department. Although Reinhardt proved to be a good officer, coming back to Aurora might not have been the best choice for him. It put him close to his father, and Dave Reinhardt found himself caught in the sweep of Buck's relentless ambitions.

Cork always figured it was Buck who was ultimately responsible for Dave Reinhardt leaving the department. When Cork resigned as sheriff and a special election was held to fill the position, Buck boasted that his son would be the next man to wear that badge. Then Marsha Dross threw her hat into the ring. Buck had a field day with that. A week before the election, he took out an ad in the *Aurora Sentinel* that read, "Dave Reinhardt for sheriff. He's the only one with the balls for the job." It got a good laugh in town, but at the polls it had a different effect. Dave Reinhardt lost by a landslide, a result that most people understood was less about his qualifications and ability than it was a backlash against his father. Dave resigned as deputy and took the job as chief of police in Yellow Lake.

"Cork. What are you doing here?" Dave accepted the hand Cork offered and gave it an agreeable shake. He was taller than his father and softer in his features.

"Looking for Buck," Cork said. "Have you talked to him today?"

"I was here earlier when Ed Larson and the BCA agent questioned him and Elise."

"What do you think?"

"I think he didn't kill the Kingbirds, if that's what you're getting at. When the shootings went down, he was home with Elise."

"That's what they both say, all right."

Reinhardt squinted at him. "What aren't you telling me?"

"Dave, I drove out here last night. Buck wasn't around."

"I know. He got home after you left. You just missed him."

"See, that's the thing. There's only one way into Skinner Lake and one way out. If Buck got home just after I left, I'd have seen him coming down that road. And I didn't."

"You reached the highway before he turned off."

"Maybe. But I headed directly to the Buzz Saw, where Buck had just got himself thrown out. If he went straight home from there, as he and Elise claim, one way or another I'd have passed him."

"Could be a lot of explanations."

"Let me hear one."

"He'd been drinking. He pulled off the road to piss."

"You were there when he was questioned this morning. Did he mention that?" When Cork didn't get an answer—which was answer in itself—he went on. "You're Buck's son, but you're also a cop, Dave. Think like one."

Reinhardt crossed his arms and leaned back against his vehicle. "Elise said Kingbird sent you here last night. Kingbird's out of the picture, so what's your interest now?"

"Aren't you worried about her safety and Buck's? With Kingbird gone, it's hard to know what the Red Boyz might do."

"Buck can take care of himself."

"He's gone a lot. That leaves Elise here alone. I'm thinking it might be best if she went to visit her family for a while."

"She's like Buck in a lot of ways," Reinhardt said. "You couldn't run her off if you tried. She's pretty handy with firearms. I'll suggest she keep one of Buck's rifles loaded and within reach."

"Going away would be safer for everybody."

"Thanks for your concern, Cork. I'll take it from here."

Reinhardt moved past him and headed toward the house. He mounted the steps, knocked at the door, and was let in. Cork climbed into his Bronco and left.

Supper was over when he arrived home. Annie had taken her brother and Trixie to Grant Park for an evening romp. Jo fixed him a roast beef sandwich and he pulled a bottle of Leinenkugel's from the refrigerator to wash it down.

"We ate on the patio," Jo said. "It's a little chilly, but if you put on a sweater it's nice. How about we sit there?"

She joined him in the cool blue that was the shadow of coming night. Cork had built the patio himself, a smallish brick affair that Jo had outlined with hostas. In spring and fall, it was a good place to eat a meal and relax. In summer, there were mosquitoes to contend with and blackflies and yellow jackets. The backyard wasn't separated from the neighbors' yards in any formal way; in Aurora, there weren't many fences. But everyone knew where their property lines ran, especially when it came to mowing grass or raking leaves.

"And?" Jo finally said.

Cork realized he hadn't said a word since they'd sat down.

"I talked to Tom Blessing, gave him a deadline for putting me in touch with Thunder."

"He didn't spit in your eye?"

"No, but he wasn't exactly quaking in his boots either."

"Will he? Put you in touch with Lonnie Thunder, I mean."

"Doesn't matter. One way or another I'll find Thunder. By the way, George LeDuc says that Alex Kingbird was seeing Henry Meloux."

"Now that's interesting."

"I'm planning on having a talk with Henry tomorrow, see what he has to say about that. He might have an idea about Thunder, too."

"Cork." From the way she said his name—a mix of tender and tough—he knew, more or less, what was coming next. "I know you promised Marsha that you'd help her, but I keep thinking that if you're alone on the rez poking around trying to find Lonnie Thunder, sooner or later the Red Boyz are going to catch you isolated out there and do something about it."

He put his beer down and nodded thoughtfully so that she could see he really was hearing what she said. Then he replied, "The people I need to talk to will be more inclined to open up if I go alone. I won't do anything stupid, I promise. And I won't be completely alone. I'll take my thirty-eight, loaded and locked in the glove box."

She drew a breath and let it out slowly. "I don't understand what's so important about bringing in Thunder now. It seems to me the damage has already been done."

Cork nodded again and then he explained: "The more players we're able to remove from the situation, the better the chances of handling it."

"*We're* able to remove? Sweetheart, you gave up the badge. And just exactly who are *we* bringing in from the other side of this situation? The people on the rez are going to be very interested to see how diligently our sheriff—and those helping her—go after Kingbird's killer, especially since all the signs point toward Buck Reinhardt."

"Elise says Buck was with her when the shootings occurred."

"Oh, now there's testimony that would convince a jury."

"I think that at the moment Marsha doesn't have any evidence to the contrary."

"She'd better find some fast. Whatever people on the rez thought of Alex Kingbird doesn't matter. The situation as they'll see it—and you know this better than anybody, Cork—is that an Ojibwe's been killed—very likely by someone who's white—and the authorities are dragging their heels. It doesn't matter what the reality is, the perception will be damning. You'll have young Shinnobs lined up around the block to join the Red Boyz."

"People rush to judgment all the time, Jo. A proper investigation moves more slowly."

"Proper investigation? You sound exactly like a white cop now." Her face changed, softened. "Cork, I'm playing devil's advocate, saying things you know are going to be said. Unless Marsha's able to wrap this up quickly, it's apt to fall apart on her. It scares me to think of you in the middle when that happens."

"I know it does. What do you want me to do?"

"I want you to step away from it." She held him with the clear blue wish of her eyes, then gave up with a sigh. "But I know you and I know you won't."

She fell silent, tilted her face upward, and gazed at the night that was crawling into the sky.

THIRTEEN

That Sunday night Annie sat in front of her computer, trying to work on the final paper for her lit class. She was asking the question: Was it really William Shakespeare who'd penned the plays that all the world loved? She'd constructed the paper to be a kind of whodunit, presenting evidence that pointed toward various suspects: Marlowe, Raleigh, Bacon, Johnson. She needed to begin wrapping it up, but she sat staring at the screen, dreadfully aware that she didn't care who'd written the plays, didn't care about the paper, didn't care about school at all. She was finished. All the seniors were finished. For the next few weeks, they were just going through the motions.

A message appeared on her screen. From Uly Kingbird. They'd IM'ed a lot while they were practicing the music they'd played that morning at church.

thanks

what4, she IM'ed back.

thought i wanted to be alone this afternoon but i didn't. the dark is no place for children and children we all are.

more dylan

more mine

pretty

pretty words don't change anything. the worlds still an ugly place.

the words come from somewhere beautiful inside you. your music comes from the same place.

He didn't respond for a minute. She wondered if he was still online.

Then another message: *i used to believe . . .*

what, she replied.

nothing. late. good night.

She sat back and stared at the screen. She was about to turn her own computer off when a final message from Uly appeared.

that every day is a chance for something better. but the truth is every day is a hole you try to climb out of. and one day you won't.

Misty took forever going to sleep. By the time Lucinda laid the baby in the crib that she'd put up in Alejandro's old room, she was exhausted. She went to her own bedroom and found Will sleeping deeply. She stood looking down at her husband and realized she was exhausted with him, too. It wasn't that he was an awful man, a bad man, he was just a difficult man, a man hard to love. Even after more than a quarter century together, he was like a foreigner to her, speaking from a sensibility she couldn't understand, following rituals she couldn't appreciate. More than anything else, it was his silence that kept him a stranger. He spoke, yes, but often in a way that felt to her like silence. Years before, she'd thought of leaving him, but she had no way of supporting herself or her boys. And it wasn't as if he was cruel to her, abused her, beat her. He never did.

When she was a girl in Los Angeles, in the backyard of her stepfather's home there was a carob tree. It had been a beautiful thing, huge and shady. Under it her mother had put a little grotto, a bathtub virgin. Lucinda spent much time under the carob, daydreaming or praying to the Virgin Mary. Then one day the tree fell apart, just fell apart. The inside, it turned out, was completely rotten. As it collapsed, a huge section of the carob tree smashed the bathtub and its virgin. These days, Lucinda often thought of her marriage as being like that carob tree: something that was rotting from the inside and would someday simply crumble.

She took a blanket from the linen closet and stretched out on the sofa in the living room. From there, she could easily hear if the baby woke and began to cry. She'd always been a light sleeper.

She closed her eyes. Against the darkness splashed the image of Alejandro and Rayette, tangled in the meadow grass, their bodies torn open by the shotgun blasts. She sat up and stared at the curtains, drawn closed over the picture window. The curtains were new. Rayette had helped choose them, and while they considered fabric she had talked to Lucinda about her childhood.

When Rayette was seven, her mother had left her with her grand-parents and gone to Minneapolis with a man named Douglas Bear. She'd promised to come back for Rayette when they were settled. That never happened. Her mother and Bear were killed in a head-on colli-sion north of Cloquet. Her grandparents raised her, but they were not young and both were dead by the time Rayette hit fourteen. She was passed from relative to relative, giving them all trouble. At sixteen she chose to make her own way. It was her luck, she told Lucinda, that the way had led to Alejandro. It felt like finding God, she confided. She didn't mean it in a sacrilegious way. It was just that she'd never known such hope before. Such happiness. He wasn't a perfect man, but he loved her, and that made all the difference in the world.

Lucinda opened the curtains and looked out the window. The house stood just beyond the town limits of Aurora. It was a one-story rambler on a large lot with two young maples in front, near the road. The backyard abutted a stand of mixed spruce and poplar. Will had given her a small section of the property for her garden, but most of the yard was grass that, thanks to her husband, was thick and velvety all summer. He kept everything perfect and orderly. It had been the same at every place they'd lived, from Camp Pendleton to Camp Lejeune, with a dozen postings, foreign and domestic, in be-tween. He was hard on the boys in that respect. No bikes left lying in the yard. No digging to China the way boys sometimes did. They both had their part in helping with the tasks, a strict duty roster that Will kept posted on the refrigerator and oversaw as rigidly as if the boys were part of his command rather than part of his family. When he retired from the military and opened his gun shop, Will had ex-pected the boys to help out there as well. Alejandro had finally muti-nied; he and Will began a battle that had seen an occasional truce but never an ending. Uly, on the other hand, never fought back. He bent beneath the weight of his father's expectations, and it hurt Lucinda to see him burdened so.

She looked toward the lights of town, which she sometimes thought of as the campfires of strangers. She left the window, returned to the sofa, and lay down. She was afraid to close her eyes, afraid of what she would see in the darkness there. Almost immediately, however, her exhaustion overtook her and she fell asleep.

She woke suddenly. It was still dark, still night. Had she heard Misty crying? She listened carefully and realized that what had waked her was the tiny squeak of the platform rocker in the corner of the living room. In the drift of light through the picture window, she saw Will's face. He looked at peace. In his arms lay the baby, asleep against his chest.

It was the only moment of beauty in that whole brutal day, but it was almost enough.

The light on Stevie's nightstand stayed on late, and when Cork went to bed, he poked his head in his son's room. The little guy was wide awake, fingers laced behind his head, staring up at the ceiling.

"Lights out," Cork said.

"Dad?"

"Yeah?"

"Is it always wrong to kill?"

Cork walked in and sat on the edge of Stevie's bed. "Why are you asking?"

"Zip Downey told me that the Kingbirds sold drugs to kids. So maybe whoever killed them didn't think it was wrong."

"Killing somebody is never the right thing to do," Cork said.

"You killed people," Stevie said. It wasn't an accusation.

"And I pray all the time to be forgiven."

"Did you think it was wrong?"

He hesitated, then answered truthfully. "I don't remember thinking about right and wrong when it happened. But I suppose somewhere in my head I must have believed it was the right thing to do."

"But you just said—"

"I know. Stevie, I hope you never find yourself in a situation where you have to decide whether to kill someone. I hope that with all my heart. Whatever people thought of the Kingbirds and whatever the Kingbirds may have done, killing them wasn't the answer. It was calculated, cold-blooded murder. It was wrong, absolutely wrong, and that's all there is to it."

The troubled look didn't leave Stevie's face. Cork had watched his son play at killing, using a stick or a golf club or an old curtain rod as a rifle. He'd never stepped in to stop it. When Cork was a boy—raised on John Wayne westerns—he'd played the same games. He believed that the real killing for which he was responsible as a man didn't come from the games of his childhood, and taking a stick away from Stevie or any other boy who fought make-believe battles wouldn't solve a thing.

"Do you understand?" he finally asked his son.

Stevie said, "If somebody killed you, I'd kill them back."

"Then I guess I'd better do everything I can to make sure I stay alive, huh?"

He ruffled his son's hair. Stevie didn't smile.

"Promise?" Stevie said.

"I promise. Going to read for a while?"

"I guess so."

Cork handed him the book on the nightstand, *The Indian in the Cupboard*. "See you in the morning." He kissed Stevie's forehead and went to his own bedroom.

Jo was almost asleep, nodding over one of her legal files that she'd brought to bed to study. Cork stood in the doorway, thinking Jo had twice asked him to promise that he wouldn't put himself at risk in whatever trouble seemed to be coming to Tamarack County. He hadn't been able to do that for her. Yet he hadn't hesitated in making that same promise to his son. What was the difference, he wondered, and if he told her, would Jo understand?

Hell, why should she? He wasn't certain he did.

Worse, he wasn't certain it was a promise he could keep.

FOURTEEN

Monday morning, Sheriff Marsha Dross was in the common area making coffee when Cy Borkman buzzed Cork through the department's security door.

"Go on ahead to my office," she called to him with an empty pot in her hand.

Cork walked into the office that twice before had been his. The first time around, he'd served nearly two terms. The second time, several years later, he'd occupied it for a brief but tumultuous three months. He liked what Dross had done to the place. She'd had the walls painted a soft sand color that reminded him of the desert and provided a pleasant backdrop for all the leafy green of her plants. She'd hung a couple of photographs on the wall. The one behind her desk showed her standing beside her father on a boat dock, both of them grinning wide. Her father had been a cop himself, down in Rochester. In the other photograph, Dross stood with her arm around Ann Bancroft, a Minnesota native and one of the world's great polar explorers. The photo was signed and was inscribed: *"To another sister who braved the ice."*

He stood at the window. The morning was overcast, promising much needed rain. Across the street was a park, a nice square of grass with a playground dead center. The playground was empty, but a small cluster of teenagers was making its way among the swings and slides, carrying book bags and packs, bumping and shoving each other in a playful way as they headed toward the high school on the far side of town.

"Coffee'll be ready in a minute," Dross said as she swept in. "Have a seat." She sat behind her desk, while Cork grabbed one of the two no-nonsense tan plastic chairs available for visitors. "What have you got on Lonnie Thunder?" she asked.

"Nothing at the moment," Cork said. "But I'm going to see Henry Meloux this morning. Seems Kingbird had been talking to him, so maybe Henry knows something. I figure it's worth a try." He hesitated before going on. "But I'm thinking, Marsha, that after I talk to Meloux, I'm finished helping with this investigation."

She sat back slowly, her face a blank of waiting.

He could have told her about his promise to Stevie and the promise he should have made to Jo. Instead all he offered was, "I'm sorry."

"You're under no obligation."

"Where are you with Reinhardt?"

She shrugged. "He swears he was home at the time of the murders. His wife says the same thing."

"What do you think?"

"At the moment, I don't have anything that contradicts them."

"Try this on for size."

He explained about not seeing Reinhardt on the road to Skinner Lake the night of the murders. She didn't seem impressed.

"It's possible you just missed him," she said. "It was dark."

"That roof rack of lights is hard to miss."

"I'll keep it in mind," she said dully.

She'd pulled back on him, probably disappointed that the help he'd promised wouldn't be coming. Maybe even more than a little disappointed.

"One more thing," he said before getting up to leave. "Just something else to consider. I'd been thinking that if Elise lied, it was done to protect Buck. But it's also possible that it's Buck who's lying to protect Elise. She's no stranger to firearms, and she has access to that arsenal Buck keeps. Lord knows she had just as much motivation as he did. She could have gone out to Kingbird's place as soon as I left."

"Thanks. I'll keep that in mind, too."

Deputy Borkman poked his head in the office. "Coffee's ready, Sheriff."

Cork stood up. "I'll pass on the coffee, Marsha."

Dross stayed seated and watched without comment as he left the room.

He drove down Oak Street heading north, out of town. As he passed the Pinewood Broiler, he glanced at the parking lot and saw Buck Reinhardt's truck alongside a couple of company trucks. He should have let it go, just kept on driving. Not only had he promised to step back from the aftermath of the Kingbird killings, what he was contemplating at the moment—pressing Buck Reinhardt for answers—was none of his business at all.

On the other hand, he still hadn't had his morning coffee.

"Hey, Cork." Johnny Papp, who owned the Broiler, greeted him from behind the counter with one of his cordial Greek smiles.

"How's it going, Johnny?"

"I'd complain, but it never does any good. Coffee?"

"Thanks."

"Menu?"

"Just the coffee."

Johnny turned away and headed into the kitchen.

It looked as if there were two or three of Reinhardt's crews having breakfast that morning, two full tables of men with T-shirts bearing the Reinhardt logo. Cal Richards, father of Allan Richards, the kid Annie had said was giving Uly Kingbird such a hard time, was among them. He was a man difficult to miss. His arms were covered with enough tattoos so that, at a distance, he appeared to have the skin of an alligator. He'd been employed for a good many years by the county to do its tree trimming, but he'd been fired for cussing out his supervisor one too many times. Buck had hired him the next day.

Dave Reinhardt sat beside his father. Dave was in uniform, the Yellow Lake Police Department patch on his right shoulder. He was talking low and hard to his father, but Buck wasn't paying any attention. Buck's eyes were full of Cork.

Reinhardt was in his midsixties. There was a story that had floated around Aurora since Cork was a kid, about when Reinhardt was a young man working for a logging outfit contracting for Weyerhaeuser. The story was that Buck could lift a McCulloch chainsaw in each hand and attack a trunk from two directions at once, so that he felled a tree in half the time it took anyone else. As a kid, Cork had believed it. When he was older, as a result of his summers in college during which he logged timber to earn tuition money, he realized how ridiculous the story was. He figured Reinhardt had started it and kept it going. He didn't doubt, however, that Buck had the strength and the balls to give it a try. Reinhardt still had the body of a man twenty years younger. His hair was white and he wore it in a long ponytail. He was handsome, knew it, and was an incurable—often offensive—flirt.

Buck Reinhardt stood up. His son put a hand on his arm, but the man shook it off. He reached Cork at the same time that Johnny Papp returned with the coffeepot.

"Put his breakfast on my tab, Johnny," Reinhardt said.

"Just having coffee, Buck," Cork told him.

"A man ought to start the day with more'n that."

"I had breakfast at home."

"But no coffee?"

"Not today."

"Something interrupt?"

"Not really."

"I thought maybe, like some of us, you had a son of a bitch pounding on your door at all hours, bothering your wife."

There were other folks eating breakfast. They'd been carrying on their own conversations, but as Reinhardt's voice rose, the other voices fell silent.

Reinhardt wore an unbuttoned shirt with the sleeves cut away and the tail hanging out of his pants. Cork nodded toward the gun belt visible across Reinhardt's waist. "What's with the hardware, Buck? Planning on shooting your scrambled eggs if they try to make a break for it? Or do you carry all the time these days?"

Reinhardt swept his shirttail back, revealing a strong side holster that nestled what looked to be a Glock, maybe a 19.

"I do when I think some crazy Indian might get it in his head to take a shot at me."

"Probably a lot of folks besides the Ojibwe wouldn't mind doing that, Buck."

Reinhardt let his shirttail fall back into place. "Why are you sniffing around my house, O'Connor? What are you after?"

"Mostly I wanted to be sure you knew that before he died, Alex Kingbird asked me to arrange a meeting between you and him."

"Elise told me. Said you didn't tell her what for."

"He felt bad about what happened to Kristi. He wanted to make things right."

"All he had to do was give me Lonnie Thunder."

"That may have been exactly what he had in mind."

"Lot of fucking good that does me now."

"I just thought you might want to know."

"That Kingbird's dead doesn't bother me at all. If I had a whiskey right now, I'd drink to the son of a bitch who killed him. That he died before he could give me Thunder, now that's a pisser. And, listen, I don't appreciate you going around telling people I've been lying about that night."

"I never said you were lying, Buck. Only said I didn't see you on the road you should've been on."

Dave Reinhardt left the table and walked to the counter. "Take it easy, Dad."

"Fuck if I will. This man's harassing me and my family."

"I don't think it's gone that far," the younger Reinhardt said.

"You taking his side?"

"I'm just advising a little restraint here, Dad."

"Or what? You'll arrest me?" Buck laughed cruelly. "You don't have jurisdiction, Davy. And though it grieves me to say so, boy, you don't have the balls neither."

Buck spun away and returned to the table. "Come on, boys," he said. "Time's a wastin' and we got trees beggin' to be trimmed."

He dropped a fistful of greenbacks on the table and led the way out, his crew following without complaint or comment. His son watched him go, then turned to Cork.

"He doesn't mean most of what he says. Buck's ninety percent bluster."

"And ten percent bullshit. Doesn't leave much for a person to cozy up to, does it, Dave?"

Reinhardt said nothing more. He headed outside, following where his father had gone. Cork turned back to the counter. "Johnny, mind putting this coffee in a cup to go?"

FIFTEEN

Henry Meloux lived on an isolated peninsula called Crow Point that jutted into an inlet far north on Iron Lake. There were two ways to get to Meloux's cabin: You used a paddle or you used your feet. Cork guided his Bronco along the paved county road north, then turned east onto gravel. He drove until he came to a tall, double-trunk birch that marked the trail to Meloux's. He parked and began to walk. For almost a mile, the trail cut through national forest land, then it crossed onto the reservation. Cork had walked the trail many times. If what George LeDuc said was true, Alex Kingbird had recently done the same.

When he broke from the trees, Cork saw the small cedar-log cabin perched at the far end of the point, set against a sky full of sluggish gray clouds. He was upwind, and in a few moments Walleye, Meloux's old dog, had his scent and let out a couple of lazy, requisite barks.

Meloux had just brewed a pot of coffee and he offered Cork a cup. Though he was an old man, in his early nineties, it was clear from everything about him that he still had a lot of road ahead before he found his way onto the Path of Souls. He walked slowly, but that was less the result of age than patience. Meloux was a member of the Grand Medicine Society, one of the Midewiwins, a Mide. His life had been engaged with healing the bodies and spirits of those who sought him out. He'd helped Cork on many occasions and, in one significant miracle of healing, he'd brought a traumatized Stevie O'Connor back to a wholeness of soul. Not long ago, Cork had been of significant help to Meloux, locating a son lost to the old man for decades, healing a wound so painful to the old Mide that it had nearly killed him. The threads that bound these two men together were many and long and ran deep.

Meloux's hair was like a long breath of white wind. He wore overalls, a flannel shirt, and scuffed boots. Cork sat with him at the table in the old man's one-room cabin, a place that felt as welcoming as home. It was furnished simply: a bunk, a table and three chairs handmade from birch, a cast-iron stove, a small chest of drawers. Meloux used kerosene lanterns. He drew his water from the lake. Twenty yards toward the trees stood an outhouse.

"Alex Kingbird," the old man said. "Kakaik. A name to be proud of."

"You called him Kakaik?"

"That was his name."

"Not legally."

"Legally?" Meloux laughed. "A man is who he wants to be."

"Who was Kakaik?"

"To me, someone who asked questions. In that, he was like you." The old Mide smiled.

"Did he come for healing?"

"I think that was not in his mind. But probably it was in his heart. He wanted to be a man of clear thought. He did a lot of cleansing."

"Sweats?"

"And other things."

"What did you think of him?"

Meloux had brewed the coffee in a dented aluminum pot on his stove. Like Cork, he drank from an old, blue-speckled enamel cup.

"If I lived in the days of my ancestors," he said, "he would have been a man I wanted as a war chief."

Walleye had settled himself in a corner of the cabin. He'd stayed alert for a few minutes, but when it was clear the men were going to pay him no attention, he dropped his head on his paws and closed his eyes.

"Henry, did Kingbird say anything to you about Lonnie Thunder?"

"Thunder. He took the name Obwandiyag." The old man didn't seem pleased with the choice. "You know about Obwandiyag of long ago?"

"No."

"He was an Odawa war chief. To most white people he is known as Pontiac."

"Pontiac. Big name for someone with a heart as small as Thunder's. Did Kingbird talk about him?"

"Obwandiyag weighed on Kakaik."

"Did you advise Kingbird?"

"He did not ask for my advice. But he did bring Obwandiyag here. Now there was a man full of fear. The white girl had died, the fault, Kakaik said, of Obwandiyag. He hoped I could help Obwandiyag find courage, find purity of spirit, find the warrior's heart."

"Did you?"

"Obwandiyag did not want my help. He left before I could do anything for him. I did not see him again."

"Kingbird was hiding him, trying to protect him, I suppose. Did he give you any idea where?"

The old man put his cup on the table. "Is it Obwandiyag you're hunting or the truth about Kakaik?"

"I think they might lie along the same path."

The Mide nodded. "There is hope for you yet, Corcoran O'Connor. I do not have an answer for you. But I have advice, if you would like it."

"I'd appreciate it, Henry."

"I would take a hawk's-eye view of the situation."

Cork waited. "That's it?"

"That is all I have to offer. Unless you would like more coffee."

Cork stood up, and Meloux after him. Walleye worked his way to his feet and padded to the table.

"*Migwech*, Henry," Cork said, thanking the old man. At the door, he paused. "A hawk's-eye view?"

Meloux shrugged. "It is a place to begin."

SIXTEEN

Lucinda often walked to the Gun Sight, bringing lunch to her husband, and to Uly as well on those occasional days when he helped his father there. She enjoyed the stroll through Aurora. That Monday, she thought it would be a good idea for both herself and Misty to get out for a while. Well-meaning people were calling and stopping by and although Lucinda was grateful, she was also weary of having to respond to their concern.

The sky was overcast but didn't seem to threaten rain. Lucinda settled Misty in the stroller, made certain the baby was warm enough, and set off.

Having to care for the baby full-time wasn't difficult for Lucinda. In truth, it gave her a sense of purpose she hadn't felt since Uly had become a teenager and pulled away, retreating into himself in the way teenagers did. A baby was a good deal of work, but a baby let you know you were needed. And the needs were so simple really, and so blessedly direct. You fed her when she was hungry, changed her diaper when she was wet or soiled, held her when she was fussy, smiled at her when she gazed up at you with her eyes full of wonder. God never took, she'd always tried to believe, without also giving. Alejandro and Rayette had been taken, but little Misty had been spared and put into Lucinda's keeping.

Will's shop was on Oak Street. Before he bought the building, the place had belonged to a florist. Whenever she first walked in, Lucinda thought she caught the faint fragrance of roses, but the scent vanished immediately, replaced by the acrid odor of the solvents Will used to clean polymer weapons.

Her husband knew firearms. He was also an expert with that other elegant instrument of warfare, the knife. He was a dealer, with a clientele of collectors worldwide. He was also an expert gunsmith and was often engaged in making something that was of custom design. They had saved carefully all their lives, and with his marine pension they easily had enough to live on. His need to work had nothing to do with finances. In a way, Lucinda believed, it kept him connected with the military life, which was the life he knew best.

He was in the back room when she pushed the buzzer. For security, he kept the door locked. There was a sign above the buzzer button that read PUSH FOR ENTRY. Will had a camera mounted outside and positioned in a way that let him see who was at his door. She heard the reply buzz and the lock release and she rolled the stroller inside.

"Back here!" he called.

At the front of the shop were rifles, shotguns, and handguns mounted in display cases behind security glass. Arrayed in the long glass counter on which his cash register sat were the knives he carried. Near the door stood a three-by-three-foot polished maple board that rested on a tripod. Will had affixed shelves to the board, on which he displayed a selection of some of the components he used in his work: barrels, actions, frames, slides, stocks, grips. The shop front wasn't an area that he'd created to feel particularly warm and welcoming. It had a Spartan, utilitarian sensibility.

She went through the open door behind the counter and into the back of the shop, where Will stood at one of his workbenches. He had several rifles laid out before him. When Lucinda came in, he left the bench and met her near the door.

"Thanks."

He took the Tupperware container she handed him, but didn't open it. She never ate lunch with him, only brought his food. In the afternoon or evening when he came home, he would hand her the empty Tupperware to wash. Music came softly from a CD player on a shelf, Neil Young's *Harvest*, one of his favorites. When he was young and courting her, he had played the guitar. They would take a picnic lunch to one of the beaches and he would sing to her and strum. He hadn't touched a guitar in years.

"It's quiet," she said. Often when she came, he was dealing with a customer.

"I didn't want to see anyone today," he said.

"Misty didn't cry at all this morning."

"That's good, right?"

"I don't know."

"You want her to cry, Luci?"

"I thought she would miss her mother."

"You feed her, change her, hold her. What would Rayette do that you don't?"

"I'm not her mother, Will."

"You are now."

"If I was Rayette, I wouldn't want her to forget me."

"She's only six months old, Luci. She doesn't understand about mothers. She understands wet and dry, hungry and full."

"There's more to a mother than that, Will."

"Whatever it is, it's coming from you now."

She looked behind him at the table where he'd just been working and where three rifles lay. "What are you doing?" she asked.

"Nothing."

"A Winchester Stealth, a Weatherby TRR, a Dragunov. These are very powerful rifles, Will. Sniper rifles."

"What do you know about rifles?"

"When you talk to me, do you think I don't listen? What are you doing with these rifles?"

"I have a buyer."

There were many things her husband was, but a good liar he was not.

"Six months ago," she said, "you sold a very expensive Robar Elite shotgun to Buck Reinhardt."

"So?"

"I know you think he killed Alejandro and Rayette. You told me as much last night."

"Go home, Luci. Take the baby and go home."

"Alejandro and Rayette are dead. Nothing we do can bring them back."

"Go home."

"We have to think of Misty now, Will. I will try to be her mother, but you must be her father. You have to be there for her, Will. You have to be there for us."

"Go home."

This time it was an order, and she understood that he was finished with listening. Whatever she said now, he would not hear.

She turned and started away.

"Luci."

She glanced back.

"Thank you for bringing me lunch."

There was so much more she wanted to do, for Will, for Uly, for Misty, for them all, but she felt powerless.

She caught Father Ted as he was crossing the yard between St. Agnes and the rectory. He wasn't a priest who wore a cassock or a clerical shirt or a collar on an everyday basis. He'd visited the day before to express his sympathy and offer his help, and he'd looked priestly then, but today he was wearing a blue denim long-sleeved shirt and jeans.

"Father Ted," Lucinda called out to him.

He turned and smiled. "Lucinda." Misty was asleep in the stroller and Lucinda took her time reaching the priest. When he looked at her closely, he seemed gravely concerned. "Is everything all right?"

"May I talk to you?" she said.

"Of course. Shall we go into my office?"

"Thank you."

They went together into the wing that housed the church offices and the education classrooms. The priest unlocked the door. The building was empty. She liked the quiet, the emptiness that was not really emptiness, she knew, because the church and every part of it was filled with the Holy Spirit. The young priest stopped at the front desk and picked up some mail.

"How is the baby?"

"She is doing well, Father. But . . ."

"But what?"

"It's almost as if she doesn't even miss her mother."

"In a way, that strikes me as a blessing."

"For her, yes. But I think of poor Rayette. Her little girl will never know her, probably never even think of her as her mother."

"You can help her with that. You can make sure she knows who her mother was and that Rayette loved her deeply."

"I will try, Father."

"Is that all?"

"No." Lucinda thought for a moment, not certain how to approach her real concern. "Father, what is the duty of a wife toward her husband?"

The priest put down the mail and lines appeared on his brow as he considered. "I would say it's to love him, to respect him, to support him, to create and raise a family with him, to help as he strives in his service to God and the Church. If we look at scripture, Ephesians tells us that a wife should respect and obey her husband."

"What if a wife is afraid of something?"

"Afraid of her husband?"

"No, no. Afraid *for* him."

"Then I think she does all that she can to help him."

"What if he doesn't want her help?"

"Can you be more specific?"

"I'm sorry, Father, I can't."

"Well then, this is what I think. But, Lucinda, it's only what I think, not necessarily advice. I think sometimes people don't really know what they want, but I've never seen a situation where giving a loving hand was a mistake." The lines on his young brow deepened and he leaned toward her confidentially. "Is there something you want to tell me, something I might be able to help with?"

"No, Father. It's all right. Thank you." Misty was awake and had begun to fuss in her stroller. Hungry, Lucinda thought. "I should get home."

"All right, then. I'll see you on Wednesday for the service and burial."

"Thank you, Father."

She left the church. On the sidewalk that ran along the street, she glanced back. Through his office window, behind the reflection of that cloudy day, the priest was watching.

When she arrived home, she heard voices coming from Uly's bedroom. Her son had stayed home from school that day, something she'd insisted on, although Will had pressed for Uly to proceed with life as usual. It was rare that Will gave in to her, but in this she'd prevailed. She took Misty from the stroller and as she headed to the baby's room, she stopped and knocked on her son's door. He didn't answer, and she knocked again, louder, and called, "Uly?"

He opened the door and looked at her without speaking, looked at her as if she was an unwelcome stranger.

"I thought I heard you talking to someone," she said.

Lucinda saw that the chair at Uly's computer desk was occupied. From the clothing the visitor wore—all black—and the black-dyed hair, she knew immediately that it was Darrell Gallagher, a boy Uly hung out with a lot these days. Darrell didn't acknowledge her, didn't even look away from the computer screen, where he was probably surfing the Internet. He and Uly spent a good deal of time on the Internet, communicating with people in cyberspace. She wished Uly would spend more time with real people in real space.

"I was just chilling with Darrell," he said.

"Why isn't he in school?"

"He took the day off to keep me company, okay?"

"Yes. Of course." She tried to think of it as a nice thing for a friend to do.

Uly smiled at the baby. "How's Misty doing?"

"She's fine."

"Hey there, *chiquita*." He gently stroked the baby's cheek. "Later, Mom." He closed the bedroom door against her.

SEVENTEEN

After his talk with Meloux, Cork stopped at the sheriff's department, but neither Marsha Dross, Ed Larson, nor Simon Rutledge was there. He left word for the sheriff to call him on his cell, then he turned to the chore he'd meant to do that day before the Kingbird killings had grabbed his attention.

He had closed Sam's Place the week after Halloween. November was always a grim month. The fall colors vanished. The stands of maple, oak, birch, and poplar lost their brilliance and became stark and bare. The days were blustery and overcast. The lake was gray, agitated, and empty. The flow of customers to Sam's Place dried to a trickle. He'd put plywood over the serving windows and hung a sign that read: THANKS FOR YOUR BUSINESS. SEE YOU NEXT SPRING. He'd tipped the picnic table against the big pine beside the lake, turned off the gas to the grill, emptied and shut down the freezer for the winter. That part of the old Quonset hut devoted to the food-service business was abandoned. The other part of the building Cork kept heated and continued to use as the office for his fledgling business as a private investigator. He was the only PI in Tamarack County and the three counties that adjoined it. His first case had involved finding Henry Meloux's son. Despite the fact that the job had, in the end, cost several lives, business afterward had been surprisingly brisk. Wilred Brynofurson, head of security at Aurora Community College, had hired him to investigate one of their environmental engineers, suspected in the theft of several computers and video projectors. His work resulted in clearing the suspect and uncovering the true culprit, the assistant director of Technology Services, a man with a serious gambling problem. He'd also done surveillance for an insurance company on a plaintiff suing for a debilitating back injury sustained when his car collided with a plumber's truck. Cork had videotaped the guy, who lived in Eveleth, climbing like a monkey all over his roof, taking down strings of Christmas lights. That one hadn't been a challenge at all. He'd served subpoenas, located a couple of bail jumpers, and tracked down Rolf and Olivia Nordstrom's daughter who'd dropped out of her first year at Augsburg College and then dropped out of sight. (After spending one day on campus, he found her living with her boyfriend—a street juggler and sometimes bar bouncer—in a crash pad on the West Bank. He didn't convince her to return to college or Aurora, didn't even try, but he did get her to promise to call her worried parents, which she did.)

Except for the work he'd done for Henry Meloux, which had been more a favor than an assignment, his PI work so far hadn't been particularly difficult. Neither had it been dangerous, and that was important. It kept Jo happy. She liked that he no longer had a job that required a Kevlar vest as part of his standard equipment.

He was on his stepladder, reattaching a corner of the SAM'S PLACE sign that had worked loose in the winter winds, when he spotted Ed Larson's cruiser turn onto the gravel access that led to the Quonset hut. He set his hammer down and watched as Larson brought the cruiser over the Burlington Northern tracks and parked in the lot. Larson got out, Simon Rutledge with him.

"Think you'll have 'er ready for fishing opener?" Larson asked as they approached.

"Provided I don't keep getting interrupted."

"Marsha asked us to stop by, find out if you learned anything from Meloux."

Cork looked down at his visitors. "In his way, he offered what he could."

"Which was?"

"Take a hawk's-eye view."

Larson stared up at him. "I don't get it."

"Neither do I."

"Does he know where Thunder is?"

"I don't think so," Cork said. "If he did, he probably would have come right out and told me."

"Take a hawk's-eye view? Is that a clue of some kind?"

"I think it's more a suggestion on how to approach the problem."

"But you have no idea what he meant by it?"

"Nope."

"Big help." Larson squinted up at Cork, blinking behind his glasses. "Marsha says you stepped back from the investigation. What's up with that?"

"Other priorities, Ed." Cork tapped the side of the Quonset hut.

"Right. Fishing opener and all." Larson looked down at the gravel, then back up. "We just finished canvassing Kingbird's neighbors."

"And they told you they didn't see anything, right?"

"Right." Larson's skepticism was obvious.

"They weren't playing games with you, Ed. Marvin LaPoint lost most of his hearing in Vietnam. When he sleeps, Mindy says it's like a freight train going through the house. She wears earplugs in bed. They're not late-night people, so they were probably sleeping when the Kingbirds were killed and wouldn't have heard anything. On the other side of the Kingbirds, the closest neighbors would be Blakeley and Gene Beatty. They usually spend Saturday nights with Blakeley's cousins in Biwabik. Big poker game, goes on all night. Blakeley and Gene usually sleep over."

"That's good to know. I thought maybe we were just being stone-walled. We also talked to a few of the Red Boyz."

"Who?"

"Tom Blessing, Daniel Hart, and Elgin Manypenny."

"And you got a shitload of attitude and nothing else."

Larson put a foot on the ladder, as if he were thinking of climbing up beside Cork. "Marsha likes Reinhardt for the murders. Doesn't buy his alibi. What do you think?"

"The alibi's thin, the motive isn't. Same's true for Elise."

"I don't know. Tough believing that a woman—a mother yet— could be that brutal. Tape up two people, back-shoot them. Speaking of which, we got prints off the duct tape. Rayette's were all over the strips used on her husband, but the tape on her wrists was clean.

We're thinking the killer had Rayette tape Alexander, and then he—or she—taped Rayette and wore gloves while they did it."

Rutledge spoke up for the first time. "I sent the tape to the BCA lab in Bemidji this morning to see if there's something we can get from fibers or anything else the roll of tape might have come into contact with before it was used for the murders."

Larson said, "Me, I don't like either of the Reinhardts for this. Too brutal. And stupid. Buck's a lot of things, but stupid's not one of them. And he'd have to know that the Red Boyz wouldn't let something like that go unanswered. It's no wonder he's carrying these days."

"So who's at the top of your list, Ed?"

"Seems to me this has all the earmarks of a drug hit. I spoke with Gordon Wingaard, our DEA guy down in the Cities, on the phone a little while ago. He's inclined to believe the same thing."

"Who did the hit?"

"Some things we know. Some things we can only speculate about. This is what we know. In California, Kingbird became a member of the Latin Lords, a gang with strong ties to the cartels across the border. The Latin Lords are a big part of the Mexican pipeline that funnels drugs to the Midwest. DEA has been aware for some time that the Lords have been using reservations as depots. Sovereign territory, for one thing. And on the reservation, so much gets tied up with family connections that people don't talk to the law. DEA has had an eye on the Red Boyz, hoping to intercept shipments, but they haven't been able to come up with anything, probably because the Red Boyz know ways on and off the reservation that none of the rest of us do."

"That's the speculation part?" Cork asked.

"DEA also speculates that the Red Boyz have been able to thin the ranks of the competition in the North Country through a disciplined campaign of intimidation."

"And so this might be the competition fighting back?"

"DEA certainly likes that possibility. They're talking to people they know, and they've promised to keep us in the loop."

Cork studied his loose sign a moment, looked up at the thick cloud cover, then dropped his gaze back to the men below. "I don't want to complicate your speculation, but there's another possibility I think you ought to consider."

"Yeah?" Larson said. "What's that?"

"Lonnie Thunder."

"I'm listening."

"According to Meloux, Thunder was running scared after Kristi's death. Kingbird took him to see Henry, hoping Meloux could help him find some courage."

"Like the Wizard of Oz," Rutledge threw in.

"Only Thunder didn't stick around long enough for the wizard to give him anything. I'm thinking that if Thunder was in a panic and afraid Kingbird was going to turn him in, he might have been desperate enough for what happened out there."

Rutledge nodded as if he liked the idea. "Which makes it even more incumbent upon us to find him."

"Yeah, well, good luck."

"The sheriff's a little ticked at you, Cork," Rutledge said. "She feels like you deserted her. Me, I think I can understand. Must be tough."

"What's that?"

"Being in the middle. Not the law, but not quite quit of it either. Situation like this Kingbird incident, with your Ojibwe friends on one side and a lot of your white friends on the other. Easier, I'm sure, just to step away and let go of any investment in the outcome. Still . . ." He shook his head in a troubled way. "I'd guess that's hard to do when you're watching it all play out in your own backyard." He started to turn, as if to head back to the cruiser, but offered what seemed to be a sincere afterthought. "Listen, would you like us to keep you apprised of our investigation?"

Cork said, "No."

"All right then." Rutledge walked away.

"Take 'er easy, Cork." Larson joined the BCA agent at the cruiser.

Cork watched them drive off under the gray overcast that had threatened rain all day but had not delivered. He turned back to his work, picked up his hammer, and pounded the next nail as if it was all that held the world together.

EIGHTEEN

That night Cork was responsible for dinner. The schedule of meals they'd all worked out for the week called for spaghetti and tossed salad. The spaghetti sauce was Prego. The salad came in a bag. This was a meal Cork could handle.

Shortly before five, Jo called to say she would be late. Opposing counsel in a trust dispute wanted to meet to discuss a settlement. Annie called a few minutes later from school to say that she and Cara Haines were going directly from softball practice to the Pinewood Broiler. Cork knew there'd been some kind of falling out between the two friends and was glad they were patching things up. He and Stevie ended up eating dinner on television trays while they watched a rerun of *The Simpsons*.

"What do you say we head over to the Broiler for a little apple pie à la mode?" Cork suggested.

"Or French silk," Stevie said, and his eyes danced with delight at the prospect.

They were halfway to the Broiler when Cork's cell phone rang. He pulled it from the pocket of his jacket and glanced at the ID. A pay phone.

"O'Connor," he answered.

There was a lot of static on the line, and Cork could barely hear the voice at the other end. "Cork, this is Oly Johnson. Got a call there's a fire at Sam's Place. We're on our way. Better get your ass over there, too."

Oly Johnson was the fire chief in Aurora.

The line went dead. Cork slapped his cell phone closed, tossed it to Stevie in the backseat, and hit the accelerator.

"What is it, Dad?" Stevie asked in a frightened voice.

"Fire at Sam's Place," Cork replied.

Cork sped through Aurora. At Second Street, he took the corner too fast and wide and barely missed hitting a pickup in the oncoming lane. He took the turnoff to Sam's Place too quickly and the Bronco drifted on the gravel road. He brought it around and shot toward the Burlington Northern tracks. He sailed over the raised track bed and pulled into the unpaved parking lot. The old Quonset hut stood solid and silent, looking no different than it had when Cork left that afternoon.

"Where's the fire, Dad?" Stevie asked.

Cork turned off the engine. "Hand me the flashlight in my toolbox back there."

Stevie unbuckled and rummaged around in the toolbox behind him, then passed the flashlight to his father.

"Wait here," Cork said. "And make sure your door's locked."

He got out of the Bronco and circled Sam's Place slowly, poking the beam here and there. Back at the Quonset hut door that faced the parking lot, he inserted his key in the lock and swung the door open. The dark inside was both familiar and unsettling. In the silence there, he realized he didn't hear any sirens coming his way. He considered the call from Oly Johnson, and understood that, of course, there was something incredibly not right about it coming from a pay phone. In his panic over the destruction of Sam's Place, he'd let himself be fooled. *Hoax?* he wondered. *Warning?* In the second before he heard the shot, he thought, *Ambush.*

The *chunk* of the round hitting the side of the Quonset hut came almost simultaneously with the rifle report. Cork spun into the cover inside Sam's Place. Another report and another round hit the wall outside, penetrated, and struck the cupboard over the sink. This time Cork was able to tell the direction from which the shot had come. A hundred yards south was a stand of poplars that surrounded the ruins of an old ironworks. It was good cover, and with a nightscope anyone who was a decent shot could bring down a target wandering in the parking lot.

"Dad!"

Cork heard the slam of the Bronco passenger door. He peered around the doorway of Sam's Place and saw the black shape of his son separate from the larger dark of the Bronco.

"No, Stevie!" he yelled. "Stay there!"

But his son had already begun to run.

In his mind's eye, Cork was seeing the image through a night-scope: the crosshairs centered on the small, moving glow; leading the target just enough to account for bullet velocity and the lope of the boy; exhaling evenly as the finger squeezed the trigger.

He launched himself from the doorway and rocketed toward his son. He hit Stevie on the fifth stride, lifted him in his arms with barely a pause, and sprinted toward the Bronco. He reached the big vehicle and dropped Stevie behind the shield of its bulk.

"You okay?" he said, breathless and scared.

Stevie nodded.

They huddled together. Cork felt his son trembling, then realized the trembling was him. He was shaking worse than if he'd been naked in a blizzard.

"You're sure?" he said.

"I'm okay, Dad, honest. I thought they shot you."

"I'm fine." Though he wasn't. Not by a long sight.

"Who is it?" Stevie asked.

"I don't know."

He tried to think, not just about the identity of the shooter but also about the shooter's location and whether the son of a bitch would seek a better firing position. The Bronco sat broadside to the old iron-works and provided good cover, unless the shooter moved.

"What are we going to do?" Stevie asked. "Do you have your gun, Dad?"

No, damn it, he didn't. "What did you do with the cell phone?"

"I left it on the seat. I can get it." Stevie started to move, but Cork grabbed his son's arm.

"No you don't. You stay right here." His big quaking hands cupped Stevie's shoulders and he looked sternly into his son's eyes. "This is what we're going to do. I'm going to open the driver's door and turn on the headlights."

"But he'll see us."

Cork didn't want to waste time explaining, but his son needed to understand.

"If he's using a nightscope, the glare from the headlights might blind him. I'll grab my cell phone and zip right back here to you and we'll call 911. If I'm hit, Stevie, you have to promise me you'll run. Run to Sam's Place and lock the door."

"No, I wouldn't leave you."

"If I'm hit, I'll need help. Use the phone in Sam's Place to make the call. Do you understand?"

"I don't want—"

"Run. That's all there is to it. Understand?" It came out harsh, but he didn't have time to make it easier.

Stevie stared at him, his eyes dark cups full of hurt. He said nothing, but he nodded.

"All right." Cork let go of Stevie's shoulders and moved toward the driver's door.

The Bronco faced the lake and like a wall shielded him from the shooter's position down the shoreline. Once he opened the driver's door, however, the dome light would give him away and for a moment he would be a perfect target. Cork hoped maybe the light would be startling enough to make the shooter hesitate and he could switch on the blinding glare of the headlights before the squeeze of the trigger came. It was a gamble with odds he didn't particularly care for, but at the moment he couldn't think of another strategy. He grabbed the door handle and yanked. The dome light winked on. He leaned in and reached for the headlight switch. The brilliance that burst from the Bronco was like white ice, freezing the gravel of the lot, the red cedar picnic table, the lone pine near the shoreline, and thirty yards of the smooth black surface of Iron Lake. Cork reached to the backseat, expecting any second to hear the bark of the rifle, though he knew he wouldn't hear the bullet that got him. He snatched the cell phone and began to slide back toward safety.

And the shot came.

He heard the report but didn't feel any impact nor did he hear the round hit. He thought the shot had gone wild.

Then he heard Stevie grunt, and his heart yanked a cord that drew every muscle of his body taut.

"Stevie!" he cried.

He pushed from the vehicle. His feet slipped on the gravel and he went down on one knee, tearing a hole in his jeans. He stumbled toward the rear wheel well where he'd left his son.

Stevie knelt on the ground, bowed forward, his hands pressed to his face. Cork dropped beside him.

"Stevie?" He touched a shoulder.

His son looked up. Blood dripped over his lips and chin. For a second, Cork stood absolutely frozen.

"I'm okay, Dad," Stevie said. "I went down when I heard the shot and I hit my nose on the bumper. Are you all right?"

Cork felt almost giddy with relief. "I'm fine," he said. "Just fine."

He flipped the phone open and 911'ed the sheriff's department. Then he put his son against the Bronco and with his own body shielded him until he heard the sirens rise out of the distance.

NINETEEN

They sat in Cork's office in the back part of Sam's Place. Marsha Dross and Ed Larson were drinking strong coffee. Cork always made his coffee strong. For Stevie, he'd whipped up some hot chocolate. He'd also put ice in a Baggie, which Stevie applied to the bridge of his nose between sips from his cup.

A small notebook sat open in front of Ed Larson and he'd already filled a couple of pages with notes. He had questioned Cork and now he was questioning Stevie, whose responses were a little nasally due to the swelling. The questioning had an interesting effect on Cork's son. It seemed to help him forget about his injury, and his answers were clear and considered.

No, he didn't see anything or anyone.

But he did hear something. When his dad was checking the outside of Sam's Place with the flashlight, he heard the bump of a canoe against rocks somewhere down the shoreline.

"In the vicinity of the old ironworks?" Larson asked.

Stevie squinted a little. Thinking, not pain.

He wasn't sure, but most of the shoreline between Sam's Place and the ironworks was sand or soft dirt. The only rocks were where the dock for the ironworks used to be.

"I don't suppose you have an idea about the canoe?"

Aluminum. Kevlar or wood wouldn't make that kind of sound.

"Why do you think it was a canoe? Why not a rowboat or even a powerboat?"

If it was a powerboat, he would have heard the motor. And if you needed to get away fast, especially if you were alone, a canoe would be better than a rowboat, wouldn't it?

Larson looked to Cork, who simply shrugged. He'd heard nothing.

Dross used a walkie-talkie to contact her people who were going over the area around the ironworks, and she directed them to take a look at the shoreline.

"Any point in getting our own boat out there?" Larson put the question to the sheriff.

"In the dark?" She shook her head. "By now the shooter's off the lake anyway."

"That was good work, Stephen," Larson said.

Stevie flushed just a little at the praise and went back to sipping his chocolate and nursing his injury.

They were just finishing up when Jo swept into Sam's Place, wearing her long black car coat and still dressed in the navy suit, cream-colored blouse, and heels she'd worn that day in court. Like a dark wind she blew past the others and knelt beside her son. She took Stevie's face in her hands and studied the damage with her sharp, ice blue eyes. Her hair was a little wild—the long day maybe, or maybe she'd run a hand through it worrying about her son and her husband—and errant strands flew out, glowing white in the light, like hot filaments. She made a sound, a rumble in her throat that Cork knew was an unhappy assessment of her son's condition.

"Put the ice back on, sweetie. We need to get that looked at." She stood up and faced Cork. "What happened?"

"I got a call that Sam's Place was on fire. When we came out, somebody started shooting at us," he said.

"Who?"

"The question of the day. Marsha's people are going over the iron-works for anything that might tell us."

Jo glanced back at the open cupboard where one of the rounds had lodged. The bullet had already been cut out, but the shelf and the counter beneath the cupboard were strewn with shards from the plates that had been shattered.

"The Kingbird business," she said.

"We don't know for sure."

"Oh?" She gave him a long, cold look. "And what else might it be?"

He had no other possibility to offer. From the silence, he guessed no one else did either.

She leaned down to her son and spoke differently, almost playfully. "And how'd your nose end up looking like something that belongs on a clown, kiddo?"

"I hit it on the bumper of Dad's Bronco. It was my own fault."

"*Your* fault? I don't think so. Come on, buster, let's have somebody look at you." She glanced at the others. "I'm taking him to the ER, all right?"

"I need to stay here for a while," Cork said.

"I'm sure you do," she said.

Stevie got up from his chair. Cork got up, too, and wrapped an arm around his son's shoulders. "You did good tonight."

Stevie grinned shyly, then said, "Whoever he was, he sure was a lousy shot."

Cork laughed and Dross and Larson joined him.

Jo didn't even crack a smile. "Let's go," she said, and ushered Stevie ahead of her.

For a few moments after they left, there was a chilly silence in Sam's Place.

"More coffee?" Cork said.

Dross waved off the offer and Larson shook his head. "I'll be up all night as it is." He studied his notes. "If the shooter was using a nightscope and he was actually trying to hit you, he was, as Stevie so aptly put it, a lousy shot."

"A warning maybe?" Dross said.

Cork went to the coffeepot and filled his cup. "There's usually something that goes along with a warning, something that explains to the idiot that he should butt out. A note, a phone call. There's nothing like that here."

"Yet," Larson said.

Cork looked at his watch. It had been nearly two hours since the shots had been fired.

Dross stood up and arched her back as if working out some stiffness. She walked to the door, opened it, and stood looking toward the ironworks. Cork joined her and watched the flashlight beams poking around in the stand of poplars that surrounded the ruins. One of the beams separated and came up a path worn along the lakeshore, a path a lot of joggers, including Cork, used regularly.

Deputy Cy Borkman stepped into the rectangle of light that fell on the ground from the opened door. He was a heavy man, a long-time deputy. He held up an evidence bag that contained a couple of shell casings.

"All we could find," he said. "Might uncover more in the morning when we can see better, Sheriff."

"All right," Dross said. "Why don't you call the guys in. We'll give it a shot again tomorrow."

Borkman handed the evidence bag to Ed Larson, who'd joined them. Larson lifted it to the light and Cork studied it with him.

"Thirty-five-caliber Remingtons," Cork said. "Good caliber for deer hunting."

"Two casings," Larson said. "He probably left the last expended cartridge in the chamber when he ran. Would make sense. I'll have Rutledge send these down to the BCA lab. If we ever get hold of Lonnie Thunder, maybe we'll find a rifle that matches the chamber marks or the marks from the firing pin."

The phone in Sam's Place rang. Cork went over and checked the caller ID. *Thunder, L.* He picked it up.

"Stop looking for me. Next time I don't miss."

"Lonnie," Cork began, but the line went dead before he could say any more. He put the phone down. "Thunder," he told the others. "Must've used his cell."

"What did he say?" Larson asked.

"Just what you'd expect. He was warning the idiot."

Dross said, "I'll do everything I can to bring him in, Cork."

"No," Cork said. "I'll bring him in."

She looked at him, surprise evident on her face. Then she nodded, getting it.

"Anything you need, let me know. Come on, Ed. We've got paper-work to do."

They left and Cork stood in Sam's Place, which was empty now but for him and a determination, cold and deliberate, to make Thunder pay.

It was a busy night in the ER of Aurora Community Hospital. A late bout of flu had hit a lot of folks hard, and both the very young and the very old showed up at the hospital dehydrated. Cork knew the admitting clerk, Sally Owens, who let him pass. Inside, he learned that Jo had just gone with Stevie for some X-rays. He went back to the waiting area and used the public phone to call home. Annie answered.

"Hi, Dad." She sounded happy. "Where is everybody?"

"Your mom didn't call?"

"No. Why?"

"There was some excitement at Sam's Place this evening. Stevie bumped his nose. Maybe broke it. We're at the hospital right now getting it checked out."

"Is he all right?"

"He's fine."

"What happened?"

"I'll fill you in when we get home. Just didn't want you worrying."

"Should I come?"

"No. We've got it under control. We'll see you in a while."

He went back to the ER and waited by the bed in the curtained-off area where Stevie and Jo had been before the X-rays. He sat for half an hour, listening to the beeps of monitors, the banter of staff, the low whispers of the ill and those who were with them. Finally Jo and Stevie returned. The bruising had spread from his nose to the area around both eyes. His son was starting to resemble a raccoon.

"How's it going, guy?" Cork asked.

"Okay." Stevie sat on the bed and lay back. He looked tired.

"Hurt much?"

"Not much."

Jo said, "They gave him Tylenol."

"What did the X-rays show?" Cork asked.

Jo sat down in the chair Cork had vacated. "They're looking at them now."

"I called Annie," Cork said.

"Thanks."

There was something immeasurably exhausting about sitting in a hospital emergency room, waiting. On more occasions than he cared to remember, Cork had felt that suck of energy. He watched Stevie's eyes flutter closed.

Jo said quietly, "When I think about what could have happened out there . . ." She didn't finish.

"It was a warning, Jo. Thunder called after you left."

"What did he say?"

"About what you'd expect. Lay off or next time he won't miss."

"Won't miss you? Won't miss Stevie? Won't miss whoever happens to be with you?"

"Jo, I told Marsha this morning that I was through helping with the Kingbird business."

"Apparently Lonnie Thunder didn't get that message. What did you tell him?"

"I didn't have time to say anything. He hung up."

"What would you have told him?"

The doctor came before Cork could answer. He was a new one, a tall kid with wire-rims and stubble who looked like he'd been on his shift too long. His name was Stiles.

"As I suspected, the nose is broken. Setting it will probably require that we rebreak it. I'm going to have you see Dr. Barron tomorrow. He'll be better able to tell you the specifics. He handles this sort of thing all the time. In the meantime, keep Stephen on Tylenol for the pain and use ice for the swelling."

Stevie was awake and listening.

"Do I have to go to school tomorrow?"

"Up to your folks, but I'd say it's probably best to take a day off, see how things go."

"All right!" Stevie gleamed.

Jo said, "I thought you liked school."

"Yeah, but I like a day off better."

* * *

At home, Annie greeted them at the back door. Cara Haines was with her. Both girls made a big fuss over Stevie, which he pretended not to like. After Stevie went upstairs with Jo to put on his pajamas, Cork told them the full story.

"We were at the Broiler and heard the police sirens, but we didn't know they were going out to Sam's Place," Cara said.

"Do you think it was Lonnie Thunder?" Annie asked.

"Seems a reasonable possibility," Cork said.

"Ike Thunder was at the Broiler, Dad." Annie was talking about Lonnie Thunder's father. "He came in after we heard the sirens."

"How did he seem?"

"Stumbling a little, like he was drunk. He was still sitting at the counter talking to himself when we left."

Cara looked at her watch. "I've got to go, Annie."

Annie walked her to the front door, and Cork headed upstairs. Stevie was already in bed. Jo sat beside him and they were talking quietly.

"You look like the Lone Ranger," Cork said. Then he said, "Stevie, I'm sorry."

"Why?"

"I got you right in the middle of things tonight."

"It wasn't your fault, Dad. And I wasn't scared for me. I was scared for you."

Almost half a decade earlier, Stevie had seen his father shot, a serious wound that had nearly killed Cork. It had taken a while—visits with a therapist, and finally the wisdom, guidance, and healing of Henry Meloux—to make the boy whole again. To a ten-year-old, five years was half a lifetime, and Cork was relieved to see that Stevie had, indeed, grown beyond the old terrors.

"What are you going to do?" Stevie asked.

Jo looked interested in the answer to this one.

"I'm not sure."

"I think it's like with a bully," Stevie said. "You don't let a bully bully you or else he always will."

"Where'd you learn that?" Jo didn't sound happy with Stevie's position.

"You told me, remember? Last year when Gordie Sumner was being such a pain in the butt."

"This is different, Stevie," she countered. "This bully has a rifle."

Stevie shook his head. "With bullies there's always something to be afraid of."

Cork said, "What scared me most was that you might get hurt."

"I'm not afraid."

Cork understood that this was true at the moment and he was proud of his son. Jo stood up and kissed Stevie's cheek. "You need rest. If you have any trouble in the night, you wake us up, okay?"

"Okay."

Cork leaned down and kissed his son's forehead. "I love you, guy."

"I love you, Dad."

"Light on?"

"Maybe for a little while," Stevie said.

Jo went to the bathroom, where Cork heard water running in the sink and the sound of an electric toothbrush. He headed to the bedroom and took the small suitcase from the shelf in the closet. He'd half filled it when he heard Jo leave the bathroom. She stopped in the doorway and watched him pack.

"What are you doing?"

"I'm going to stay at Sam's Place until this business is finished. I think it's safest for everyone. If Thunder gets it in his head to pull off a few more rounds, I don't want any of you anywhere near me."

Her eyes went cold and her voice was all frost. "You're going after him."

"I'm not going to just let this thing lie." He went to the closet and pulled out a hooded sweatshirt that was hanging on a hook.

"You won't be happy until one of you is dead, is that it?"

"There's no way I can make you understand, Jo. I'm not even going to try. This is just the way it's going to be."

"Goddamn you, Cork." She said it quietly so that Stevie, in his bed down the hall, wouldn't hear.

He snapped the suitcase closed.

"What do I tell him?" she said.

"Tell him I'm squaring off with a bully."

"This bully has a rifle."

"With bullies there's always something to be afraid of."

She went to him and put her hand on his arm, as if to restrain him. "You were all set to step away from this."

"Thunder changed my mind."

"And I can't change it back." She dropped her hand. "This is so fucking macho stupid."

"Lock the doors," he said, and moved past her.

He took his .38 police special from the lockbox in the closet and pulled the gun belt with the basket-weave holster from the shelf. He went to the basement and from the locked cabinet took his Remington and cartridges for both firearms. Upstairs, Jo stood in the kitchen, near the back door.

"Cork, please don't go. Please just let Marsha and Ed and their people handle this."

"Their people don't know the rez. Nobody on the rez will talk to their people. You know that." He understood her fear, he really did. He wished she understood him. He tried one more time. "Jo, can't you feel it? It's like we're standing on an ocean shore watching a tidal wave come at us. Something big and awful is taking shape and it's going to hit this county and everyone in it. I can't just stand by and let that happen."

"You're exaggerating, Cork."

"Am I? Two people have been brutally murdered already. The Red Boyz aren't going to let that slide. Buck Reinhardt wants Lonnie Thunder dead, and to make that happen he's probably more than willing to go through all the Red Boyz and anyone else who stands in his way."

"Including you."

"It doesn't have to come to that."

"But it could," she said.

"Not if I find Thunder."

"This argument feels hopelessly circular. And I know I'm not going to convince you, so just go."

"About Stevie tomorrow—"

"I'll take care of Stevie. Just go." She put a hand on his chest and gave him a light shove toward the door.

Now he felt pushed out, which didn't sit well with him. But leaving was what he'd wanted, right? Even so, he hesitated, trying to think of something reasonable to say, something that would relax the tension between them. Jo just stood there and stared at him, resigned and unhappy, and finally he simply turned and left.

All the way to Sam's Place, Cork felt a vague unsatisfactory anger. At himself, at Jo, at all the stupid people who'd done stupid things lately and all those who were poised on the brink of doing still more stupid things. He pulled into the parking lot and stopped in almost the exact spot where he'd been when the shots were fired. He sat gazing at the old Quonset hut, which was a dull gray in the dim light from the gibbous moon visible behind high, thin clouds, and he couldn't help feeling that Jo was right. He'd abandoned his family. Again.

He had no idea if what he was doing was the right thing. It had felt right at first, but now he was uncertain. Maybe if Jo had sent him off with hugs and kisses and encouragement, that would have made the difference. Or maybe it was simply that her arguments were reasonable and he saw now that he was just too damn stubborn to listen.

Shit.

He climbed out of the Bronco, grabbed his suitcase and his firearms, and headed inside. Sam's Place still smelled of the coffee he'd brewed earlier. He got sheets, a pillow, and a pillowcase from the corner cabinet where he kept such items for just such situations as this. He made up the mattress on the bunk. He stripped out of his clothes and took a pair of gray gym shorts and a clean T-shirt from the things he'd brought. He turned on the lamp that sat on the old nightstand, which he'd constructed from lacquered birch limbs. He turned out the overhead light. He turned back the covers, crawled into bed, and lay awake a long time, unable to close his eyes. *All that coffee,* he told himself. In his head, he reviewed the day, a loop tape that replayed a dozen times, never leading him anywhere certain, anywhere safe.

Finally he grabbed a book from the small selection he kept sandwiched between bookends on the nightstand. A collection of Robert Frost. He turned to one of his favorite poems and began reading:

Two roads diverged in a yellow wood . . .

TWENTY

In the days when he wore the badge, Cork had collared Ike Thunder at least once a month, usually for being drunk and disorderly or driving while intoxicated. The D and Ds he would often let ride, particularly if Ike's offensive behavior was mostly verbal. Ike, when he got drunk, talked mean, but he seldom carried through with the threats he made. It was hard for a man missing most of an arm, most of a leg, and all of an eye to do much damage, especially someone as small as Ike. Cork often put him in a holding cell and simply let him sleep it off. The DWIs were a more serious matter, and Ike finally spent six months as a guest of the Tamarack County Jail for the repetition of that offense. It cured him of the driving, but not the drinking. Ike took to confining himself to the North Star Bar, at the southern edge of the reservation, a place he could easily bum a ride to with one of his cousins. If he couldn't get someone to give him a lift home, Fineday, who owned the bar, would let him sleep on a cot in a corner.

Ike Thunder was a war hero, a decorated Vietnam vet who'd gone away with a young man's fervor and come home with two Purple Hearts, a Silver Star, half a body, and a well of bitterness so deep, all the alcohol in the world couldn't fill it up. He'd left behind a girl who loved him and who, when Ike came home so terribly damaged, swore that she loved him still. They married and had a son, Alonso. Rachel Thunder was a pretty woman, small like her husband. From early on it was clear that their son, whom everyone called Lonnie, was going to be an enormous human being, a circumstance that greatly troubled the diminutive Ike. When he was a little drunk, which was often, he would take to speculating on the true paternity of the boy. When he was roaring drunk, which was not so often back then, he would sometimes try to abuse Rachel, not a wise choice for a man with only one good eye, one good arm, and a leg made of plastic. Rachel, who'd grown up tough on the rez, had no trouble dealing with Ike, usually with the aid of a baseball bat that she kept handy and, Cork had heard, that she'd dubbed Excalibur. By the time Lonnie turned four, Rachel had had enough. She left her husband and took her son to Chisholm, where her sister lived and where she got a job working for a small trucking firm. An ice storm the day before Thanksgiving that year coated everything in silver as slippery as mercury. On her way home from work, Rachel fell on a steep slope of sidewalk, hit her head, and died from the cerebral hemorrhage that resulted. Lonnie was returned to Ike, who raised him on his disability pension and the life-insurance money he received from Rachel's death, claiming he was doing the best he could for a boy who was probably not even his own.

Thunder lived in a small clapboard house a couple of miles south of the old mission, near the center of the rez. The house had been built by his grandfather, an excellent carpenter. Ike was good with the tools his grandfather had taught him how to use and he kept the place up. Occasionally he earned extra money custom making furniture. His product was amazingly good, but his delivery timetable was always questionable, for two reasons: It took a man with one arm a lot longer to get the project done, of course; but in addition, Ike was often too drunk to work.

The morning after the shots were fired at Sam's Place, Cork pulled off the road and parked in the bare dirt beside Thunder's house. It was another overcast day, with a cool wind out of the northwest. He got no answer to his knock. He walked to the shed that had been built as a garage but was now Thunder's workshop. The door was unlocked and he stepped in. The shed had a good smell to it: the fragrance of sawdust and raw wood released at the bite of the crosscut tooth and the shave of the plane. A half-completed chest of drawers sat on the old floorboards. The wood was probably maple, the color of dark honey. The shed was neat and spoke well of the enterprise that took place there. Cork had heard that Thunder altered all his tools to accommodate the use of the prosthetic arm he wore. Still, Cork would have loved to see how the man managed his work.

Lonnie Thunder didn't live with his father, but he did live on his father's land. Cork followed an old rutted lane that cut between the house and the shed and led into a stand of mixed pine and aspen. The ground was hard and dry, but the lane held tracks from wide SUV tires. Lonnie Thunder drove an off-road Xterra. There hadn't been a good rain in a long time, so Cork knew the tracks weren't recent. After ten minutes of walking, he spotted the trailer, an old silver Airstream up on blocks. Thunder's Xterra wasn't there. Even so, Cork drew his .38 police special from its holster and stepped off the lane and into the trees. He circled carefully and approached from the back. He put his ear to the trailer but heard nothing. He peeked through a window where there was a crack between the curtains inside. Although mostly he saw dark, Cork could still see clearly that the place had been trashed. He crept to the door. The metal around the latch was damaged where someone had used a pry bar to pop the door open. The door was still ajar an inch. Cork eased it open farther until there was a gap wide enough for his head. He looked in, satisfied himself the trailer was empty, then stepped inside.

The television screen was shattered. Dishes were smashed. Lamps had been slammed against the walls. The mattress on the bed had been sliced to shreds. The sheriff's people had been out here after Kristi died and had found a supply of crystal meth and the disgusting photos and videos. They'd have been thorough, but not destructive in the way of the devastation Cork saw now, which seemed to him less the result of ransacking than anger. Blind, raging anger. Destruction for destruction's sake.

"Don't move."

The instruction came at his back, and Cork obeyed.

"Morning, Ike," he said.

"What are you doing here, O'Connor?"

"Looking for Lonnie. Mind if I turn around?"

"Holster that handgun first."

Cork put the .38 away.

"Okay, turn around," Ike Thunder said.

Cork found himself facing the barrel of a shotgun. Ike held the stock snug against his right shoulder. The double hook at the end of his prosthetic left arm tugged at a couple of rings he'd anchored in the stock, giving him a firm grasp on the firearm.

"What are you doing here?" Thunder asked again.

"Looking for Lonnie."

"You and everybody else."

"Everybody else do this?"

Thunder's eyes wandered over the destruction. "No idea who did it."

"It wasn't the sheriff's people?"

He shook his head. "They didn't leave it like this."

"When did it happen?"

"Found it this way a couple of days ago."

"Does Lonnie know?"

"I got no idea what that boy knows."

"Why didn't you report it to the sheriff's office?"

"Think they'd care that Lonnie Thunder's trailer's been tore up? Hell, I figure it was Buck Reinhardt, come looking for Lonnie, sending him a message with all this mess."

Cork thought the same thing. "Mind putting the shotgun down?" he said.

Thunder lowered the barrel. He stood in the doorway. Behind him, the sun broke through clouds and Thunder suddenly cast a shadow, longer than he was tall, across all the debris that littered the floor. Where the face of that shadow would have been was a broken picture frame that held a photograph of Lonnie, maybe twelve years old, grinning from ear to ear, standing beside a multiple-point buck he'd brought down. Ike stood beside him in the photo. Lonnie was already a head taller.

"Know where Lonnie is?" Cork asked.

"Haven't seen him in a couple of weeks."

"Would've been about the time Kristie Reinhardt died."

"That'd be it."

"You didn't answer my question, Ike. Do you know where Lonnie is?"

"No idea."

"Care to speculate?"

Thunder's eyes narrowed. "What do you want with him?"

"He took a few shots at me last night. I'd like to talk to him about that."

"Talk? Yeah, right."

"Okay, I'd like to beat the crap out of him. Better?"

"Truer."

"My boy was with me. He could've been hurt."

Thunder's left eye was artificial and it was fixed in a dead gaze off to the side of Cork's face. His other eye showed just about as much emotion. "Lonnie shot but didn't hit you? Must've had to be he didn't want to. He's a good shot."

"He called me afterward."

"Yeah? What'd he say?"

"Told me to quit looking for him. Told me next time he wouldn't miss."

"That's more'n he's said to me in six months." Thunder slipped his hooks free of the rings on the shotgun and deftly scratched at the stubble along his jawline. "You were looking for him? Buck Reinhardt hire you to find him?"

"You know about Alex and Rayette Kingbird?"

"I heard about 'em. Heard Reinhardt was behind it. Hell, he's probably the one did this."

"It appears he's got an alibi for the Kingbird killings."

"Sure. He's white and he's rich."

"I'd like to know where Lonnie was when those folks were gunned down."

Thunder looked surprised, then perturbed. "You're thinking Lonnie might've had a hand in that? He's not the brightest spark from the fire, but he wouldn't do something like that. Hell, he thought the world of Kingbird. All those Red Boyz did."

"I'm thinking Alex was going to turn him over to the sheriff. Maybe hoping to keep the peace and take the heat off the Red Boyz."

"They can handle the heat."

"I'd like to talk to Lonnie about it."

"Seems like that's something he definitely don't want. Lonnie don't want something, that's all she wrote."

Cork made a final appraisal of the destruction. "Whoever tore this place apart, they find Lonnie, it won't be pretty."

"Lonnie takes care of himself."

"I hope you're right, Ike. Mind?" He indicated he wanted to leave.

Ike Thunder moved back and Cork exited the trailer. Thunder followed him, swinging his stiff artificial leg as they headed back to the house.

At his Bronco, Cork said, "You've modified all your firearms for that hook of yours?"

"Yeah."

Cork gave it a moment, then said, "Heard you were at the Broiler last night. Heard you showed up after the shots were fired over at Sam's Place."

"I got no idea when Lonnie fired them shots. Len Boudreau gave me a lift into town. Helped me deliver a cedar chest to Darwin Dassel, then he dropped me at the Broiler."

"How'd you get home?"

"He had some kind of meeting at the fire hall, picked me up after."

"Len, huh?"

"I got work to do," Thunder said.

"I find Lonnie, want me to say hey from you?"

"You find Lonnie, you'll have your hands too full to be doing much of anything 'cept saving your own ass."

TWENTY-ONE

By noon the sun had come out and it was warm enough to have lunch outside. Annie and Cara Haines sat on the wall of one of the brick planter boxes that lined the entrance to Aurora Area High School. Five years earlier the district had consolidated with several of the smaller districts surrounding Aurora, and a new high school had been built. Annie hadn't paid much attention at the time, but she understood there was a lot of discussion about the location of the building. The site that was finally chosen was a large meadow near the gravel pit at the edge of town. From the windows of the rooms facing west, the tall gravel conveyor was visible, rising from the pit like a long-necked prehistoric beast spitting rock. East, the view was of the parking lot in front of the school, and beyond that, the houses of Aurora, side by side, lining the streets that headed toward the lake nearly a mile distant.

"I'm thinking of going camping this weekend," Cara said. "Maybe Slim Lake. Want to go?"

"I'll be helping my dad at Sam's Place."

"Right. Fishing opener. My dad says your dad should wait to start the season."

"Why?"

"All this trouble with the Red Boyz. The shots last night. He thinks folks will stay away from Sam's Place for a while. Actually, he thinks I should stay away from you."

"Me?"

"Yeah."

"He's serious?"

Cara looked toward the parking lot where a group of guys were clustered around Gary Amundsen's red '67 Mustang convertible. Gary's father owned Amundsen's Auto Body, and both Gary and his father were car freaks.

"About nights, he's serious. Once it's dark, he doesn't want me hanging with you. He's afraid of what he calls 'collateral damage.'"

"That's so bogus."

"I don't know, Annie. What if we'd been with your dad last night?"

Allan Richards came out the front door with two other boys. Richards was a tall kid with a bad complexion and an attitude to match. He tossed a green tennis ball in the air as he walked. As he passed, he glanced at Annie and Cara with a dismissive *whatever* look and headed toward the red Mustang. Annie didn't pay much attention. She was trying to decide if she should be pissed at Cara or Cara's father.

"Kind of a sunshine friendship," she finally said.

"He'll get over it. Give it a couple days. And we can, you know, still do the library and stuff."

"What about Slim Lake? He was okay with that?"

"I didn't ask him. Anyway, it would be away from town, away from your dad. Kind of out of harm's way."

Annie saw Uly Kingbird and Darrell Gallagher crossing the parking lot, coming from town. She'd been surprised to see Uly at school that week. She'd figured that because of the tragedy in the family, he'd be home for a while. But the Kingbirds, she remembered, were not a family that cried. She hadn't had a chance to talk to him, but he seemed okay. Even though the temperature was easily in the high sixties, Gallagher wore his long black leather coat, à la *Matrix*. As they got nearer, Allan Richards pointed their way and said something to his buddies gathered around the Mustang. He started walking a course that would intercept them. A couple of the other boys trailed after him.

"Hey, Red Boy," Richards called. He was still tossing his tennis ball.

Uly kept walking, as if he hadn't heard.

"Hey, I'm talking to you." Richards stepped in front of Uly and Gallagher, blocking their way. "You deaf or just stupid?"

Uly said, "I'm just going inside, okay?"

"No, it's not okay." Richards grinned and glanced back to see if the others around Amundsen's Mustang were watching. "I think you should take the day off, because the truth is, I can't stand being in the same building with you."

He tossed the ball at Uly. It bounced off his forehead and Richards caught it. Uly tried to move past, but Richards stepped in his way.

Gallagher said, "Why don't you just leave him alone."

Richards turned and bounced the ball off Gallagher's forehead in the same way he'd done it to Uly. "Why don't you make me, freak-boy."

Gallagher made no move against Richards, just stood silently with his hands in his long black coat.

"Go on," Richards said to Uly. "The Red Boyz aren't welcome here."

"I'm not one of the Red Boyz."

"Know what we do to Red Boyz around here? Open 'em up with buckshot, that's what."

He popped the ball off Uly's forehead again. This time Uly followed it back. He tackled Richards. Together they fell backward and ricocheted off a green Taurus wagon, knocking the side mirror from its mount. They hit the pavement with Uly still in Richards's grasp. The car alarm on the Taurus began to bleat mercilessly. Richards was taller and heavier, but Uly was all rage and he wrapped up the bigger boy in the furious hug of his arms as they wrestled. Annie leaped from the planter box and raced toward the Taurus. The Mustang crowd came, too. They formed a loose circle around the two kids writhing on the asphalt. Annie moved to intervene, but Gary Amundsen blocked her way.

"Let them finish it," he said.

"Get out of my way, Gary."

Annie tried to move around him, but Randy Shaw slipped next to Amundsen and stood with him shoulder to shoulder, forming a human wall.

"You heard him," Shaw said. "It's between them."

Annie tried once again to maneuver around them, but Shaw

reached out and shoved her roughly back. Anger flared red in her vision. She responded to his shove with one of her own, far fiercer than his had been. He hadn't expected it. His eyes showed his surprise and he stumbled backward and fell over Uly and Richards. As he went down, he hit his head on the door handle of the Taurus. He came to rest in a heap on top of Richards, who'd finally managed to pin Uly beneath him. For a moment it was chaos on the ground as they all fought to separate.

Then Amundsen yelled, "Hey, stop it, you guys. Randy's bleeding bad."

Shaw seemed confused. He reached a hand to the back of his head, and when he brought it around in front so that he could see, his face went white. His palm and fingers were dripping red.

"Jesus," he said. "Oh shit."

Uly and Richards separated and stood up. Shaw struggled to stand and finally found his feet. He turned the back of his head toward Amundsen. "Dude, is it bad?"

"I can't tell, Randy. There's too much blood."

Amundsen was right. Blood welled up bright crimson through Shaw's blond hair and fell in huge drops onto the black asphalt. Annie's rage vanished, replaced by a terrible fear.

"Break it up, guys! Break it up!" Mr. Bukoski, who taught math, shoved his way through the circle of boys. He was more Mack truck than man, and he was the school's head football coach as well. "Let me see." He took a good look at the back of Shaw's head, his fingers sifting through blond hair and blood. "Might take a stitch or three, but you'll be fine. Here." He yanked a folded handkerchief from his back pocket and put it over the wounded area. "Hold that there. Come on." With his bloody hand on the boy's shoulder, he turned Shaw toward the school. "Kingbird, Richards, O'Connor. I want you in the office. Now. And that's my car. Somebody's going to pay for a new mirror."

Annie trooped with the others behind Mr. Bukoski and Randy Shaw. When she passed Cara, who still sat on the planter box, Cara mouthed, *You were awesome, girl.* Annie made no reply and followed the others into the dark of the school building.

* * *

When she got the call, Lucinda was in the middle of changing Misty. She lifted the baby, whose bottom was clean but still bare, from the changing table and carried her to the phone in the hallway. *Aurora Area High School,* the caller ID indicated. Her thought was that Uly had forgotten something important and wanted her to bring it, a request he'd made occasionally in the past.

When the principal explained to her what the situation actually was, she assured him that her husband would be there soon. She called Will.

"It's Uly," she told him. "There's been some trouble at school. A fight. A boy was hurt."

"Uly do the hurting?" He sounded almost hopeful.

"I don't know. Can you go? I have the baby."

"I'll take care of it, Luci."

She spent the next hour and a half worrying. A call from school hadn't been uncommon with Alejandro, but Ulysses never got into trouble. He was too quiet, something Will complained about. It was true that Uly didn't talk much. He lived inside himself. But his father was the same way.

She'd just put Misty down for a nap when she heard the car pull into the drive and the thump of car doors slamming. She reached the kitchen just as the side door opened and the two walked in. Ulysses came first, looking sullen, as always. Behind him, Will didn't look too upset.

"Go on to your room. I'll let you know what I decide," he said to his son's back.

"Yes, sir."

Uly skulked past his mother without looking at her.

"Are you all right?" She reached out and held him back gently with her hand. She looked into his face. "You're not hurt?"

"I'm fine, Mom." He didn't pull away, but waited until she'd removed her hand, then moved on.

With an old, familiar hurting in her heart, she watched him leave her.

Will took off his jacket and hung it neatly on a hanger he kept on a peg near the back door. He never tossed his coat over the back of a chair, never left his shoes in the living room, and he never suffered this kind of laxity in others. His military training.

"He's been suspended for the rest of the week," he said. "I'm hungry. What do we have for lunch?"

"What happened?"

"He got into it with a couple of other boys. One of them ended up with a bloody head."

"Bad?"

"Looked worse than it was. Head wounds are like that."

"Two boys? He was fighting with two boys?"

"The principal couldn't get a straight story from anybody, so what really happened is still unclear. They were all suspended. Including Anne O'Connor."

"Annie? What did she have to do with it?"

"Not sure. Like I said, the kids were all pretty tight-lipped." He opened the refrigerator and peered inside. "How about heating up some of that leftover lasagna?"

"You told Uly you'd let him know what you decided. Decided about what?"

"Appropriate punishment."

"Punishment? He's been suspended, isn't that punishment enough? And I know Uly. Whatever happened, he didn't start it."

He spoke with his head deep in the refrigerator. "There are rules, Luci. One of the rules is that you don't get into trouble at school."

"But you're happy he fought back."

"Of course I am. Someone attacks, you have to respond. If you don't, you lose respect and it's important that the enemy respect you."

"Enemy? Will, these are just high school kids. And this isn't a war."

He pulled out the pan of lasagna, folded back the aluminum foil that covered it, and sniffed. "Life *is* war, Lucinda." He held out the pan for her to deal with.

TWENTY-TWO

Cork drove across the rez to the old mission, a small one-room building in the middle of a large clearing. The mission, nearly a hundred years old, had fallen into disrepair, but several years earlier a priest known affectionately as St. Kawasaki had spent a lot of his own time and resources to restore the structure in order to celebrate Mass there periodically. Most Shinnobs on the rez who were Catholic were used to driving to St. Agnes, in Aurora. They always appreciated, however, a service in their own community.

Behind the mission, bordered by a wrought-iron fence, was a cemetery begun when the mission was first built. It was an assortment of gravestones, chiseled markers, crudely wood-burned plaques, and crosses. There were also a number of grave houses, which were low wooden structures built over the burial plots, an old Ojibwe tradition. Two open graves lay waiting to be filled. On the following afternoon, the bodies of Alexander and Rayette Kingbird would do the filling.

Cork leaned against the fence. The afternoon was sunny and warm. He wrapped his hands around the top rail and felt all the heat the black iron had absorbed. It was from the sun, of course, but he knew it could just as well have come from the fire of the collective anger contained in the burial ground. So much death dealt out so unfairly, betrayal in every form—hunger, disease, outright murder. His grandmother's people were interred here, and their blood ran hot in his veins. Still, he was more Irish than Ojibwe, and he observed that his own shadow lay outside the fence. It was only because of the angle of the sun, but in that convergence of circumstance, he saw the accusation that had dogged him all his life. In Tamarack County, a place where history was a litany of lies and a long saga of distrust, he was considered neither Ojibwe nor really white. He understood that he would always stand outside the fence.

He left the mission, drove a quarter mile east, and turned onto an old logging road overgrown with timothy grass and wild oats. The road cut along a ridge that overlooked the clearing. He pulled to the side, parked, and grabbed his binoculars from the back of the Bronco. He climbed to the top of the ridge, which was thick with second-growth jack pines. The mission was clearly visible, a small white box in the middle of a field of green. A single road—Mission Road—bisected the clearing. West, the direction from which Cork had come, the road led toward Allouette. East, it headed toward the back side of the Sawbill Mountains, where it dead-ended in difficult bog country. He lifted his field glasses and was able easily to follow the gravel road west about a mile, where it curved out of sight among the pines. The dust kicked up by his Bronco still hung, ghostlike, in the corridor that ran between the distant trees. East, the road ran straight and he could see even farther. He swung the lenses toward the mission. The open graves of the cemetery were like black eyes staring back.

The clearing was empty now, but tomorrow it would be filled with people from the rez. Cork wouldn't be among them. He'd be up there on that ridge with his binoculars.

Take a hawk's-eye view, Meloux had advised.

White men didn't have a name for the ridge, but the Ojibwe did. They called it Kakaik after the great war chief. It was the name Alexander Kingbird had taken when he formed the Red Boyz, a name with a simple meaning: Hawk.

Jo poured water into the coffeemaker on the counter. She kept her back to Cork.

"I'm sorry," he said. "I was on the rez, out of cell phone range, otherwise I'd have been there, you know that."

"I didn't need you there, Cork. I told you last night I'd take Stevie to Dr. Barron." Her spine was an iron pole. "That's not the point, anyway. The point is that I worried myself sick when I couldn't get hold of you to tell you what the doctor said. I saw you lying dead out there somewhere with your back torn open just like the Kingbirds."

"I'm sorry, Jo."

"But not sorry enough to step back from this whole Kingbird mess, huh?" She turned and gave him a look that could have frozen fire. "How'd you sleep last night?"

"Restless."

"Restless?" She almost laughed. "I don't think I slept at all."

They stared across a silence that lay between them. Finally Cork said, "Where's Annie?"

"Upstairs."

"What did she have to say?"

"Not a lot. She shoved the Shaw boy. He hit his head and bled all over everything. She's been suspended from school and from soft-ball."

"Ouch. What did the Shaw kid do that made her shove him?"

"Why don't you go up and get the story from her yourself."

He walked out of the kitchen.

"Would you like some coffee when it's ready?" Jo called to him.

"Yeah, save me a cup, thanks."

"I'll be glad to bring it up."

He paused in the dining room and turned back. Through the door-way, he could see her standing at the counter. The offer to bring his coffee to him upstairs was, he understood, a small bridge across the chasm that had been her anger.

"Thank you," he said. "I'd like that."

He found Annie in her room, lying on her bed, staring up at the ceiling. Her leather ball glove was on her left hand. In her right was an old softball, scuffed and dirty. She didn't see her father at first. Cork stood in the hallway just outside her room, watching her toss the softball and catch it in her mitt. She was a slender young woman, with red hair that was often untamed and a face that freckled signifi-cantly in summer.

"Hey, slugger. Hear you did some damage today," he said.

She took the glove off, nestled the softball in its palm, and set it on the bed beside her. "It was an accident."

"The damage maybe. How about the shove?"

"What did Mom tell you?"

"Not much. I'm mostly in the dark."

He strolled in and sat next to her. She stared at her left hand, which looked so much smaller now that her big glove was gone.

"What's the story?" he said.

"Allan Richards started giving Uly Kingbird a lot of crap. You know, about his brother and all. It was pretty hurtful stuff. Uly finally lit into him. Richards is way bigger, so I went over to, I don't know, try to help somehow. A couple of other guys stepped in to stop me. Shaw was one of them. I tried to get around him. He shoved me. I shoved him back and he went down. That's about all there is to it."

"Except for the gallon of blood he lost."

"Yeah, except for that."

"What do you think?"

"Huh?"

"About the whole situation," he said.

"I probably shouldn't have shoved him."

"Why not?"

"I don't know. I guess you shouldn't respond to violence with violence?"

"That's a question."

Annie dumped the softball out and slid her glove back onto her hand. She gave the leather palm a couple of hard thumps with her fist.

"The truth is, I don't know that I'd do anything different," she finally said. "Those guys were total jerks."

"Okay. As long as you're willing to accept the consequences. Your mother told me you've been suspended from school and from the softball team."

Her eyes narrowed in anger. "That part's unfair."

"School or the softball team?"

"Softball."

"Are you suspended permanently?"

"I can't play in the game on Friday. Winning the conference depends on this one. So if we lose, it's as good as permanent."

"I'm sorry, kiddo. That's hard, but under the circumstances, understandable."

She didn't respond for a minute. Finally she said grudgingly, "I suppose it's like you said. If I think it was the right thing to do, I need to accept the consequences." She picked up the softball and slapped it into her glove. "I just wish I'd done some damage to Allan Richards while I was at it."

Cork couldn't help smiling. "So how did Uly do with the Richards kid?"

"He had him for a while, but Allan's a lot bigger. Kind of a David and Goliath thing, only Uly didn't have a slingshot. Am I, like, grounded or anything?"

"I'll talk to your mom, but I think missing the playoff game is enough." He stood up. "Your mom and I are going to the visitation for the Kingbirds tonight. You want to come?"

"Yes, thanks. Dad?"

"Yeah?"

"When I was a kid and I had to take the garbage out at night, I was scared sometimes that there were things hiding in the bushes. You know, monsters and stuff. I was always sure they were going to jump out and get me."

"What about it?"

"That's how I feel right now. Not about me specifically, but about everybody and everything here. It feels like there's something scary hiding in the bushes, you know what I mean? I keep thinking that any moment it's going to leap out and . . . I don't know what exactly, but I'm kind of afraid."

She looked up at him as if she expected her father to put her fear to rest.

Cork gave her the only thing he had, which was company in her concern. "Hell, Annie, I'd be a liar if I said I wasn't scared, too."

TWENTY-THREE

The visitation was held at Nelson's Funeral Home. Annie had been there over the years for other visitations and memorial services. Also, when she was a sophomore, she'd gone on a field trip organized by her biology teacher, Mr. Dexter, an odd man, short and balding, full of gruesome stories about the strange parasites he'd seen inhabit people's bodies when he was a Peace Corps worker somewhere in Indonesia. The mortician had taken the class on a tour of the prep room, explaining how he prepared a body for burial and showing them the instruments and the bottles of chemicals. It had seemed alien and cruel and unnecessary to Annie. Why not simply let go of the body in the same way the spirit did?

Nelson's was one of the nicest of the old houses in Aurora. Bigger, more luxurious homes had been built on Iron Lake, but Nelson's, with its gingerbread trim, its wraparound porch, and its cupola, seemed elegant in a way that suggested there was some sort of etiquette to the aftermath of dying. The biological stuff of body preparation Annie could do without, but some of the traditions that accompanied death felt right, like the visitation. Gathering to offer comfort and to remember the life that had gone before the death seemed fundamental and natural to a transition that Annie thought was probably more difficult for the living than for the dead.

Annie and her family paused at the door to the room where the visitation was in progress. On the tour she'd taken, the mortician said that it had once been a grand dining room and held a table that could have easily seated twenty. Now it contained two dark-wood caskets placed side by side, a number of flower arrangements, several photographic memorials that had been created on poster boards and positioned on display tripods in the corners of the room, and a lot of people talking quietly. Her mother signed the guest register while her father wrote a check to the St. Agnes Early Education Fund, which the Kingbirds had designated for memorial contributions.

Annie went on ahead. Across the room, Uly stood peering at one of the poster memorials. She wandered over, but he was so intent he didn't notice her. He seemed to be focused on a photograph of him and Alexander standing together on a white diving raft in the middle of a lake. Uly was short and skinny; Alexander was much taller, much older, a young teenager with a developing physique. He wore a broad smile. Uly stared warily at the camera, as if he was on a raft drifting out to sea.

"Where was it taken?" Annie asked.

"North Carolina, I think. Lejeune," Uly said. "Probably just after we moved there."

"Alexander looks happy. You look like you just lost your pet turtle."

"Alex liked moving. He was good at it. Dad would get a new posting, we'd hit a new base, a new town, and Alex was out the door getting to know the place, the people. Charisma. He had it in spades."

"You didn't like moving?"

Uly shook his head. "Staying in one place seemed better. Safer. Till we moved here." He thought a moment, then smiled. "Alex got us kicked out of base housing once."

"How?"

"I'm not sure exactly. It involved a cherry bomb, a bag of dog crap, and the base commander. Alex was never much impressed by authority. It was the only time Dad ever hit him. Slapped him across the face." He wasn't smiling anymore. "That part I remember." He turned to her. "Sorry about today."

"It wasn't your fault. I really like the way you lit into Allan Richards. He's such an asshole."

"I wanted to kill him," Uly said. "If I'd had a gun, he'd be dead."

The pupils of Uly's eyes were a swirl of green, and what Annie saw in them made her think of the threatening look of the sky before a hailstorm. She struggled to find a way to help him out of the dark hole into which he seemed to be sliding. "I've been thinking. What if we did another piece for church? Everyone loved what we did last Sunday."

"I don't think so."

"You don't have to give me an answer right away."

"He just did."

Annie turned and found Darrell Gallagher at her shoulder. He was dressed, as usual, entirely in black, which should have been appropriate for the occasion, but somehow felt instead like an insult. The sly smile on his face made everything about him feel off.

"You have an annoying habit, Gallagher, of butting in on other people's conversations."

"And you have an annoying habit, O'Connor, of breathing," he shot back.

"Think about it, Uly," she said.

He didn't answer. He turned away in Gallagher's company and drifted off. Why did Uly hang with someone like Gallagher? she wondered. But she knew the answer: Being alone was worse.

"Are they in there?" Stevie asked. He nodded toward the polished, closed caskets at the other end of the room. His black eyes and the bandage over his nose made him look like he'd gone through hell, which he had. Jo had taken him to see Dr. Barron that morning, and the repair procedure had been scheduled for Thursday. At the moment, Stevie didn't seem much bothered by his broken nose.

"Not them," Cork said. "Only their bodies."

"I know that. Their souls are gone and stuff. I meant are their bodies really in there? It's not just for show?"

"They're really in there. Why wouldn't they be?"

"They were pretty messed up, right?"

"That's probably one of the reasons the caskets are closed."

Stevie stared at the two coffins as if trying to imagine Alexander and Rayette Kingbird lying inside on the soft satin, their bodies ripped apart by buckshot.

Lucinda Kingbird stood near the caskets talking with a constant stream of people. Cork spotted Will Kingbird standing alone a good distance from his wife, his hands clasped behind him, looking like a soldier at parade rest. Although he'd been born and raised on the Iron Lake Reservation, he hadn't made an effort to reconnect with his Ojibwe roots when he returned to Tamarack County. The Shinnobs who'd come to the visitation, Rayette's relatives mostly, spoke to him only a moment before moving on. It was the same with the others who'd come, many of whom were parishioners from St. Agnes. Kingbird wasn't the kind of man who invited long conversations.

"See Annie by the poster board over there?" Cork said to his son. "Why don't you go keep her company for a few minutes?"

Once Stevie had gone, Cork headed toward Kingbird.

"Will," he said in greeting.

They shook hands, firmly and briefly.

"I just want to say how sorry I am about Alexander and Rayette."

Kingbird's eyes were dark—his Anishinaabe heritage—and they were difficult to read. Also an Anishinaabe trait. But there was something that made Kingbird's eyes different from other Shinnobs. The Anishinaabeg loved to laugh, and in their eyes there was always a spark of humor. Not in Kingbird's eyes.

"You know," Kingbird said, "you were probably the last person to see Alex alive."

"No, that would have been whoever killed him."

"I can tell you who killed him. Buck Reinhardt."

"A lot of good law enforcement people are looking hard at that possibility, Will, and they're not finding any evidence."

"Looking hard? An investigator name of Rutledge came to my shop yesterday. I told him about the customized Robar shotgun I sold Reinhardt. He said there wasn't much they could do with that. Said you can't prove anything with buckshot the way you can with a bullet. He told me Elise Reinhardt swears her husband was home when Alex was killed. Know what I told him? Give me an hour with Reinhardt and I'd get the truth out of the son of a bitch."

"This isn't that kind of war."

"Once the shooting starts, there's only one kind of war."

Cork kept his voice low, not wanting to disturb the others at the visitation, and said, "Will, I'm sorry about what's happened, I really am, but I don't think it helps to think of any of this in military absolutes."

"I'll tell you about the military. When I was a kid, didn't matter if I did a thing right. If my old man had it in his head to hit me, he'd hit me. The corps, you do a thing right, it means something and they remember. You think I'm rigid. I think I'm consistent. I see the world in terms of consistency. Reinhardt killing my son is entirely consistent with the man Buck Reinhardt has always been."

"I'm not going to disagree with you, Will, but your thinking seems a little narrow to me. Reinhardt wasn't Alex's only enemy."

"He's had enemies for a long time. It wasn't until Buck Reinhardt lost his daughter that somebody killed him. You're going to tell me that doesn't prove anything. That's because you see yourself as a reasonable man and reasonable men don't rush to judgment. You have any idea how many times I've seen reasonable men stand by and do nothing while the worst shit you can imagine goes down?"

Cork didn't reply. His attention had been grabbed by a contingent of the Red Boyz who'd appeared in the hallway outside the viewing room. He knew them all: Tom Blessing, Daniel Hart, Elgin Manypenny, Rennie Decouteau, Jessie Hanks, and Bobby Oakgrove. Most were young, eighteen or nineteen. They'd dressed neatly, in clean dark pants, white shirts, some colorful vests. They all wore their hair long. Some had braided it, others let it fall loose beneath a leather band or a folded bandanna bound about their heads and adorned with an eagle feather. In the Ojibwe culture of long ago, the eagle feather signified that a warrior had killed another in battle. What it meant to the Red Boyz, Cork didn't know.

Will Kingbird saw where Cork was looking. He turned, and both men waited for the Red Boyz to drift in.

Lucinda Kingbird did not want to be there. She did not want to have to talk to these people who offered her kindness in a time they believed must be terrible for her. She did not want to feel bad for not being full of the emotions they expected. The cordial smile she wore wearied her. She wondered, as she had from the beginning of this whole tragic mess, if she truly was different from other people; if, because she did not feel like grieving for her son, something was terribly wrong with her.

She had never fit in. She had never felt as if she was somewhere she could call home. In Aurora, people were pleasant to her, but it was clear that she was an outsider. She was not white, nor was she Ojibwe. She was Latina; she spoke with a slight but noticeable accent. In Tamarack County, no one seemed quite certain what to make of her. Although Will had grown up here, he'd made no effort to reestablish his connection with his people. He was comfortable as an outsider. Lucinda believed she should have been, too. When she'd married a career marine, she'd become a nomad, a chronic outsider. Over time, she should have adjusted. But she'd never grown used to feeling different, feeling watched. She'd only grown accustomed to feeling alone.

"There shoulda been a wake."

Lucinda turned at the sound of the old voice and found Tillie Strangeways staring at her in accusation. Tillie was Rayette's great-aunt, an old woman who reminded Lucinda of an apple long fallen off the tree: leathery, bitter, shriveled to a little ball of wrinkles. She was a caustic old woman who referred to Lucinda as "that Mexican." She was accompanied by Ginger, Rayette's cousin.

"Good evening, Tillie," Lucinda said, and put on her cordial smile.

"Why didn't you hold a wake?" the old woman croaked. "They don't do that in Mexico?"

"Grandma," Ginger said.

"All I'm saying is there shoulda been a wake. Two, three days. With singers."

Lucinda hauled up as much graciousness as she could summon. "My husband made all the arrangements."

The old woman squinted and scanned the room. "Where's the baby?"

"I told you, Grandma," Ginger said. "Justine's taking care of Misty tonight."

Tillie Strangeways seemed shocked, though Lucinda suspected it was all drama. "Justine? That girl don't have the sense God give a retarded cow."

Ginger offered Lucinda an apologetic look and said to the old woman, "Come on, Grandma. Let's go see Uncle Leonard. He's talking about making fry bread for after the funeral tomorrow."

"Leonard? Fry bread?" Everything seemed to shock Tillie. "That boy couldn't fry a rock."

Whatever that meant.

As soon as the women left, Lucinda saw Jo O'Connor coming her way. She was tired, but once more tried to smile.

"Lucinda, I'm so sorry." Jo hugged her gently.

She and Jo worked on the education committee for St. Agnes and helped with the Christmas pageant every year. In a hopeful sort of way, she felt close to Jo.

"I didn't know Alexander well, but I knew Rayette and I thought she was a wonderful mother and a fine person," Jo said.

I didn't really know Alejandro either, Lucinda wanted to tell her. *And if a mother doesn't know her son, who does?* Long before this terrible thing happened, she'd lain awake nights wondering if she loved Alejandro enough. But how can you love someone you don't know? And now, with all these well-meaning people around her, she wondered why grief was not tearing her apart.

"How's Misty?" Jo asked.

"She is wonderful."

"If there's anything I can do to help, please let me know."

There was something, yes, but Lucinda couldn't say it, not there, not like this, with so many around to hear.

"Thank you," she said instead. "You have always been so kind."

They stood a moment, and Lucinda thought from the way Jo gazed into her eyes that maybe she had divined what was on Lucinda's mind and was waiting for Lucinda to ask. It was as if she was offering Lucinda permission to speak the unspeakable. Lucinda opened her mouth, knowing suddenly that she would ask, right there, ask the unspeakable of this woman who was as near to a friend as Lucinda had.

Before she could say a word, however, the Red Boyz walked in.

Lucinda knew some of them. The one named Blessing she certainly recognized. An odd name, she'd always thought, because he never seemed to her to be concerned about what God had given him. Whenever she'd seen him in Alejandro's company, he'd looked stern and unhappy. Now he looked worried.

He spotted Will first, who was standing with Jo O'Connor's husband. He spoke to Will in a voice that could be heard above all the others in the room, "Your son, our brother, was a great man. We've come to pay our respects."

Nothing about Rayette, Lucinda thought with disapproval.

Will opened his hand, gesturing toward the caskets. "Then pay them."

Blessing hesitated and eyed Cork O'Connor. "I heard what happened last night. Don't say I didn't warn you about Lonnie Thunder."

Lucinda could see the anger in O'Connor's face, but he spoke so quietly in reply that she couldn't hear what he said. Whatever it was, it made Blessing laugh in a brutal way.

"I'll pass that along to him," Blessing said. "Threats from an old man. He'll get a real kick out of it. Make his day."

"You said you came to pay your respects." Will opened his hand again toward Lucinda and the caskets beyond her. "I suggest you do that."

Blessing made his way across the room with the other Red Boyz following. He stood before Lucinda and drew himself up in a formal way.

"I'm sorry for your loss. We give you our promise that whoever did this will pay. Kakaik was our friend, our brother, our leader. Kakaik was a great warrior."

Out of the depth of her weariness, Lucinda stared at him.

"His name was Alejandro," she said, and turned away.

TWENTY-FOUR

They drove home from the visitation separately and Cork parked his Bronco behind Jo's Camry in the driveway. Once inside, they spent a while around the kitchen table over the usual O'Connor nighttime fare: cookies and milk. Stevie went upstairs to get ready for bed, and then Cork went up to say good night. His son scooted over to make room on the mattress and Cork sat down. Trixie, who'd settled herself at Stevie's feet, crawled up and wedged herself between them.

"Are you going back to Sam's Place?" Stevie asked.

"Yeah, buddy, I am."

"Somebody might shoot at you again."

"I'm thinking that, for them, once was enough."

"Then why are you still staying at Sam's Place?"

"Just playing it safe."

"Because of us, you mean. Me, Annie, Mom."

"Don't forget Trixie." Cork scratched Trixie's head, behind her ears. The dog's tail thumped the mattress with a slow beat.

"You don't want us around if there's more shooting, right?"

"That's right."

Stevie looked troubled. "You said you wouldn't do anything that would get you hurt."

"I'm kind of in a spot there, guy. It doesn't seem to matter what I do, people still shoot at me."

"They're afraid of you. And they oughta be."

"You think so?"

"Uh-huh." He nodded seriously. "Is Mom still mad at you?"

"What makes you think she's mad?"

"When Mom's mad, everybody knows it." Stevie yawned.

"She's coming around."

"She's just worried. Moms do that." His eyes seemed to be getting heavy.

"I'll leave the light on if you want to read a little while."

Stevie shook his head.

"'Night, buddy." Cork bent and gave his son a kiss on the forehead. "Sleep tight."

"'Night, Dad."

As he left the room, Cork turned off the light. Behind him, he heard his son mumble dreamily, "'Night, Trixie."

He paused at the open door to Annie's room. His daughter sat at her desk, facing her computer. The glow from the monitor surrounded her shoulders and head like a halo.

"So, without school taking up all your time, what's on your agenda tomorrow?" he asked.

Annie spun around in her chair to face him. "I don't know. Run first thing in the morning. Finish my term paper. Mom says since I'm home all this week, I'm responsible for dinners."

"Sounds reasonable."

"Maybe I'll try some new recipes from that cookbook Aunt Rose sent me."

"Adventurous." He leaned against the door frame and smiled.

"Dad, I'm worried about Uly Kingbird."

"How so?"

"It's never been easy for him here. Now it's even worse. And he won't ask for any help."

"I'm sure Will and Lucinda are doing all they can." He saw the sour look on her face. "What?"

"Parents are clueless."

"Oh?"

"I could tell you stories."

"About you? I'm all ears."

"Someday, maybe, when I'm past being grounded for life." She smiled, but only briefly. "Uly's dad isn't like you."

"Is that good or bad?"

"Uly doesn't talk about it, but I get the feeling Mr. Kingbird rides him all the time. Uly can't do anything right."

Cork came in and sat down on the bed. "Let me tell you about Will Kingbird. His mother died when he was very young and his father remarried a woman with several children of her own already. Will's father was an alcoholic. Not a mean drunk, but chronic. Had trouble holding a job. His second wife finally got tired of his drinking and left. I think she was a White Earth Shinnob and just went back to her people. Will pretty much took care of his old man after that. When Will was seventeen, his father hanged himself. It was Will who found him. Pretty soon after, he joined the marines and left Aurora.

"Will Kingbird can be a demanding perfectionist. He's responsible in the extreme. From what I gather, his choice of profession—a career soldier—often put his life at risk. He's pretty much a loner. And he has trouble expressing his emotions. As I understand it, these are all characteristics of children of alcoholics. There's more to him than that, of course, but it explains a lot."

Annie thought for a while. "How do I help Uly?"

Cork shook his head. "I'd say offer what you can, whatever you're capable of offering. But if he doesn't want your help, I don't think there's much you can do."

"I don't want to just turn my back."

"I didn't say you should. Try to be there if he decides he needs you."

"And the rest of the time butt out?"

"Pretty much."

"That's not real specific."

"Best I can do. Anything else?"

"No."

"Good night, then."

"'Night, Dad."

He found Jo in her downstairs office, working late for her clients. She looked up when he came in. Behind her glasses, her blue eyes were huge. Her hands lay in a pool of light cast by the lamp on her desk. Her face was shadowy.

"I'm taking off for Sam's Place," he said.

"Still think you need to leave?"

"I do."

"'I do.' Doesn't that come just after 'till death do us part'?" She stared at him and he made no reply. "Are you going to the funeral tomorrow?"

"Not exactly."

She took her glasses off and sighed. "I'm not even going to ask what that means."

"It means I'll be home for dinner. Annie says she's going to cook up a storm while she's suspended."

"We'll set a place for you."

He thought he ought to kiss her good-bye, but he wasn't sure it was something that she wanted at the moment, so he simply said, "Good night, then."

"Cork," she said as he turned away. "Please be careful. And call me when you're safe inside Sam's Place."

He crossed the room and leaned down to her. She reached up, put her arms around his neck, and held him in a kiss.

"I'll be careful," he promised.

At the corner of Oak and Second, before he reached the road to Sam's Place, he pulled over and took out his cell phone. He tried Thunder's number, as he had several times that day, and again got no answer. Maybe Thunder didn't want to talk. Maybe he was hiding somewhere deep in the woods, somewhere he couldn't easily charge his cell phone. What about Thunder did he really understand?

He considered Will Kingbird's philosophy of the world: consistency. What were the consistencies in Thunder's behavior? Thunder had disappeared immediately after Kristi Reinhardt's death. If what Meloux had said was true, Thunder was a man very much afraid. He'd probably gone into hiding, somewhere he believed no one could find him. Yet he'd risked coming into town to take a few potshots at Cork, a stupid thing. Cork wasn't entirely convinced that killing Alex and Rayette was consistent with what he knew about Thunder. It took a lot to kill in cold blood. But a rash action was consistent with fear. Fear and stupidity: Maybe these were the constants in Thunder's behavior.

Then Cork realized consistency ran both ways. Was *he* predictable? If a kid like Thunder could fool him into an ambush, what did that say?

Cork turned around on Oak Street and headed to Grant Park, at the southern end of the open field that lay south of Sam's Place. He turned off his headlights and pulled into the parking lot, where his was the only vehicle. From the glove box, he took his .38 and from his toolbox a Maglite. He flipped the switch on the cab's dome light so that it wouldn't come on, got out, and closed the door quietly. In the ambient light from town, he found the jogging path that had been worn into the ground cover along the lakeshore and that ran all the way to Sam's Place. He crept along the path, putting his weight on the outside of his soles, as he would if he were stalking game. Approaching the copse of poplars that surrounded the old ironworks from which Thunder had fired the night before, he paused. To enter the trees, he needed to leave the path, but the field was full of brown wild oats and milkweed and thistle, dead since November, gone brittle. There was no way he could move through them soundlessly.

He got a break. A wind rose off the lake and pushed through the branches of the poplars with a loud rustling that masked any noise he might make. He slipped among the trees. It was dark in the copse and he moved like an animal on the prowl: creep and pause, creep and pause. He was a dozen yards from the ruined wall of the ironworks when he spotted a green glow that, after a moment, he realized was the face of a wristwatch turned up for someone to check the time. He positioned himself behind the trunk of the nearest poplar, aimed his Maglite and his .38 in the direction of the glow. He hit the light switch.

"Don't move!" he shouted. "I have a gun."

The figure froze in the ice white beam of light.

"Put your hands on your head. Now turn around slowly."

The figure was dressed in camouflage fatigues. When Cork saw the familiar face, he almost laughed.

"Marsha?"

"Can I put my hands down, Cork?" she said.

"Go ahead."

"And that flashlight's blinding me."

He killed the light and walked to her.

"How long have you been here?" he asked.

"Since just after dark."

"No sign of Thunder?"

"Nothing yet. If he was out there, that light of yours scared him away."

As his eyes adjusted to the dark around them, he spotted a rifle with a nightscope propped against the wall. "Thanks," he said. "You could have had one of your guys do this instead."

She shrugged. "I knew it was a long shot. And a deputy I'd have to pay." She stared toward the lake, where the night kept her blind. "I feel bad about all this, Cork. I asked you to help, next thing you know Thunder's shooting at you and Stevie. I'm sorry."

"Not your fault." Cork leaned against the top of the wall, which, in its fallen state, came just above his hips. "Look, I think I might be able to get a lead on Thunder."

"How?"

He explained about his interpretation of Meloux's enigmatic advice.

"You think Thunder will be at the funeral tomorrow," Dross said.

"Maybe not in actual attendance, but I think he might be in the general area, close enough so that he can see what's going on."

"Why?"

"Curiosity. Loyalty. Loneliness. Take your pick."

"You want someone with you?"

He shook his head. "Best done alone."

Dross checked the ghostly green-white glow of her watch. "I don't think Thunder's coming tonight. I know you like him for the Kingbird murders, but don't go out on a limb, okay? I still believe Reinhardt had the motivation and the nature, and we'll keep hammering at that alibi of his till it breaks."

Cork pushed off from the wall. "Let's get out of here."

The sheriff picked up her rifle and slung the strap over her shoulder. They left the ruins, walked out of the trees, and paused together on the jogging path.

"Where are you parked?" Cork asked.

"In town. Didn't want anyone making my vehicle."

"Want a ride?"

"I'll hoof it, thanks." Dross looked toward the lights on the far side of the empty field. "When you had the job, Cork, did you ever wonder if you were doing the right thing?"

"When didn't I?"

"Yeah." She smiled, but even in the dim light, Cork could see how weary the gesture was.

They separated, heading in different directions, both stumbling in the dark.

TWENTY-FIVE

Wednesday morning Cork was up at first light and at the house on Gooseberry Lane before anyone was stirring. He shook Annie gently awake and asked if she wanted to run with him. In ten minutes, she was dressed and ready to go. They jogged to Grant Park to warm up, stretched there, then began the real business. They followed the shoreline of Iron Lake past the old ironworks and Sam's Place, turned inland, and headed up to North Point. They turned around at the end of the peninsula in front of the old Parrant estate, then backtracked to Oak Street, headed west to the high school, and finally home. It wasn't a long run, only eight miles.

Five years earlier, Cork had entered his first marathon. Eighteen months ago he'd taken a bullet in his left thigh. He wasn't a young man. Rebounding fully took him longer than he'd expected. He was back in the rhythm now and glad of it. Annie, who was in marvelous shape, could have danced rings around him while they ran, but she held back. He appreciated that she seemed to enjoy his company.

The sun was well above the trees, the day warming up nicely when they walked into the kitchen. Jo was pouring herself a cup of freshly brewed coffee. A box of Froot Loops stood on the kitchen table near a bowl that was empty except for a spoonful of milk and a few soggy cereal bits. Cork grabbed a glass from the cupboard and went to the sink to run himself a cold drink of water.

"Thanks for the run, Dad," Annie said.

"Anytime."

She went up to shower, and Cork took a mug from the cupboard and filled it with coffee. "Where's Stevie?"

"Upstairs running a comb through his hair. He's not exactly happy about going back to school today." She dropped a couple of slices of bread into the toaster. "And you're not exactly not going to the Kingbird funeral today. Whatever that means."

"What it means is that I'll be observing, but not close enough to be observed."

"You'll be out on the rez, then. Alone?"

"That's the plan."

"Do me a favor, will you? Call me when you go and call me again as soon as you're back in cell phone range, just to let me know you're okay."

"I will, I promise." He finished his coffee and ran water in the cup to rinse it out. "I'll be home for dinner."

The toast popped up, but Jo ignored it. She moved close to him and took his face in her hands. "I know it must seem sometimes that I want you to change, but I don't, Cork. I love who you are. It's just that it's so hard worrying about you."

"I wish I could tell you to stop worrying."

"Like asking me not to breathe." She kissed him and let him go. "Take care of yourself, cowboy."

The funeral was scheduled for noon. Two hours before it began, Cork was on the ridge above the old mission, his Bronco parked out of sight among the trees below. He had his Leitz binoculars and, just in case, his Remington. He was dressed in sage-colored jeans and a green flannel shirt. He wore a dun-colored ball cap with LEINENKU-GEL'S across the crown. The sun was high at his back. The clearing below was a field of tall grass full of wildflowers just beginning to blossom. At its center stood the old mission building, white as a block of ice.

As he waited for things to begin, Cork thought about his discussion with Marsha Dross at the ruined ironworks the night before. She said she was hammering at Reinhardt's alibi. Cork had awakened that morning with an idea about Reinhardt. Depending on how things went with Thunder today, he'd decided he might have a crack himself at breaking Reinhardt's story.

Half an hour before noon, he spotted a glint of sunlight off glass or metal on a hilltop on the far side of the clearing. He'd chosen his own position on the ridge knowing that, with the sun behind him, there'd be no reflecting light to give him away. The hill on the other side faced east, directly into the morning sun. And the sunlight had given something away.

Cork shifted his position and used his knees to steady his binoculars. He studied the locus of the reflection for several minutes. The glint from the hilltop came and went. More and more, Cork was convinced it came from someone who, like him, was observing the mission with field glasses.

When the first of the vehicles appeared in the distance on Mission Road, he turned his attention back to the clearing. It was the priest's car. Not far behind were the Kingbirds. The vehicles continued to come and people parked around the mission and spilled out. Mostly they were Shinnobs from the reservation. Cork recognized many of the Red Boyz. George and Sarah LeDuc were there, as were many of the tribal council members. Cork figured they'd come not so much for Kingbird, who'd been seen as a troublemaker, as for Rayette. There were easily a hundred people present. Lonnie Thunder was not among them.

The small mission was clearly not large enough for the gathering, so Father Ted held the service in the meadow. He was assisted by Ben and Kevin Olson, two altar boys whose mother was full-blood Ojibwe. Uly Kingbird played the guitar. Because the day was so still, Cork could hear the playing and the voices of the mourners when they sang "Amazing Grace" and "Morning Has Broken." A few people stepped forward to speak, but none of the Red Boyz. Cork knew that if Alexander Kingbird were alive, he'd have spoken eloquently. Tom Blessing, to whom the duty should have fallen, remained silent.

When it was finished, the people drifted back to their vehicles and began to depart, all heading toward Allouette, where a postfuneral meal was being served at the community center. Only one vehicle did not follow the others. Tom Blessing's black Silverado headed the other way. A mile beyond the clearing, Mission Road turned east toward the Sawbill Mountains and wove its way through miles of uninhabited bog country.

Cork lifted his binoculars to the hill on the far side of the clearing. The reflection had vanished.

Cork kept his distance. He didn't have to worry about losing Blessing. The spring melt—what little there was that year—had left the low-lying areas soggy, but the red dirt and gravel roads were dry and dusty. Cork followed the choking cloud kicked up by the big tires on Blessing's Silverado. Technically, they were still on Mission Road, though once it passed beyond the mission itself, the Iron Lake Ojibwe called it *ginebig,* which meant snake. The road curled and twisted, following the contours of the hills. It shadowed, more or less, the southern edge of the Boundary Waters Canoe Area Wilderness. Between the hills lay marsh and treacherous bogs edged with tamaracks, white cedars, and black-ash trees. Cork had driven the road in summer when swarms of mosquitoes often formed a gray, shifting fog in the marshy areas. The soggy ground and the mosquitoes made this region unattractive for habitation, and there were no resorts or summer cabins along the way. The road had been cut for logging, and the logging had been done in the winter, when there were no mosquitoes and the ground was frozen hard. It dead-ended far short of the Sawbills and was maintained only because it offered access to two remote entry points for the BWCAW. If Thunder wanted to hide where no one would look for him, he'd chosen a pretty good place.

Cork suddenly realized that he'd broken from the ghost of dust that had hung over the road in Blessing's wake. He pulled to a stop, glanced back, and saw no side access where Blessing could have turned off. He continued another fifty yards until he found a stretch of dry, solid ground off the road that was shielded by a stand of tall sumac. He parked the Bronco out of sight, then walked back. He located the crush of undergrowth that marked the place where Blessing had left the road, and he discovered a blind of brush that had been built to hide the trail Blessing had followed. As he stood before the blind, he heard the approaching growl of another engine and the crunch of gravel under tires. He didn't have time to get back to his Bronco. Instead, he ran to the other side of the road where he threw himself down among cattails that edged a small marsh.

Half a minute later, a red pickup appeared. As soon as it broke from the dust, it stopped. Cork couldn't see the driver. He heard a door slam and figured whoever it was, they were doing exactly what he had done and were looking for the place where Blessing had turned. He peered carefully through the wall of cattails and saw the figure study the trail Blessing had followed into the trees. When Cork realized who it was, he stood up.

"Dave!"

Reinhardt turned and Cork saw that the man was carrying. Dave Reinhardt had the weapon up and in a two-handed grip in an instant. He didn't fire, but he also didn't lower the weapon. He stared at Cork, looking surprised and unhappy.

"What are you doing here?" Reinhardt said.

"Same as you, I imagine. Trying to find Thunder."

Reinhardt holstered his handgun and Cork crossed the road.

"Was that you on the east side of the clearing?" Cork asked.

Reinhardt was dressed in khakis, a brown sweater, dark blue running shoes, a brown ball cap. "You spotted me?" He looked pained.

"The reflection off your field glasses."

"Where were you?"

"The ridge west of the mission."

"You saw Blessing take off and you followed him?"

"Yeah. Didn't realize you were behind me."

"I didn't realize you were ahead. I thought all that dust was Blessing's." He swung a hand toward the trail behind the blind. "Where do you figure he's headed?"

"I don't know. I've got a good map though."

Reinhardt followed Cork to the Bronco, parked beyond the sumac. Before heading to observe the funeral, Cork had grabbed a topographical map of the area. He took it from the glove box and spread it on the Bronco's hood. Reinhardt looked over his shoulder.

"I figure we're here." Cork tapped the map with his finger. "Half a mile north is Black Duck Lake, just this side of the Boundary Waters. If I were Thunder and I wanted to be somewhere that would give me a quick back-door escape, I'd choose a place like Black Duck Lake. A fifty-rod portage puts him on the Myrtle Flowage, inside the wilderness area. Hard to follow him there."

"Half a mile," Reinhardt said. "Ten minutes on foot, and he wouldn't hear us coming."

"You're reading my mind, Dave."

Reinhardt parked his pickup truck next to the Bronco behind the sumac. Cork took his binoculars and Remington and the two men followed where Blessing had gone. Cork would have preferred to stay off the trail, but on either side were bogs where an unwary step could put a man in the relentless grip of quicksandlike muck. They walked without speaking, not even a whisper, and watched the woods ahead.

They hadn't gone far when they heard the sound of the Silverado returning. They scrambled off the trail and dropped behind the trunk of a fallen cedar. In a moment, Blessing's truck appeared, Blessing alone in the cab. The Silverado passed them and disappeared among the trees as it headed back toward the road. They waited until it was well out of sight, then crept back onto the trail. Reinhardt nodded in the direction of Black Duck Lake, signaling to Cork that he thought they should continue. Cork nodded his agreement and they moved on.

Several hundred yards farther, the trail ended at a small log structure. Just beyond it was the blue of the open sky above Black Duck Lake. The log structure wasn't exactly a cabin. It was small and square, maybe eight feet on each side. There was no chimney or stovepipe, not even any windows, just a door. Cork thought maybe it was an old trapper shelter. It didn't look like the kind of place anyone would want to stay permanently, but if you were Lonnie Thunder it might be a reasonable spot to hide while you considered your next move.

Cork put four cartridges into the Remington's magazine and jacked one into the chamber. Together, he and Reinhardt approached the closed door. Reinhardt put his ear to the weathered wood. From inside came a sound loud enough that Cork heard it, too: the rattle of paper being crumpled. Reinhardt drew his handgun and reached for the knob, an antique-looking thing of dirty white porcelain. He exchanged a look with Cork, then flung the door open and they rushed inside. Sunlight shot in with them, throwing their shadows long across the dirt floor. From a dark corner came a desperate scramble. Cork spun left just in time to see the tail end of a chipmunk disappear through a hole in the chinking between the logs. He did a three-sixty, a full-circle survey of the room. There were empty beer cans and empty cans of Hormel chili and Vienna sausages. There were empty potato chip bags and candy bar wrappers. There was the smell of disuse, of desiccation, of stale beer. But there was no Lonnie Thunder.

From the corner where the chipmunk had scampered away came the glint of cellophane. Cork looked closer and saw an empty package of Double Stuf Oreos. The dirt floor was full of boot prints, but it was impossible to tell how recently they'd been made.

"Somebody's been living here," Reinhardt said.

"Probably Thunder. No sleeping bag or blankets. Looks like he's cleared out."

Cork stepped outside. Near the lake, he found a fire ring. The ash and char were cold.

Reinhardt joined him and said, "Blessing must've been expecting that his cousin would be here. Maybe it means Thunder'll be back."

Cork eyed the small lake. "I think he hasn't been here in a while."

"Then why did Blessing come?"

"Maybe this was the last place he knew his cousin had been. I get the feeling Thunder doesn't trust anybody now."

"Not even the Red Boyz?"

"I believe Kingbird was ready to give him over. And if you don't trust the guy who heads up the gang, who do you trust?"

Reinhardt looked over his shoulder at the log structure. "He might come back."

"It's possible. But there are a lot of other empty places out here where a man can hide. Who knows, maybe he's left the rez for good. I don't think there's any point in us sticking around here."

Cork started back the way they'd come. He stopped at the trap-per's shelter, where he noticed something on the walls. Dozens of small black scars were burned into the wood.

"What's that?" Reinhardt said.

"Looks like somebody's branded the wood."

"Those are the letter *R*."

"For Red Boyz. From what I understand, when you become one of them, you're branded."

Reinhardt scanned the area around them and nodded. "If I was going to put somebody through some secret kind of initiation, espe-cially one that involved a branding iron, this is the kind of place I'd choose. Out here, nobody'd hear you scream."

They didn't talk until they reached their vehicles, but the whole way, Cork was thinking. Blessing had come directly from the funeral, maybe hoping to catch Thunder at the hidden trapper shelter. But Thunder wasn't there. That might indicate that Blessing wasn't in contact with Thunder anymore, which was interesting because they were cousins, and if Thunder didn't even trust family, he was a man truly afraid. Cork understood that he was lucky last night to have es-caped with only warning shots. Thunder had become the kind of enemy Will Kingbird probably feared most, one who was unpredict-able.

"This is way out of your jurisdiction, Dave," Cork said as he stowed his Remington in the Bronco.

"Hell, you've got no jurisdiction anywhere," Reinhardt pointed out.

"Buck send you?"

"Right," Reinhardt said, with a bitter laugh. "Buck's opinion of me seems to be at an all-time low. Since Kristi died, he's become pretty unbearable."

Cork wanted to say Buck had always been pretty unbearable, but he held off. Instead he said, "You figure it'll help things with your father if you deliver Thunder?"

"Head on a platter, isn't that how it's done?" Reinhardt opened the door of his pickup. "If I decide to come back here one of these nights, you want me to let you know?"

"Yeah. Probably good to have company, especially at night."

Reinhardt got into his truck, backed onto the road, and shot west, toward Aurora. Cork delayed a few minutes, waiting so that he wouldn't have to eat Reinhardt's dust. He thought it must be hard having a father like Buck, a man unloving and unlovable in so many ways. Yet Cork had the feeling that love was the one thing Dave Reinhardt desperately wanted from his old man. Hell, didn't every son?

TWENTY-SIX

Three thirty in the afternoon was too early for the drinking crowd at the Buzz Saw. The place was empty of customers when Cork walked in. Faith Hill was on the jukebox. Seneca Peterson was perched on a stool, reading a book that lay open on the bar. She glanced up and, with a disturbed look, watched him approach.

"Sorry, Seneca," he said, taking the stool next to her. "This'll only take a minute, then I'm out of your hair."

He glanced down at the book: *We Want Freedom: A Life in the Black Panther Party.*

"Sad and unsettling," she said.

Cork realized her dour look had nothing to do with him. "Pleasure reading?"

"For a class I'm taking at ACC," she said, referring to Aurora Community College. "The politics of resistance. The Black Panther movement was well articulated, had admirable goals and able leaders. They just couldn't fight a whole political, social, and judicial system that was dead set against them." She marked her place with a paper coaster, slid from the stool, and slipped behind the bar. "What can I get you?"

"A Leinie's."

"Original?"

"Dark."

"Glass?"

"Just the bottle's fine."

She popped the cap and brought him the beer, along with a coaster. "Start a tab?"

He put a twenty on the bar and said, "One'll be enough." While she went to the register, he took a sip. The beer was ice cold and felt good going down. "Remember the other night when I was in here?"

She set the change in front of him. "Sure. You asked about Buck Reinhardt."

"I asked where he might have gone after you kicked him out."

"And I told you if he was going home he'd probably hit Tanner's on the Lake."

"I checked. He wasn't there. He also wasn't at the Silver Horse, the casino bar, or the Four Seasons."

"That was the night the Kingbirds were murdered. Now that was truly tragic. I knew Rayette. Liked her." She leaned on the bar. "And because you couldn't find him, you think Buck did it."

"I think in his own mind he had good reason to do it. Do you think he did it?"

She smiled with a secret understanding. "I knew the minute you walked in that you weren't here for the beer."

"Really?"

"I've never seen you here in the middle of the day. You drink in the evening or at night. What I call dismally responsible."

"Predictable?"

"That, too."

"You didn't answer me. Do you think Buck did it?"

She reached under the bar and brought up an opened pack of American Spirits and a Bic lighter. She tapped out a cigarette and reached for an ashtray. "The day after the murders, a couple of cops came in to talk to me. Captain Larson and a state cop."

"From the BCA, actually. Simon Rutledge."

"Yeah. Cute in a family-guy sort of way." She lit the cigarette and blew smoke out of the side of her mouth, careful to keep it away from Cork. "They asked me about Buck, how drunk was he, was he belligerent, what time did he leave, did he say where he was going. They didn't ask me the question you just did, do I think Buck killed the Kingbirds."

"What would you have said?"

"I'd have told them no."

"Why?"

"Because Buck's predictable, too. Saturday nights he comes in, drinks three or four rounds of CC and ditch water."

"What the hell is that?"

She gave a rich laugh. "That's how he orders Canadian Club and soda. At ten thirty sharp he finds something to complain about, makes a big pronouncement that he's going elsewhere to finish getting shit-faced, and he leaves. Always ten thirty sharp. Last Saturday he was worse than usual, carrying on with his racial slurs about the Ojibwe, so I shoved him out the door a little early."

"Any reason ten thirty is the witching hour?"

"That's when Brit gets off work."

"Brit? Would that be Brittany Young?"

"Yeah."

Cork knew her, one of the women who served food and drink at the Buzz Saw. Tall, long blond hair, good figure. A way about her that suggested that if you tossed her a flirt, she'd catch it with a soft glove.

"Something going on between her and Buck?" he asked.

"I'm just telling you what I've observed." She took a long draw on her cigarette and studied him. "I used to watch you in church, you know? When I was a kid."

"No kidding? Why?"

"Jenny and I took First Communion together. I would try to imagine what it was like being the daughter of the sheriff. I thought it would be pretty exciting. But you're not sheriff anymore, so I'm wondering what your interest in all this is."

"I promised some people that I would look into it."

She stared at him, and he remembered that when she was younger and still attended Mass, she seemed like one of those kids who had the mysteries of the faith all figured out and found them amusing.

"I heard someone shot at you the other night," she said.

"Yeah."

She shook her head. "Being your daughter would be too hard. Too much worry. Look, I'll throw in one more observation. I don't know if it'll help you, but here it is. Brit's put on weight lately, and it isn't from overeating."

"Is she on the schedule today?"

"Starts at five thirty."

Cork checked his watch. Quarter to four.

Seneca straightened up and arched her back. "I've got a chapter to read before class tonight, and you've got a beer you've barely touched."

"One more question. You happen to know where she lives?"

He caught Brittany Young polishing her nails. Her toenails. She came to the door walking on her bare heels, wads of Kleenex jammed between her toes. She wore a loose-fitting black T-shirt and gray sweats. She had a pink towel wrapped like a turban around her hair. She smelled clean, of some floral soap. She looked pissed when she opened the door, then she looked puzzled.

"Yeah?"

"Brittany, I'm Cork O'Connor."

"I know who you are. What do you want?"

"Do you have a minute to talk?"

"I'm in the middle of something."

"This won't take long, and it might help a friend of yours."

"Who?"

"Buck Reinhardt."

She thought it over, then stepped back and let him into her apartment.

It was bare bones inside, thrift-store décor: a beat-up sofa, a beat-up love seat, a scratched coffee table, a standing lamp, all of it arranged on an oval braided rug the color of beef gravy, none of it matching. In the small dining area, which was separated from the tiny kitchen by a counter, was a cheap dinette set that had recently been painted white. The one item in the place that looked new and expensive was a television with a thirty-five-inch screen, situated on a stand so that anyone lounging on the old sofa would have a good view. The television was on—an Adam Sandler movie—but muted. A bottle of dark red nail polish stood on the coffee table.

Brittany stayed on her heels all the way to the sofa where she plopped down and stared up dismally at Cork. She didn't ask him to sit.

"So how is it you think I can help Buck Reinhardt?" she asked.

"Are you aware he's the primary suspect in the Kingbird murders?"

"How could he be? He was home when that happened."

"And you know this how?"

"I heard it around."

"Then maybe you heard around that it's only a matter of time before that alibi collapses. Nobody's buying it. The sheriff's people never believed it for a second and they're doing everything they can to break it. Pretty soon the whole truth'll come out."

"Why should I care?"

"Mind if I sit?"

She pursed her lips and nodded toward the love seat. As Cork settled in, she bent and began removing the wads of tissue from between her toes.

"Got a name for the baby yet?" Cork asked.

She came up fast and stared at him with surprise.

"Let me ask you another question," Cork went on. "Does the Buzz Saw provide health coverage for its employees?"

She eyed him warily. "No."

"Have you got health coverage?"

"Yes. Not that it's any of your business."

"Buck pay for it?"

"Look, you need to leave," she said, doing her best to sound incensed.

Cork leaned toward her in a confidential way. "Brittany, I know that Buck was with you the night the Kingbirds were killed. If you come forward, it's the best thing you could do to help him."

"Right."

"The sheriff's people aren't the only ones convinced that his alibi is a lie. He's at the top of the Red Boyz's hit list. If you don't help clear his name, it could very well cost him his life."

She frowned and didn't look convinced.

"I'm not after Buck," Cork said. "I'm after the man I believe is responsible for the Kingbird killings, and I think that's Lonnie Thunder."

She started to speak but held back. Then a mean little gleam came into her eyes. "That's not who Buck thinks did it."

"No? Who does he think?"

"Elise."

"What makes him believe that?" Cork asked, trying to maintain a neutral response.

"He has this shotgun, some kind of special thing. When he got home Saturday night—"

"After he'd been here?"

"Yeah."

"What time did he leave?"

"Midnight, maybe twelve thirty."

"Okay, go on."

"So he gets home and Elise has this shotgun in the living room. Buck can tell it's been fired. She claims she used it to scare off a cougar that had been sniffing around the place."

"Buck didn't buy that?"

"He says that ever since Kristi died, Elise has been crazy. Doesn't sleep, drinks too much. He says sometimes she scares him."

"Scares Buck?"

"That's what he says." She looked away, stared at the television where there was only movement, no sound. Her mouth went thin as a pin. "He was going to leave her, then Kristi died."

"Leave her? And marry you?"

"A ring and a father for our baby, that's what he promised."

Cork thought that as fathers went, Brittany could have done a lot better for her child than Buck Reinhardt. And as a husband, Buck was hardly a prize. But none of that was Cork's business. He had what he came for and he stood up.

"I'm going to be talking to the sheriff in a bit, Brittany. I'm going to tell her everything you've told me. It'll clear Buck, but a lot of shit's going to hit the fan."

She gave a brief bitter laugh. "Like that's never happened with me before."

"The sheriff's people will want to talk to you. If they were to ask, is there any way you can prove Buck was with you that night?"

"Have 'em talk to Mrs. Schickle in apartment 113. She's better than a damn watchdog. Never sleeps, sees everything."

"Thanks, Brittany. You've been a real help."

She went back to pulling tissue from between her toes. "I just hope to God Buck sees it that way."

On his way out, he stopped at apartment 113. Mrs. Schickle was indeed an all-seeing eye, and when Cork gave her his business card and explained that he was helping the sheriff's department, she was only too happy to talk. He had the feeling that even if all he'd shown her in the way of authority was a bubble gum card she would just as eagerly have told him everything.

Outside in the parking lot, Cork looked back at the building. It was an ugly box of tan brick three stories high, one of the new constructions on the west side of town that had been thrown up as Aurora continued to grow. It wasn't the kind of place anybody lived permanently. Brittany Young probably saw it as a stop on her way to the sprawling house Buck Reinhardt had built on Skinner Lake. There was always the possibility that it might work out better for her than it had for either the current or the previous Mrs. Reinhardt, but Cork didn't hold out much hope. Because Buck was the constant in the equation, the outcome, he suspected, was dismally predictable.

TWENTY-SEVEN

When Elise Reinhardt opened the door, her hand held a small glass full of whiskey and her eyes held a look full of mean. Her gaze shot from the sheriff to Ed Larson, to Simon Rutledge, and finally to Cork.

"We already gave to the widows and orphans fund," she said.

"Elise, I wonder if we can come in and go over a few things with you." The sheriff was firm but not unpleasant.

"Again?"

"It's important."

"I can see that from the backup you brought." She stepped aside and waved them in. "Hell, let's get this over with. I've got a steak to grill."

They came in and stood clustered in the living room. Though it wasn't particularly dirty or cluttered, the place felt neglected. Flowers drooped in a vase on a table. The air in the room carried a distant unpleasant odor, like dirty socks.

Elise crossed her arms. "Sit down if you want. I'd offer you something to drink, but that might encourage you to stay."

"We'll get through this as quickly as we can, Elise," Dross said. She didn't sit. "The night the Kingbirds were killed, what time did Buck get home?"

"I told you already. Told you a dozen times."

"Could you tell us again?"

"It was maybe fifteen minutes after Cork left."

"What time would that have been?"

"Nine fifty, give or take a couple of minutes."

"What were you doing when he got here?"

"Exactly what I was doing when Cork left. Listening to music and drinking Macallan." She held up her glass.

"And after Buck got home, what did you do?"

"Went to bed."

"Anything unusual occur that night?"

"Not that I can think of."

"Once Cork was gone, you didn't leave the house?"

"Nope."

"And you're positive about the time Buck came home?"

"I am *so* fucking positive. And *so* fucking tired of being asked."

"Do you think Buck killed the Kingbirds, Elise? Is that why you're lying?"

She looked startled by the accusation. "I'm not lying."

"Elise, we have a witness, someone who's willing to swear that Buck wasn't here at ten. Or eleven. Or even midnight."

Elise gathered herself. "So, our word against his."

"Hers."

A slight disturbance ran across her face. "Whatever."

"We know where Buck was during that time, and it pretty much assures us that he didn't kill the Kingbirds."

"Well, there you go."

"You think it makes no difference that you lied?"

"Sue me." She took a sip of the drink in her hand.

Simon Rutledge said, "Mrs. Reinhardt, when we first interviewed you, you said you weren't sorry Alexander Kingbird had been murdered."

"I'm still not. Like I told you before, he ran the Red Boyz. He's hiding Lonnie Thunder. You ask me, all the Red Boyz need to be dealt with."

"By killing them? The way you killed the Kingbirds?"

"Me?" She looked truly shaken.

"When your husband came home, you had a shotgun in the living room, one that had recently been fired. We've been told your husband thinks you killed the Kingbirds."

"Who told you that?"

"The woman he was with from ten thirty until midnight the night the Kingbirds were killed."

Elise blinked and put her drink down. "That son of a bitch. That goddamn son of a bitch." She shook her head and huffed a sour little laugh. "All this time I thought he'd killed them, killed them for Kristi. I'd have lied my way into hell for him after that. But there he was, rutting with some whore instead."

"What were you doing with the shotgun?" Dross said.

At first, Cork wasn't sure Elise Reinhardt had heard the question. She seemed distant. He wondered if she was imagining Buck "rutting with some whore," as she'd put it. Finally she focused on the sheriff. "I heard the dogs going crazy in the kennel out back. I thought maybe we had a bear nosing around and I got the shotgun. Turned out to be a cougar. I discharged the shotgun into the air and the thing ran off."

"Can you prove this?"

Everyone waited. Elise seemed to enjoy the drama of the moment. At last she crooked a finger and said, "This way."

She led them through the maze of the house to a back door. Outside, the afternoon was waning. Sunlight shattered as it fell through the pines and it hit the ground in pieces. The day was still pleasantly warm. They followed Elise to a fenced-in area that included a kennel and a short run. A couple of gray bird dogs came bounding to greet her. They leaped up, put their paws on the fence, and shoved their noses between the mesh.

"Good boys," Elise said, and rubbed their muzzles. She walked down the fence line a few yards with the dogs pacing beside her eagerly. "Here." She pointed toward the ground.

The tracks lay at the center of a large patch of sunlight. They'd been made in the wet dirt around an outside spigot that jutted from the ground and had probably been put there to clean the kennels.

Ed Larson, who'd been quiet so far, said, "Elise, how do we know these tracks were made that night?"

"Never saw a cougar around here before."

"Can you prove that?"

"Tell you what, Mr. Smartypants. How about you make me prove it?"

Dross said calmly, "Where's the shotgun, Elise?"

"Locked in the gun case."

"May we see it?"

She looked exasperated. "Do you really think I killed the Kingbirds?"

"If you didn't, there's no reason for us not to see the shotgun, is there?"

She eyed them all as if she finally realized she was surrounded and outnumbered. "Come on."

She led them back to the house and once again through the maze of Buck Reinhardt's random construction to a denlike room hung with hunting trophies and with two large mahogany gun cases set against opposite walls. She dug in the pocket of her jeans and pulled out a small key ring. She unlocked one of the cases, reached in, and lifted out a shotgun, which she handed to Ed Larson.

"Robar," he said, with real admiration. "Nice piece."

"Buck had it custom built."

"Mind if we keep it awhile?"

"Be my guest."

The cell phone in its leather case on Marsha Dross's belt began to bleat. "Excuse me," she said. She stepped away and answered, "Dross." She listened, then said, "I'll be there as soon as I can." She slipped the phone back into place and said to Elise, "You might want to come with me."

"Yeah? And why's that?"

"We just got a call, shots fired out on County Road Eighteen, Elise. It looks like Buck was the target."

"Did they hit him?"

"Apparently not."

"Too bad."

"Would you care to come?"

"If he was dead, maybe. Right now, I'd rather finish my drink."

* * *

By the time Dross, Larson, and Cork pulled their vehicles off the road and parked behind the deputy's cruiser, it was dusk. Simon Rutledge hadn't come with them. He'd asked Elise if she minded his staying so they could talk a little more. She'd agreed, but only if he had a drink with her. Rutledge had said he could live with that.

On the far side of the road were two trucks from Reinhardt's Tree Service. One was a big utility truck with a hydraulic bucket for trimming high branches. The other was Buck Reinhardt's personal pickup, replete with the big rack of lights on top of the cab. Another vehicle was parked there as well, a cruiser from the Yellow Lake Police Department.

Buck was talking with Deputy Cy Borkman, who was taking notes. Dave Reinhardt stood close by. Two men sat on the rear bumper of the bucket truck. One was Adrian Knowles, who wasn't much more than a kid, though he had a wife and an infant son to support. The other was Cal Richards. Richards was smoking a cigarette. He had his shirt sleeves rolled up high enough to show most of the long green dragon tattoo on his right arm. Neither of the men bothered to stand up when Dross and the others arrived.

Borkman separated from them and met Dross in the middle of the empty road.

"So what have you got, Cy?" the sheriff asked.

"Happened an hour ago now. Buck's working in the bucket, doing some trimming." He pointed toward the telephone lines that shadowed the road.

"Buck?" Dross said. "Buck was doing the trimming?"

Borkman shrugged. "Guess he likes to keep his hand in the actual business. His crew says he still hefts a pretty mean chainsaw."

"Okay, go on."

"They're all focused on the work, got their backs to the road. They hear a vehicle approach, but they don't take any notice. Suddenly, bang-bang. They spin around, see the vehicle speed off west down the road."

"Did they give you a plate number or a description?"

Borkman shook his head. "Sun was in their eyes. Dark SUV was all they could say."

"You told me on the phone the shots were fired at Buck. What makes them think he was the target?"

"There's a bullet hole in the bucket. A foot to the left and six inches higher and there'd be a bullet hole in Buck."

Buck seemed to have had enough of being ignored. He strode onto the asphalt and called out as he approached, "Got anything to say about me carrying now?"

He was, in fact, wearing his gun belt.

"Did you shoot back, Buck?" Dross asked.

"The son of a bitch was out of range by the time I cleared my holster."

Dave Reinhardt had followed his father to the middle of the road. "Dad called me on my cell, Marsha. I thought maybe I could help."

Dross said, "That's okay, Dave. Buck, I understand nobody got a clear look at the shooter or the vehicle. Is that correct?"

"Indians," Buck said. "I'll give 'em this, they're smart when it comes to being sneaky. Bushwhacked me with the sun in my eyes. Couldn't see a thing."

Bushwhacked? Cork thought. Reinhardt had clearly seen too many Randolph Scott movies.

"Why do you say 'Indians'?" Ed Larson said. "I mean, if the sun was in your eyes and you couldn't see."

"Who else wants me dead?"

Cork found himself imagining the line.

"So the truth is, you really didn't see anything that might help identify the assailant?" Larson said.

"The smell," Cal Richards said from the bumper of the truck.

"Smell?" Dross swung her gaze toward Richards.

"Yeah, greasy war paint." Richards laughed. Knowles laughed, too.

A vehicle appeared on the road, coming from the east where the sky was slipping into the dark blue-gray that was the shadow of evening. Its headlights were on. The group moved off the asphalt and onto the shoulder near Reinhardt's trucks. They all were silent as the vehicle approached and passed. A white pickup. The driver eyed them as he cruised by and headed toward the rosy glow in the west.

Dross said, "Buck, I talked to Brittany Young this afternoon. She told me you were with her the night the Kingbirds were killed. She's willing to sign a sworn statement to that effect."

"Okay. So?"

"She also told me you think Elise killed the Kingbirds."

"I'm not saying nothing about that."

"You don't have to. We already spoke with Elise."

Buck looked a little worried. "You tell her about Brit?"

Dross said, "She knows."

"Ah, Christ."

"Do you still think she killed the Kingbirds?"

"Hell, a lot of vengeance in that woman these days. Add enough booze and she's up to just about anything."

"We have the shotgun she took from the gun case the night of the murders."

"My Robar Elite? What the hell are you doing with that?"

"Dad," Dave Reinhardt said quietly at his father's back, "the Kingbirds were killed with a shotgun."

Buck spun around. "You think I'm stupid, boy? I know that. I want to know how they got it."

"Elise allowed us to take it," Dross said.

Buck shook his head. "Stupid cow. Hanging herself."

"Dad," Dave said, his voice still quiet but full of edge now, "they won't be able to tell much, if anything, from the shotgun, so it doesn't hurt Elise."

"What did she say about having the shotgun that night, Buck?" Dross asked.

"Elise is your wife, Dad. You don't have to answer these questions."

"Elise can take care of herself, boy. She told me she shot at a cougar, Sheriff."

"Did you believe her?"

"Hell, no. I've never seen a cougar around my place."

"She showed us some tracks near the kennel. Cork's seen cougar tracks before. He says these do, in fact, look like they were made by a cougar."

"Well, what do you know? Maybe the bitch wasn't lying."

"What else did she say?"

"Dad, don't answer any more questions," Dave said. "Marsha, this is inappropriate. My father shouldn't be giving statements that could be used against Elise."

Buck turned on his son. "Don't be telling me what I can and can't say. I think she killed the redskins. There. How's that for a statement?"

"Jesus," Dave said.

"Fuck you, boy. You had it in you, it'd be you asking the questions instead of some skirt."

Dave Reinhardt grabbed his father by the shirt collar and shoved him against the side of Buck's pickup. "That mouth is going to get you killed one of these days. And you know what, Dad? I'm going to turn cartwheels on your coffin." He let go. "I'm out of here. You're on your own." He stomped toward his cruiser.

Buck watched him go, then straightened his shirt and laughed. "Finally the boy's got some balls."

A few more minutes of questioning and it became apparent that neither Reinhardt nor his crew had anything more to offer. As they parted, Dross said, "Buck, I highly advise that you stay close to home for a while, until we get a better handle on this whole situation."

"Piss on the Red Boyz," he responded. "I got me a bodyguard." He tapped the Glock holstered on his hip. "Come on, boys. Let's call it a day."

Reinhardt and the other men got into their trucks. Cork crossed the highway with Dross, Larson, and Borkman. They watched the trucks take off and head toward Aurora.

Dross said, "You better get on back to the office, Cy, and do the paperwork. I'll be there shortly."

"Yes, ma'am." Borkman slid his large bulk behind the wheel of his cruiser, turned around on the asphalt, and followed where the other two vehicles had gone.

"A dark SUV," Larson said. "Not much to go on."

Cork said, "Lonnie Thunder drives a dark green Xterra."

Dross shook her head. "Why would Thunder go after Buck? Doesn't really get him anything."

"He's not operating in a predictable way," Cork said. "Too scared to think straight, maybe."

"I'd love to have him behind bars, take him out of this whole equation." Dross looked where the sun had set, leaving only a red glow above the trees, as if from a distant fire. "What I'd really love is to be on vacation in Aruba. Come on, Ed. We've got paperwork."

After the others left, Cork stood a moment in the gathering dark. It was quiet on the long straight stretch of empty highway that burrowed through the pines. He wished he believed the quiet would last.

TWENTY-EIGHT

Once they'd left the community center in Allouette where the post-funeral gathering had been held, Will, Lucinda, and Ulysses had exchanged no more than a dozen words in the car. At home, Will changed his clothes and said he was going to the shop. Uly headed out "to hang with Darrell for a while." Lucinda was left alone with the baby, who'd been unusually quiet all day. She laid Misty in the carrier, which she sat on the kitchen table so the baby could see her as she worked. Lucinda spoke constantly to her granddaughter, fully realizing that the infant had no way of understanding. But babies needed the sound of a loving voice. And for Lucinda, too, the sound of a voice, even if it was her own, was comforting.

For years Lucinda had often suffered long hours of silence, with no one to talk to. When her boys were young, things had been different. Alejandro had been an adventurer, exploring the territory of every new posting, every new home. He would report to her what he'd discovered. He talked about his school, his teachers, his classmates. He made friends easily and he told her about their houses and their families. In this way, he kept her connected to his life. Uly was quieter and the things he told her seemed more like secrets he was sharing. She felt special being allowed into his private world this way. As they'd grown, however, the boys had changed. They'd become increasingly like their father, and more and more they closed themselves off from her. Maybe it was that way with all boys as they stumbled through adolescence. She didn't know. She often wondered how different things would have been if she'd had daughters.

Although none of them would be hungry soon—they'd eaten after the funeral—she set about making tamales. She knew that preparing a meal would keep her grounded. Once a month or so, Will drove her to Duluth where she bought corn husks and other foodstuffs at a market that specialized in Latino goods. Tamales had been one of Alejandro's favorites, a dish he often requested on his birthday. She didn't think about this consciously as she began, but in the middle of everything, the realization of what she was doing hit her and she almost cried. Almost. As she had since the beginning, she took her grief and shoved it deep inside, telling herself that the man buried this day was not the brave boy who loved tamales. That boy had left her years before. As for Rayette, Lucinda simply refused to allow herself to think about her at the moment. Force of will. A practiced soldier's wife.

When Will came home, the dining room table was set. Misty was sleeping in her crib in her new room. Uly was in his bedroom with the door closed. It was dark outside. Crickets chorused through the open windows, their chirring coming in on a warm spring breeze. Will washed up, knocked on Uly's door, and they all sat down at the table. No one commented on the tamales.

Near the end of the meal, Will said, "I heard someone took a couple of shots at Buck Reinhardt." They were the first words he'd spoken since saying grace.

"Did they hit him?" Uly asked.

Will stuffed the last forkful of tamale in his mouth. "Missed."

"Maybe they were just trying to scare him," Lucinda said.

Will looked at her as if she was stupid. "What would be the point? You scare someone to keep them from doing something you don't want them to do. Reinhardt's already killed Alex. No way to keep him from doing that now."

"You think it was the Red Boyz?" Uly said.

"That's what I think." Will shook his head. "Screwups. Bunch of screwups. Alexander didn't teach them anything useful."

"Like what? How to kill a man?" Lucinda was suddenly full of fury, a deep anger that seemed to come from nowhere and that spilled out at her husband. "Why would anyone want to teach that? Why doesn't someone teach how to live together without killing? Now that would be useful."

She threw her napkin on the table, grabbed her plate, and took it to the sink. At her back, neither her husband nor son said a word. She stood staring out the window into the dark where the crickets, in their way, kept up a lively conversation.

"Yes," Will said quietly. "How to kill a man."

She heard his chair slide across the carpet as he moved back from the table, then she heard him walk from the room. She looked over her shoulder. Uly was staring after him.

Annie was at her computer when the message from Uly Kingbird appeared on her screen.

r u there

yes, she typed back.

meet me at st agnes . . . important

when

15 minutes

ok

The May night was warm. There was no moon yet and Annie walked in and out of the darkness between the islands of light under the streetlamps. She loved spring in Minnesota. It was never a long season. Winter left reluctantly and summer usually came immediately after and with a vengeance that included mosquitoes and blackflies. But for a couple of weeks in May, everything felt new and clean and hopeful. This feeling was just one more treasure Annie wanted to lock away in her heart when she left Aurora for college.

Uly was already sitting on the steps in front of St. Agnes. There was a little light above the entrance that was always on at night, as if inviting the lost to come inside, though the doors were actually locked. Uly sat on his shadow. He looked up when he heard Annie approach. She sat down next to him.

"Thanks," he said.

"It's not a big deal. What's up?"

Uly had a small stone, which he nervously juggled in his right hand as he spoke. "I'm going to do something."

"Okay. What?"

The stone went up and came down. "Do you believe in hell?"

"You mean like with the devil and all that?"

"I'm not talking about some cartoon devil with a tail and a pitchfork. I mean a place where you're in eternal torment, where nothing will ever get better."

"I don't believe there's anything like that after we die, Uly, but I think for a lot of people that's their life."

"Yeah, tell me about it." He held the stone in his hand and stared at it. "You told me once that you wanted to be a nun."

"I used to. I don't know anymore."

"There's nothing I ever wanted to be. Except dead, sometimes."

"Don't say that, Uly. What about your music? You've got so much talent. More than anybody else I know." She shifted and faced him with her whole body. "Look, it's just this place, these people, Uly. Once you graduate and leave Aurora, the world'll be full of possibility."

"Alex left and came back and they killed him."

"You're not Alex."

He finally threw the stone. Annie heard it hit the pavement and bounce away. "Sometimes I wish I was. He had guts." He stood up, shoved his hands into his pockets, and stared hard where he'd thrown the stone. "Nuns pray for people."

"It's one of the things they do."

"Pray for me, Annie."

She stood up. They both cast shadows that lay on the church steps like small animals, black and huddled. "You're scaring me, Uly."

A sad smile appeared on his face. "Me? Scaring somebody? That's a switch." He looked away, into the night. "Look, I've gotta go. Something I've gotta do."

"I'll come with you."

"No. I need to be alone now." He hurried away, as if he was already late for whatever it was that was calling him.

"I'll do it, Uly!"

He stopped and turned back. "Do what?"

"I'll pray for you."

He thought about that and nodded gratefully. Then he left, and she watched him move swiftly through the islands of light until finally the darkness took him altogether. She sat down on the steps of St. Agnes, bowed her head, and kept her promise.

Will came into the baby's room, where Lucinda sat in a rocking chair, feeding Misty a bottle of formula. "I'm going back to the shop," he told her.

"Now?"

"I won't be able to sleep anyway. Maybe if I get tired I'll lie down on the cot there. Don't worry if I don't come home till late."

"All right," she said, because she knew whatever she said it wouldn't matter. Will was going and that was that.

After he left, she rocked Misty and sang to her softly. When the baby was asleep, Lucinda laid her in the crib and went to the big picture window, in the living room, that looked out over the front yard. She was watching for Uly, who'd headed off earlier, borrowing her car, saying he was going to the library, though she didn't believe it for a minute. She was worried about him. She'd always been worried about him, worried that he would break under the weight of all his father laid on him. Will was usually clear about what he expected of his sons. He was good at laying down the law. He wasn't good at forgiving when the law was breeched. And he was a complete failure at letting his sons know when he was proud of them. It must have seemed to Alejandro and Ulysses that he had never been. Which wasn't true. He simply didn't know how to tell them so.

She lay down on the sofa, and without realizing it, she drifted off. She woke to a distant scream and thought at first that Misty had awakened. Then she realized the sound was coming from sirens racing through Aurora. Like a bad dream they faded away and the soothing *chirr* of the crickets returned and once again she slept.

TWENTY-NINE

When the phone rang, Cork was asleep in the bunk at Sam's Place. Over the years, particularly in the days when he was sheriff of Tamarack County, he'd become accustomed to being hauled out of bed at god-awful hours, and he was awake instantly and across the dark room to the telephone.

"O'Connor," he said.

"Cork, it's Bos." Bos Swain, one of the dispatchers for the sheriff's department. "The sheriff asked me to call. She figured you'd want to know. Buck Reinhardt's been shot. He's dead."

Homicide was always startling news, yet as he dressed to head out to the scene, Cork found himself thinking, *Of course.*

Buck Reinhardt had been killed at 10:35 P.M. as he left the Buzz Saw and made his way across the parking lot toward his truck. He was shot once in the head with a high-caliber bullet fired, witnesses said, from a wooded rise on the other side of the highway, a distance of approximately seventy-five yards.

"A tough shot," Dross said, eyeing the rise from where she stood near Reinhardt's truck. "Lighting's not great, parking lot's full, a lot of interference."

Ed Larson, who was standing next to her watching his team finish with the crime scene, said, "With a scope and a steady hand, about anybody who knows how to handle a rifle could make the shot."

Dross shook her head. "Killing a man, that's not a cakewalk. Takes a lot of determination."

"Scared people do it all the time," Larson said, "and then wonder how the hell it happened."

Dross turned from the rise and looked at her investigator. "Do you really think it was fear that killed Buck Reinhardt?"

Cork, who'd been leaning against the tailgate of Reinhardt's truck with his arms crossed and his mind working on the incident, asked, "Witnesses see anything?"

"Nobody we've interviewed so far," Larson said. "The shots were fired, Buck went down, and everybody scrambled for cover. They all agreed where the shots had come from, but that's about all they've been able to tell us."

Cork came away from the truck. "Shots? He was hit only once."

"A second round was fired after he went down. Burrowed into the asphalt beside his body. We dug that one out."

"Whoever it was knew enough about Buck to know he'd be at the Buzz Saw tonight. They just took up their position and waited," Cork said.

"Who knew about Buck?" Dross asked.

Cork shrugged. "Just about anybody who'd spent five minutes asking. Wasn't any secret he did most of his drinking here. And he drank a lot."

They all turned and watched as Reinhardt's covered body was lifted onto a gurney and wheeled to the ambulance. The small crowd that had gathered around the entrance to the Buzz Saw watched, too. A minute later, with no flashing of lights or other fanfare, the ambulance pulled away.

"Does Elise know?" Cork asked.

Marsha said, "I sent Cy Borkman and he broke the news."

"How'd she take it?"

"According to Cy, with a little water and on the rocks."

"What about Brittany Young?"

"Pretty shaken up. One of her friends took her home."

In the woods on the rise, deputies were going over the area with halogen beams. Occasionally, a bright flash indicated that the scene was being documented with the department's digital camera. BCA agent Simon Rutledge emerged from the pine trees, looked both ways, then crossed the highway.

"Anything?" Dross asked.

Rutledge grinned and held up a plastic evidence bag. "Found the place in the pine needles where our shooter laid down to wait, and we got a shell casing. No tracks or anything else yet."

"Nobody saw the shooter leave the woods?" Cork asked.

"Nope," Larson replied.

"Hiked out probably," Rutledge said. "What's the nearest road?"

"That would be Lowell Lake Road, about half a mile that way." Dross pointed north, up the highway.

Rutledge said, "Any houses there? Anyone who might have seen a car sitting along the side of the road?"

Dross shook her head. "That stretch is deserted."

"Still, you may want to get someone over there to look for tire impressions from a vehicle parked on the shoulder."

Larson got on his walkie-talkie and raised Deputy Pender, who was on the wooded rise. He explained what he wanted and told Pender to take one of the other deputies with him.

A red pickup slowed on the highway in order to pull into the parking lot. It was stopped by Deputy Minot, who had instructions not to let anyone in. After an exchange between deputy and driver, the pickup came ahead and parked in an empty slot near the door to the Buzz Saw. Dave Reinhardt got out and walked toward his father's truck.

"Where is he?" he said.

"His body's already gone, Dave," Dross replied. "The autopsy'll be done first thing in the morning."

"How'd it happen?"

Dross explained what she knew.

Reinhardt stood with his hands clenched at his sides. "Red Boyz," he said.

"We've got nothing at the moment that points toward anyone, Dave. There's still a lot of groundwork to do."

Reinhardt looked at her. In the light of the parking lot lamp, his face was white and hard, like new plaster. "Are you blind or just stupid, Marsha?"

Dross said evenly, "It seems to me the stupid thing would be to rush to judgment."

"Hey, Dave!" Cal Richards broke from the crowd at the door to the Buzz Saw. He slipped under the crime scene tape and came toward Reinhardt. He was still wearing the coveralls he'd had on when the shots had been fired at Buck earlier in the day. He looked stunned. Or drunk. Most probably some of both. "The shits, man. He's buying you a drink one minute, the next minute his head's all over the parking lot. Jesus."

"Mr. Richards, you need to step back behind the tape," Dross said.

Richards gave her a *screw you* look and made no move to comply.

"I'll be happy to have a deputy escort you," Dross said.

"All right, all right." Richards lifted his hands to stave off her move. "Dave, let me buy you a drink?"

Dave Reinhardt said, "I'll be there in a minute, Cal."

Richards turned, ducked under the tape, and returned to the bar.

"What are you going to do?" Reinhardt asked. The question was directed at Dross.

"Conduct a thorough investigation that will end in a lawful arrest, Dave."

"Just like you've arrested Lonnie Thunder for killing Kristi? And how about the Kingbirds? Got any leads there? Your investigations have all the speed of a car with square wheels, Marsha."

"There's a lot going on, Dave. We're doing the best we can."

"Yeah, right." He stood a few seconds more, looking at his father's truck, looking at the asphalt that had been chalked with an outline of Buck's body. "Fuck," he said and followed Richards to the bar.

"He's right," Dross said. "We're getting nowhere."

They all looked at her. Finally Larson said, "Okay, so what now?"

"Let's finish up here. Wrap up the interviews, pull it to a close on the rise, see if Pender has come up with any impressions on Lowell Lake Road. Then let's go back to the office, do the paperwork, go home, and try to get some sleep. We'll start on it all again first thing in the morning."

Rutledge raised his hand, as if he were in geography class. "Marsha, you mind if I drop in on Elise Reinhardt, keep her company in her grief?"

"Kind of late, isn't it?" Ed Larson said.

Rutledge gave a little shrug. "She told me this afternoon that she seldom goes to bed before two. She said she drinks until she can't keep her eyes open, otherwise all she sees when she lies down is her daughter's face. I think she could use a little sympathetic company."

Dross said, "Simon, I'm so tired I wouldn't care if you painted yourself yellow and pretended to be a taxi."

"Then I'll see you all in the morning."

He left them and headed toward his Cherokee, which was parked at the far end of the lot.

Ed Larson frowned. "If I didn't know better, I'd say he's taking advantage of a woman in a vulnerable position."

"Elise vulnerable?" Dross laughed. "Yeah, like a Brink's armored car. I'm sure he's got something besides her grief on his mind. You headed home, Cork?"

"I think I'll buy Dave Reinhardt a drink first."

"Suit yourself."

She turned to Larson and they walked away, talking quietly.

Inside the Buzz Saw, the shooting seemed to have had an energizing effect. Though it was late, nearing one A.M., the place was still jumping. Cork spotted Reinhardt and Cal Richards sitting together on stools at the bar. Reinhardt already had three empty shot glasses in front of him, and as Cork watched, another patron came up to Dave, offered his condolences, and signaled the bartender to give the man a round. Cork waited until Reinhardt and Richards were alone again, then he took the stool next to Buck's son.

"Just want to say I'm sorry, Dave."

Reinhardt, who sat hunched forward over his line of empty glasses, glanced his way.

Cork lifted a hand to signal for a drink. "Everybody knows Buck could be a son of a bitch—"

"Hell," Cal Richards broke in from Dave's other side, "he took pride in being a son of a bitch."

"But he was still your father," Cork went on, "and I'm sorry for your loss."

"Thanks." Reinhardt said it grudgingly.

Jack Sellers, who was tending bar, brought three glasses of what-

ever scotch it was Reinhardt and Richards were drinking. Cork handed
him a twenty and told him to keep the change.

"You know if anybody's told Elise?" Reinhardt said.

"Cy Borkman broke the news," Cork told him.

"How'd she take it?"

"Pretty well from what I understand."

"I'll bet. Probably proposed a toast." He picked up the drink Cork
had bought him and downed it.

"I get the impression Buck hadn't been particularly husbandly
toward her of late."

"Hell, Buck never worried about being anything to anybody," Cal
Richards said, after gulping his own drink. "He was just fine with who
he was."

A rattlesnake's just fine being a rattlesnake, Cork thought, *but
that doesn't mean you want to cozy up to it.*

"Buck was a rare one," he said instead.

Reinhardt nodded in agreement. "A man spends sixty years on
this earth, there ought to be somebody sheds a tear when he's gone.
He could be a mean old bastard, sure, but he was my father, goddamn it."

Cork picked up his own glass, but held off drinking. "Fathers can
be hard to please."

"I remember your old man," Reinhardt said. "He didn't seem too
bad."

"I lost him to a bullet, too."

"That's right, I remember. Sorry."

"Long time ago, Dave. It passes."

Reinhardt stared at the line of empty glasses. "I tried so hard to do
something he'd be proud of. Too late now."

Cal Richards said, "I know something you could do."

"Yeah? What's that?"

"Get the prick that shot him."

Cork leaned to the side and looked across Reinhardt's back at
Richards. "You got any idea who that might be, Cal? 'Cause the sheriff would love to know."

"You're a cop, Dave," Richards went on, unperturbed. "That's what cops do, figure shit out. Hell, you couldn't do any worse than that bitch who's wearing the badge."

Cork said, "Cal, anybody ever tell you that you've got all the charm of a gas station toilet?"

"Fuck you, O'Connor."

Reinhardt's fist hit the bar. "I know who did it. The Red Boyz."

"You *don't* know that, Dave," Cork said. "And even if it was one of the Red Boyz, which one? Let Marsha and her people handle this."

Richards said, low and seductive, "Show that bitch, Dave, and make your old man proud at the same time."

Jack Sellers came down the bar. "Last call, boys."

"One for the road, Dave?" Richards said. "On me."

"Sure, why not?"

Sellers eyed Cork, who declined with a shake of his head.

People had begun to stand and put on their coats and slowly make their way toward the front door. Sellers brought two final shots and set them in front of Dave Reinhardt and Cal Richards.

Richards lifted his glass. "Here's to Buck, and to finding the god-damn coward son of a bitch who sent him to his reward."

Both men tilted their heads and threw the shots down their throats. Reinhardt fumbled with his wallet, pulled out a twenty, slipped it across the bar, and slid his butt off the stool.

"I don't think you're in any condition to drive, Dave," Cork said.

Richards, who'd had a lot to drink himself but seemed at the moment to be handling it better, said, "I'll see he gets home."

Cork watched them join the slow, steady exodus, then he got up as well and called it a night.

THIRTY

T he baby's crying, Mom."

Lucinda opened her eyes. Uly stood beside the sofa, in his pajamas, his eyes barely open, his hair wild from sleep. Lucinda stirred and realized she was under a blanket, the blue one she kept in the hall closet.

"How did this get here?" she asked, trying to come fully awake.

"I put it over you when I got in last night. You looked cold."

"Thank you, Ulysses." She sat up and rubbed her eyes.

"Want me to get Misty?"

"I'll take care of her."

"Where's Dad?"

"At the shop. He slept there last night, I imagine."

"At the shop." Uly looked at her as if he knew it was a lie, because it had been one of the lies over the years. Sleeping at the shop. Along with: Gone to the Twin Cities to deliver a custom order. Or: He went to a gun show. Before that, when Will was still in the Marine Corps, it was much easier. She would simply tell the boys that their father was on special-duty assignment for a few days. "Whatever," Uly said, and shuffled back to his room and to bed.

It was early, although already well past dawn. Beyond the living room picture window, long morning shadows fell across grass still wet with dew. The birds were going crazy in the trees. In Alejandro's old bedroom, the baby cried for her first feeding and changing of the day.

Lucinda threw back the blanket and rose to her life.

After she'd taken care of Misty and brewed coffee for herself, she tried calling the shop. No answer. Of course. She wondered why she even bothered. After her own breakfast of oatmeal and half a grape-fruit, she went to the bedroom she shared with Will, and she opened the top dresser drawer. Inside was a cedar case the size of a small loaf of bread that Lucinda proceeded to open. The case contained the medals and ribbons Will had received during his service as a marine—Purple Heart, Vietnam Service Medal, Meritorious Service Medal, Combat Action ribbons, Good Conduct Medal, Drill Instructor ribbon, Presidential Unit citations, Kuwait Liberation Medal—as well as his dog tags and an extra set of keys to the shop. Lucinda took out the dog tags, wrote down the last four digits of his social security number, then put everything back into the case except the keys to the shop. She bundled up little Misty and secured her in the car seat, got behind the wheel of her Saturn, and drove to Will's shop. His van wasn't there, but she parked at the curb anyway and walked to the door.

Through the shop window, she could see that inside everything was dark. No surprise. She rang the buzzer but got no response. She used the key to unlock the door. As soon as she was inside, she reached out to key in the disarm code—the last four digits of Will's social security number—on the alarm pad beside the door, but she was surprised to see that the alarm was already disengaged. This was unheard of because Will was more than just careful about locking up and turning on the alarm; with a shop full of firearms, he was maniacal about security. There were bars on the windows. The door had been special ordered and the lock carefully chosen for strength. A camera monitored the doorway day and night.

"Will?" she called toward the rear of the shop.

Receiving no answer, she returned to the car and disengaged the car seat, Misty still buckled inside. She went back into the shop and set the car seat on the counter. She used another key to unlock the door to the back room. Before she entered, she hesitated, aware that she was about to trespass on Will's sanctuary. Finally she eased the door open and groped for the light switch on the wall. The shop was suddenly illuminated. No Will. No cot. Only the air full of the mixed smells of gun oil and cutting oil and solvent, the rows of shelving neatly stacked with cardboard boxes that held components for the firearms Will constructed, and the floor and the work areas clean, the way Will always left them. Except for the emptiness of her heart and a profound determination that came to her out of the silence of that room, Lucinda was alone.

When she arrived for work that Thursday morning at the Aurora Professional Building, Jo O'Connor found Lucinda in the waiting area of her office.

"Luci?"

Fran Cooper, Jo's secretary, smiled from her desk and said pleasantly, "I explained to Ms. Kingbird that you had a full agenda today and I'd be happy to schedule her for an appointment as soon as you had an opening."

"I asked to wait," Lucinda said. She didn't want to get the secretary, who'd been kind to her, in any trouble.

"That's fine, Fran. Shall we go into my office, Luci?"

"Thank you."

It was nice inside. Warm, civilized, Lucinda decided. Not like Will's shop, full of bits and pieces of cold metal that created instruments of death. Here there were only books. And two plants that were well cared for. And a chair for her to sit in. And on the other side of the desk, a woman who was willing to listen.

"Would you like some coffee, Lucinda?"

"No, thank you."

"How is little Misty?"

"She's well. Ulysses is watching her for me. He's very good with her."

"What can I do for you?"

Lucinda looked down at her hands, folded in her lap. They were old hands, she thought, dried and cracked now because, with the baby, she was always washing them. She felt old, like her hands. Old and lost and frightened.

"I want to leave my husband," she said in almost a whisper.

She glanced up and was relieved to see that Jo didn't seem shocked or disappointed.

"Is there a particular reason?" Jo asked.

"I have lived for twenty-six years with a man I do not know. I know his voice, his walk, his smell. But his heart, his mind?" She shook her head.

"Does Will know how you feel?"

"I think my husband does not care how I feel."

"Have you talked with him about this?"

"No."

"Has he abused you, Luci?"

"Never."

"Is there something that's precipitated your decision? Is he involved with someone else, or are you?"

Lucinda hesitated. "Involved?"

"An affair."

Lucinda considered this and finally said, "No."

"Do you love him?"

This she didn't know how to explain, but she knew she had to try.

"I was sixteen years old when we met. I had a cousin who was a marine. He introduced us. Will was so handsome, so respectful, so full of bravado. He is the only man I have ever had. I have followed him around the world. I have given him sons. I have tried always to respect him." She stared deeply into the soft blue of the other woman's eyes. "Is that love?"

Jo reached across the desk and took Lucinda's hands in her own. "Oh, Luci, there's so much that's good in that. Are you sure you want to leave him?"

Lucinda looked into the other woman's face and saw compassion there and she felt something like gentle fingers reach into her heart and slowly tug it open. She began to cry, softly at first, then huge sobs that shook her whole body. Jo came to her and embraced her and all the grief that Lucinda had been holding back with her denials flooded out.

"My boy, my Alejandro, gone," she wailed, rocking in Jo's arms. "And Rayette, *bonita* Rayette. All gone, all gone. Oh, God. Oh, Mother Mary, please help me." She wept and wept and at one point drew away and tried to explain. "Will never cries. He does not understand. It is weakness to him."

"You go right ahead," Jo said, stroking Lucinda's hair. "Cry all you want, all you need to."

"I should have done something, protected my Alejandro. I should have stood up to Will."

"Luci, what happened isn't your fault. You can't blame yourself."

"If only I had done more for my little boy. My Alejandro. My poor little Alejandro."

Lucinda wept until she felt as if she'd touched the bottom of her grief, a place she'd been afraid to go. When the tears finally subsided, Jo reached to a box of Kleenex on her desk and drew out several tissues and handed them over.

"Sometimes, Luci, when something tragic happens to a couple, it sends them spinning off in frightening directions, away from each other, full of blame, recrimination, guilt. Hasty, regretful decisions can result. Before you make a final decision about your marriage, would you be willing to talk to someone? I could recommend some very good counselors."

Lucinda shook her head. "I'm afraid now. Afraid for Uly and for Misty. They should know they are loved. Children need that. With Will, they will never know. I need to protect them. I need to make sure they know they are precious." She began to cry again, but quietly this time. "Alejandro . . . maybe if Will had been different with him . . . maybe he would still be alive. Maybe none of these awful things would have happened."

"You blame Will for what happened?"

Lucinda wiped her eyes with one of the tissues Jo had given her. "I know it's not fair. But I can't help feeling that Will drove Alejandro away. I do not want that for Ulysses or Misty."

"Luci," Jo said in a careful voice, "it's my understanding that the instructions Alexander and Rayette left direct that you and Will together be Misty's guardians. Is that correct?"

"Yes."

"Leaving Will now could be a problem."

"What do you mean?"

"I'll have to look into the matter, but there could be some dispute over who would be awarded custody of Misty. If you separate, it may become the court's responsibility to decide."

"You mean Will would raise them?"

"I'm only saying that who raises them could be in dispute. Let me do some checking, and in the meantime, would you consider talking with someone about your relationship with Will? If these issues can be worked out without the dissolution of your marriage, wouldn't you rather that?"

"I suppose I could speak with Father Ted."

"That would be a good beginning. But if you decide in the end that separating from Will is what you want to do, I'll help you do that."

"Thank you."

Jo touched Lucinda's cheek with her palm. "Are you all right?"

"Yes. I am now."

They walked together from the office, and in the hall they hugged.

"There's a way through all this, Luci. I'll do my best to help you find it."

"You are a good friend," Lucinda said.

She left feeling not so alone nor so afraid, holding in her heart the warm hope her good friend had given her.

THIRTY-ONE

By the time Cork finally rolled out of bed, the sun was already high and the dew had long ago evaporated from the grass. He scratched all the usual places and began making coffee. While the old Hamilton Beach on the counter was doing its thing, Cork showered, shaved, and brushed his teeth. He was just buttoning his blue denim shirt when there was a knock at the door. He opened up and found George LeDuc standing in the shade of Sam's Place, looking like a man carrying a gorilla on his shoulders.

"Perfect timing, George. Coffee's ready." Cork stood aside and let his friend in. He poured cups of java for them both, then they sat at the table while a slender finger of sunlight came through the east window and nudged their shadows across the floor.

"You heard about Buck Reinhardt?" Cork said.

"The news ran through the rez like a man on fire." LeDuc sipped his coffee. "Whoa."

"I like it strong," Cork said.

"Strong? You could strip varnish with this."

"Did you drop by just to insult my coffee, George?"

"Fanny Blessing's house burned down last night. Burned to the ground."

"Is Fanny okay?"

"She wasn't there. She was feeding quarters into a slot machine at the casino when it happened. Came home around four A.M. and the place was gone."

"How about Tom?"

"Spent the night at his girlfriend's. Didn't know about it until this morning."

Cork shook his head. He wasn't fond of the Blessings, either Fanny or her son, but this was a shame. "Burned to the ground, you say."

"It's so far from everything else around it and it was the middle of the night. Nobody noticed."

"Any idea how it started?"

"The fire inspector's out there right now. But I have a guess." LeDuc sipped his coffee and made a face. "First, this. I've been authorized by the tribal council to hire you."

"For what?"

"If I hire you, what we talk about here is confidential, right? Privileged?"

"That's right."

"Then tell me you'll take the job."

"How can I? I don't even know what the job is."

"Here's a retainer." LeDuc pulled a check from his pocket and handed it across the table to Cork.

"Five thousand dollars?"

"Are you hired?"

"All right, I'm hired. Just tell me what's so confidential."

"This morning about two thirty, a couple of guys in ski masks broke into the Decouteau's place, dragged Rennie outside, and beat the crap out of him. Rennie's one of the Red Boyz, you know."

"I know. Did they beat him up on general principle or was there a specific reason?"

"They wanted to know where Tom Blessing was. And Lonnie Thunder."

"Did he tell them?"

"He didn't know anything about Thunder, and he swears he kept his mouth shut about Tom Blessing and his girlfriend. Probably true since, as of this morning, Blessing is fine and dandy. Pissed off, of course."

"Has Decouteau talked to the sheriff?"

"He doesn't want to have anything to do with the law. The Red Boyz are saying they'll take care of things."

"Christ."

"Exactly." LeDuc stared down at his coffee, as if trying to decide whether another sip was worth it. "You don't suppose it was just a coincidence that the Blessing house burned?"

"Yeah, and pigs fly out my butt." Cork finished his coffee and headed back for more. "With Alex Kingbird gone, Blessing leads the Red Boyz. Makes him a good target. Three men, you say?"

"That's the word."

"White?"

"Yeah."

"Figures."

"You got an idea?"

"I might." Cork stood at the counter, full in the sunlight. He could tell the day was going to be a warm one. "George, I really think the sheriff ought to know about Rennie Decouteau."

LeDuc pushed his coffee away for good. "No offense meant here, Cork, but the sheriff hasn't exactly been Wonder Woman in taking care of things lately."

"She's had a lot to take care of. Look, George, what is it precisely you want me to accomplish?"

"We want to know who killed the Kingbirds. We want to know where Lonnie Thunder is. We want to know who beat up Rennie Decouteau. And we want to know who burned down the Blessings' place."

"What about who killed Buck Reinhardt?"

"We don't care about Buck. There are more than a few Shinnobs would give a medal to the guy who shot him." LeDuc stood up, preparing to leave. "I'm thinking hiring you is what might be called a convergence of common interests. I'd guess the sheriff wouldn't mind at all if she knew you were working the rez. I know you got a rock in your shoe name of Lonnie Thunder that you'd be happy to get rid of. And the council's concerned that if we don't get some answers soon, we'll have scared people, red and white, hauling out their hunting rifles and looking to shoot something other than whitetails."

"A lot of what you're asking is what I've been doing anyway, George. So what's the five grand for?"

"Anything you find out, you come to us with it first. We decide what the authorities know. The truth is, there's a lot of concern about how all this is going to affect the casino. We don't want folks staying away because they hear there's some kind of Indian war going on."

"So a lot of this comes down to worrying about money."

LeDuc nodded at the check lying on the table. "Is that going to be enough? If you need more, don't be shy about saying so."

Cork shrugged. "What's a nice coffin cost these days?"

Cork found Enos Minot and Ari Ostrowsky standing at the edge of the square of char and ash that had been the Blessing house. Minot was one of Marsha Dross's deputies. Ostrowsky was a volunteer fireman. Together, they were the Tamarack County Fire Investigation Unit, an entity Cork had created when he was sheriff. Both men had completed training with the National Fire Academy, the Minnesota State Fire Marshal, and the Minnesota BCA. They were both small and complemented each other well. Enos was laid-back and thoughtful. Ari was like a sheepdog, running around the scene trying to shepherd all the disparate elements into a cohesive and understandable whole. They loved their job.

Cork parked his Bronco on the road and walked toward the two men, who were conferring over clipboards.

"Enos, Ari," he greeted them.

"Hey, Cork," Ari said with an eager and affable grin. "What brings you out here?"

"Working for the Iron Lake Ojibwe, Ari. This is the rez, and they're concerned. You guys got any idea what happened here?"

Enos shook his head. He was mostly bald, and in the warm, late-morning sunlight, his bare scalp glistened with a thin sheen of sweat. "This will be a tough one, Cork. The structure's almost totally destroyed. Gonna be a bear trying to pinpoint the origin of the fire. If we just had some wall left standing . . ." He shook his head again.

Ari, who wore a Minnesota Twins cap, waved off his partner's concern. "We'll get to the bottom of it once we're able to move in there and start sifting. Still too many hot spots."

"Any way to tell the time the fire started?" Cork asked.

Enos nodded. "When we interviewed Ms. Blessing, she indicated she returned from the casino about four thirty A.M. The place was still burning but the walls had already collapsed. At most, we think, the fire started a couple hours earlier."

"So, around two thirty?"

"That's in the ballpark," Ari said.

"Was Fanny the one who reported it?"

"Yeah. Called from a neighbor's house a couple of miles down the road."

"How was she?"

Enos ran his hand over the top of his head, then wiped the sweat on his pants leg. "By the time we got here and had a chance to interview her, she'd calmed down. I heard that earlier she was pretty hysterical."

"Know where she is?"

"Went to stay with a relative. A cousin, I think. I've got the name and address if you want it."

"Thanks, we'll see. Has her son been around?"

"Tom?" Enos pointed toward the old gas station across the road. Parked in the shade of a willow on the east side of the derelict structure was Tom Blessing's Silverado. "He's been there watching us most of the morning. We interviewed him. He claimed he was at his girlfriend's house all night. Sheriff's going to follow up on that."

Ari bent and picked up a charred piece of wood that blackened his fingers. "Nobody even noticed. The yin and the yang of this beautiful isolation."

"I'm going to talk to Tom," Cork said. "You guys sticking around for a while?"

"Yeah. We haven't been able to get to the heart of things yet," Enos said. "And the investigator for the insurance company's on his way up from Duluth. Want to be here when he arrives."

"Thanks, guys."

"You betcha, Cork," Ari said. The men turned their attention back to their clipboards.

Cork headed toward the old derelict gas station across the road. It looked much the same as it had when the photographer from *National Geographic* had immortalized it in the pages of that publication. Though the accompanying article had been about the problems of the rez, to Cork the old gas station was a different kind of symbol. He saw something admirable in it, something that spoke of tenacity, of endurance in the face of neglect and all the other elements that worked to break it down. In a way, it was like the spirit of the Ojibwe.

In the shade of the willow, Tom Blessing lowered his window.

"*Boozhoo,* Tom," Cork said in greeting.

"Waubishash," Blessing said, reiterating the name he'd taken as one of the Red Boyz. He wore sunglasses and stared at Cork from behind the big black lenses.

"I'm sorry about your mother's house."

"Not as sorry as she is," Blessing said.

"I heard about Rennie Decouteau. How's he doing?"

"His name is Kaybayosay. And he's been better."

"I heard the Red Boyz are considering a response."

The dark lenses of Blessing's sunglasses reflected the burned-down house. "News to me. The Red Boyz got nothing on their minds but being law-abiding citizens."

"Any idea who beat up Decouteau?"

"I told you, his name is Kaybayosay."

"Fine. Any idea who messed him up?"

"Same piece of shit who did this, don't you think? Came looking for me here, didn't find me, took it out on my mother's house, then grabbed Kaybayosay and took it out on him."

Cork had to admit it seemed like a reasonable read of the incidents. "Look, Tom—"

"Waubishash."

"As hard as it's going to be to restrain yourself and the Red Boyz, nothing's gained by going off half-cocked. Let the sheriff's people do their work. They'll get to the bottom of things."

Blessing gave a derisive laugh. "Right."

"How long you figure on staying here?"

"Longer'n you, I imagine." Blessing crossed his arms and went back to staring across the road.

Blessing was right. There wasn't anything more for Cork to do there. He went back to his Bronco and left.

Yellow Lake was fifteen miles southwest of Aurora. It was only slightly smaller than the county seat and had its own police force. The police shared a building with the volunteer fire department, which was located on a corner across the street from a lakefront park. The view was lovely: green grass; blue water; dark pines; and a sky full of clouds, like angels' breath on a cold morning.

Dave Reinhardt was seated at his desk, leaning over an opened manila folder, head bowed. He wore his khaki uniform. When Cork came in from off the street, Reinhardt jerked upright, as if he'd been napping, and he quickly slid a desk drawer closed.

"Paperwork used to put me to sleep, too, Dave. That and late nights." Cork walked across the little office and into the reek of whiskey.

Reinhardt picked up a Bic pen that had been lying on the papers in the open folder. He began tapping the desktop with the point of the pen. "What can I do for you, Cork?"

"For starters, you can stop trying to appease your father."

"I don't have the slightest idea what that's supposed to mean."

"No? You have any idea what the word 'Ojibwe' means?"

"Like I give a flying fuck."

"Loosely translated, it means to pucker up. Now, a lot of Shinnobs accept the theory that the name came from the way the Ojibwe sew their moccasins, with a little pucker to the stitch."

"Is this going somewhere?"

"There's another theory. This one holds that the Ojibwe got their name because they used to roast their enemies slowly over a fire until they puckered up. The point is this, Dave. Any more Shinnob houses get burned down, any more Shinnobs get worked over, I'll tell the Red Boyz who to look up. And I just might tell them about the old way of dealing with an enemy, if they don't already know."

"You're talking riddles I got no answer for, O'Connor."

Cork leaned his hands on the desk and bent toward Reinhardt. "Dave, don't become Buck. With all due respect, those are shoes not worth filling."

Reinhardt's eyes were webs of red lines. The booze and lack of sleep, Cork figured. "Who do you think you are, O'Connor, passing judgment on my father?"

"I knew him my whole life, Dave. I don't like speaking ill of the dead, but that man's ghost needs to be put to rest. And no matter how much you drink, you're not going to resurrect him with a whiskey bottle."

"Get out of here."

"Marsha Dross isn't stupid. She's going to figure you out. Me you can ignore. Marsha and her badge, they've got you trumped six ways from Sunday. Start using your head, Dave, before somebody gets hurt."

Cork walked back into the beautiful day, leaving Reinhardt alone in his office, plagued by a bad hangover and a badly misplaced sense of duty.

THIRTY-TWO

Lucinda Kingbird knew the man who stood on her porch in the shade of the early afternoon, although she could not remember his name. There was a title that went with it, something military. He had been at Alejandro's home after she discovered the bodies that horrible Sunday morning.

"Yes?" She held Misty to her shoulder, gently patting to bring up a burp. She did not open the screen door.

"Ms. Kingbird, I'm Captain Ed Larson, from the sheriff's department. We met the morning your son was killed."

"I remember."

"I'd like to speak with your husband. Is he home?"

"No."

"I stopped by his shop, but it was closed. Do you know where he is?"

"He's away."

"Away? Out of town, you mean?"

"I think so, yes."

"You think so?" The policeman looked puzzled. "When did he leave?"

"Last night."

"What time?"

"I do not know. I was sleeping."

"Do you have any idea where your husband was last night around ten thirty?"

"Why are you asking these questions?"

"Ms. Kingbird, last night at approximately ten thirty, Buck Reinhardt was murdered."

"*Madre de Dios*," Lucinda said involuntarily. She looked at the policeman. "You are here because you think Will did this thing?"

"We don't know who did it, Ms. Kingbird. As part of our investigation, we need to know the whereabouts of anyone who might have reason to have wanted Mr. Reinhardt dead. Do you see?"

"Yes. You think that because people say this Buck Reinhardt killed my Alejandro and Rayette that we would want him dead. That is ridiculous."

"Nonetheless, Ms. Kingbird, we need to check. So, you have no idea where your husband was at ten thirty last night?"

"We buried my son and daughter-in-law yesterday. It was a very hard day for us. We were tired. I went to bed here. My husband, I suspect, went to bed at his shop."

"And then left town without telling you?" When Lucinda didn't reply, he went on, "Do you expect your husband home soon?"

"Later today perhaps. Maybe tomorrow. How was this man killed?"

"He was shot in the parking lot of a bar. A high-caliber rifle was used. It would save your husband and me a lot of trouble if you'd have him give me a call when he returns."

He pulled a card from his wallet and held it out. Lucinda opened the screen door and took it.

"How's the baby doing?" the policeman asked, finally smiling.

"She is fine and beautiful," Lucinda replied, forcing a smile in return.

She watched the policeman leave, then she closed the door and dressed Misty for a trip outside. She went to the bedroom, opened the top dresser drawer, and from the small cedar box took the extra set of keys for the Gun Sight.

By the time she reached Will's shop, Misty was asleep in her car seat. Lucinda lifted her out carefully and the baby didn't wake. She punched in the code to disengage the alarm, then opened the back room. She hurried to a tall rifle case that stood against the west wall and used one of the keys to unlock it. When she opened the door, she was confronted with a rack of what she knew were heavy-caliber rifles, her husband's private collection. There was an empty slot where a rifle was missing. Lucinda thought about the three weapons she'd seen laid out on Will's work table a couple of days before, and she realized the Dragunov was gone.

"Oh, Will, Will," she whispered, her heart full of despair. "What have you done?"

THIRTY-THREE

The procedure to repair Stevie's nose was scheduled for one P.M. in one of the hospital's day-surgery rooms. Both Cork and Jo were there to see him wheeled in. It was, Dr. Barron had assured them, a rather quick and simple procedure. The nose would be rebroken and set correctly. Stephen wouldn't feel a thing, and his face would be just fine afterward, eventually showing no sign that his nose had ever been damaged. Stevie hadn't seemed to mind the idea. What was most important to him was another day off from school.

Cork walked with Jo to the waiting area after they rolled Stevie away.

"Are you okay here by yourself?" he asked.

"I told you I would be. Go do whatever it is you have to do."

She wasn't angry with him, which was a little unusual. Earlier, when he'd told her he had something important to do and asked if she would mind waiting alone for Stevie's procedure to be finished, he'd expected her to respond coolly at best. Instead she'd nodded thoughtfully and replied, "It's about the Kingbird and Reinhardt business, I suppose."

"Yes."

"Who are you helping now?" She waved off the question even before he had a chance to reply. "It doesn't matter. Whatever it is, it's important to you, so go."

Now he kissed her briefly in the waiting area. "Thanks. I'll be home as soon as I can."

She grabbed his hand as he turned to leave. "Come home tonight.

Come home and stay. Whatever danger you believe there might be, I'd rather we all faced it together. We need you. I need you. Please."

Cork said, "I'll be home, I promise."

He left the hospital and drove north, out of Aurora, keeping to the back county roads until he reached the trail to Meloux's cabin, where he parked the Bronco and began the hike to Crow Point.

Meloux wasn't in his cabin. Neither he nor Walleye were anywhere in sight. Cork walked to the end of the point, where there was a stone fire ring in which Meloux often burned sage and sweet grass and cedar. No one was there and the ash in the fire ring was old and cold. Cork thought maybe the Mide had hiked into Allouette, which was a good six miles distant. It was a trip Meloux made at least once a week, in all weather, despite his more than nine decades on the earth. If Meloux had gone to Allouette, there was no telling when he might return.

Cork walked back to the cabin and stood looking across the meadow. The wild grass was tall and green and already there were flowers: oxeye daisies and marsh marigolds and violets. The wind blew and the grass, shining in the sun, moved like waves of green water. Cork lifted his face and caught the scent of wood smoke. It came on the wind, which was out of the east. Now he knew where to find the old Mide.

The path led past the outhouse, through a stand of birch, to the eastern shoreline of Crow Point. In a little clearing that edged the lake stood a small sweat lodge. The embers of a fire still smoldered in front of the structure's opening, which was covered with a blanket. Near the fire was a pitchfork and next to the pitchfork lay Meloux's old mutt, Walleye, fast asleep. Cork was downwind and the animal did not have his scent.

Meloux built a new sweat lodge twice a year, in early spring and late fall. He constructed the frame of young, flexible willow limbs bound together with rawhide prayer ties. The frame formed a hemisphere that was seven or eight feet in diameter and, at the center, arched five feet off the ground. It was covered with a tarp that was overlaid with blankets, both layers used to keep the heat in and the light out. Cork had helped Meloux build several sweat lodges over the years, and he knew that a shallow bowl had been scooped in the earth inside. In that bowl, Meloux would have carefully arranged the Grandfathers, the five stones that had been heated in the fire in front of the lodge until they were searing hot. Meloux had employed the pitchfork to carry the Grandfathers inside. Sometimes the old Mide used the sweat lodge in his healing ceremonies; sometimes he used it simply to cleanse himself and prepare for clear thought. Cork didn't know if the old man was alone, and he didn't want to disturb Meloux, whatever he was involved in. He picked up a small stick and broke it to announce his presence to the dog. Walleye's eyes shot open, and his head popped up. The old mutt looked ready to bark a warning, but recognized Cork and slowly pushed to his feet. He lumbered over and Cork gave him a good patting, and the two of them settled down near the smoldering fire to wait.

Nearly an hour passed before the old man emerged. He pushed back the blanket over the opening and came out naked, his skin flushed red, his long hair white and dripping wet. He was alone. He glanced up and saw Cork, but said nothing, instead making his way down to the lake, where he waded in. Cork knew the lake hadn't warmed enough yet from the winter ice to be comfortable. The water could still cramp a man's muscles instantly. But the old Mide showed no sign of discomfort as he bathed himself and drank to replenish the water his body had lost. Cork lifted the blanket that had been folded on the ground and offered it when the old man returned. Meloux's skin had lost the red flush from the heat of the sweat lodge, and he looked refreshed and relaxed. He drew the blanket tight around him and said, "I'm hungry."

They returned to the cabin, where Cork found a pot of stew waiting on the stove. He stoked the fire and began heating the stew while Meloux dressed. When the food was hot, they sat at Meloux's table and ate. Neither of them spoke. When the meal was finished, Meloux said, "We will smoke."

He took a small pouch of tobacco and a pipe whose bowl was carved of maroon stone and whose stem was wood and they walked to the fire ring at the end of Crow Point, Walleye padding quietly behind. The wind had died. The water of Iron Lake was blue and still, as if the sky had leaked onto the earth. The old Mide offered tobacco to the four cardinal directions, then filled the pipe and lit it. The two men shared the smoke in silence.

Meloux finally spoke. "Something is out there, Corcoran O'Connor, something that eats the light. I have had a vision, but I do not understand it. It is something to be feared, enough to scare this old Mide. I have been trying to cleanse myself, to sweat out the fear so that I can meet this dark, hungry thing and know its face."

"I'm sorry if I disturbed you, Henry."

The old man waved off Cork's apology. "I did not even know you had come."

"This dark thing, Henry, is it about the killing of the Kingbirds and Buck Reinhardt?"

"Buck Reinhardt is dead?"

"He was shot last night."

The old Mide shook his head. "Those are dark things, but I do not know if they are part of what I saw. When I am rested, I will try again."

In a way, Meloux's words echoed Annie's comment just a couple of days earlier, when Cork had talked with her after her suspension from school. She'd been afraid, too, and had likened it to something scary waiting to leap from the bushes.

"Why have you come, Corcoran O'Connor?"

"I thought I followed your advice, Henry, but I'm still confused." Cork explained about how he'd interpreted Meloux's enigmatic advice about taking a hawk's-eye view in his search for Lonnie Thunder. He related his observation from the ridge above the cemetery during the Kingbirds' funeral and how that had led to the old trapper shelter where Thunder had been, but not to Thunder himself. By the time Cork finished his story, the old man was grinning widely.

"You're staring at me like I'm an idiot, Henry. What did I do?"

"Your way was one way of looking at the problem. It was very . . . creative," the old man offered graciously.

"But it wasn't what you meant."

"Alexander Kingbird took for himself a name with greatness." The old man fell silent while Cork puzzled.

"Kakaik," Cork said. "Hawk."

He mulled this over as Walleye got up from where he'd settled and nudged his head under Meloux's old hand. The Mide gently stroked his old friend's coat.

"Okay, Henry, are you telling me to look at things as Kakaik looked at them? Is that what you meant by a hawk's-eye view?"

"Sometimes, Corcoran O'Connor, you remind me of a turtle. You move slow, but you get there."

"I'm not sure that's a lot of help. How does it get me to Lonnie Thunder?"

"If I knew where Obwandiyag was," he said, using the name Thunder had taken as one of the Red Boyz, "I would tell you. I only know the way, not the destination."

"How can I look at things the way Kakaik did if I don't really know who he was?"

Like two polished stones the old Mide's dark eyes held steadily on Cork.

"Wrong question, huh?" Cork shook his head. "Are you saying that before I can understand his thinking, I need to know who he was? Henry, I don't think anybody knows who he was. Do you?"

"I can tell you about the man I knew, but that is only part of the whole." Walleye settled down at the old man's feet. Meloux caressed the dog as he spoke. "When he first came to me, Kakaik was like you are now, always asking questions. He wanted to know how, in the old ways of The People, a boy became a man. I explained *giigiwishimowin*, how a boy would seek a dream vision. He came back many times after that and we talked about many things. He was a man seeking to understand himself and his place, and I think, too, he was a man becoming something he did not expect."

"What was that, Henry?"

"Anishinaabe."

Meloux stood. It was clear he'd said all he had to say to Cork. Walleye struggled to his feet, and they walked back to the cabin. Cork thanked the old man.

"Henry, when you understand what this thing is that eats the light, will you let me know?"

Meloux nodded, then added, "If it does not eat us all first."

THIRTY-FOUR

After visiting Meloux, Cork took an old logging road east, one that didn't appear on any map. He made his way to County 15 on the far side of Iron Lake and drove to Allouette, on the rez. He stopped at LeDuc's store, spoke briefly with George, then walked across the street to the large community center, which housed the tribal offices, the community health program, several meeting rooms, a gymnasium, and a recreation room. The Red Boyz could often be found at the center, shooting pool or shooting hoops. Cork checked the gym, which was being used at the moment by Ani Sorenson, who coached the Iron Lake Loons, the girl's basketball team for the rez. She was taking a number of adolescent girls through drills. Basketball was serious business in the Indian community, and although the season was officially over, Sorenson and the girls kept working on their game. In the recreation room, he found Benny Fullmouth all alone, shooting pool. Fullmouth was twenty years old. He'd dropped out of high school at sixteen and spent the next couple of years getting into trouble—a lot of it triggered by drinking—and heading toward serious jail time. As far as Cork knew, Fullmouth had been clean since joining the Red Boyz. Like all the other gang members, he wore his hair long. At the moment, it was held back with a red bandanna tied around his head. When Cork walked in, Fullmouth glanced up from the table then completed his shot. In the quiet of the room, the crack was like a rock splitting.

"*Boozhoo*, Benny," Cork said.

"What do you want?" Fullmouth circled the table, studying the placement of the balls.

"Five minutes."

"I'm busy."

"You talk to me, it might help nail the person who killed Kakaik."

Fullmouth leaned down to eye an angle. "Somebody already took care of that."

"I don't think Buck Reinhardt killed Kakaik."

"Right."

"Buck had an alibi, one that's standing up. He wasn't anywhere near the rez the night Kakaik and Rayette were killed."

Fullmouth bent, laid his cue across the bridge of his hand, and shot. The cue ball struck the seven and sent it popping into the corner pocket.

"I want one thing from you, Benny."

"Yeah? What's that?"

"Tell me who Kakaik was."

Fullmouth gave him a look that said Cork was an idiot and went back to studying the table.

"You cleaned yourself up when you joined the Red Boyz, Benny."

"What of it?"

"Was it Kakaik who made you do that?"

"It's what you do when you become one of the Red Boyz."

"Must've been tough. How'd you manage it?"

Fullmouth drilled the side pocket with the next shot.

"He made you go through *giigiwishimowin*," Cork said.

Fullmouth straightened up. "If you already know the answer, why ask the question?"

"You had a vision?"

"Yeah, I had a vision. And it won't do you any good to ask."

"It made you one of the Red Boyz."

"It made me ready to be one of the Red Boyz."

"Kakaik did the rest?"

"Look, what he did was help me see that when I was a kid, I thought only about myself. If I was going to be one of the Red Boyz, I had to think about The People."

"That's what the Red Boyz are about? The People?"

"We're about warriors. We're about brothers. Hell, the Red Boyz are better than brothers. Kakaik asked me to be one of them. He asked *me*."

"And what are the Red Boyz about, Benny?"

"About purifying. Ourselves and the rez."

"The tribal council doesn't look on the Red Boyz too kindly."

"All they care about is fucking with the BIA and keeping the casino running. That's got nothing to do with being *ogichidaa*." Which meant being a leader, a protector of the people and the land. "Kakaik was a great *ogichidaa*." Fullmouth threw his cue on the table and tore open his shirt. He thrust his left shoulder into view. A scar, a branded *R*, was burned into the skin. "He gave me this when I became one of the Red Boyz. If he'd wanted me to cut off a finger, too, I'd've done it."

"Do all the Red Boyz go through *giigiwishimowin*?"

"You can't be one of us if you don't."

"Do you all seek the vision in the same place?"

Fullmouth looked at Cork suspiciously, but finally said, "Yeah."

Cork said, "Let me guess. You go out from Black Duck Lake. And when you return, he brands you, and you become one of the Red Boyz."

From Fullmouth's reaction, Cork could see that he'd guessed correctly, and he understood now why Blessing had made the pilgrimage to the lake after Kingbird's funeral. To the Red Boyz, it was a place of power.

"Your five minutes are up." Fullmouth headed to a soft-drink vending machine.

"What about Lonnie Thunder?"

"He isn't one of the Red Boyz." He fed a dollar into the machine and looked over his choices.

"He says he is."

"Fuck what he says."

"What did Kakaik think of Thunder?"

"That he could help the son of a bitch."

"Is that why he asked Thunder to be one of the Red Boyz?"

"He didn't. Waubishash wanted Thunder in. They're cousins."

"I know."

Fullmouth poked a button and after some internal clunking, the machine delivered a twenty-ounce plastic bottle of Sprite. He pulled out the bottle and shook his head. "Thunder, he wanted to be one of us for all the wrong reasons."

"Which were?"

"He's big, likes to throw his weight around. He thinks that's what we're about. That and dealing dope."

"You don't deal?"

Fullmouth unscrewed the cap on the Sprite, took a long sip, and followed it with a loud burp. "No, man. Staying pure, that's what the Red Boyz are about. And helping other Shinnobs to stay pure. We find someone dealing on the rez, we don't mess around. We kick ass."

"Lonnie was dealing. And he was doing worse than that with young Shinnob girls. How come you didn't kick his ass?"

"We didn't know anything about that. Even Waubishash won't take his side now."

"You'd kick his ass now?"

"Up to me, we'd cut his balls off and stuff 'em down his throat. Nothing but trouble comes from him. But he's done that bug thing."

"Bug thing?"

"Found a rock somewhere and crawled under it."

"You don't know where he is?"

"If I did, I wouldn't be shooting pool right now."

"Benny, I think Thunder might have killed Kakaik."

Fullmouth stared at Cork. "You're shitting me. Why would he do that?"

"I think Kakaik was prepared to turn him over to the sheriff."

Fullmouth thought it over. "Kakaik would've killed Thunder before he gave him over to the cops. Hell, he should have killed him to begin with. Would've made everybody happy. The Red Boyz, the cops, even that crazy old Reinhardt."

"Is that the Red Boyz way?"

"That's the way of the warrior, O'Connor. Old man like you, I don't expect you'd understand that."

"If I found Thunder and turned him over to you, what would you do with him?"

"You mean after I slit his throat?"

"Is that how all the Red Boyz feel?"

"We're brothers. One heart, one mind."

"Nice talking to you, Benny."

THIRTY-FIVE

Annie had prepared a good stroganoff, which she served with beets and a tossed salad. Jo volunteered to do the dishes. Cork and Stevie cleared the table, then went into the backyard for a little batting practice while there was still enough light. Stevie's nose was taped, and Cork didn't want to risk damaging it again—at least right away—so they used a Wiffle ball and a plastic bat. Trixie wasn't a bad outfielder, chasing after whatever Stevie hit.

As the evening faded and night crept in, Cork called a halt and Stevie reluctantly went with him inside. His son headed upstairs to put on his pajamas while Cork tracked down Jo, who was in her office, going over papers at her desk.

"You mind doing the bedtime routine with Stevie?" he asked.

Jo took off her reading glasses and gave him a puzzled and slightly concerned look. "I thought you were going to stay here tonight."

"I'll be back. I just want to talk to Will Kingbird."

"What about?"

"Alexander. I'm trying to get a feel for what his thinking about Lonnie Thunder might have been at the end."

"So you can find Thunder, bring him in, and jail him?"

"I'm beginning to believe that even if I find him, I might not be able to jail him."

"Why?"

"Will you take a rain check on that answer? Just until I get back?"

"All right." She got up and came to where he stood in the doorway. She put her arms around him. "I hate to sound like a broken record, but please be careful, Cork."

* * *

Lucinda laid Misty in her crib for the night, then sat on the living room sofa, bone tired and ragged with worry. No word from Will, and the dark, monstrous fear of what he might have done weighed on all her thinking. Her husband had killed before, as a very young man in Vietnam, and later as part of Division Recon, involved in Direct Action missions, especially in what he called prisoner recovery. He was not only an excellent sniper, he was trained in many ways to kill with quiet efficiency. He sometimes got calls in the night and was gone for days. When he returned, though he wouldn't speak of where he'd been or what he'd done, it was as if he carried bodies on his back. Was it any wonder he was so closed? Who would want to talk of such things? Who would be proud of it? After he'd become an instructor at Lejeune, the night calls and sudden deployments stopped, but there were still times when he'd vanish and lay the blame on the corps when Lucinda knew it was not so.

The doorbell pulled her from her black thoughts and from the sofa. When she opened the front door, Cork O'Connor stood on the porch, smiling cordially.

"Evening, Luci. Is Will at home?"

"No, he's not."

"At the shop?"

"He is out of town." She saw disappointment in his eyes. "Is there something I can help you with?"

"I wanted to talk to him about Alexander."

"You could talk to me." She opened the screen door. "Would you like to come in?"

"Thank you."

When he was inside, she asked, "May I get you something? Coffee maybe?"

"Nothing, thanks."

She returned to the sofa; he sat in the maroon easy chair usually occupied by Will.

"What would you like to know?" she asked.

"I'm not exactly sure, Luci. I'm trying to find Lonnie Thunder."

"The young man who gave the drugs to the Reinhardt girl."

"Yes."

"I don't think I can help you."

"I'm wondering about Alexander and his state of mind regarding Lonnie Thunder and the Red Boyz before he was killed."

"His state of mind?" She laughed, though not with humor. "That's like asking me what the coffee table is thinking. Alejandro almost never spoke to me about what was on his mind."

"What about Rayette? Did she say anything that might have been of help?"

Lucinda thought of the wonderful talks with her daughter-in-law on those Sundays they rode together to church. The memory made her terribly sad.

"She said Alejandro was quieter lately, even more than usual. She thought he was worried."

"About Buck Reinhardt?"

"I don't know." She thought again. "The last time I saw Alejandro alive he said something to me. He said he understood his father better now. The responsibility, he said, of a family was great. Me, I didn't think that Rayette and Misty were difficult, so perhaps he wasn't talking about them."

"The Red Boyz?"

"Rayette told me that many of the Red Boyz looked to him as they might have a father. Now I will tell you something that is what I think but Alejandro never spoke to me about it, so it might be nothing. When he came back here, he was not the Alejandro I knew. He was like a clay pot, hardened in the fire. It was difficult to be with him. But he changed again after he married Rayette and especially after Misty was born. I think—and this is my own thinking—that he found what he'd always been looking for."

"And that was?"

"Home. He found home." Lucinda heard the side door open and the sound of someone in the kitchen. "Will?" she called eagerly.

"No, Mom. Just me."

Ulysses walked into the living room. His friend Darrell Gallagher was with him, wearing the horrid black leather coat that fell below his knees, and the black hair so purposefully cut askew, and the black look on his face that made her cringe, not with fear but with the thought that here was a child who hadn't been loved in a long time. She didn't like Uly being so often in his company, but her son had no other friends. Perhaps this was true of Darrell, too.

"Hi, Uly," Cork O'Connor said. To the other boy he said, "You're Darrell, right? Skip Gallagher's grandson?"

"Yeah," Gallagher replied in a flat voice.

"I haven't seen your grandfather in a while. How is he?"

"Old," Gallagher said.

"Going to my room," Uly said. He didn't wait for his mother to reply.

Lucinda's eyes followed where Gallagher had gone. "Do you know his family?" she asked Cork O'Connor.

"He doesn't have much family to speak of. Lives with his grandfather. I know Skip from way back. He was a state trooper for a long time. A crusty old guy. I can't imagine he relates very well to a teenager."

"All that black," Lucinda said, shaking her head.

"Goth, Luci. A lot of kids seem to be into it."

"Have I helped you at all?" she asked.

"I think so." He stood. "I appreciate your time. When do you expect Will back?"

"I don't know." She hesitated, then said, "There's something else. I don't know if it's important."

"Go ahead."

"I'll tell you what I think about Alejandro and the Red Boyz. This is my own thinking. He never talked to me, but I have thought a lot about it. I think that Alejandro joined the marines for two reasons. I think he wanted his father's approval, and I think he wanted a place to belong. I don't think he found either. For him the marines were not what they had been for his father. I think he became involved in that gang in Los Angeles because he was still looking for a place to belong. I think he did not find it there, either. When he came back here, he was still searching. With the Red Boyz, I think, he found that place. And with Rayette and Misty, he finally felt that he had a home. Maybe it is just what I want to believe, but I think that for a little while he was happy."

"Thank you, Luci." He walked to the front door and she followed. "Is Misty doing okay?" he asked when he was standing on the porch.

"She is an angel. She is a blessing."

"I wish they all were," Cork O'Connor said.

She closed the door and thought, *They all begin that way.*

Cork drove to the rez and took the cutoff to the place where Fannie Blessing's house had stood. The moon had risen, only a half-moon but bright enough in that isolated area to cast shadows. Cork parked in front of the old gas station across the road from the patch of black ash that was all that was left of the Blessings' home. He grabbed his Maglite, got out, and walked to the derelict building. In its day, the place had not only dispensed gas and a few of the sundry items essential to fishermen and campers, it had also been a garage with a bay for vehicle repairs. Elmer Waybenais, a full-blood Ojibwe, had owned the station, and his son, C.J., had been the mechanic, one with a good reputation. Elmer Waybenais was long dead, and C.J. had taken a job at the Tomahawk Truck Stop, where he still had a good rep, particularly with diesel engines. Cork walked to the wide door of the garage area. The door was down, locked, and the windows where the glass had long ago been shot out by vandals were covered with newspaper. Cork flicked on the Maglite and looked closely at the newspapers.

When he'd talked that morning with Tom Blessing in the shade of the willow next to the ancient building, he'd noticed that the newspapers covering the garage windows were white, not yellowed with age. It was a small detail that he hadn't given any importance. After he talked with Benny Fullmouth and with Lucinda Kingbird, the detail suggested something to him. He'd been trying from the beginning to figure out what Alexander Kingbird had meant when he'd said he would offer Buck Reinhardt justice, a statement that in light of all the apparent circumstances made little sense. In Cork's thinking, to offer justice, Kingbird would have had to hand Thunder over to the sheriff, which would have been a betrayal of the Red Boyz. Turning Thunder in might have had another unwanted consequence as well. Thunder wasn't likely to be grateful for the move, and probably wouldn't be inclined to be silent about things the Red Boyz would prefer remained secret. If it was true that the gang was warehousing drugs for the Latin Lords, Thunder might be more than willing to cut a deal that would keep him out of prison. So putting Thunder in the hands of the cops probably wasn't what Kingbird had in mind.

Illuminated by the Maglite, the date on the newspaper that had been used to cover the garage door windows was clear: one week earlier, to the day. No wonder the paper was still so white. Cork tore the newspaper away from one of the glassless windows and shot the flashlight beam inside, where it reflected off a headlight. He ran the beam left and right across the grill and hood of the vehicle inside. It was a dark green Xterra, the same kind of vehicle Lonnie Thunder drove. Cork tried the door to the office part of the old building, which was secured with a new hasp and padlock. The long windows were boarded up with plywood that had rotted over time. Cork kicked the plywood with the flat of his foot and the wood splintered. A few more kicks and he broke his way in. He eased through the splintered opening. Inside he found a cot set up on the dusty floor. Beside it was an overturned orange crate with a Coleman propane lamp on top. Under the cot sat a gym bag full of rumpled clothing. Lying on the blanket that covered the cot was a vehicle license plate: RedStud.

Jo sat with her back propped against the headboard of their bed, her reading glasses in her hand. She'd set her book aside in order to listen to Cork, and now she asked, "So what does it mean?"

Cork paced their bedroom as he talked. "Thunder was at the old trapper's cabin at one point, then he was gone. He took those shots at me at Sam's Place, then he was gone. He did the drive-by of Buck Reinhardt, then he was gone. The question I've been asking myself lately is how could Thunder have been out so much and not have been spotted by someone? The answer is that he wasn't. Lonnie Thunder's dead. He's been dead for some time."

"And you think it was Tom Blessing who was driving his SUV?"

"Probably. This morning I thought he was parked out there to watch the investigators go through the rubble of his mother's house. It's more likely that he just wanted to make sure no one got nosy around the old gas station."

"The vanity plate you found. He took that off the SUV to keep from being so conspicuous?"

"That would make sense. Unless you fired a few rounds from the driver's seat in order to get noticed, a dark green SUV wouldn't attract much attention. I'm betting the plates on there now were stolen."

"Why go through all that trouble to make people believe Thunder's still alive?"

Cork sat on his side of the bed. "I think I'm responsible. I told Blessing I believed that Thunder had a good motive for killing Kingbird. Blessing played on that and led me right along."

"That still doesn't answer the question of why. Unless Blessing killed Kingbird."

"Or was trying to cover for whoever did."

"How do you find out?"

Cork stared for a moment at the open bedroom window. A breeze came through and the curtain trembled. "I think someone needs to make Blessing an offer he can't refuse."

"Someone?"

Cork turned to Jo. "It's best if this is a conversation we never had."

"You're scaring me."

He reached out and took her hand. "If this is about what I think it's about, we should all be scared."

THIRTY-SIX

Friday morning they ran a course that, near the end, brought them to Sam's Place. Annie slowed down in the parking lot and stopped at the picnic table under the red pine. She stood looking out at Iron Lake, which at that moment seemed to her to have exactly the characteristic its name suggested: a thing intractable and enduring. With so much about to change in her life—leaving home for college, going out on her own—she wanted to believe some things would be forever.

Her father jogged up behind her, breathing hard.

"Tired?" he asked.

"Just wanted to stop for a minute, Dad. Okay?"

"Sure." He sounded a little grateful.

She glanced back at the old Quonset hut. "Feels strange not working at Sam's Place the weekend of fishing opener."

"I think the fishermen'll survive. Too many other things on my plate at the moment. Maybe next weekend."

"The Kingbird stuff, right?"

"Yep, the Kingbird stuff." Her father sat on the picnic table and used the bench as a footrest. "Are you going to the playoff game this afternoon?"

The Aurora Blue Jays were hosting, home field advantage.

"Coach said I could sit on the bench with the team, even though I couldn't suit up," she said.

"It'll be hard, I imagine."

"We'll do okay. We're a team."

"Hard on you, I meant."

"It sucks, but that's the way it is."

"Who's pitching in your place?"

"Meg Greeley."

"She won't last more than four innings."

"Kris Evans will relieve her. She'll bring the game home just fine."

"I'll try to be there."

"Thanks."

"I'm proud of you, you know that, don't you?"

She stared at the hard morning blue of the lake and didn't meet his eyes. "Thanks." She turned toward Grant Park, south beyond the vacant field. "Let's finish the run."

At ten A.M. Cork was parked in the driveway of the burned-down Blessing home. He'd been waiting fifteen minutes when he saw Tom Blessing's Silverado coming from the south. Blessing hit the cross-roads, took a right, and half a minute later, pulled up behind Cork's Bronco. They both got out.

"*Boozhoo,* Tom. Beautiful morning, huh?"

"This better be good, O'Connor."

"Good, I don't know. Necessary, definitely."

"You said you knew something about the fire."

"I've got a confession, Tom. I lied."

"What's going on?"

"You tell me."

Cork turned back to his Bronco, opened the back door, and pulled out Lonnie Thunder's license plate: RedStud. He handed it to Blessing, who stared at it, and then darted a look toward the old gas station across the road.

"His Xterra is still there, Tom, although he's not. But you know that."

"This doesn't prove anything." Blessing flung the plate into the ruins of the house as if he were throwing a Frisbee. It landed with a clatter and a small puff of ash.

"It makes a pretty good case for aiding and abetting."

"Big deal."

"Maybe a good case for murder as well."

"What are you talking about?"

"Thunder's dead, Tom. Did you kill him?"

"You're crazy."

"Or did Kakaik?"

"What makes you think he's dead?"

"Because on the rez you can't get around for very long without someone spotting you. Nobody's seen Thunder in a while."

"He split. He knew he was fucked if he stayed, so he left."

"When?"

"I don't know. Couple of days ago."

"How? His Xterra is still here."

"Got a ride."

"Who with?"

"One of the Red Boyz."

"Which one?"

"Fuck you. I don't have to answer your questions."

Blessing turned away, ready to leave, but he stopped when he saw the line of vehicles coming down the road from the west.

"Maybe you don't have to answer my questions, but I think you're going to want to answer theirs."

The vehicles—half a dozen dusty SUVs and pickups—turned into the drive and blocked any hope Blessing might have had for an escape. George LeDuc led the procession in his Blazer. Chet Everywind was with him. When they got out, Everywind was cradling his deer rifle. The others, Ojibwe all, left their vehicles and sauntered over, putting Blessing at the center of a ring of men and rifles.

Blessing's eyes swung right and left. "What is this?"

LeDuc spoke. "Cork stopped by my place this morning, Tom, and we had a long talk. After that, I spoke to a few of the others here. We decided to form our own gang. We call ourselves the Red Menz 'cause we're a little older and a little wiser."

"What do you want?"

"The truth, Tom. Just the truth."

"Going to beat it out of me?" Blessing tried to laugh, but it came out feebly.

"We thought we might go about it another way."

LeDuc nodded and two of the men—Jack Gagnon and Dennis Mc-Dougall—grabbed Blessing's arms. They were both big men, but it didn't matter. Blessing didn't put up a struggle. He kept his eyes on LeDuc, while the men bound his outstretched arms to the grill of his Silverado.

"Lester," LeDuc said, "get your stuff."

Lester Neadeau was a master plumber. He went to his truck and came back with a propane torch and a flint striker.

LeDuc said, "I'm going to ask you some questions, Tom—"

"My name is Waubishash."

"First question: What happened to Lonnie Thunder?"

"Fuck you."

LeDuc signaled Neadeau, who opened the valve on the torch, and sparked a flame with the striker.

"You've been branded before, Tom. This shouldn't be much different. Jack, Dennis, let's see some red skin."

The two men tore open Blessing's shirt, exposing his hairless chest.

"Lester," LeDuc said.

Neadeau stepped up to Blessing and moved the torch toward the young man's bared chest. The sharp blue tongue of flame licked Blessing's skin. Blessing screamed and Neadeau stepped back.

"You brought violence to the rez," LeDuc said. "You brought fear, you brought dishonor—"

"We brought power," Blessing cried.

"Power? Hooking the Reinhardt girl on dope is power? Using our own girls in the way Thunder did was power?"

"We didn't hook the *chimook* girl," he said, using the unflattering Ojibwe slang for white people. "She was already deep into meth. And it was Lonnie who used those girls, not the Red Boyz."

"He's one of you."

"He wasn't."

Cork said, "Wasn't? Don't you mean isn't?"

"What happened to Lonnie Thunder?" LeDuc said again.

Blessing refused to reply. LeDuc nodded to Neadeau, who started the torch toward Blessing's chest.

"He's dead," Blessing said, a second before the flame connected.

"Who killed him?"

"He killed himself."

"Sure he did. Lester, a little more flame."

"I'm not lying," Blessing said. "Kakaik gave him a choice. He could kill himself or Kakaik would do it for him."

"Why did Kingbird want him dead?"

"He didn't want him dead, but it was the only way. Lonnie stole drugs from the Red Boyz. He traded them for sex with the Reinhardt girl and used them to get what he wanted from those others. He didn't know how to walk the path of the warrior and he jeopardized us all. He wouldn't turn himself in and he threatened he'd tell everything he knew about the Red Boyz if Kakaik tried to turn him over. Killing him was the only answer."

"So he killed himself?" LeDuc looked unconvinced. "How?"

"Kakaik offered him a choice, gun or knife. The gun had one bullet in it. We were all there, all the Red Boyz. Lonnie knew he was a dead man. He took the knife and cut his own throat."

"While you all stood there and watched?" LeDuc's position shifted and his face dropped into shadow. "Watching a man die—a cousin—that's not an easy thing."

Blessing looked full into the sun, but he didn't blink. "When he died, I had more respect for him than any time when he was alive. He finally acted like a warrior."

"What did you do with his body?"

"Threw it in a bog."

LeDuc glanced at Cork. Cork said, "Who killed Kingbird?"

"If I tell you, I'm a dead man."

Cork moved close to Blessing and leaned near the man's face. "It was the Latin Lords, wasn't it, Tom?" From the look in Blessing's eyes, he could tell that he'd hit the mark. "Was it about the drugs?"

Blessing was silent. The wind picked up suddenly, and the smell of char and ash from the burned ruins blew over them all. Against the hard blue sky, a hawk rode the current, its wings slicing the air like knife blades.

"They killed him because Kakaik was no longer one of them," Blessing said. "He was one of us."

Cork said, "The Lords sent him out here to help control the drug traffic, didn't they? To deal with the competition and extend the pipeline. That's why he created the Red Boyz. But in the end, his loyalty was here, with you."

Blessing gave a nod. "He wanted to end the drug connection. He thought it weakened us, dishonored us."

"And the Latin Lords weren't happy?"

"They sent men to talk to him."

"Talk?"

"We spent Saturday afternoon with them, Kakaik and me. I thought there was an understanding. I thought they left. Then they came to me the next morning, after Kakaik was killed. They said I was the head of the Red Boyz now, like it was something that was theirs to offer."

"How many were there?"

"Two."

"Their names?"

"Manny Ortega and Joey Estevez."

"You knew them before?"

"Ortega's the Latin Lord we always deal with. He's like a businessman. Comes in from Chicago. Estevez comes with him, brings muscle. He was trained by Los Zetas, the assassins of the Mexican cartels. He's death in a pair of lizard-skin boots."

"An enforcer. How'd they get here?"

"The way they always do. In a floatplane."

"That landed at Black Duck Lake?" Cork said.

"Yeah."

"Isolated. And let me guess, the drugs are warehoused somewhere out there? They deliver and you distribute?"

Blessing nodded.

"Where?"

"All over, but mostly little places no bigger than a fart, kind of towns people think of as safe."

"Good money in it?"

"You got no idea."

"But Kakaik was going to end the deal, so the Latin Lords killed him and put you in charge."

"They said if I got any ideas like Kakaik had, I'd end up the same way. They said wouldn't I rather be rich and alive."

"You shot at me and my son and pretended to be Thunder. Why?"

"I didn't shoot at you. If I shot at you, you'd be dead. I just shot. I was trying to scare you off. I didn't want you poking around on the rez. I figured it was safe putting the blame on a dead man."

"What about Reinhardt? Why shoot at him?"

"I was hoping to put a little fear in him, too. And, hell, that was just the kind of stupid thing Lonnie would do."

He was probably right, Cork thought. "The Red Boyz have anything to do with the shooting in the Buzz Saw parking lot?"

"That wasn't us," Blessing replied.

Cork nodded. For the moment, he'd let it lie. "You said the Latin Lords come in a floatplane. How do they get around from there?"

"They keep a Tahoe parked at the warehouse."

"You have any proof it was these men who killed Kakaik and Rayette?"

"I know it was Estevez. He was always looking at Kakaik like he'd love to cut him into little pieces because Kakaik wasn't afraid of him."

"The sheriff's people are going to want proof."

"Sheriff's people?" LeDuc said. "This is rez business."

"Hold on, George," Cork began.

LeDuc cut him off. "You believe he's telling the truth?"

"Yes."

"Then Shinnobs will handle this."

"It's too big, too dangerous."

"I'm not giving you a choice." LeDuc squared himself in front of Cork. "In this, you are Anishinaabe or you are white. You can't be both."

LeDuc's face could have been cut from sandstone and his eyes carved from agates. He and Cork were old friends, but in this business LeDuc was *ogichidaa,* protector of his people and their land. Cork understood this, but for him it was not a question of being Shinnob or white. It was a concern that arose from an ingrained and deeply felt respect for the law, something as much a part of who he was as the color of his skin or the mixed blood that ran through his veins.

"If we try to handle this on our own, George, and it goes south, the consequences could be enormous," he argued quietly. "Good men here could be killed. Or just as bad, they could become murderers."

"A man who kills a murderer is not himself one."

"That's not how the law will look at it, George."

"White man's law. This is our land, and our laws decided things here a long time before white people came." LeDuc was not angry, but his voice had the sharp edge of a honed knife. "Go now or stay. The choice is yours, Cork. If you go, you go without shame. But if you stay, you are one of us and you are with us in whatever we decide. I will discuss this no more."

Cork turned from LeDuc and studied the faces around him. He knew these men, respected them, and would have been proud to stand with them. He knew no better than they did the end of this affair. There was enormous risk involved and these men were prepared to accept it. Cork knew that stepping back was the safe thing to do. But he also knew that he could not.

"*Anishinaabe indaaw,*" he said to LeDuc. I am Anishinaabe. I am one of The People.

LeDuc gave a nod, almost imperceptible, and it was done.

Cork faced Blessing again. "If you wanted to talk to these men, they'd come in on the floatplane and dock where the Tahoe is parked?"

"Yeah."

"What if they thought you were going to be as difficult to deal with as Kakaik?"

Blessing stared at Cork, then his eyes moved across all the other men who were present. "It would get ugly."

LeDuc said, "It's already ugly."

He reached to his belt and drew out a hunting knife that was sheathed there. He walked to Blessing and held the blade up. Sunlight skated along the edge. He reached out and cut the bonds that held Blessing to the Silverado's grill. Blessing shot his right hand toward the place where Neadeau's torch had burned him, but stopped short of touching the wound. He stood tall before the others.

LeDuc said, "We're all one people, Waubishash, and our enemy is the same. We should fight together, don't you think?"

Blessing held still, caught in the intensity of LeDuc's eyes. Then he nodded and said, "I'll make sure the sons of bitches come."

THIRTY-SEVEN

Will came home in the late afternoon. He walked in the door without a word about where he'd been, hung his jacket in the closet, and spoke with his back to Lucinda, who was on the floor entertaining Misty with a rubber pig that squeaked. "Where's Ulysses? He was supposed to wash your car, but it's still covered with dust."

"He's at Darrell Gallagher's house. They're playing some kind of video game. He said he might be there until late."

Will left the closet and headed toward the kitchen. He would not look at Lucinda. "Gallagher," he said. "I don't like the feel I get from that kid."

"Uly says he writes poetry."

"Hitler wrote poetry."

"Uly says he feels sorry for him. The boy is lonely. He has no friends except for Uly."

"There's usually a good reason someone has no friends."

She watched him walk away from her. "Will, I know what you did."

That stopped him. In the doorway to the kitchen, he turned and stared at her.

"I know you killed Buck Reinhardt," she said.

"Reinhardt's dead?"

His surprise seemed so genuine that Lucinda suddenly doubted all the horrible conclusions she'd come to.

"Two nights ago, the night you left," she told him. "He was shot with a rifle from a distance."

"A night shot?"

"Yes."

"And you think I did this?"

"I went to your shop yesterday morning. You weren't there, and the Dragunov was missing."

"The Dragunov? Jesus." He quickly returned to the closet and grabbed his jacket.

"Will?"

"Not now, Luci."

He hurried out the door and was gone again.

The baby smiled and reached for the pig, but Lucinda barely noticed. She was thinking about Will and his surprise at the news about Reinhardt. Perhaps he did not kill the man. She was so ready to feel relief. She didn't know for sure where he'd been, but that was not unusual. As always, she had her suspicions.

The Blue Jays won the regional playoff game in a dramatic finish. One run down, bottom of the seventh and final inning, Cara Haines hit a double to right field that brought two Blue Jays across home plate. Stevie sat with Cork in the stands, and they both went crazy, along with the rest of the home crowd. They waited for Annie behind the bleachers, and she came with her teammates, who were headed to the locker room. She said a bunch of the girls were going out to celebrate; she'd probably be home late. Cork told her to have a good time.

It was almost six thirty when Cork and Stevie walked back to the Bronco in the school parking lot. "We could go home and I could fix up something to eat, or we could go to the Broiler and have some fried chicken. What do you say, buddy?"

Stevie grinned. "No-brainer, Dad."

"Let's call your mom, see if she'll join us."

He tried her work number, but the line was busy. He tried again when they pulled into the Broiler parking lot. This time she answered.

"I was on the phone with Lucinda Kingbird," she explained. "Will's being held in the jail."

"What for?"

"He confessed to the murder of Buck Reinhardt. I'm on my way over to the sheriff's office now."

"Do you want me there?"

"I can't imagine what for, but I'll want to talk to you later, I'm sure. Don't go out of cell phone range, okay?"

"I'll be here."

"Oh, Cork? How'd they do? The Blue Jays?"

"Just a second." He handed the phone to Stevie. "Your mom wants to know how your sister's team did."

Stevie took the phone. "Kicked butt," he told her.

Will looked so tired Lucinda wanted to weep. Hold him and weep.

"Thanks, Cy," Jo O'Connor said to the deputy who'd brought Will in.

"Let me know when you're ready to leave." The deputy tapped the buzzer on the wall next to the door to make sure she knew how to summon him, then he stepped outside.

"Oh, Will." Lucinda reached across the table, but he pulled his hands away and dropped them into his lap.

"What are you doing here?" he said to Jo.

"Lucinda asked me. She'd like me to represent you. I told her I would, if you agreed."

"Nothing to represent. Open-and-shut case. I killed the son of a bitch who killed my son. That's all there is to it."

"Why not let the sheriff's people handle it?"

"They were doing nothing. I got tired of waiting."

"How did you do it, Will?"

"I shot him."

"Could you be more specific?"

"I knew he liked to drink at the Buzz Saw. I took up a position on a rise across the road where there was cover and a good field of vision. When he came out, I shot him."

"What did you use?"

"My Dragunov. It was an easy shot."

"Easy shot? That's not what the sheriff's people think."

"For a trained sniper, it was a cakewalk, believe me."

"Where's the Dragunov?"

"I got rid of it. Threw it in a lake."

"What lake?"

"I don't know. I wasn't thinking too clearly."

"Where did you go after that?"

"Drove, just drove."

"Drove? Where were you parked when you shot Reinhardt?"

"Down the road."

"Could you be more specific?"

"About half a mile north, where Lowell Lake Road comes in."

"Okay, where did you drive to?"

"What difference does that make?" he said.

"Will, she's trying to help," Lucinda said.

"Yeah, and what'll this help cost? Because I'm thinking that in my situation, a public defender would do as well."

"For right now, Will, let me represent you. It's what Lucinda's asked. And I'll let you know when I'm ready to begin charging for my services, which is not yet, okay?"

He thought it over and agreed with a slight nod.

"Can he come home?" Lucinda said.

"No, Lucinda. They haven't charged him yet, but they're going to hold him. Because it's the weekend, they have until Monday to make a decision. Then they'll have to charge him or let him go."

Lucinda looked deeply into her husband's eyes. As always, it was like staring into a starless night sky. *Where is the light, Will?* she wondered. He seemed not to care what was ahead for him. But she cared.

"I'll bring you something if you'd like," she said. "Is there something, Will?"

"Nothing. I don't want anything, Luci. Who's watching Misty?"

"Uly. I called him at his friend's house and asked him to come home."

"You told him about me?"

"Yes."

"Did he say anything?"

"No." Then, "Yes. He said the man deserved it."

"Will," Jo O'Connor said, "I don't want you talking to anyone unless I'm present, is that understood?"

"Yeah."

She looked at Lucinda. "We should go."

"May I kiss him good-bye?"

"Of course."

Lucinda walked around the table to Will. He held himself rigid, and when she kissed his cheek made no sign that he'd felt it.

Jo signaled the deputy, who came in and escorted Will away. The sheriff was waiting outside. She said to them, "Could we talk in my office?"

Lucinda followed the sheriff through the department. No one looked at her oddly, looked at her like a woman whose husband had killed one of their citizens. And Jo O'Connor walked gracefully, as if it was natural for her to be in this place, and that helped Lucinda not to feel so helpless.

When they were inside the office, the sheriff closed the door. "Please, have a seat. Would you like some coffee?"

"No, thank you," Lucinda said.

"No thanks, Marsha."

The sheriff sat at her desk. Outside the window behind her, the sky was almost dark. Along the edge of the western horizon lay a pretty blue-green afterglow that reminded Lucinda of the color of a dress she'd once owned, long ago. The memory had a happy feel, though she couldn't say why. It gave her a much needed sense of hope.

"Mrs. Kingbird, I'm Sheriff Dross."

"I know."

"Your husband is in serious trouble."

"I understand."

"He's confessed to murder, but all of us here who've spoken with him are a little confused."

"Why?" Jo asked.

"We weren't really looking at him for the crime. Because of the possible connection between Reinhardt and the murders of Alexander and Rayette Kingbird, he was a person of interest to us, of course. Still, I'm at a loss to understand why he came forward on his own." She looked to Lucinda. "Can you help me?"

The woman didn't wear a badge or a uniform. She had a powder blue turtleneck sweater with the sleeves bunched just below her elbows. Her hands were large and bony, not pretty hands, though the nails were carefully manicured. She wore no makeup, and Lucinda saw lines at the corners of her mouth and eyes that told her the woman often smiled. This was someone, Lucinda thought, who might understand. But she couldn't say what was in her heart, not to this woman, not to Jo, who was her friend, not to anyone.

"I don't know why he would do such a thing," she said.

The sheriff seemed disappointed. She turned her attention to Jo. "His confession may be enough to charge him. He certainly had motive and opportunity, and from his background we know he had the ability. It's in the county attorney's hands now, but there are things about all this that, frankly, trouble me. I'd like to talk with him some more."

Jo said, "I'll need to be there when you do."

"Of course."

"Is that all, Marsha?"

The sheriff looked again to Lucinda, who could tell she was being given one more chance to open her heart. Lucinda stared beyond her, out the window to the west, where the blue-green afterglow had faded away, replaced by the dark of night.

"All right," the sheriff said with a note of resignation. "I'll be in touch."

THIRTY-EIGHT

W e need to talk, Luci."

They stood in the parking lot of the sheriff's office under the glare of a halogen lamp high above them. Jo O'Connor's face was an odd color, a kind of pale violet, and she looked troubled.

"Are you hungry?" Lucinda asked.

"I haven't eaten since lunch."

"Let me make you something at my house and we can talk."

"Thanks. That would be great."

When she pulled into the driveway, Lucinda saw Ulysses standing at the picture window, watching for her. She parked in the garage, waited until Jo arrived, and the two women walked together into the house.

"What's up with Dad?" Uly asked as soon as they'd passed through the door.

"They're keeping him," Lucinda replied.

Uly gave Jo a pleading look. "It's got to be, like, you know, justifiable homicide or something, right?"

"They haven't charged him yet, Uly. Maybe they won't."

"They shouldn't. I mean talk about justice."

"Your father will be fine," Lucinda said, trying her best to sound reassuring. "He's safe and Mrs. O'Connor will help us get him out."

"Sure," Uly said. "Yeah, he'll be fine. Thanks, Mrs. O'Connor."

"Misty?" Lucinda asked.

"I put her down, Mom. She cried for a little while but went to sleep, maybe half an hour ago. Can I go back to Darrell's?" He looked at Jo O'Connor. "We're in the middle of this awesome online video game. It's called Kings of Chaos."

"Will you be late?" Lucinda asked.

"Maybe."

"Is it all right with Mr. Gallagher?"

"Yeah. He likes Darrell to have company."

"I suppose it will be all right then."

He went to the closet and grabbed his jacket from a hanger.

"Good night, Ulysses. Be good," Lucinda said.

"I wish you wouldn't say that."

"It's what I always wish."

"Yeah, well it always sounds like you think I'm up to something."

"It's just what parents say."

"Whatever." He shrugged his jacket on and opened the front door. "I'll see you tomorrow, Mom. 'Night, Mrs. O'Connor."

"Good night, Uly."

The front porch shivered as he clumped down the steps. Lucinda walked to the window and watched him jog into the night.

"He's going through a difficult time," she said.

"I understand."

"He really is a good boy."

"I know."

She turned to Jo. "He wants to be a musician."

"He's very good."

"Yes." She brightened a little. "I have tamales. I make them myself. Would that be all right?"

"That sounds delicious, Luci."

When everything was ready, they sat at the kitchen table and ate. Without Will and Uly there, the house was quiet and felt empty. Lucinda was grateful for the company. Through the preparation of the meal and the eating, they'd talked about small things: church, Uly's music, Annie O'Connor's college plans, and sweet little Misty. When the meal was over and they'd taken the plates to the sink, Jo leaned against the counter and said, "Luci, let's talk about Will. Do you think he killed Buck Reinhardt? I need you to be honest with me."

"Will . . . Will has killed men, this I know. He has trained men to kill other men. These were his jobs in the marines. But this man, I think he didn't kill."

"Why do you believe that?"

"I thought at first he did. But . . ."

"Go on."

"You won't understand," Lucinda said.

"I'll try."

She looked at the wall above the kitchen table and tried to find the right words. "Whenever Will returned home from a mission, one that involved killing, he was—" She was embarrassed, but struggled on. "He was always eager to make love. I think that for him it was part of how he dealt with the killing. He was very different in those times. Vulnerable. I'm ashamed to say this, but I loved those moments, even when I knew what had come before. He needed me. Do you see?"

"And this time?"

"He was cold. Only cold."

"I understand, Luci. I'm not sure it would convince a jury, but let's assume that it's true. Why would he lie about killing Buck Reinhardt?"

"I don't know."

"Do you know where he was when Reinhardt was shot?"

Lucinda had a damp dish towel in her hand. She began to fold it carefully.

"It's important, Luci."

She opened the door under the sink and hung the dish towel on a rack there. She straightened up and finally looked at Jo O'Connor.

"From almost the start of our marriage, Will would disappear sometimes. Just leave. A day or two. He always had a cover story. Some military operation. He couldn't say where. Orders. Sometimes this was true, but sometimes when he came back, I knew it wasn't. I never pushed him about it. Two, maybe three times a year this would happen. When he left the marines, it continued. He had different excuses. Delivering a special order for a customer. A gun show. A reunion with some of his old friends from the service. The last couple of years, he hasn't even bothered with excuses. He just goes. He knows I won't say anything. Or Ulysses. It's one of the things we never discuss."

"Do you know where he goes?"

Lucinda bent and opened the bottom drawer beside the sink. She dug under the pot holders she kept stored there and brought up a cardboard coaster and a book of matches. Both held the image of an orange flame against a solid black background. Under the flame were the words SLOW BURN BAR. DULUTH'S HOTTEST SPOT. She handed the items to Jo.

"I found the matchbook in the pocket of his coat when I took it to the cleaners last year. The coaster Uly found a few months ago when he vacuumed his father's car. I told him his father had picked it up when he met one of his old marine buddies. I told him it wasn't important. But I've also seen credit card bills with charges from this place."

"What do they mean?"

"When we spoke in your office and I told you I wanted to leave Will, you asked me if I thought he was involved with another woman. I said no. That wasn't exactly the truth. I have always suspected that Will visits prostitutes when he's gone." She watched Jo O'Connor's face for surprise or condemnation. She saw neither, and she went on. "Because of his duty, we were sometimes separated for long periods, and a man is a man. I accepted that. I have never been afraid that he would leave me for some other woman. And I always thought it was better to have a man than to be alone, especially with two boys. There are worse things than a husband who sleeps with prostitutes."

"You think he may have been with a prostitute the night Buck Reinhardt was shot?"

"I think so, yes."

"I can understand why he would lie about that. But if he was with someone else, I can't understand why he would lie about killing Reinhardt." Jo rubbed her forehead and thought for a moment. "Luci, if he was with another woman, a prostitute, and we find this woman and she verifies that Will wasn't even in Aurora when Reinhardt was shot, it would go a long way toward getting him released." She reached out and put a hand gently on Lucinda's arm. "Would you like to help Will?"

"Yes."

"Would you let me tell my husband these things? He's a licensed private investigator. If Will was with someone, Cork might be able to find out who she was and talk to her."

"Will won't like it, me interfering this way."

"This isn't just for Will. This is about your life, too, Luci. And Uly's and Misty's."

She felt confused and afraid. "I don't understand why he would lie about murdering Buck Reinhardt."

"Let's take it one step at a time. First let's do our best to prove that he couldn't have done it. Then we'll talk to him about the lie, all right?"

The weight of everything felt so heavy. She wanted so much to have the burden lifted, or at least shared. She looked into the face of her friend, into Jo O'Connor's blue eyes, into their comforting certainty.

"All right," she agreed.

In the next moment, she found herself in her good friend's embrace, weeping a torrent of blessed tears.

Cork examined the matchbook and the coaster. "Should be easy enough to find. But if Will's been keeping company with a lady of the night, she could be difficult to track down and even then it might be impossible to get anything useful from her. I never knew a hooker to give up a john without some leverage being used on her, and I've got none."

"Money?" Jo suggested.

"Are we on the Kingbirds' nickel?"

"Cork, do what you have to. We'll worry about sorting out the finances later."

They sat on the sofa in the living room. Stevie had long ago gone to bed. Trixie had drifted downstairs and settled herself in the middle of the floor, her eyes blinking drowsily as she watched them talk. The windows were open and a night breeze blew through, bringing from the backyard the random and sonorous notes of the wind chimes that hung beside the patio.

"Does Will know?" Cork asked.

"No."

"If he's lying about Reinhardt, he has his reasons. He won't be happy that we're interfering. An argument could be made that we ought to let him go down whatever road he's chosen."

"I think Luci's is the better argument, that what Will does affects not just him, and shouldn't she and Uly and Misty have some protection."

"All right."

"What's that mean?"

"That I concede your point. Besides, the truth is, I'm intrigued. If Will's lying about killing Reinhardt, I'd love to know why."

"The question of the day. I think we ought to get him out of jail before we ask him that one."

Cork glanced at his watch. "It's almost eleven. I couldn't make it to Duluth tonight in time to do any good. I'll go tomorrow. I've got two meetings in the morning, one with LeDuc and the other with Marsha Dross. Then I want to stop by Sam's Place. I can head down after that, early afternoon."

"Cork." Jo turned on the sofa so that she faced him fully. She reached out and put her hand gently against his chest, over his heart. "I don't tell you this often enough, I know, but I so appreciate you. I feel lucky that you're my husband. I love you very much."

Cork was caught by surprise. "Thank you," he said. "Where did that come from?"

"It doesn't matter. I'm going to try to be better about making sure you know how much I love you and how much I value you."

"You're not dying, are you?"

She laughed.

"You know I feel the same way about you," he said and kissed her. "And you're right. We should say it more often."

They were in the middle of another kiss when Annie walked in. "Get a room," she said. She dropped into the easy chair.

"Congratulations on the game," Jo said. "How was your evening?"

"Fun. How was yours?"

"Odd," Jo replied. "Will Kingbird confessed to shooting Buck Reinhardt."

In Annie's face, Cork saw not only surprise but also dismay. The first words out his daughter's mouth were, "Poor Uly."

In her room, Annie sat down at her computer and IM'ed Ulysses Kingbird.

r u there

She waited for a reply that didn't come. She tried again, same message with the same result. Finally she typed *here if u need me.* She got ready for bed and lay down. Once more she kept a promise she'd made a few days earlier.

"Dear God, please take care of Uly."

THIRTY-NINE

Cork ran early Saturday morning and he ran alone. When he began, the streets were empty and the houses dark. Iron Lake, when he reached the shoreline, was a cauldron full of black water and gray mist. He ran north until the rising sun threw a warm glow into the sky and turned the tops of the pine trees orange, then he turned and ran back. By the time he returned to Sam's Place and began the final leg, the sun was up fully and the lake was dotted with boats.

Fishing opener in Minnesota.

At home, Cork found that Stevie was the only one awake. The little guy had poured himself a bowl of Cheerios and milk, set up a television tray, and was watching a cable wildlife program while he ate. He barely noticed his father coming in. Cork showered, groomed, and quietly dressed. He wrote a note to Jo, which he slipped under an empty coffee cup that he put on the kitchen table, and he left.

He drove to Allouette, on the reservation. In the back room of LeDuc's store, he met with George and the others who, with goofy grins, continued to refer to themselves as the Red Menz. Tom Blessing was there. They drank coffee that Sarah LeDuc brought from the Mocha Moose next door.

At seventy, LeDuc was the oldest, though his vigor rivaled that of any man present. He took one of the two folding chairs, as did Lester Neadeau, also an elder. Cork and the other men sat on overturned crates or stood leaning against a wall.

"What did you say to them?" LeDuc asked.

Blessing, who'd been instructed to sit on several bags of Purina Puppy Chow that LeDuc had stacked in the center of the room, said, "I told them I wanted new terms. I told them that with all the trouble here, it was more dangerous to move the stuff than before. Anything less than sixty percent of the gross wouldn't cut it."

"Sixty percent? They must've thought you were crazy," Cork said.

"I told them I was open to negotiation. That's when they said Ortega would come to discuss the matter."

"When?"

"He'll fly out of Chicago tomorrow, arrive around noon. I said I'd meet him at the dock on Black Duck Lake."

Cork said, "They'll be planning to say hello to you the same way they did to Alexander and Rayette Kingbird."

"I'm not afraid," Blessing replied.

LeDuc folded his arms and leaned back in his chair. "We need to be ready for them."

They spent another hour planning the reception for the Latin Lords, and when they were all agreed and each understood his part, they broke up and went their separate ways.

Cork returned to Aurora and drove to the sheriff's department. Cy Borkman, who was on the contact desk that morning, buzzed him through the security door. On the other side, he nearly bumped into BCA agent Simon Rutledge, who had a cup full of coffee in his hand.

"Morning, Cork," Rutledge said.

"You sound chipper, Simon."

"And why not? Beautiful day."

"You a fisherman?"

"Yeah, but I never go out on opener. Like battling the crowds at a department store on the day after Thanksgiving. Peace and quiet is a big reason I'm on the lake. Care for some coffee?"

"I can get it myself." Cork pulled a cup from a stack of Styrofoam disposables near the coffeepot.

"We're all in the sheriff's office," Rutledge said.

"I'm right behind you."

Marsha Dross was seated at her desk. Ed Larson stood behind her, looking over her shoulder at some papers she held. They both glanced up when Cork walked in and he had the sense that his presence had caused them to cut off their conversation.

"Sorry I'm late," Cork said. "A little business to take care of first."

"Anything to do with finding Thunder?" Larson asked.

"Personal," Cork said.

He took one of the empty chairs and Rutledge took the other. Larson remained standing at the sheriff's shoulder. A beam of sunlight the color of a pine plank slanted through the east window, looking solid enough to walk on.

Dross folded her hands and said, rather formally, "Have you made any progress in finding Thunder?"

"Finding him? No. I do know he's still on the rez."

"I suppose that's something." She exchanged an enigmatic look with Larson before continuing. "And you're still convinced he's responsible for the Kingbird killings?"

"I may have to revise my thinking on that."

Larson said, "DEA believes strongly it was a drug-related hit. I agree."

Cork shrugged. "Who am I to argue with DEA?"

"So basically you have nothing new?" Dross said.

"Basically," Cork said. "How about the Reinhardt shooting? Anything new there?"

"You mean aside from Will Kingbird's confession?" Larson said.

"You believe his confession, Ed?"

"Why shouldn't I? We didn't exactly beat it out of him." Larson gave him a piercing look. "Unless you know something we don't."

They all sat eyeing one another while dust slid down the plank of sunlight.

"I don't know what that would be," Cork said.

Dross glanced at her watch. "Then I guess there's not much more to talk about this morning." She folded her hands on the desk and stared at Cork until he stood. "Keep us informed, okay?"

"Sure, Marsha." He nodded to Larson. "Ed."

Rutledge stood up, too. "I'll walk Cork to his car."

Across the street from the sheriff's department, the park was full of children, giddy on that warm Saturday morning, bathed in the promise of spring. Rutledge stood by Cork's Bronco eyeing the park and smiling broadly.

"Chase has a track meet this afternoon," he said, speaking of his teenage son. "I'd love to be there."

"But you won't?"

"Duty calls."

"What's going on, Simon? Back there in Marsha's office, I had the feeling we were all playing ring around the rosy. What do you guys know that I don't?"

"There's a rumor floating around that you've been retained by the Iron Lake Ojibwe, Cork."

"I'm not going to say that's true, but supposing it is?"

"How does it go in the Bible, the line about no man serving two masters?"

"Gospel of Matthew, and I don't think it applies. We've all got parallel interests here, it seems to me, Simon. Everyone's concerned with the same truths."

"Same truths, maybe. Not necessarily the same outcomes."

"All the Ojibwe want is justice."

"And what exactly is that, Cork? Seems to me a little like the story of the blind men and the elephant. Everyone has a different interpretation." Rutledge had been grinning affably, but now he stopped. "Remember one thing. We're the cops. We can hold stuff back. You hold something back from us, it's different."

"I know the rules, Simon."

"I'm sure you do." He shook Cork's hand cordially in parting and took a last wistful look at the park.

FORTY

On his way out of town, Cork stopped at Sam's Place to pick up some cash, which he kept in a safe he'd installed in the floor. When he pulled up to the old Quonset hut, he saw a boat tied to the dock, near the picnic table, and a man and a boy standing at the serving windows. They watched him hopefully as he got out of his Bronco and walked toward them.

"Morning," he said.

"Hi. You run the place, right?" the man greeted him.

"That I do."

"Are you open today?"

"Usually I would be, but I'm running a little behind this year. I'm looking at next weekend for sure."

"Oh." The man glanced down at the boy, who didn't look as if he was having the best of days. "We come every year for opener, always make a stop at Sam's Place. Kind of a tradition."

"I'm glad to hear it. How's the fishing?"

"Not even a nibble so far," the boy said, his disappointment obvious.

"Have you tried casting a line off North Point?" Cork said.

"No," the man answered. "We were south."

"There's a drop-off about fifty yards to the west of the tip of the point. Usually good in early season. Give it a try. And I hate to send you to the competition, but if you dock at the Four Seasons in town, they serve a pretty mean cheeseburger. Of course, they'll charge you double what you'd pay here."

The man smiled at the boy. "What do you say?"

"That sounds okay. I'm hungry."

The man offered Cork his hand. "Thanks."

"Good luck with those walleyes."

He watched them head to their boat and cast off, and he felt guilty for letting them down. He liked the idea that people counted on Sam's Place, that they appreciated it enough to make it a part of their tradition. This created a different kind of contract with the public, it was more than just delivering good food. But there was nothing to be done about that now. He went inside to grab the money he'd come for.

It took him a couple of hours to drive to Duluth. Much of the way he thought about what had been planned at LeDuc's store that morning. Dangerous business with the very real potential of ending badly. Good men might be hurt or killed and if that happened, how could it possibly be explained? Fortunately it would all go down on rez land, and the Iron Lake Ojibwe were good at keeping secrets. Or were they? Somehow Dross and the others had learned that he'd been retained and was now in the service of the Ojibwe.

But there was another, even deeper concern for Cork. He'd spent much of his life trying to prevent violence, yet here he was, party to a plan that almost ensured it. Was there some other way to confront an organization like the Latin Lords, for whom killing seemed to come as easily as sleep? He'd wrestled with the urge to talk to Marsha Dross, but he'd given his word to LeDuc, and he would stand by that. Besides, bringing in law enforcement would lead eventually to disclosures that would put a lot of the Red Boyz behind bars. It made sense for the Ojibwe to handle the situation. In the end, what Cork hoped was that the show of solidarity among the Anishinaabeg, the closing of the ranks between the young and old warriors, would be enough in itself to convince the Latin Lords that this was territory they should abandon. Whatever happened, for better or worse, he would be a part of it. In what was to come, he was one of The People.

When he arrived in Duluth, he was greeted with a fine day in the harbor city. The hills rose to the west, steep and green, and the streets that ran down toward Lake Superior were rivers flooded with the gush of spring sunshine. Two freighters lay anchored outside the harbor, awaiting permission to enter the port. They looked like black whales stranded on a blue beach. The Slow Burn Bar turned out to be on Superior Street, within sight of the harbor and the Lift Bridge. Cork parked at the curb and headed to the door. In the glass display out front was a poster hyping the Follies that occurred every Saturday night. The graphic illustration seemed to be suggestive of the Folies Bergère: a dance line of women lifting their dresses to show dark stockings and frilly underthings. Cork noted that the names of the featured performers, which were printed below the illustration, were all male.

Inside, the Slow Burn was quiet and, compared to the bright afternoon outside, dark. A dozen small, round tables were set about the central floor area, which was outlined with small booths lit by Tiffany-style lamps. Along one side of the room was a raised platform, a kind of stage, where performances—the Follies, perhaps—could take place. A beautifully restored wood bar with a long beveled-glass mirror behind it stretched almost the entire length of the back wall. Above the bar at one end hung a television, the only one in the place, tuned at the moment to a home-remodeling program but with the sound muted. The Slow Burn smelled of fine old wood and only faintly of booze. Two booths were occupied by couples. In another booth near the front sat a solitary drinker, a young woman, reading a book and sipping a Bloody Mary.

The bartender looked to be in his thirties, hair shaved to a shadow, wearing a loud Hawaiian shirt. "What can I get you?" he asked.

"Do you have Leinie's on tap?"

"Only Honey Weiss."

"What do you have in bottles?"

"Everything."

"Give me a Leinie's Dark, then."

The bartender brought the bottle, a glass, and a coaster. Cork handed him a twenty. "Keep the change," he said.

The bartender looked at the bill, then at Cork. "You're buying more than beer, I'm guessing."

"I'm interested in a man."

"Honey, aren't we all?"

From his jacket pocket, Cork pulled the photo of Will Kingbird that Lucinda had given to Jo. He held it out for the bartender to get a good look.

"Familiar?"

"Who wants to know?"

"His wife."

"Can't help you."

Cork took another twenty from his wallet and laid it down. The bartender's hand swallowed it. "I still can't help you. Honestly, I've never seen the guy."

"He might have been here Wednesday night."

"Ah. Bondage-à-Go-Go."

"Bondage-à-Go-Go?"

"S and M lite. A lot of straights in the crowd. Kenny's behind the bar on Wednesday nights. You could come back then. Or you could talk to Mistress Imorg over there." He nodded toward the woman drinking alone and reading in the booth up front.

"Mistress Imorg?"

"Her professional name. Otherwise she goes by Sue. She's a Wednesday-night regular."

Mistress Imorg, otherwise known as Sue, appeared to be in her late twenties. She was slim and had blond hair pulled back in a long ponytail. She wore glasses with slender, rectangular frames. She was dressed in a white sweater and jeans and sported pink sneakers on her feet. Her nails and lipstick matched her shoes.

"Mistress Imorg?" Cork said.

The woman looked up slowly and didn't speak.

"Could I buy you a drink?"

The woman continued to stare and to hold to her silence.

Cork produced a business card and set it on the table. "I'm looking for information on a man who may have been here last Wednesday night."

She glanced at the card. "Let me guess," she said in a flat tone. "A wife who doesn't understand."

"Not exactly. May I sit down?"

She considered him. Her eyes were chips of jade. She closed her book and nodded for him to sit on the other side of the table.

"Mistress Imorg," Cork said. "A dominatrix?"

"In the business, also known as the top."

"Why 'Mistress Imorg'?"

"Do you really care?"

"Yeah, I do."

A little smile crept across her pink lips. "It's from an episode of the old *Star Trek* series, the first one, with Kirk and Spock. They find a planet where women dominate men. The men are called Morgs, the women Imorgs. The men speak of the women as the givers of pain and delight." She took a sip of her Bloody Mary. "What about this man you're interested in?"

"He's in trouble. I'm trying to help."

Cork explained about Will Kingbird.

"So if he was here," Mistress Imorg said, "he couldn't have been in your little town doing what he's confessed to doing?"

"That's right."

"You're convinced his murder confession is a lie?"

"His wife is. She thinks he was here on Wednesday night."

"If so, maybe he'd rather be known as a murderer than a man who enjoys bondage."

"That seems extreme."

"How much do you know about S and M, Mr.—" She glanced at the card Cork had given her. "—O'Connor?"

"About enough to fill a matchbook cover."

She spent a good half minute studying him. Her sharp jade eyes never left his face. Finally she leaned forward and said, "Buy me that drink you offered, then I'll educate you."

Cork headed to the bar. When he returned, Mistress Imorg was reading again. He saw that it was a novel, *Great Expectations*. "For my master's thesis," she explained as she closed the book. "Dickens wrote during the Victorian age, a time of incredible moral contradictions." Cork put the drink down and slid into the booth. She took the celery stalk from the glass, delicately tapped it clean, and set it aside.

"Some people, Mr. O'Connor, have to be tied up to be free," she began. "Those who don't understand bondage believe it's about sex. Generally speaking, it isn't. It's about catharsis. It's about people who hold such a tight grip on their lives that they desperately need a way to let go and bondage is their liberation. I have clients—we call them bottoms—who head major companies or are doctors or lawyers. These are very successful, very powerful people. For them, the moderate sadomasochism I offer isn't a sexual aberration so much as it is a meta-phor through which the psyche speaks of its suffering and its passion. Strength can be a terrible burden. It's a constraint, which often can be relieved only in moments of abandonment, of letting down and let-ting go."

"You sound like a therapist."

"In a way, I am. I offer clients a release that allows them to con-tinue their daily living without the deep desperation that might threaten their normal lives, their families, their jobs, their mental health. But I'm not like your average MSW or PhD with a diploma hanging on the wall. People who go through accepted therapy are re-luctant enough to reveal that fact. Imagine my clients. I'm sure there are those among them who would go to extreme measures to hide their proclivity."

Cork pulled out the photograph of Will Kingbird that Lucinda had given him and slid it across the table. "Is this man one of them?"

She took the photo, but her face gave away nothing. "Part of what I promise my clients, Mr. O'Connor, is discretion."

"Look, I don't want to resort to threats, but I could probably make your professional life difficult. I have friends on the Duluth police force."

She almost laughed. "You think I don't?"

Cork sat back. "Sorry. I'm just a little desperate here. You have to understand that Will's wife has been through a lot lately. Now her husband's in jail for a murder he probably didn't commit. Lucinda be-lieves he was with a prostitute on Wednesday night and she's accepted that. How much worse could this be?" He opened his hands toward her. "If you can, Mistress Imorg, help her. Please."

She sat perfectly still, studying him carefully, weighing his words. Finally her eyes softened and she said, "My name is Sue."

FORTY-ONE

It was almost six thirty when Deputy Duane Pender escorted Will Kingbird into the small interview room. Kingbird sat at the table across from Cork.

"Buzz when you're finished," Pender said.

"Thanks, Duane." Cork waited until Pender was gone, then said to Kingbird, "I just came back from Duluth, Will. I had a long talk with Mistress Imorg this afternoon."

Kingbird's face had been slack with disinterest, real or feigned, but now his whole body reacted as if electricity had just passed through it.

"You weren't anywhere near the Buzz Saw when Buck Reinhardt was shot."

"What the hell are you doing?" Kingbird said.

"Lucinda asked me to help."

"I don't want your help."

"I was helping Lucinda."

"Damn her! Goddamn her!"

"What did you expect? That she'd stand by and let you sacrifice your life, hers, and Uly's?" He leaned across the table. "What are you doing, Will?"

"Stay out of this, O'Connor."

"It's too late."

Kingbird slumped back in his chair and closed his eyes a moment. "Does Luci know?"

"I came straight here to talk to you first."

"You son of a bitch," Kingbird said in a tired voice. "You've got no idea what you're doing."

"Give me an idea, Will."

Kingbird's eyes were full of exhausted anger. "Know what I've always hated most about you, Cork? You're always so goddamned ready to understand. You should've been a priest."

"Do you want to be the one who talks to the sheriff's people, Will, or should I go to Lucinda and she can tell them?"

"I'd love to shoot you right now, you sanctimonious son of a bitch." Kingbird stood up, turned his back, and walked away. He stared at the wall where someone had scratched an empty heart into the oatmeal-colored paint. "You don't understand. How could you understand?"

"I don't need to understand."

"I'm not a freak. I'm not a pervert." He slammed his fist against the heart scratched on the wall.

Pender stepped in.

"It's okay, Duane," Cork said.

Pender considered Kingbird, nodded to Cork, and backed out.

"Will, the only thing that's important to me is that you didn't kill Reinhardt. Somebody's going to tell the sheriff's investigators, and the question is, who? That's the initial question anyway. The next is probably why you lied in the first place."

In the silence, he could hear Kingbird's deep breathing and the scrape of the man's fingernail as he traced the empty heart on the wall.

"Are you covering for someone, Will?"

Kingbird finally turned to face Cork. He spoke carefully. "It should've been me who killed Buck Reinhardt. I don't know who pulled that trigger, but it should've been me. I waited around for the cops to do things their way. Hell, they never were going to get to the bottom of it. Then somebody—I don't know, maybe one of the Red Boyz—acted like a man and took the bastard out. But it should've been me."

"You're trying to tell me you're protecting someone and you don't even know who?"

"Whoever it is, he did my duty. The only honorable thing left for me was to cover his back."

"And to do that you'd take his punishment?"

"I'd take the responsibility. What judge or jury would go hard on a father who killed the killer of his son?"

"Big gamble, Will."

"I've spent most of my life weighing the odds in life-or-death situations. I've come out on top so far."

Cork shook his head. "Good luck convincing the sheriff's people. It would be best if Jo was here when you talk to them."

"I don't want Luci to know any of this."

"She won't get the details from me. Whatever you and Jo decide about Luci is between the two of you."

Cork was present, along with Jo, when Kingbird told his story. Cork confirmed what he knew of it from his interview in Duluth. Kingbird gave the same reason for lying that he'd given Cork earlier. When they'd exhausted their questions, Dross, Larson, and Rutledge left the room. They were gone ten minutes, and when they returned, the sheriff told Kingbird they were processing his release. In less than an hour, he was free. Cork took him home, then drove to Gooseberry Lane where his own house lay deep in the blue of twilight. Before he went inside, he used his cell phone to call George LeDuc.

Annie had already fed herself and Stevie, and both kids were watching television. When Cork walked in, Jo was in the kitchen, had a couple of cheese sandwiches ready to grill, and was opening a can of Campbell's tomato soup. Cork took over the sandwiches while Jo saw to the soup.

"What did you think of Will's story?" Cork asked.

She looked up from stirring. "Which part?"

"His reason for the false confession. That he felt duty bound to cover for whoever it was who'd done it."

She shrugged. "I was more concerned with just getting him out of jail. Why? You don't buy it?"

"Pretty thin, it seems to me. I think he was covering for someone, but not someone unknown to him."

"Who?"

"It would have to be someone worth going to jail for. And for Will, who would that be?"

Jo thought about it. "He doesn't seem close to anyone except his family."

"Exactly."

She laid the wooden spoon against the side of the soup pot and turned to Cork. "I can pretty much assure you it wasn't Lucinda."

"So that leaves?"

She looked at him with incredulity. "Uly? You can't be serious."

Cork tapped the griddle with the side of the spatula. "Just thinking logically. The kid helps Will in the shop, knows how to handle a firearm. He's got motive. I don't know where he was that night, but if I was Marsha Dross, that's what I'd be finding out."

"If they'd questioned Uly, I'd know it," Jo said. "And if they're thinking what you're thinking, why haven't they?"

"I don't have an answer for that one. Maybe they know something I don't."

"I'm sure they have their secrets, Cork. As much as you'd like to think you're still on the inside, you're not. Besides, you've kept things from them, haven't you? Everybody has their secrets."

He flipped the sandwiches. "Do we?"

"Come on, I know you don't tell me everything."

"When it affects you, I do."

"Right."

"Do you keep things from me?" he asked.

"You have no idea what I've protected you from." She smiled coyly and kissed his shoulder.

"Soup's bubbling," he said. "Do you think Will's going to tell Lucinda the whole truth about the Slow Burn?"

Jo returned to stirring and was quiet for a moment. "I don't know. I doubt it. I get the feeling that, in their marriage, truth is the exception rather than the rule. No, let me rephrase that. Disclosure is the exception. They seem to hold so much in. I don't know what's kept them from bursting apart."

"I'm going back to the Kingbirds' this evening with George LeDuc."

"Whatever for?"

"There's something we need to talk to Will about."

"What would that be?"

"It's between Will and LeDuc and me."

"Now who's keeping secrets?"

Cork slipped the spatula under one of the sandwiches and lifted it off the heat.

"I think the grilling is done," he said.

Will said almost nothing to her when he walked into the house following his release. "Where's Uly?" he asked in a surly tone.

Lucinda was in the rocker, feeding a bottle to Misty. "He's spending the night at a friend's house."

"A friend? You mean the Gallagher kid."

"They're friends, Will."

He whirled away, tornado dark in his mood, and headed toward the bathroom. "I'm going to shower."

He was gone a long time, over an hour. Lucinda put Misty in the crib, then sought Will, who was sitting on the bed in their room, staring at the wall.

"Will?"

He looked up, startled.

"I want to speak with you," she said.

He stood and turned away from her. "I'm not going to talk about it, Luci."

"Please, Will."

Now he spun back. "Don't you ever go poking your nose in my business again."

"Poking my nose? I was trying to help."

"I don't need your help."

She flung open the gate to her own anger, something she almost never did. "Then what am I here for, Will? What am I even doing in your life?"

"You're my wife."

"And what is that? Wife. Tell me what you think I should do as your wife. Am I here to help you? Comfort you? Or just to feed you and clean up after you? What, Will? Because I don't know what I'm supposed to do. I have no idea."

"You . . . you're . . . ," he sputtered. His Ojibwe eyes as he stared at her were like shells over hard nuts. For a moment Lucinda was afraid that for the first time in all their years together, he was going to hit her. Instead, he looked down at the floor, and she saw all the iron go out of him. "I don't know what to do, Luci."

"Oh, Will, talk to me. Please."

He lifted his face, full of desolation, and spoke barely above a whisper. "It was Uly."

"Uly? What do you mean?"

"When you told me the Dragunov was missing, I checked the security tape. He's there, Luci, on the tape. He's helped me at the shop a hundred times. He knows where I keep the spare keys. He knows the code to disable the alarm. He came into the shop, took the Dragunov, and that night Reinhardt was killed. He helps me test my custom rifles. He's an excellent shot. It was Uly, Luci. Uly killed the man he thought shot his brother."

"And that's why you lied? To protect Uly? You were going to take the blame?"

"We already lost Alex. I couldn't let them take Uly, too."

"Oh, Will, Will." She crossed to the corner where he stood like a child lost in the dark. She took him in her arms.

"What are we going to do?" he asked.

"I don't know, Will. We'll figure out something."

It was an unusual moment, delicious in a way, comforting Will, something she hadn't done for a very long time. In her mind she cast about for a way to save her only son and wondered why she didn't feel fear or panic or share Will's miserable despair. Instead calm had descended and with it the absolute belief that she could find a way for them out of the dark. In that moment, she felt strong enough for all of them, all of those she loved.

The doorbell rang. Will tensed and pulled away.

"I'll get it," she said.

It was Cork O'Connor and with him was George LeDuc, whom she'd met at both the visitation and the funeral for Alexander and Rayette. Cork said, "Good evening, Luci. Is Will home?"

"Yes, but I think he doesn't want to talk to anyone."

"It's important."

"I'm here," Will said at her back. He took her hand and stood beside her.

Cork said, "Could we talk out here, Will?"

"All right. Wait inside, Luci."

He joined Cork O'Connor and George LeDuc on the porch, and Lucinda busied herself in the kitchen, making decaf coffee, thinking perhaps their visitors might stay for a few minutes after they'd talked with Will, though honestly she didn't want them there. She didn't want anything to break the connection she'd made with her husband. Finally Will came back in, alone.

"What did they want?" she asked.

"Nothing." He held out his hand and said, "Come and sit with me, Luci. Just sit with me awhile on the porch."

For a moment, she didn't move.

"You asked me what I wanted you to do as my wife. Right now I just want you to sit with me. Would that be all right?"

They sat on the porch steps looking at the night sky, and although they didn't talk, and the question of what to do about Uly was still before them, unanswered, there was something magnificently hopeful about staring into the dark together.

FORTY-TWO

In the gray that preceded the Sunday dawn, they gathered at the mission, arriving in dusty pickups and SUVs. Arthur Villebrun drove up in his rusted, misfiring '87 Impala because, he explained, his wife needed the truck to go to Eveleth for their niece's First Communion. A couple of the men had handguns that previously they'd fired only in target practice, but most brought the rifles they used for hunting game. As day broke over the clearing, they stood next to the cemetery behind the mission, drinking coffee and eating doughnuts that George LeDuc had brought from the Mocha Moose. A few of the men smoked while they waited for the Red Boyz. No one said much. They'd greeted Will Kingbird and told him he was welcome, and though their faces gave nothing away, their eyes lingered a long time on the rifle that hung from a strap slung over Will's shoulder, a Winchester Stealth painted in camouflage and with a powerful Leupold scope.

Tom Blessing's black Silverado was the last vehicle to arrive. The others had come from the west, from the direction of Allouette, but Blessing drove in from the east, from the bog country. As the Silverado approached, a red dawn began to bleed into the clouds along the horizon behind it. Cork watched the pickup come across the clearing where the meadow grass stood so high that he couldn't see the wheels, and for a brief time it looked to him as if Blessing was guiding a small ship across a dark green sea.

Red sky at morning, he thought.

Half a dozen young men were hunkered down in the bed of the pickup, and when Blessing parked, they all stood up with their rifles in hand and stared mutely down at the older men already gathered. Blessing got out of the cab and walked to where LeDuc and Cork stood together. Blessing looked as if he'd aged lately, from the weight of many pressing concerns.

"Everyone here?" he asked.

"We are now," LeDuc said.

"All right then. Follow me."

"Hold on a minute. I think something needs to be said."

Lester Neadeau called out, "You're already head of the tribal council, George. No need for speechifying."

The men laughed.

LeDuc said, "I'll keep it short." He looked over those gathered beside the cemetery in the half-light of a day yet to break. "A lot of years ago, when I was no older than most of you Red Boyz, I fought in Korea. Dennis and Jack there, they both fought in Vietnam. Harvey served in the Gulf War. And Will Kingbird, hell, is there a continent you haven't fought on? In these wars, in far-off places, we risked our lives for our country. The fight today is for our people and the land of our people. In the days of our grandfathers, there was ceremony before a battle. I don't know what it was. A lot's been lost over the years. But we haven't lost our spirit, I can tell you that. We haven't lost our courage. And we haven't lost our knowledge of who we are." He stood tall and he strode among the men, looking into the face of each one. "We are The People," he finished and lifted his rifle above his head. "We are Anishinaabe."

The men shouted and whooped. LeDuc turned to Blessing. "Now we're ready. Lead the way."

Most of the men climbed into two vehicles: LeDuc's Ranger and Neadeau's Blazer. Kingbird got into the Bronco with Cork. Trailing behind Blessing, who returned the way he'd come, they drove east on miles of dirt and gravel, twisting among bogs and sliding between high ridges, eating dust and chewing silently on what lay ahead.

"Where exactly is the warehouse?" Kingbird finally asked.

"On Black Duck Lake. Not a place anyone goes anymore, if they ever did. Too shallow for good fishing, not particularly picturesque or accessible. Being on the rez helps keep it isolated."

Kingbird squinted at the red sky. "You heard of Jeb Stuart?"

"Civil War general, right?"

"One of the best the South had. Know what he said when someone asked his secret for winning a battle? Said you had to get there the firstest with the mostest. If I was this Ortega, I'd be there hours ahead of when I said I would, and I'd come well armed."

"That's why we're heading out before daybreak. And the Red Boyz have been out there since yesterday, watching for just such a possibility."

"Ortega might also be thinking seriously of not coming that way at all."

"We thought of that. The Red Boyz have someone posted at all the important road junctions on the rez. They spot the Latin Lords, they radio that info to Blessing."

"You thought this thing through pretty carefully," he said.

"This is Ojibwe land. The Ojibwe know how to defend it."

Blessing finally pulled to a stop where the access to Black Duck Lake split off. One of the Red Boyz jumped from the truck bed and dragged the blind aside. After the three vehicles had passed, he put the blind in place and bounded back into the truck. The procession continued slowly along the narrow track to the old trapper's cabin, where once again a blind was hauled aside, exposing a faint, rugged trail that followed the shoreline east.

The warehouse had been built on a small cove at the southeast end of the lake. It was a simple rectangle about the size of a two-car garage. There were no windows and only one wide door that ascended on rollers. Camouflage netting made it difficult to see from the lake and probably impossible to spot from the air. Cork figured it wouldn't have taken the Red Boyz much more than a weekend to put up a structure like that. It sat a dozen yards back from the lake. On the shore, two portable ten-foot aluminum docks on wheels were beached and, like the warehouse, had been covered with camouflage netting. Blessing had told them that the Tahoe the Latin Lords used whenever they visited the rez was parked inside the warehouse.

The tops of the pines that edged the water were burning with yellow sunlight as morning broke over the lake. Bobby Oakgrove, one of the Red Boyz, stood sentry in front of the warehouse. The vehicles parked along the trail and the men piled out.

"Anything?" Blessing said to Oakgrove.

"A few loons arrived for breakfast, nothing else."

LeDuc scanned the woods around the warehouse. "Let's get those vehicles back up the trail and out of sight. Then find yourselves a place in the trees to settle in and we'll wait."

Kingbird said, "And what? When they arrive we just open up on them?"

"More or less," LeDuc said. "Unless you want to greet 'em with a handshake."

There were a couple of quiet laughs among the men.

"I figured we'd give them a chance to talk first," LeDuc said seriously. "Maybe we can reach an agreement."

"The only agreement men like this accept is that you die and they don't. This is war," Kingbird said. "If they come, and if they're smart, they'll make a couple of flyovers to reconnoiter. With the sun up, any reflection off the windshields or chrome on those vehicles will give us away. We shouldn't just move them. We should cover them with netting, if possible."

"Do you have more netting?" LeDuc asked Blessing.

"All you need."

"Anything else?" LeDuc said to Kingbird.

"Yes. If they have any concern that the Red Boyz might give them trouble, and again, if they're smart, they'll come prepared. By that I mean with men and with good weapons. I expect these people can afford both. If it was me, I'd come in with assault rifles, AK-47s or maybe XM8s. We give them a chance, they'll simply lay down a sweeping fire that'll cut the woods and everything in it to shreds. We'll probably take them down eventually, if we don't lose our cool, but a lot of us will go out with them."

"That doesn't sound good," LeDuc admitted.

"And there's another problem. They all die. I don't think you want them all dead."

"No?"

"My guess is that the Latin Lords would just send someone else, more men, more weapons, and next time you won't know when they're coming. I think there's a way you might get everything you want and that will keep the Latin Lords away for good."

"I'd love to hear what it is," LeDuc said.

"It's going to take someone familiar to them, someone with the guts to pull it off." He scanned the gathering and his eyes settled on Blessing, the young man who'd taken the name of the war chief Waubishash.

Without hesitation, Blessing said, "What do you want me to do?"

The plane came not long after, hours before Ortega had told Blessing they would arrive. Just as Kingbird had predicted, it made several passes over the lake, almost scraping the tops of the pines that enclosed the warehouse. Cork, with his field glasses, could make out the face of the pilot and the man sitting next to him. The floatplane completed a final loop and came at the water from the north. The lake was so calm that Cork could see the reflection of the plane racing along the surface as the floats touched down. The plane taxied toward the shore. As it neared land, the passenger door opened and a man clambered out and nimbly leaped to the pontoon and from there to solid ground. He had an assault rifle slung over his shoulder.

Cork and Kingbird lay behind a hastily constructed blind of branches and brush forty yards west of the warehouse. Prone between them lay Elgin Manypenny, barely seventeen and the youngest of the Red Boyz present that day. He held a walkie-talkie in his right hand. The fingers of his left loosely gripped a nice Ruger Mark II that rested on the ground beside him. Each of the groups positioned among the trees and hidden behind blinds consisted of a mix of Red Menz and Red Boyz. Each had a designated leader and instructions, generally speaking, concerning what to do in several possible scenarios that Kingbird had talked them through. LeDuc and Blessing together had made the decisions about the makeup of the groups and chosen a radioman for each. There'd been some grumbling, but in the end every man accepted and understood his assignment. Kingbird had deployed them in such a way that there wasn't a square foot of ground anywhere around the warehouse that was not in their field of fire, but he was also careful to place them so that they didn't risk shooting each other. There was nowhere for the enemy to hide. The skill and efficiency with which he'd organized the operation that morning had impressed Cork and the other men. Kingbird had been given the responsibility for instituting any firing action that might be necessary, and each group awaited his command.

Cork had begun the morning still hoping that bloodshed could somehow be averted. But if what Kingbird predicted proved true—that the Latin Lords had come with men and with firepower—he knew any hope for a peaceful resolution was almost dead. With so many guns and so much tension, there was only one way for this confrontation to go and only one question in the end: Who would be left standing?

"Walking point," Kingbird whispered, as the lone gunman moved toward the warehouse.

The man circled the structure, then studied the trees and the trail that ran along the lake toward the trapper's shelter. Finally he walked back to the plane and signaled. The pilot cut the engine and the props ceased spinning. Another man climbed out carrying a rope, which he attached to the nose of the plane. He tossed the line to his cohort onshore, who caught it and tugged until the pontoons touched solid ground. He tied the line to an aspen sapling a dozen feet inland. From the description Blessing had supplied, Cork recognized the second man as Estevez, the enforcer. He was compact, with a head like a block of polished maple and a scar that ran diagonally from just above his left eye to his right jaw. Blessing said he'd heard it had been made by a machete.

The pilot disembarked next. This was Ortega. Blessing said that Ortega always piloted and that he claimed he could land a plane on a postage stamp. He joined the other two men on shore and they talked.

"Only three?" Kingbird whispered to Cork over Manypenny's back. "That doesn't feel right."

The men walked together to the warehouse, where Ortega checked the lock.

"Give Blessing the word," Kingbird said to Manypenny.

The young man spoke quietly into the walkie-talkie. "Now, Waubishash."

From a distance up the trail came the diesel clatter of an engine approaching and the rattle of suspension negotiating the rough terrain. The three men at the warehouse came instantly alert. Ortega and Estevez stayed in view, but the third man slipped the assault rifle off his shoulder and disappeared behind the warehouse.

In a minute, Blessing arrived in his Silverado. He stopped twenty yards short of the warehouse and got out. He walked to the other men and they shook hands. The third man slid around the corner of the warehouse and stood behind Blessing. If Blessing was aware of the rifle at his back, he gave no sign.

Blessing spoke with Ortega and Estevez. He pointed to his watch and then to the plane and said something that made the others laugh. They talked quietly for another minute or so, then Blessing began to gesticulate fiercely and his voice rose, so that Cork could hear him.

"No. There's no negotiation. You're on Anishinaabe land. In Chicago, in L.A., things may be different, but here what the Anishinaabeg say goes. Here, *we* make the rules."

In a blur of motion, Estevez had Blessing pinned to the warehouse. The sound of Blessing's body slamming against the door exploded the stillness of the morning. Before Blessing could recover, the third man had his assault rifle inches from Blessing's temple.

"Now?" Manypenny asked anxiously. His fingers were tight around his rifle and he gripped the radio fiercely. He held his body tense and his breathing was shallow and fast.

"Relax," Kingbird said. "If we try anything now, they'll kill him. And something about this is still off."

Manypenny yanked his eyes from the scene in front of him and looked nervously toward Kingbird. "What do we do?"

Before Kingbird could reply, a familiar old voice hollered, *"Boo-zhoo."*

George LeDuc had come from out of nowhere. While the attention was focused on Blessing, he'd opened the door of the Silverado and, using it as a shield, he'd laid his rifle through the open window and sighted on the men.

"What the hell does he think he's doing?" Kingbird whispered.

"Go home, old man," Ortega called out in a jovial tone. "Go home and take a nap."

"I might do that," LeDuc allowed. "After you let my young friend go."

"Old man, you should choose your friends more wisely. This one, he won't be your friend long." Ortega squinted at LeDuc and grinned. "What is that you're holding? Hell, that rifle's as old and worthless as you."

"The bite of an old bullet will hurt as much as a new one."

"You're outnumbered, *jefe*."

"There are only three of you. Target practice for me."

"Only three?"

Ortega whistled and from the plane spilled three more men, all carrying assault rifles. They spread out quickly along the shoreline.

"The rear guard," Kingbird said with satisfaction. "That'll be all of them."

"Old man, if I give the word, what's left of your body won't even feed the worms. Put the rifle down and we'll talk."

"Let my friend go and we'll talk."

Ortega shook his head slowly, as if he couldn't quite believe this old man. "*Cojones,*" he said and laughed. He spoke to Estevez. "Let him go."

Estevez released his hold on Blessing and stepped back. In that instant, Blessing tackled Ortega and threw him to the ground.

"Now!" Kingbird said.

"Fire!" Manypenny cried into his walkie-talkie, then took up his rifle.

Kingbird pulled off the first round. A red bloom appeared on the warehouse wall directly behind the man holding the assault rifle and he collapsed. From all sides of the woods enclosing the warehouse came the crackle of gunfire. The men on the shoreline staggered, and one by one they went down, their bodies rent by a hail of bullets and their weapons unfired. Estevez drew a huge handgun from a holster under his jacket, but Cork, who'd had the man in the sights of his Remington the whole time, put a round into his shoulder and Estevez spun to the ground.

"Go, go, go!" Kingbird yelled and leaped to his feet.

"Close in!" Manypenny hollered into his walkie-talkie.

They rushed the warehouse, sending up war whoops as they came, a sound to put ice in the blood of the fiercest enemy, and they enclosed the fallen Lords in a loose circle of readied weapons. Blessing still fought with Ortega on the ground. Ortega had produced a knife and was trying to wrench his hand free of Blessing's grip in order to use it.

"That's enough!" LeDuc shouted.

Suddenly aware of the situation that had developed around him, Ortega ceased his struggle. He let go of the knife and it fell to the dirt with a soft thud. Blessing pushed himself free of the man, stood up, and took his place with his comrades.

"Check the others," Kingbird said, gesturing to Cork and Many-penny.

Cork checked two of the Lords who'd formed what Kingbird termed "the rear guard." They'd each sustained multiple gunshot wounds and were stone dead. He waded through reddened lake water to where Elgin Manypenny stood over the third member of the rear guard. The youngest of the Red Boyz, a kid who shaved at most once a week, stared down into the face of another kid not much older than he. Incredibly, the Latin Lord was still breathing.

"What do we do?" Manypenny asked Cork.

Kingbird called to them, "Put a bullet in their heads to be sure."

Manypenny put the muzzle of his rifle inches from the head of the kid in the water, then hesitated.

"I'll do it," Cork told his young companion.

"No," Manypenny said. He fired point-blank and turned quickly away.

Cork took care of the other two, then called out, "It's done."

Though badly wounded, Estevez was still moving. He pressed a hand to his right shoulder, where his jacket was soaked with blood, and he tried to sit up.

"Help him." LeDuc signaled to Gagnon and McDougall, who grabbed the wounded man and yanked him to his feet. Estevez's tan, Latino face had gone white—loss of blood or shock or both—but he angrily shook off the hands of the Shinnobs who'd lifted him.

LeDuc loomed over Ortega. "Get up," he ordered.

Ortega stood slowly. He looked at Blessing then LeDuc. "Going to scalp me?"

LeDuc said, "We're going to give you a choice. You can fly out of here, or you can be burned alive along with the drugs in that warehouse."

"You're kidding." He stared into LeDuc's eyes and saw that the Ojibwe leader had spoken truly. "Hell, I'll fly out of here."

"There's one thing you have to do first."

"Yeah? What's that?"

"Kill Estevez."

"What?"

"This is the father of Alexander Kingbird," LeDuc said, indicating Will. "He demands justice. It's right that he should see this man die. Toss me his pistol." LeDuc reached toward Neadeau, who'd picked up Estevez's weapon. When LeDuc had the pistol, a nine-millimeter Beretta, he ejected the clip and emptied it of all but a single round. He slapped the clip back into place, worked the round into the chamber, and held the firearm out toward Ortega. "Kill him and you're free."

"We're Latin Lords. We're *hermanos*," Ortega said defiantly.

"All right," LeDuc said. "Then you burn with your brother. Tie him up," he ordered.

"Wait," Ortega said.

The smell of burnt powder lay heavy in the air. The sun, a fiery ball just risen, burned across the lake. The men stood waiting in the charged silence of the morning.

"All right," Ortega finally said.

LeDuc handed him the weapon. "Everyone clear away." LeDuc and the other Anishinaabeg retreated a few yards, leaving Ortega alone with Estevez.

The two *hermanos* faced each other, standing in sanguine sunlight, casting shadows that stretched across the ground three times as long as the men were tall. Ortega raised the pistol until the barrel was level with the other man's eyes.

"Fuck you, *puta*," Estevez spit at his executioner.

No more than five feet separated the two men, but a long silence separated one moment from the next. Ortega stood as if cast from bronze, his arm outstretched. Then came the crack of the exploding cartridge powder. The bullet pierced Estevez's forehead, slammed against the back of his skull, shattered the bone like a china plate, exited tumbling amid a bloody spray of fragmented brain, flattened itself against the tempered hasp of the lock on the warehouse door, and fell to the ground. The end of a journey, Henry Meloux might have said, that had been meant for it from the moment it was born out of molten lead.

"Put the gun down," LeDuc said in the stillness that had returned.

Ortega set the Glock in the dirt at his feet.

"Arthur," LeDuc called. "You get that?"

Arthur Villebrun raised a cell phone that he held in his right hand. "I got it."

LeDuc walked to Ortega. "What we have is video of you shooting this man, this Latin Lord, who you called *hermano*. We don't care what you tell your other brothers, but whatever it is you better make damn sure it keeps them from ever coming back to the Iron Lake Reservation. We don't want you and we don't want your drugs. And I can't imagine you want this video getting into the hands of the other Latin Lords. Who knows what they might think?"

"I can go?" Ortega asked, clearly skeptical.

"That was our bargain."

He eyed the warehouse. "You're really going to burn all that merchandise? It's worth a couple million dollars."

"We measure its worth differently."

Ortega let his gaze march across the faces of all the men still standing that morning, then he considered those dead. He turned and walked slowly back to his plane. He released the line tied to the sapling and shoved the plane away from shore. He hopped onto the float and climbed into the cockpit. The engine coughed, caught, and the props began to spin. He turned the floatplane toward the exit of the cove and guided it onto the body of the lake. In a couple of minutes, the plane lifted off, took a long curl toward the south, and vanished beyond the hills.

LeDuc turned to Will Kingbird. "The man who killed your son and your daughter-in-law is dead. Are you satisfied?"

"I would rather have killed him myself," Kingbird replied.

"This way is better for everyone." LeDuc spoke to all the men gathered there. "The dead and the drugs we'll burn. The Tahoe will disappear in the bogs. In the old days, there would be songs and stories about what happened here this morning. This is a different time. What we've done can never be spoken about. Never. We're all in this together and our safety depends on our silence. But in our hearts, we will always know what we did for The People today. Build a fire now. A big fire. And let's burn what doesn't belong here."

FORTY-THREE

Will came home smelling of fire but Lucinda didn't ask where he'd been. She said, "Are you hungry?" and she fixed him huevos rancheros, one of his favorites, and gave him coffee and sat with him while he ate.

"Where's our son?" he asked.

"He went to early Mass," she said. "We can still make the late service at church, if you'd like."

"I'd rather just stay here with you," he said.

When he was finished eating, she washed the dishes while he showered and shaved. He called her to the bedroom where she found him naked, and for the first time in forever they made love. Afterward she lay against him, and although she wondered where he'd been and what he'd done, she didn't ask. After a while, he spoke to her quietly. "There's still Uly," he said.

Cork and his family made the late service. As he went through the Sacrament of Reconciliation, he considered deeply what had occurred that morning, the carnage of which he'd been a part. When he looked into the cup of red wine at the rail, he thought about the blood of the five men slaughtered at dawn. Returning to the pew, he knelt and prayed, explaining that the dark and hungry thing Meloux had seen in his vision had to be the Latin Lords. He told himself and God that although killing was never good, it was sometimes necessary, and that it had been essential that the Ojibwe deal with the Latin Lords before the youth of the reservation were swallowed by that darkness. In the end he accepted that he didn't know if those five men had died for anything but he was certain they'd been killed for something, and in the balance between the elements that made the world better and those that made it worse, what had happened that morning at Black Duck Lake was for the best. He could live with it. He would have to.

In the parking lot, a sheriff's cruiser was parked next to Jo's Toyota. When the O'Connor family left the church, Deputy Cy Borkman got out.

"Morning, everybody," he said. Borkman was a heavy man and as he smiled in the sunlight, the loose flesh of his face folded into deep, easy creases. "Cork, the sheriff would like to see you."

"What about, Cy?"

"I'm not at liberty to say."

"All right. Let me take my family home and I'll be there directly."

"I think you'd better come now. You can ride with me."

"Sounds serious."

Borkman didn't reply, just stood squinting against the glare of the sun, waiting.

Cork kissed Jo. "If this is going to take long, I'll call."

"I'll save you some lunch," she promised.

Cy Borkman had begun his law enforcement career when Cork's father was sheriff of Tamarack County. Cork had known him all his life and considered him a good friend. "Come on, Cy," he said as they pulled out of the parking lot. "What's up?"

Borkman shook his head. "Can't say."

"Can't or won't?"

"You'll know soon enough."

"Is it bad?"

Borkman turned onto Oak Street and headed south, toward the sheriff's department. "Sure going to be bad for someone," he said.

Cork smiled, trying to make it as affable an expression as he could muster. "Bad for me?"

Borkman drilled him with a frank look. "What's the matter? Got a guilty conscience?"

Cork let it go and for the rest of the ride listened to the squawk of the cruiser's radio and to Borkman, who jawed enviously about all the reports of big fish caught the day before. Borkman ushered him through the security door and escorted him to the sheriff's office, where Marsha Dross and Simon Rutledge were waiting.

"Thanks, Cy. We'll take it from here." When the deputy was gone, the sheriff said, "Have a seat, Cork. Would you like some coffee?"

"No, thanks." Cork took the empty chair. "What's this about, Marsha?"

"We know who killed Buck Reinhardt."

Cork was truly surprised. "That's great. Are you going to tell me?"

"Actually, I'll leave that to Simon, since he's the one responsible."

Rutledge sat on the sill of an open window, relaxed, with his legs crossed. He wore faded jeans, a white shirt under a navy cardigan, and New Balance walking shoes. He looked like a college professor about to address his class, pleased with what he was going to present.

"You remember the night Reinhardt was killed, after we finished at the Buzz Saw, I made a rather late visit to his wife, Elise."

"I remember," Cork said. He recalled the joking speculation that Rutledge had more than business on his mind.

"I figured she was bitter already and dealing with a good deal of grief over the death of her daughter, and once she learned about her husband's faithless behavior she'd probably added anger to the mix. It seemed to me a volatile combination, one that might drive a person to do something as extreme as murder. Call it a hunch."

"A hunch?" Dross laughed. "Come on, Simon, you put it together like a chemical formula."

Rutledge smiled and went on. "When we interviewed her earlier, she told us she usually didn't go to bed until well after midnight, when the booze finally put her under. She was up when I got there, and as a matter of fact, had a drink in her hand."

"A little surprised to see you, I imagine," Cork said.

"Absolutely. But you know me, Cork. Utterly charming. She invited me in, offered me a drink, which I accepted, and we had a little chitchat about this and that, during which I mostly sympathized with her situation. She was pretty well lubricated and I steered the conversation toward the killing. I assured her we'd get the shooter. All we had to do was locate the rifle that had been used, and I was sure that wouldn't be too difficult since we had an expended cartridge, which would give us plenty to go on. Unless—I added this as a dramatic afterthought—the shooter had the presence of mind to get rid of the weapon. Right away, I could see a kind of desperate realization in her eyes, which she tried to cover by undoing the top button of her blouse."

"And did her action distract you, Agent Rutledge?" Dross asked.

"A lesser man maybe. Me, I simply bid her good night and drove away. Or appeared to drive away. A couple of hundred yards down the road, I killed the headlights, parked, and hoofed it back to the Reinhardt place, which I intended to keep under surveillance all night if need be. Wasn't necessary. Within twenty minutes, Ms. Reinhardt comes out of the house, stumbles down to the lake, and throws something in. After the lights finally go out inside, I wade into that cold water and come up with a very nice-looking Weatherby Mark Five. I took it to the BCA lab in Bemidji to have them check for a match against any impressed action marks on the shell we found at the crime scene. We got the results this morning. The rifle Elise Reinhardt threw into the lake is the same weapon that killed her husband."

"Ed Larson is out there right now with a warrant for her arrest," the sheriff said, finishing the story. "We thought you'd want to know."

"Thanks."

"Some cases," Rutledge said, "you know what the truth is but you're never able to accumulate the evidence to prove it. But every once in a while, it gets handed to you on a platter."

"But some cases you're never sure what the truth is," Dross said. "Any headway tracking down Lonnie Thunder, Cork?"

"I hate to admit it, Marsha, but I'm giving up the search for Thunder. As nearly as I can tell, he's gone from the reservation, gone for good."

"Do you still think he was responsible for killing the Kingbirds?"

"No."

"Nor do I," the sheriff said. "I'm with Ed Larson on this one. I think it was a drug hit. We'll keep working with the DEA, but we may never know the truth of what happened out there. I hate leaving the case open. I'm sure the Ojibwe will have a lot to say about that. I think what we do now is focus on shutting down the Red Boyz operation."

"I don't think that'll be a problem," Cork said. "I get the feeling they're already disbanding and that some of the older men will be taking them under their wings. In the end, I think good things will come out of this."

"There's something else I think you ought to know," Dross said. "We're holding Cal Richards and Dave Reinhardt pending charges of arson."

"How'd that happen?"

"Richards got drunk at the Buzz Saw last night, started spouting stuff about beating up one of the Red Boyz and burning out another. Talk about dumb. Seneca Peterson called us. When we brought him in for questioning he buckled in ten minutes. Claimed to be proud of what he'd done. Dropped the dime on Dave Reinhardt while he was at it."

"Reinhardt, now there's a shame. Never thought he was a bad guy," Rutledge said.

"His old man really screwed with his head," Cork said. "Have you picked him up yet?"

Dross nodded. "He's all lawyered up, but he's also feeling pretty bad since we told him it was Elise who killed his father. I'm thinking that after it eats on him awhile, he'll talk." She sat back in her chair and took a deep breath. "I'm hoping things in Tamarack County quiet down now. The last week has shot the budget to hell. And I could use a good night's sleep."

"Me, I'm heading home," Rutledge said, pushing away from the windowsill. "Always a pleasure working with you folks."

"How'd your son do in the track meet yesterday?" Cork asked as Rutledge headed for the door.

"Like I told him last night on the phone, losing builds character. I'm just proud he was out there trying." He turned with a smile and headed out the door.

In the quiet after Rutledge had gone, Dross turned her chair and looked out the window at the park across the street. "It's been a tough week, Cork. There were times I wished to God I wasn't the sheriff."

"I suspect there'll be a lot more of those before you retire."

She swung around and faced him. "Thanks for all your help. You put a lot on the line when you didn't have to."

"I'd say, 'Any time,' except Jo would kill me." Cork turned and walked to the door. "Get some rest, Sheriff," he said over his shoulder. "You deserve it."

FORTY-FOUR

The baby's cry pulled Lucinda from her husband's arms. She went to see to Misty. The phone rang and she heard Will answer. She changed the baby's diaper and put her in a new outfit, little Oshkosh overalls that had been a gift from one of the families who'd come to the visitation for Rayette and Alejandro. When she came into the living room with the baby in her arms, she found Will standing at the picture window, gazing out at the beautiful Sunday morning. He turned to her and looked happy.

"What is it?" she asked.

"That was Cork O'Connor on the phone. The sheriff is arresting Elise Reinhardt for killing her husband."

"They're sure it was her?"

"Cork says there's proof. I told him I was afraid it had been Uly, because of the missing Dragunov and all. He told me he thought it might have been Uly, too. He figured we'd be relieved."

"Oh, Will." She felt a flood of relief, of gratitude, of happiness.

"That still doesn't answer the question of why Uly took the rifle," Will said.

"You can ask him yourself." She nodded toward the road, visible through the window, where she saw Uly walking from town, carrying the overnight bag he'd taken to Darrell Gallagher's house.

At the driveway Uly stopped for a minute, staring back toward Aurora.

"Sometimes he looks so lost it breaks my heart," Lucinda said.

"At that age, Luci, everybody's lost." Will put his arm around her shoulders. "Tell me an age we aren't." He strode to the front door and called out, "Uly, could we talk to you?"

Uly dragged his feet up the steps like a man mounting the gallows.

Lucinda put the baby on the floor and sat down with her. She had Misty's pink rubber pig in her hand, which squeaked whenever she squeezed. She made the pig squeak and Misty smiled and tried to reach for the toy.

When Uly was inside, Will said, "Sit down."

Uly set his overnight bag on the floor and dropped onto the sofa. If he was surprised or pleased to see that his father had been released from jail, he didn't show it. He put his hands together, almost as if he expected to be handcuffed, and he looked up at his father with a face ready to sulk. "What did I do now?"

"We just got word that they're arresting Buck Reinhardt's wife for his murder."

Uly often hid his emotions behind a wall of feigned indifference, but the news had a visible effect. His whole body relaxed and his dark eyes lost their stony aspect and looked, in fact, as if they were about to melt.

"I don't understand, Dad," he said. "Why did you tell them you did it?"

"Because I thought you killed Buck Reinhardt."

Uly looked stunned. "I killed him?"

"What other reason would you have for taking the Dragunov?"

Uly didn't reply right away. His eyes settled on the baby, whose hands grasped at the pig in Lucinda's hand. "I was going to kill him. I decided I couldn't."

"That's a good thing," Will said.

"I thought it was the kind of thing you would do."

Will sat down beside his son and said, "I don't want you to be me, Uly. I don't want anyone growing up to be what I am."

"Don't say that, Will," Lucinda broke in.

"It's true, Luci." He put his hand on his son's shoulder. "There's so much about my past that I would undo if I could, Uly, so much about who I am that I would change. I'm proud of who you are. I don't tell you that enough, but I am. I'm proud of the man you're becoming. I'd rather have you picking up a guitar than a rifle. It seems to me the world could use more music and less gunfire, son."

Uly looked uncomfortable, but said, "Thanks."

"Where's the rifle?" Will asked.

"I've been keeping it at Darrell's house."

"I'd like it back today."

"I'll go now, if Mom'll let me borrow her car again. But he might not be home. He was thinking of going fishing with his grandfather. If I can't get it back today, I'll pick it up first thing tomorrow morning and drop it off at the shop after school. Okay?"

"That'll be fine." Will stood up as if he was finished, but he said one more important thing. "Uly, when I thought it was you who killed Buck Reinhardt and I thought about the possibility of losing you, it was one of the hardest things I ever faced." Then he said something Lucinda had never heard from him before. "I love you, son."

Uly stared at his hands and finally said, "Can I go?"

"Sure."

Uly lurched from the sofa and walked to the kitchen, where he took the extra set of car keys from the drawer where Lucinda kept them, then he headed out the door.

"I think I embarrassed him," Will said.

Lucinda gazed up at him and smiled. "I love you, Will Kingbird."

Misty gurgled and flailed. Will bent down and lifted her in his arms.

"You always wanted a daughter to complete this family, Luci. The Lord works in mysterious ways, I guess." He gave the baby a gentle kiss.

Late that night, Annie sat at her computer, trying to bring to a close her term paper on the true authorship of the works attributed to William Shakespeare. She was drafting her conclusion, which was basically an admission that the truth may never be known and an assertion that, in the end, the truth was pointless. She figured she'd end with something sappy, maybe a line of full alliteration, something she thought Ms. Killian, her English teacher, would love.

Does it matter who created the rose? she typed. *The important thing is that its beauty exists for all to enjoy. So it is with the words and the wisdom the world has credited to William Shakespeare.*

She wasn't sure if she liked it, but she was sick of writing. Then Uly Kingbird IM'ed her.

r u there

yes, she replied.

thank u

what for

your prayers helped

good

do u have more

for u

a friend

who

does it matter

The only friend she knew that Uly had was Darrell Gallagher.

i'll pray, she replied.

There was a long pause. She waited patiently for what turned out to be Uly's final message of the night: *pray hard.*

FORTY-FIVE

Cork slept better than he had in days, and he rose early and refreshed. He slipped into his running gear and hit the street while the rest of Gooseberry Lane was just beginning to crawl into Monday morning. Normally he would have asked Annie if she wanted to run with him, but he knew she'd been up late the night before finishing a paper for her English class, the last major obstacle to a clean graduation. A couple more weeks of classes without much substance, a week full of ritual closure, and she was free. Softball practice in preparation for the state championship would fill her afternoons, but that was pure joy for her. As the sun rose over Iron Lake and put down a gold carpet under his feet, he felt like a man rich beyond his dreaming.

He ran a route that took him past Sam's Place, where he stopped for a few minutes. The lake was the color of gemstones, sapphire water and topaz light, and above it two flights of geese arrowed north. He ran his hand along the wall of the Quonset hut and felt as if he was connecting with an old, neglected friend. His plan that day was to begin again the preparations to open the following weekend. There was a lot to be done, but he was looking forward to focusing on something simpler than all that had occupied his time and mind in the last week. He was looking forward to Aurora returning to normal, to settling into the quiet, unremarkable slide into summer, to the usual preparations for the migration of tourists that would come as surely as those flocks of Canada geese.

When he returned home, Annie was finishing her breakfast at the kitchen table.

"Dad," she said, shoveling in the final spoonful of oatmeal, "you should have gotten me up."

He pulled a tumbler from the cupboard and began to fill it at the kitchen tap. "Unfortunately you take after my side of the family, kiddo, and need all the beauty rest you can get," he joked.

She crumpled her napkin and threw a fastball that caught him in the back of the head. "It's best anyway," she said. "I'm meeting Cara. We're walking to school together."

"Finish that paper?"

"Yeah, and I could live forever without reading another play by William Shakespeare. Or whoever."

Jo entered the kitchen just in time to overhear the comment. "Someday you'll understand there's more to life than activities involving balls, Annie."

Annie looked at her father and they both burst out laughing.

"You know what I mean," Jo said, but she laughed, too.

"And with that profound advice ringing in my ears, Mother dear, I bid you adieu." Annie picked up her backpack and danced out the door.

"Stevie," Jo called toward the living room. "Get a move on, guy. I'll drop you off at school on my way to work." She poured herself a cup of coffee and sipped as she turned to Cork. "So what's on your agenda today?"

"Sam's Place. A lot to do to get ready for next weekend. You know, I'm really looking forward to opening the place up."

"You always do, sweetheart." She kissed him, tasting of coffee.

Cork headed upstairs to shower, passing his son on the way. Trixie wasn't far behind. She had one of Stevie's sneakers in her mouth.

"I'm teaching her to fetch my shoes," Stevie explained.

"When you get her to mow the lawn, let me know." Cork ruffled his son's hair and moved on.

As he stepped out of the shower, he heard Jo pull out of the driveway in her Camry. He shaved and was almost dressed when he heard another vehicle pull up and park out front. He looked through his bedroom window and saw George LeDuc's truck at the curb. LeDuc got out and Henry Meloux with him. Cork pulled his boots on and headed downstairs. He reached the door just as the bell rang.

"*Anin*, Henry. *Anin*, George," he said, using the more formal Ojibwe greeting. "Come on in." He moved aside to let the men enter. He couldn't read their faces. "Coffee?" he offered.

"No," Meloux replied. LeDuc shook his head.

"What's up?" Cork asked.

LeDuc said, "Henry showed up on my doorstep this morning. He told me he had to see you."

"Well, here I am."

The old Mide spoke: "I told you, Corcoran O'Connor, that I had a vision of a dark, hungry thing."

"I remember, Henry."

"I have finally seen this thing clearly. It came to me before sunrise. It has the face of a youth. And I saw it standing in a meadow, surrounded by many bodies, also young. This dark thing was drinking their blood."

"Do you know what it means, Henry?"

"I am not sure. But the meadow is a place I know from the stories I heard when I was a boy. It is called Miskwaa-mookomaan."

"Red Knife," Cork said. He knew the name, too. It had come up a few years earlier when the school district was debating the site for the new high school. They'd elected finally to build it on the place where, long before, the Ojibwe had slaughtered a hunting party of Sioux.

"One more thing, Corcoran O'Connor. I saw your daughter, Anne, among the bodies covered with blood."

"Where is Annie?" George LeDuc asked.

"She left for school. She's probably there by now."

Then Cork thought about what Will Kingbird had told him, about Ulysses taking the rifle from the gun shop. Will had been afraid his son had taken it to kill Buck Reinhardt, but maybe Uly, a boy misunderstood and much picked on, had a different purpose in mind all along.

Cork grabbed the telephone in the hall and dialed Annie's cell phone. The phone rang and rang and finally went to voice mail. He tried not to panic. Annie always turned her phone off before she went into school. It was a rule.

He hurried to the kitchen and grabbed the keys to his Bronco. He shouted to LeDuc and Meloux as he headed out the side door, "I'm going to the high school." He didn't wait for an answer.

He backed out of the drive in his Bronco and shot down Gooseberry Lane. He thought briefly of calling the sheriff's office, but he had no proof that anything was going to happen, today or any other, just the vision of an old man. Besides, it would take him only five minutes to get to the high school. And what could possibly happen in five minutes?

FORTY-SIX

Annie had just turned off her cell phone and was coming into the school parking lot with Cara when Uly Kingbird called to her. He was standing beside the red Saturn his mother usually drove.

"Annie, can I talk to you?"

"Go on," Cara said. "I'll see you inside." She headed toward the school entrance where a late-arriving bus had parked and its student riders were spilling from the door.

Annie put her cell phone in her purse and crossed the parking lot to Uly. He looked terrible, disheveled, red eyed, as if he hadn't slept at all. "Uly, what's wrong?" she asked.

"Could we talk? Please? In private, in the car?"

"Sure. We need to make it fast, though. We don't want to be late our first day back after suspension."

Uly got in the driver's side. Annie went around to the passenger door and slid in. Uly grabbed the steering wheel and squeezed, as if he were choking a snake. The tension in his body and the pain that twisted his face frightened Annie.

"What is it, Uly?"

"I don't know what to do, Annie."

"About what?"

"Last night I went over to Darrell's house. I had to get one of my dad's rifles."

"What was it doing over there?"

"Long story. I've got it in the trunk. I'm taking it back to the shop after school."

"Sorry. Go ahead."

"Darrell was all pissed off when I got there. His granddad and him had been fighting, I don't know what about. Darrell said he was going to add him to the target list."

"Target list?"

"It's this list we keep. Whenever somebody's really been an asshole, we put him on the list. Then we shoot him."

"What?"

"Darrell's granddad keeps a lot of firearms around: pistols, rifles. We go out and set up bottles somewhere and shoot the hell out of them. Each bottle is somebody on the list. It's just a way to, you know, deal with stuff. It's not serious. At least I never thought it was. Last night, Darrell starts saying things that scared me. He said it was time to take care of the target list. He said he had a plan all worked out. He wanted us to do it together."

From the school came the ring of the final bell, calling students to homeroom.

"He said what we'd do is lock the doors, chain them from the inside so nobody could get out. He has them, the chains. He showed them to me. And the locks. Then we'd sweep through, taking down anybody we wanted to."

"What doors, Uly?"

He stared at the school and nodded in its direction.

"Oh my God."

"I told him it was crazy, Annie. He's like, 'Dude, the whole fucking world is crazy. In the end, you've got only one choice. Do you go out with a bang or a whimper?' It's something he got off the Internet. He says it all the time."

"We've got to tell somebody."

"Who?"

Annie thought a moment. "Let's start with Ms. Sherburne." The school psychologist, who was also Annie's softball coach.

Uly's face went sour. "I don't know. I've talked to her about stuff before. We don't, you know, connect. And what if I'm wrong? Darrell already takes a lot of crap. If this got out, Jesus, he'd like have to move or something."

"What if you're not wrong?"

"I don't know, Annie. I thought about it all night long and I just don't know."

"Look, if he's talking this way, he needs help even if he's not really thinking of doing anything."

"Why? I mean sometimes I've thought how great it would be just to shoot all the assholes. That's why we had the target list."

"But would you, Uly? Would you really shoot them?"

He stared at the school building and finally shook his head. "No."

"Would Darrell?"

Uly thought it over. "All right," he said at last, though he didn't sound totally convinced.

They got out of the car. The parking lot was empty and quiet. Annie knew they were already late for class, but they needed to talk to Ms. Sherburne and would be even later. They walked silently to the front entrance. Annie reached out and pulled the door handle. The door opened just a little then stopped. Annie yanked and heard the metallic rattle of a chain on the other side and in the last moment of her mind working clearly, she thought, *Oh God. Darrell Gallagher.*

Once when she was much younger, she'd been trapped under a diving raft on Otter Lake, the back of her swimsuit strap snagged on something she couldn't see, couldn't reach back to release herself from. She'd struggled desperately. Seconds seemed too few and at the same time endless. Her mind took in everything, including the useless details of her situation—the soft green light of the water; the bubbles gathered along the bottom of the raft, like frog eggs; the velvet algae on the raft chain—but understood almost nothing in a useful way. The lake pressed around her, against her, isolated her, entombed her.

That's how she feels now, as if she's underwater, struggling to fight her way out of an airless tomb, moving too slowly, unable to think clearly, to breathe, to release herself from the terror that has gripped her.

She's alone. Uly's no longer beside her. Where he's gone, she cannot say. Her cell phone is in her hand—how did it get there?—and her thumb is pressing the power button.

She stumbles away from the chained front entrance, out of the shadow of the portico, and into sunlight. Without really thinking, she turns and sprints for the doors at the south end of the building. Her feet seem mired in mud, dragging like dead things. Through the windows of the classrooms, she sees students milling about, settling gradually into their desks for homeroom, oblivious. The south doors appear suddenly in front of her. She grasps the handles and yanks. These, too, are chained and locked.

Gallagher, she understands, has trapped everyone inside.

Think, Annie, she tells herself. *Think.*

She remembers the entrance for the school kitchen, where deliveries are made, which is never used by the students or faculty. She spins and heads north.

The cell phone plays a twinkling tune to let her know it's powered on now and she punches in 911 as she races along.

Tamarack County Emergency Services.

Annie knows that voice, a woman's voice, but a face doesn't come to her.

This is Annie O'Connor, she cries into the phone. *I'm at the high school. Darrell Gallagher has a gun. He's going to kill people.*

Have you seen the gun, Annie?

No, but I know he has it. He's locked the doors and trapped everybody inside.

Officers are on their way, Annie. Are you in the school?

No, I'm outside.

Stay there and don't go in.

But she's already at the kitchen service entry and she pushes inside, snapping her phone closed as she goes.

The moment she enters she hears from somewhere in the distant interior four rapid cracks—*bam bam bam bam*—like a fist smacking against lockers in the hallways. She runs through the kitchen. Morning sunlight glances off stainless-steel countertops and sinks and commercial-size stoves. Two women in hairnets are frozen in the act of pulling big mixing bowls from the cabinets. They stand as if posed, heavy women with arms uplifted, glittering silver bowls cupped in their fleshy hands. It reminds her of a painting, some Renaissance thing about a pagan offering she should know because she studied it—didn't she?—in her humanities class.

Get out! Annie yells as she passes them. *He has a gun! He's shooting in the school!*

She doesn't wait to see if they respond.

Three more cracks in rapid succession echo down the empty hallway as Annie enters. She looks left, a clear view all the way to the main doors where light floods through the windows and down the polished tiles until it hits an obstruction, a dark oblong, lying crossways on the floor, that breaks the stream of light and begins a flow of its own, a dark and glistening stream. She thinks of a deer her father hit years ago when she was with him in the Bronco and she remembers how the animal lay across the road in just this way, bleeding, dying, then dead as she stood there with her father, watching helplessly as what neither of them could stop transpired.

Screams ricochet off walls at the other end of the hall.

Bam-bam. Bam-bam.

Two doors down, Iris Surma, the librarian, sticks her head out.

Darrell Gallagher has a gun! Annie cries in her mind. But does she speak it? She's not sure.

The librarian replies, her words like wood blocks that Annie gathers in her head and slowly puts together to construct their meaning: *We can't get out. The doors are locked.*

Annie points back the way she's come. *Through the kitchen. The service door is open.*

Iris Surma beckons behind her. *Hurry!* Eight students rush out and make a beeline for the cafeteria. Ms. Surma pauses and motions frantically for Annie to come with them. To Annie, it seems like a scene from an old movie where people stand on a pier waving to a boat that has already sailed.

Annie turns away from the librarian, turns toward the body on the floor.

It's Lyle Argus, she discovers, one of the two security people in the school. He lies on his side, his arms outstretched toward the chain on the door. He stares beyond the reach of his empty hands, and Annie, who believes absolutely in heaven, wonders, as she kneels beside him, what those sightless eyes see now.

Bam-bam. The shots sound as if they're coming from the second floor. *Bam-bam-bam-bam.* The north stairwell disgorges students and several teachers, who stumble into the hallway. They rush toward the main entrance and Annie lifts her hands to stop them. *It's locked! Go through the cafeteria to the kitchen door!*

Some hear and swing in that direction, but many of them continue past Annie, leaping over the body of Lyle Argus in their hurry to reach the chained entry where they bunch like driven cattle. Annie's cell phone bleats and she realizes it's still in her hand. The call, she sees, is coming from Cara's phone.

Cara?

Annie, I'm shot, she says, her voice barely audible.

Where are you?

South stairwell.

I'm coming.

Behind her as she rises, those grouped at the chained entrance kick uselessly at the doors.

Her legs move as they do when she runs in the mornings with her father, without her thinking of them or even feeling them, really. She passes an open classroom where Mr. Henning, who teaches geography, sits on the floor with his back against the wall, cradling a student's head in his lap. In the middle of Mr. Henning's blue shirt is a huge red continent, like one of those he teaches about, but it's a continent whose shape she doesn't recognize. Mr. Henning looks at her as she passes, and he is crying.

A long trail of blood on the hallway floor leads to the girls' bathroom and disappears under the door. Annie leaps over the blood and races on.

She approaches a corner and sees three black spiders crawling across the wall ahead. Nearer, she realizes they're bullet holes that radiate cracks across the surrounding white plaster. She turns the corner and her legs carry her down another hallway, past closed gray lockers, past closed classrooms where the sound of desks scraping across floors tell her barricades are being erected. More gunshots—so many it sounds like corn being popped—and she reckons them to be coming from the direction of the main doors. She tries not to think of her classmates who've crowded there, desperately hoping to escape.

She rounds another corner and is at the south stairwell.

Cara lies at the bottom of the stairs, her face a bloodless white. She still clutches her cell phone in her hand. Her long legs, so graceful on the ball field and beautiful to watch, are sprawled under her, limp and twisted. She stares at Annie out of eyes that seemed to have turned into two dark tunnels. Annie glides to her and kneels.

Can't feel, Cara whispers.

Annie lifts the bottom of Cara's soggy sweater and sees the blood welling up. There is so much she can't see the hole the bullet has made. The blood comes from somewhere deep inside her friend and pours out so quickly that it is dark purple. It runs onto the polished floor and begins to snake away.

Annie . . .

Hush.

She wipes at the mess and locates the wound, to the right of Cara's navel. She presses her hand there, but bruise-colored blood continues to slip under her palm and feed the snake on the floor. Annie lifts her hand away, and in the next moment she has taken off the Reebok she wears on her right foot, has yanked off her white cotton sock and folded it into a compress that she lays over the wound as she presses again.

She hears the cry of many sirens outside.

Hang on, Cara. Hang on, girl. I'm right here with you. You're going to be fine.

"Oh, I don't think so," comes the voice of Darrell Gallagher at her back.

His voice was ice on her fevered thinking. She felt as if she was waking from a bad dream, only to discover a worse reality. She turned her head and looked over her shoulder, keeping her hands on the compress against Cara's wound. Gallagher stood in the hallway in his long black coat. Visible beneath it was a vest full of ammunition clips. He held a handgun pointed loosely in her direction. He looked oddly calm. On the floor of the hallway where he'd just walked, his boots had left red prints. Streaks ran down his black coat, like dark red veins. Blood, Annie realized, though not his own. She thought for an instant of pleading with him, but she understood clearly that it would be useless. She understood, too, that her own death was upon her, and in that moment, she received a blessing she could never have guessed. Serenity descended and a wonderful, peaceful acceptance filled her. She looked into Gallagher's eyes, where there was no hint of pity, and she said, "God forgive you, Darrell."

His reply was a lazy smile as he raised the gun and aimed at her head.

"Darrell!"

Uly's shout came from down the hallway.

Gallagher kept his gun trained on Annie while he looked behind him. The smile became a short laugh as he watched Uly Kingbird approach. "Son of a bitch. You decided to join in the fun after all."

Uly carried a rifle. The one he'd picked up at Gallagher's the night before, Annie figured. He stopped a dozen yards from where Gallagher stood.

"Put the gun down, Darrell," he said.

"But I just got started," Darrell replied amiably. "Still a lot of people on the target list."

"It stops now."

"I did you a big favor, Uly. Took care of that asshole Allan Richards. You should've seen him. He tried to hide in the girls' bathroom. Cried like a baby before I shot him."

"Darrell, put the gun down."

"We can make history together, bro. Go out with our names in lights. It's what we planned."

"Not my plan."

"Come on, Uly. Don't punk out on me now."

"I'm not with you, Darrell."

"Maybe not yet. But, hell, I'll give you a choice."

Gallagher swung his arm away from Annie and brought his gun to bear on Uly.

"I pull the trigger and you go down and I waste O'Connor anyway. Or you join me and they put our names in the history books," Gallagher said. "With a bang or a whimper, dude. The choice is yours."

From outside came the scream of more sirens. Annie could hear a commotion at the main entrance, the sound of the doors being battered.

"You got three seconds, bro. Decide."

"All right," Uly said. He sounded sad and defeated. "I'm sorry, Annie." He looked past Gallagher and into her eyes and his own dark eyes seemed tired beyond measure. "If I don't do it, he will." He lifted the rifle and fit the butt to his shoulder. He jerked his head to the right. "Move, Darrell. You're in the way."

Gallagher grinned, opened his arms wide in welcome, and said, "My man." He stepped to the side.

At the same moment, Uly adjusted his line of fire, following Gallagher. He squeezed the trigger and a round exploded from his rifle. The bullet struck Gallagher in the chest, bore right through him, and tore a hole in the back of his black leather coat as it exited. The round dug into one of the stairs a couple of feet from Annie's left shoulder. Gallagher dropped in a heap where he stood. His head hit the floor with a resounding crack and his gun clattered across the tiles.

Uly lowered his rifle. He said to Annie in a stone voice, "I had to get him to move. I was afraid I might hit you." Then he laid his rifle down, put his back against the nearest wall, and slid to the floor. He covered his face with his hands and began to cry.

Annie stared down at Cara. The white cotton sock she'd used as a compress was soaked red, but blood no longer welled up under it. Cara's chest no longer rose, not even faintly. Her lips didn't move, nor did her closed eyelids tremble. She was gone, Annie knew, gone without a sound, without a final sigh or gasp or rattle, simply gone. Beneath Annie's hands, she'd slipped away.

"Annie?"

She felt a light touch on her shoulder. Lifting her eyes, she found her father bending low beside her.

"Dad."

"Are you okay?"

"No."

"Are you hurt?"

"No." She looked again at her friend. "She's dead."

Her father knelt and put his fingers to Cara's neck. "Yes," he said. He cupped his hand gently under Annie's arm and eased her up. "Come on, sweetheart. Come with me."

"No." She pulled away, stepped past the body of Darrell Gallagher, and went to Uly Kingbird, who sat hunched over, sobbing. She settled beside him, put her arm around his shoulders, and with her bloody hands gathered him in. He laid his head against her breast and she held him. And while he wept she prayed for them both and for them all.

FORTY-SEVEN

Killing Spree a Mystery
BY ERICA CORTEZ
Star Tribune Staff Writer

Authorities in the isolated northern Minnesota town of Aurora are struggling to find a motive for the killing spree at the local high school that left 9 people dead and 5 injured. Among the dead were 7 students, a teacher, and a security guard. Before leaving home for school that fateful Monday morning, 16-year-old Darrell Gallagher also shot and killed his grandfather, Vernon (Skip) Gallagher, a retired state patrolman. Local law enforcement officials, with the aid of the FBI, are still trying to understand what drove the troubled teenager to cold-blooded murder.

"He was a loner, real quiet. He got picked on some, but he never really fought back," said Gary Amundsen, one of Gallagher's classmates. "I don't think anybody knew him very well. But nobody expected this."

No one saw the bloodbath coming. Relatives and friends of the family say that Darrell Gallagher was a troubled young man, but not violent. His father abandoned the family shortly after Gallagher was born. Gallagher's mother died of leukemia when the boy was ten years old. He

was being raised by his grandfather. Those who
knew the family well say there was sometimes
conflict between Gallagher and his grandfather
but never any physical violence.

According to school officials, Gallagher was a
bright student who didn't perform to expectations.
He was part of a special program designed to help
low-motivated students, but in Gallagher's case
the program seemed to have failed.

"We worked with Darrell to identify areas of
interest that might engage him in the curriculum,"
said school principal Lindsay Munoz. "He liked
to write and draw, but he didn't have any desire
to apply these abilities. We were still looking for
ways to engage him."

Juanita Sherburne, psychologist at Aurora Area
High School, commented, "It's not uncommon
for teenagers to feel a sense of isolation and
disaffection. It's also not uncommon for students to
be picked on by classmates. But no one anticipates
that a student will react like Darrell did. I don't
know how anyone could have predicted it."

So what went wrong with Darrell Gallagher?
What drove a troubled teenager over the brink to
commit unbelievable violence? As law enforcement, school authorities, and the people of
Aurora, Minnesota, continue to ask this question,
maybe an answer will be found. For the moment,
as with so many school shootings, the ultimate
reason remains a mystery.

The state girls' softball sectional playoff was delayed a week while
the people of Tamarack County tried to deal with the aftermath of the
shootings. The Aurora Blue Jays, when they finally played, lost badly,
nine to one. The heart had been knocked out of them.

The town of Aurora was besieged by the media, most of whom

had all the sensitivity of a ripsaw. The flood of television and radio and print reporters was swelled by gawkers who descended like locusts.

Graduation that year was a solemn affair. The governor and the state's two senators came to address the graduating seniors. They spoke of reconciliation, of keeping eyes on the brighter horizon, of moving on.

And moving on was exactly what happened with the reporters and the politicians and the interest of the rest of the nation. Once a year, for several years, as the anniversary of that terrible day approached, a little airtime and a little column space—less and less each year—was given over as a perfunctory nod to the event. But the truth is that tragedy remains tragedy only for those who experience it. For everyone else it becomes history.

Haled as a hero, Uly Kingbird was besieged with requests for interviews. *60 Minutes,* the *Today* show, *Larry King Live* all wanted to talk to the young man who'd been both the friend and the end of the enigmatic Darrell Gallagher. On his son's behalf, Will Kingbird declined them all. Uly hated the publicity. He spent a good deal of time in counseling trying to deal with the shootings, and at Cork's suggestion, he accepted the help and guidance of Henry Meloux as well. In late August, shortly before school was to begin again, Will Kingbird sold the Gun Sight and moved his family to Des Moines, Iowa. Lucinda confided to Jo that they hoped Uly might have a better chance of escaping the notoriety and putting together a more normal life. Uly—who kept in touch religiously with Annie over the years—would ultimately find refuge in his music and eventually achieve modest fame as a musician in the mold of his idol, Bob Dylan. He was often accompanied on vocals by his niece, a beautiful dark-haired singer named Misty Kingbird.

Annie O'Connor didn't go to Madison to play softball for the University of Wisconsin. The shootings altered her course and directed her down a different path.

In the years after, in those nights when she would wake to the sound of gunfire that proved phantom, when her pulse raced and her breath came fast and shallow and she waited for the bullet that was never fired, Annie O'Connor would remember how, in comforting

Uly Kingbird in the midst of his grief, she had for a while been able to forget her own. She would grieve, yes—in a way, never stop grieving—but Annie understood that for her there was a way through grief, through sadness, through hate and anger and all the anguish and confusion of the world. It was a path that in a strange way led through the hurting hearts of others, a path that she believed always led to God. And throughout her life Sister Anne would follow it.

On a clear day in late August, Cork O'Connor sat in the cabin of Henry Meloux, smoking tobacco with the old Mide. Outside, Stevie played in the meadow grass with Walleye, trying to coax the relaxed old mongrel into chasing butterflies with him. On the table between Meloux and Cork lay a .38 police special and a Remington Model 700. The rifle Cork had used for hunting since he was a young man. The revolver his father had carried as sheriff of Tamarack County, and Cork, too, when he was sheriff.

"Why not sell them?" the old man suggested.

"That just puts them into someone else's hands, Henry."

"There will always be other rifles, other guns, Corcoran O'Connor. I can't keep them all."

Through the open window, Cork watched his son play and his heart felt heavy. "I've killed men, Henry, and convinced myself it was the right thing to do. Now I lie in bed nights thinking about Darrell Gallagher. In his own mind, I'm sure everything he did was justified."

The dark creases at the corners of the old man's eyes deepened and Meloux nodded thoughtfully. "In the woods sometimes I find the bones of deer left by the wolves that brought them down. If a deer had a rifle and could shoot the wolves, I expect it would do just that."

"My life has been steeped in bloodshed, and God help me, some of that was because I wanted it that way. Once you turn to violence as an answer, Henry, it's hard to stop looking there first. I don't want my son growing up to be me. I don't want him to be able to pick up a gun and have it feel like he's shaking hands with an old friend."

Meloux, too, looked through the window and watched Stevie at play in the meadow. "I have been told, Corcoran O'Connor, that the heart has two chambers. I believe it because I do know that the heart has two sides. One is love and the other is fear. One creates, the other destroys. Not every person kills, but every person could. It is how the Great Spirit created us. I do not pretend to understand why; I only know it is so."

"Maybe you can't alter the human heart, Henry, but you can remove the weapons. Maybe not so many people would kill then or so many die."

The ancient Mide gave his head a faint shake. "Handing me your firearms won't by itself change anything."

"It's a start."

"All right," the old man agreed, though his voice betrayed his skepticism. He reached out with his wrinkled, spotted hands and drew the weapons toward him. "They'll be here when you need them."

"I won't be needing them, Henry."

"We will see."

They left the cabin and walked into the sunlit meadow.

"Time to go, Stevie," Cork called.

His son bestowed on Walleye a prolonged patting in good-bye and came trotting to his father's side.

"*Migwech*, Henry," Cork said.

Meloux smiled and gave a small shrug, and Cork knew exactly what the old Mide was thinking. It didn't matter.

Together, father and son walked the path toward the woods that edged the meadow. Halfway there, Stevie said, "I'll race you, Dad."

"Okay, but wait until I say go."

Stevie poised himself as if at a starting line.

"On your mark," Cork said. "Get set."

And he took off.

"Hey!" Stevie yelled at his back.

In a few seconds, Stevie had caught up. He ran past Cork, his arms pumping hard, his small strong legs carrying him away. Cork slowed and, as he watched his son, his beloved son, racing away from him, he was struck with an overwhelming and inexplicable sadness. In only a moment, Stevie had sprinted out of the sunlight, entered the shadow of the deep forest ahead, and disappeared from his father's sight.